# BAD GIRL CREEK

*Jo-Ann Mapson*

# Bad Girl Creek

*A NOVEL*

COMPASS PRESS

AN IMPRINT OF WHEELER PUBLISHING, INC.

Published in Large Print by arrangement with Simon & Schuster, Inc. in the United States and Canada.

Compass Press Large Print book series;
an imprint of Wheeler Publishing Inc., USA

Set in 16 pt Plantin.

*Library of Congress Cataloging-in-Publication Data*

Mapson, Jo-Ann.
  Bad Girl Creek / Jo-Ann Mapson.
     p. (large print)  cm. (Compass Press large print book series)
  ISBN 1-58724-126-9 (hardcover)
  1.  Women gardeners—Fiction.  2.  Physically handicapped women—Fiction.  3.  Female friendship—Fiction.  4.  Floriculturists—Fiction.  5.  California—Fiction.  6.  Large type books.  I.  Title.

[PS3563.A62 B33  2001b]
813'.54—dc21                                         2001047353
                                                          CIP

In memory of Susan D'Antuono

and

to JPvL

for the rainy night in Boston
& every single day after

We thank with brief thanksgiving
Whatever gods may be
That no life lives forever
That dead men rise up never
That even the weariest river
Winds somewhere safe to sea.

—SWINBURNE
"The Gardens of Prosperine," 1866

# *Summary*

I should like to enjoy this summer
  flower by flower,
As if it were to be the last one for me.

—ANDRÉ GIDE, *Journals*
  May 18, 1930, tr. Justin O'Brien

# 1

## *In All Fairness*

A FEW WORDS ON COMPOST
from the gardening journal of Sarah DeThomas

Dearest Phoebe,

If you dig deep enough in this garden, you're likely to come across my red cowboy boots. I wore the soles out, dancing with no-good men on sawdust-covered floors, and regret not a moment. Likewise you'll find the alligator flats for which I could never find a suitable replacement, and the smart black pumps I wore when I married Kenny. Those shoes turned out to be far more intelligent than I was, I'm forced to admit, but one must always have black pumps handy—weddings, funerals, at my age these occasions all blur together.

The reason I buried my shoes, you see, is that I never understood the point in throwing away leather when it could be used as mulching material. The same holds true for nylon stockings, which make grand supports for wobbly stalks or fledgling trees.

Therefore, I believe I can honestly state with ecological impunity that I am present in this land now and always. It's your land, for a while at least, my dear. Consider its future well. Build ticky-tacky houses on it if you like and make a neat profit, or subdivide and sell it to rich people. You may on a lark opt to grow flowers again, for which this journal may come in handy, or you may choose to simply allow the dirt to rest. Allow me to offer up one final cautionary, my darling girl. This patch of earth will never be free of me. In all ways, I remain—

Your loving aunt,
Sadie

P.S. In case you're wondering, the flower I most hate to leave behind is *Buddleia globosa,* or summer lilac, commonly known as butterfly bush. Originally an import from Peru, it first blooms in spring but will with care continue throughout the summer. Oh, it's lovely, and rather like opening a singles' bar for butterflies. At times they feed so thickly you'd swear the flowers are animated. Intoxicating scent—something between wild raspberries and good red wine. If the afterlife smells anything like that, I'm sure I won't mind dying.

SO ENDS PAGE ONE of the ledger Malcolm Colburn, Sadie's attorney, hands to me just before he must take his urgent phone call. Next to me, my brother James frowns over his own pages. I have to close my book because I don't want to cry in front of Stinky. Hanging tough's been a point of honor with me all my life. If someone says a mean word to me, James'll beat the tar out of him, but if I shed one tear, he teases me endlessly.

"Well, what did yours say?" he finally asks me.

James and I have been on the outs lately. The reasons vary, but one thing I know for certain is that I didn't help matters by staying on at the farm after Sadie died. She insisted I give up my apartment six months ago since I was spending all my nights at her place anyway. Mr. Colburn requested that for security reasons I stay "on the premises until he got the estate settled," and now I understand why. What's the point of moving out when I'd only be coming right back?

"Something about her favorite shoes," I tell James, leaving out the news that Sadie has apparently left me the farm, a revelation that is making me a little breathless, although with my compromised heart I never know what exactly makes it skip. "How about yours?"

He flips the pages and shakes his head. "It's her financial investment journal. Every penny accounted for, can you believe it?"

My brother, James, AKA Stinky, has the angled face of a Kennedy, more JFK than poor doomed John-John had. He's a little darker in complexion than they were, but he gives off that same good-breeding pheromone. Women look at James and immediately want to have his babies. Then they find out he isn't as rich as a Kennedy and go back on the Pill. "Really?" I say, waiting to hear about the dollar amount, but if indeed he got any, James doesn't crow over his riches.

"Yeah. Some kind of lesson for me, I suppose. I guess this means we split the cash and you go shoe shopping, huh?"

Before I can answer, Malcolm hangs up the phone and smiles the way lawyers do when they know they're billing by the hour. "Just so you understand, Sadie asked that the ledgers be in your hands when I explained the terms of your inheritance." He chuckles. "I can't tell you how many times I was forced to oblige that woman's bizarre sense of humor. I'll miss her. James, you're the recipient of Sadie's liquid assets and investments. Phoebe, you're the new owner of the farm."

I'm shocked. I always assumed Sadie would leave everything to some pet cause, and during her lifetime she had many.

"But that's not fair," James says, and Mr. Colburn peers over his tortoiseshell reading glasses and sighs.

"It's what she always wanted," the lawyer says patiently. "Once a year your aunt met with me to update her will. Over the thirty years

6

we knew one another so many of her wishes changed I often suggested we write this document in pencil. She directed certain paintings to particular museums, then, when she got her dander up over the way some curator spoke to her at a party, she aimed them elsewhere..."

At once I remember the incident with the Historical Society. Sadie had a huge collection of Cannery Wharf photos; turn-of-the-century stuff, documenting the town when the roads were dirt and everyone rode horses. When the Society biddies deemed the pictures "unimportant," Sadie gave them to a local photographer who now sells their reprints and as a result has become a millionaire. My aunt—she wrote scathing letters to the newspaper, volunteered at the library, rode a horse in the Valley Fourth of July parade dressed as Lady Godiva (flesh-colored leotard, long blond wig, sunglasses). One thing was for certain, the Bayborough gossip columns could always count on Sadie for material.

"James," Mr. Colburn says, "there's only one issue that ever remained the same, and that is what I just read to you." He takes a sip of water from a clear glass and sets it down on his blotter. "Now, other questions? Or may I continue?"

James sits back hard in the oak chair and I can hear it creak under his weight. My only and older brother has put on a few pounds hanging out with the wine-and-cheese crowd over at Bay Links. Poor James. His life is all

7

about investments, and not just financial. He wants so badly to fit in with the money people he must attend a soiree every night of the week. Not that I have a great deal of experience with parties, mind you, but I imagine that's tough on a guy in his forties. Tiring. And in a way, I sympathize. He's only thinking what I'm thinking. Sadie was supposed to leave him her land to develop, and then he could get super-rich. She'd leave me her money because of my "special circumstances," and I wouldn't have to suffer the indignities I had in the past. What am I going to do with a farm?

I place my hands on the push rims of my wheelchair and turn so I am facing the window instead of Mr. Colburn and his wall of multi-hued law books. There's a pocket garden outside. A forked eucalyptus tree with jigsaw bark planted between artfully arranged river rocks and sweet alyssum. When the breeze blows around Bayborough-by-the-Sea, all you can smell is purple-and-white alyssum. People here are mad for it. They stuff it in window boxes, grow it in hanging baskets. I don't know. To me that smell's kind of like dime-store bubble bath or spilled honey. So many other flowers have nicer scents, and are prettier besides. White roses, for instance, can't be beat for perfume, and to me that once-a-year treat when tulips bloom—it's as if the fields are covered in the tongues of angels. Even if some parts of me don't work so great, I know I have excellent floral taste.

With all my compromised heart I love

Sadie's farm. Shortly before she went into the hospital for the last time, we sat on her front porch drinking sun tea and watching the crows dive-bomb the sunflowers that grew along the fence line. Every year she made Florencio plant a row especially for the birds, saying "One for the rook, one for the crow, one to die, and one to grow."

"Isn't that just an old wives' tale?" I asked her.

I remember she answered, "Not at all. Crows are smart little buggers with foxy minds and very few morals. Not unlike Kenny," she said, smiling faintly at the mention of her first husband, out of whom she had wrestled this forty-acre farm. The property had been in his family for at least a couple of generations. She said he owed her big time for the heartache he'd caused her, what with the other women and the drinking and on more than one occasion, raising his hand to her. I've never been married, not even come close, but Sadie was, twice. The second guy, Howard, was a lot older than she was, and when he died Sadie kind of hung up her interest in long-term relationships. She was never idle, though. Aunt Sadie accomplished so much in her lifetime that I couldn't really feel too sad when she passed away. Imagine if your résumé included climbing to the base camp of Everest. She knew all kinds of famous people. When I was a kid, she let me read the letters over and over, didn't even care if I got jelly stains on Eleanor Roosevelt's stationery. At various times in her life, not counting America, my aunt lived in three different countries. Sure, there were financial ups and downs, but never once did she let go of this property. Now it's mine. How am I going to afford the upkeep?

My mind reels with the notion of paying workers' wages, rotating crop cycles, harvesting the flowers she sold up and down the California coast, in short, being a businessperson, which really is more up James's alley than mine.

"What about the cars?" James is saying now. "The Jag and the Benz. Who did she leave those to?"

Mr. Colburn ruffles his papers. "Well, I suppose vehicles fall under the description of the ranch equipment since they're on the premises..."

"Get out," James says, slapping the edge of the desk in disbelief. "What in the Sam Hill is my sister going to do with a luxury car? With two of them?"

I look down at my legs, wanting to apologize to them for his insensitivity. They still work, after a fashion, just not well enough to mambo. My legs and I have learned to appreciate this chair. It opened the door out of Shriners' Hospital into the real world. My birth was "traumatic," and my spine took the brunt of it. The larger problem's my heart. Among other childhood illnesses, I had rheumatic fever, which caused me to spend a year in bed. I'm small as a result of all of that, and my heart's as worn out as an old lady's who deserves a good rest. I buy my khaki slacks in the girls' department. Likewise my purple high-top sneakers, which rest against the chrome foot plates quite symmetrically. So what if a thirty-eight-year-old woman wears tennis shoes everywhere? The "differently abled" deserve a little style, and the soles of my shoes never wear out.

"Maybe I'll get the cars converted to hand controls, James," I inform my greedy brother. "Drive the Jag on even days, the Benz on odd ones."

Color rises in his cheeks like a fever. Like Father, James has the same quick-to-Irish temper. Me, I take after Mother, who has dark eyes, even darker straight hair, and this stoic exterior not even a pickax can penetrate. She's a puzzle to me, often upset to the point of hand-wringing, but deep inside, where nobody can see, I suspect she has an Irish peat fire of a heart.

"Oh, really?" James says. "What do you plan to use for money, Pheebs?"

"How about I roll myself out onto Ocean Avenue and hook for it?"

We look at each other for a few moments, exchanging the bald-eyed challenge of a good old-fashioned sibling stare-down. When we were kids, I'd stare at James until my eyes dried up like prunes.

Mr. Colburn rubs his face. "I thought that when Sadie died days like this were behind me for good. You're excused, the both of you. Stop at Kathryn's desk and sign the papers she

11

has waiting for you. Then go somewhere and have lunch and settle this everlasting argument before you send me to the grave next to your aunt's."

Which would be difficult since we scattered Sadie's ashes at sea. "James will have to pay for lunch," I say, "seeing as how he has all the money."

"No problem," James quickly replies. "You can drive."

A PERSON SPENDS OVER thirty years in a wheelchair, she learns the perks and makes no bones about working them in her better interests. The River Grill, just across the road from Mr. Colburn's law office, is packed with tourists as usual, implying a long wait. All I do is park my chair at an angle in front of the hostess and look famished, and what do you know, suddenly there's this great table for two available immediately.

"I hate it when you do that," James says under his breath as the waitperson rushes to bring us bread and butter.

"Do what?" I ask, fanning myself with the menu.

"Act crippled."

"James, James, James," I say. "I've just inherited a forty-acre farm, not to mention two luxury automobiles. I'd hardly call that crippled."

He gives me a dirty look and holds the

menu up in front of his face like one of those sun reflectors that give you maximum tanning rays. I check out the restaurant. The River Grill's okay, but I prefer diners, like Katy's in the Valley. River Grill serves "California cuisine." Basically that means there's sure to be two not terribly spicy Mexican dishes, Caesar salad plain or with chicken, and five kinds of fatty, grease-sodden hamburgers. I scan the menu and decide James will order the bleu cheese burger with fries and a side order of ranch dressing. Though it's like playing Russian roulette with your arteries, he's addicted to the brief rush saturated fats deliver. The Caesar salad looks good to me, that and a Thirsty Lizard, one part grape-fruit juice to two parts ginger ale. When the server returns, James gestures to me—ladies first—and I tell her what my brother wants, leaving off the ranch dressing.

"You two must know each other very well," she says. "And for her?"

"Caesar salad," James says.

"Will that be all?"

"Oh, if it isn't too much trouble, could you bring me a side of ranch dressing for those fries?" James adds.

I grin.

"I don't know what you're so damn happy about," he says as we work our way through our lunches. "You're the one who stands to lose. Have you ever heard the term *land-poor?* Why don't you let me sell the farm for you? Real estate prices around here are astro-

13

nomical. With the kind of money you'd get, you could move yourself into a first-rate ground-level beachfront condo on the Links, Pheebs. We could hire a contractor, have him install ramps; downsize the kitchen counters so you can cook all that healthy crap you love. With a few carefully considered investments you'd be set for life. You wouldn't even have to make those little clay people anymore." He sips his coffee, makes a face, and adds more cream.

"I like making those little clay people, James. People like them, too, at least enough to buy five dozen or so every month. Sculpting's what I do, James."

"Fine, we'll get you a house with a separate outbuilding to use as an art studio." He starts drawing a blueprint on a napkin, as if some wiggly pen marks will convince me to part with Sadie's farm.

I don't need a separate outbuilding to make my art. All it takes is a flat surface, your basic oven, and Fimo clay. In my hands, when the clay takes shape, I feel whole and useful. No one sees my chrome wheels, pretends I'm not there, or shushes their children when they stare at the unusually small woman who doesn't walk. They simply admire my work, don't care who made it, and are willing to part with money for it to be theirs. The bulk of my line is mobiles of naked women. Lest it sound like I'm prurient, these women are in no way pornographic. Nosiree. They're mythic, like goddesses, and not some New Age-y crap, either, but strong women, with outstretched arms ready to embrace whatever joy life hands them. In the light of a window, they fly untethered above the pull of the earth. Depending on my mood, I add red curly hair, gray pubic thatch, a big toothy smile, or earth-mama breasts. From the hips down, the clay's less defined because to me legs are not important. My ladies are amusing to buyers, I guess, because I continue to get orders. I string the clay women on fishing line and hang them off two intertwined wire arms. When the mobile is properly hung, all you have to do is blow a puff of breath their way. My ladies are happy to twirl all day in circles. To me, each one is a pilot. You won't find a flight attendant among them.

JAMES DRIVES ME BACK to the farm and unloads my wheels. I get out of the car and into my chair without any help and wheel myself up onto the porch. We sit there a moment, each of us figuratively running our hands over the space between us. Yes, it's less awkward now than it was in Colburn's office, but it still needs major smoothing.

"Aren't you going to invite me in? I promise I won't steal anything."

"Another time, James," I say, without turning to look at him in the doorway. "Nothing personal, I just have a lot to think about and I'd appreciate some privacy."

"Well, take care, Phoebe," he says. "You know I love you, right?"

Yes, I know, I think to myself. And I also know how much you'd like to manage my life along with your investment portfolio. "Same here, James."

"I'll call you tomorrow."

And the day after that, and the next, I think, until you wear me down and this place is a land developer's dream come true and I'm stuck in some stupid condo with rules as to how much distance there needs to be between each tree I plant. "Fine," I say, thinking there's no rule I have to answer the phone.

He drives away in his Jeep Grand Cherokee. It's white with those tacky gold wheel rims— a dead giveaway that he's trying too hard to better his station. Every Friday he has it "detailed." Nobody outside California has heard of that term. If I say, "Oh, you got your car washed," it annoys James to no end. But what am I supposed to say? "You got your car hand-washed, hand-vacuumed, and, lest we forget, professionally scented in your choice of aroma for five times what they charge at the drive-through?" Unfailingly, James chooses new-car scent.

Suddenly I'm tired. Florencio, Sadie's farm manager—he's mine now, I guess—walks up to the porch. "That car of your brother's? The *numero uno* most frequently towed car in California."

"Is that right?"

"*Si,* I hear this on *Car Talk*. Good show, *Car*

*Talk*. I learn much, even though the brothers have difficult accent." Florencio heads off to the barn and I'm left alone on the porch hearing ghostly echoes of Sadie's gardening advice. *Hang mothballs in peach trees. Roses love graywater. Crush the cloves of garlic a little before you plant them*...or was that onion? Why me? I have to wonder. What is an eighty-five pound woman going to do with a flower farm? Maybe it's true that pondering the end of her life, even the wisest woman goes a little dotty.

I TIDY UP THE KITCHEN as best I can, swiping the tile counters and washing the spoon and bowl left over from my breakfast oatmeal. Then I roll myself into the living room and look at the oil portrait of my late aunt where it hangs above the river rock fireplace. It was painted when Sadie was in her thirties, probably around the age I am now. The major difference is I will never look like anyone but myself, whereas Sadie, in this incarnation, closely resembles Lauren Bacall. Her silvery blond hair is styled in a short pageboy. A turquoise comb holds one side to keep it from falling in her sultry, follow-you-everywhere eyes. She's dressed in a black turtleneck sweater and sporting a single strand of pearls. Her smile could mean a number of things: she's been flirting with the artist, or just cracked an off-color joke, or pulled a prank on someone—like she did on James and myself.

"Sadie, there are so many questions I want to ask you," I say, and my voice trembles because I would give this farm to James in a heartbeat if it meant I got my aunt back.

There are no answers except the echoes that move about this room with the cathedral ceiling and first edition books and good art and old leather furniture. Every stick speaks her name, and I'm all ready to settle down to an old-fashioned pity party, to wallow in my predicament until I'm good and soggy, when a knock at the door ruins everything.

Through the screen I spy a tall black woman, maybe mid-thirties. The sun is at her back, which makes her skin appear so dark I can hardly make out her features. The farm doesn't get much in the way of door-to-door sales-people. Anyone who shows up here is either asking for work, looking to buy flowers, or turns out to be a real estate agent. "Yes?" I say, in what I hope sounds like an authoritative tone.

I have to give the woman credit. She doesn't shy at my chair, or bend down on one knee as if she's speaking to a child, the way most people do. She just tilts her chin and states her business. "I was wondering if this ranch boarded horses, and if so, what the rates are, and if you think the owners would possibly con-sider some work in trade for payment."

I get the impression this sentence has been rehearsed, tried out at a few places before landing on my doorstep, and has yet to work in her favor. "Um, it's not a ranch, it's a flower farm, and it's mine."

She sighs and looks away. Only then do I see her profile, strong and dignified. There's a slight overbite to her mouth that makes me wish I had skipped orthodontia. Her mouth is her face's one imperfection, totally charming, and somehow it makes me immediately warm to her, even though the rest of her, especially the tiny braids that cover her head, looks like supermodel material. "Thanks for your time," she says, and turns to go.

As she steps off the porch, I see a beautiful black horse tied to the fence rail. "Hold on a minute," I call out, pushing open the screen door and wheeling myself to the porch via the ramps Sadie installed when I was a teenager. "I know a lot of people in this valley. Tell me what you're looking for; maybe I can help. Wow, the day really warmed up, didn't it? You want a glass of water? How about lemonade? My name's Phoebe," I say, and thrust out my hand.

"Well," she says as her dark fingers close around mine, "my horse could sure use a drink."

AN HOUR LATER, Ness Butler and I have drained the ice tea pitcher and each been to the bathroom. We've covered her early years, growing up in Oakland, then moving to San Jose; touched on me at Shriners', and are rapidly approaching present day circumstances. "Where were you boarding the horse before now?" I ask.

19

She looks across the fields of sunflowers, heads heavy and bending toward the earth. The blackbirds are absolutely ransacking them. "Until a couple of weeks ago, I was a farrier on the Patrini Ranch. It's a racehorse training facility and working ranch year round."

"I'm sorry, but what's a farrier?"

"You know, like blacksmiths used to do, shoeing horses."

"Really? Are there a lot of women horse farriers?"

"Oh, honey. It just might be the last bastion of the old boy network. Not to mention the race issue! There are a handful of us."

"Why did you leave?" I know I'm prying, but I'm curious why she'd leave a job she worked so hard to get.

Ness sets her empty glass down on the porch. "Believe me, it was time to get the hell out of Dodge, me and old Leroy Rogers there. And before you ask, no, I didn't name him."

"I was just about to. Where are you living now?"

She laughs a slight, flinty laugh. "You'd be surprised how many places a girl and horse can find to camp this time of year. Down by Bad Girl Creek's nice. Fresh water, lots of birds to watch, and the stars make for great company. I have a nice camp set up."

"Oh, my goodness," I say. "Are you telling me you're homeless?"

She gets that elegant, proud look on her face again. "This book I've been reading says I should tell folks 'I'm in a transitional phase.' "

"In other words, homeless."

"Hey, it's not like I can't afford to rent a room. I have money to tide me over until I find my next job. The problem is Leroy. His needs reach a little beyond a carport, you know?"

We both look at the horse that by now Florencio has eating out of his hand. Using an old brush he found in the barn, he's burnished the gelding to a satiny gleam, given him all the carrots I had in the fridge, and fetched him a bucket of water, probably the bottled stuff, not the tap. As if on cue, Leroy lifts his tail and does his business. "Not exactly box-trained," I say and we both laugh.

I picture in my mind how the Valley highway stretches east forty miles until it hooks up with U.S. 101. All along its edges there are houses, farms, and acres of grassy rolling hills turned golden under the summer sun. As you move north, sprawling green fields of agricultural farms unfold where all manner of California produce is grown and harvested. Trucks rattle by full to the brim with gleaming tomatoes, and if you roll down your window, it smells like freshly made bruschetta. There are entire fields devoted to the artichoke, and in July, a festival for garlic. A hobo wouldn't starve to death traveling this route, but Ness Butler isn't a transient, she's looking for a place where someone will allow her to send down a single root. It's difficult to imagine there isn't one barn in the Valley that won't board her horse. "Did you try Vista del Oro?"

She nods. "No room at the inn."

21

"The Gables? They have a huge barn."

"Full up. And Happy Valley has been sold to a winemaker. Horses on their way out, grapes on the way in."

"Yeah, I heard something about that. If the grape crops are lousy they'll make gourmet vinegar."

Meanwhile, Florencio walks the gelding around the fields left fallow these past few years when Sadie was ill. He's all puffed up, like he just found something worthwhile to do, and I suppose he has, since I haven't asked him to work on anything. There's something about a black horse that brings out—in certain men—a conquistador spirit. Florencio, in his straw hat and white shirt, is muttering to Leroy so close to his muzzle he might be telling him a secret. I point. "Check that out. And people go on about the bond between women and horses."

Ness looks down at her lap, where her hands lie neatly folded on her blue jeans. "Phoebe?"

"Yeah?"

"You seem to love horses."

I touch the armrests of my chair; feel the comfortable leather, worn to familiar softness. "Oh, I do. From a distance, anyway. I've never actually ridden one, but they're like art, aren't they? Have you ever seen DaVinci's drawings of horses? No? Oh my gosh, incredible. My aunt has this book—"

"If I was to sign Leroy over to you, would you promise me not to sell him to the dog-food people?"

My heart breaks. Slowly, deliberately, like I'm Leroy moving toward the carrot Florencio holds out, I come to the conclusion that there must be enough insurance on this farm to cover one horse and any possible accidents. I look over at the flowers bending in the afternoon wind. At Leroy's tail swishing as Florencio walks him across this farm. At my few pieces of large statuary in the flower bed, gathering a fine sheen of moss. "Ness, tell you what. Leroy can stay here until you get things figured out. But you'll have to buy some hay. All we have around here is fertilizer and straw, you know, for mulching the flowers." Suddenly the thought occurs to me that perhaps mulching is what happens at this time of year, and that if I'm going to stay here, I had better read Sadie's gardening journal.

Ness stands up and comes over to me. As if she belongs on Sadie's land more than I do, she smells like some kind of tart flower. Her arms encircle my shoulders and chair, and her skin is smooth and warm. "Bless you, Phoebe."

I guess she has me right then, because I am a sucker for anyone who hugs my chair.

Living careful is something I've done my entire life. I can't afford to catch things like pneumonia, so I stay out of drafts. I eat healthy so that my heart, bless its hardworking faulty chambers, will stay as strong as it can. When I was at Shriners', and the therapists were urging me toward an electric wheelchair, I held firm on the self-propelled kind. There were people who needed that motorized kind of help and there were people like me, who could lift weights and work hard at staying strong, even if they don't do so well at walking. Even if it meant getting stuck sometimes, even if it meant the occasional humiliating fall, I wanted to be the one propelling myself. Sadie would approve of what I've done. She'd have broken out a bottle of champagne. James, however, will grill me. *How much do you know about this person? Did you check her references? Can you describe the nature of her character?* "I turned thirty-eight three weeks ago," I say, but I don't tell her my birthday was the day after my aunt died. "How old are you?"

"Thirty-five last December."

"Do you mind if I ask you what Ness stands for?"

She puts her hand over her mouth. "Oh, please. Anything but that."

"Why not? Is it Elliot Ness? Did your mother have a crush on that guy in *The Untouchables*?"

She laughs. "Not that I know of. My granny named me Preciousness. Which I never was by the way, and with a name like that, you find a nickname as soon as humanly possible. That's my deepest secret, and it had better stay that way, you hear? I can't afford to have folks find out that a female horse shoer looking for new clients is named—oh, don't make me say it twice."

"I understand. What about poor Leroy? Who named him?"

"Some racist idiot I thought I loved. Leroy

24

and I've been friends twelve years now. I don't even know of a single marriage that's lasted that long, do you?"

The only one that comes to mind is my parents'. They were together long enough to have two children, a mortgage, and good insurance. When my father died, my mother completely switched personalities and left us kids baffled. Occasionally that bafflement turns to misery, because she deals with her problems in one of two ways: traveling or meddling. Sometimes I wish she'd get married again, just so it would take the heat off me, but widowhood suits her—there are cruises to take, causes to fight for, and best of all, so much free time to tell me how little she approves of my life. "Not really," I say.

"That's right," Ness continues. "My feeling is a man will let you down, but a horse, now there's a true partnership."

I try to think what questions I could ask her that are important yet not too probing, something in the way of what a landlord might ask a prospective tenant. But I'm not any good at that, and as usual, I lead with my heart. "Does that mean there's currently no man in your life?"

Her eyes glitter, and I can tell I've touched a hurt that's barely scabbed over. "No man for me. How about you?"

"Ha." I'm flattered she'd think there was one, impossible as it is with me in the chair. "Well, you want my humble opinion," I say. "Except for Florencio, most men suck. Wait until you meet my brother Stinky. Let's just say he's aptly named."

She grins and stretches her arms above her head. I envy the long, ropy muscles that flex and uncoil. She can lift any feed sack a man can, or my chair with me in it. She's smart and laughs at my jokes. "Did you always want to be a farrier?"

"Heck, no. I had my sights set on a large animal veterinarian practice. Never could scrape the money together for school. But I'm good at what I do. I like it. What about you?"

"I'm doing it," I tell her, pointing to the mobiles hanging in my aunt's windows. "I make these clay ladies. Little People, the shop off Ocean Avenue across the highway? They sell them."

She runs her fingers over the naked women hanging from the mobile. "Interesting in a weird sort of way, Phoebe," she says. "What else have you done?"

I point out the clay flower women in the garden. Imagine cabbages, but instead of leaves, women's faces emerging. Ness smiles politely. Then we go indoors and I show her my other work. "This is a mask I did a few years ago," I say. It's the most realistic thing I've ever attempted, and most people remark on it, but what Ness Butler lingers over is the mermaids. A year ago I was on an oceanic kick, and outfitted this whole season of clay ladies with swirling scaly green tails, even glue-gunned their behinds to various shells Sadie had collected in her travels. When my aunt's pain got too bad and the morphine wasn't kicking in quickly enough, the mermaids amused her. I remember making this one, curling it around her index finger like a ring. Sadie would shut her eyes, doze for a while, then wake with a start, and before the pain could grab hold of her and squeeze too tightly, she'd focus on the mermaid. *That's me before too long, Phoebe,* she'd say, and I knew she was referring to her funeral wishes, cremation and ashes scattered off the coast.

"This is some kind of palace," Ness says, looking up at the wooden ceiling crisscrossed with massive old beams. "Reminds me of that hotel in Yosemite. Ever been there?"

I shake my head no. "Not a lot of national parks with wheelchair ramps. But I've seen pictures of El Capitan and Bridal Veil Falls."

"You could see a whole lot more on horseback," Ness says offhandedly, as she wanders through the living room looking at Sadie's paintings. "Nice art you have here," she is saying. "If a body could get up mornings and look at paintings while she drank her coffee, the whole day might go better, huh?"

"Maybe."

So I know a lot more about Ness (Preciousness!) than James would give me credit for. She works hard, is resourceful, and loves her grandma. She appreciates art, but if she doesn't like something, has enough backbone to say so. Yes, she's homeless, but that's a temporary thing, and she's proud of herself

27

and desperate enough to give Leroy to a good home before she'd sell him.

We're approaching the kitchen when I ask, "Ness, do you like to cook? It's one of my passions."

"Just point me to the pots and pans. I can cook vegetarian lasagne and squash casseroles and breads so full of whole grains they sand the plaque right off of your teeth. I don't eat red meat 'cause all it does is support the cattle industry, which is wrecking the planet." She quickly claps a hand over her mouth. "But I don't judge people who want to eat it."

"It's okay," I say. "I hear you on that score. I only have one more question. How much rent do you think you can realistically afford to pay?"

"Three-fifty, until I get me some new clients," she says. "Are you asking me what I think you're asking me?"

"I am."

She looks away and says softly, "Oh, Phoebe."

And so in the space of a month I find myself having scattered my beloved aunt's ashes at sea and having received an embarrassment of riches, including a forty-acre farm, two luxury automobiles, a horse to keep my farm manager happy, my first ever roommate, and who knows, maybe a friend.

"I need to see about the hay situation for Leroy," she says excitedly. "You think Florencio would mind if we borrowed the truck?"

"I have a car," I tell her. "In fact, I have two of them." She follows me out to the garage, where the black Jag and the yellow Mercedes sit gassed up and ready to rumble. Sadie sold the farm pickup to Florencio when she got sick, but every day he starts her cars up like any minute she'll be back. "You think the Jag's trunk will hold a bale of hay?"

"Damn, girl," is all Ness can say when I throw her the keys.

*Ness*

# 2

## *Breaking Camp*

WHILE I PACK UP MY THINGS, the creek trickles along, sliding over the rocks and fallen oak limbs like it's humming a lullaby. At night I'd've given anything for it to sound that way, calming, reassuring, but the truth is not even a fifth of whiskey could have settled me down. I wanted to be anyplace else, to be anybody else, but me was who I got stuck with. Now it feels strange to leave my camp. I can't say I was comfortable here, but I did feel at home.

Poor Leroy—I've got him so loaded up he looks like a pack mule—my sleeping bag, a cooking pot tied to the saddle horn, my carrying case of shoeing equipment looped over that. I circle the campsite twice to make sure no trace of me is left behind. Sometimes things look clean, but you scratch the surface and it's a whole different story. Something always stays behind when you leave a place, even if it's just bent weeds or the smooth patch in the dirt where you laid out your bedroll. I tell myself not to feel so bad about the damage I did here, that Mother Earth knows how to renew herself just fine and maybe someday I'll believe it. Likely a year from now, some hiker will stop to soak his toes in the water and never in a million years guess that just where he's sitting, my life's most major drama unfolded. It's not like I want to dwell on it, but how can I not, when it feels as if I dwell *inside* the unthinkable?

Well, it's getting close to dinnertime, and I know I should leave, but I might sit just a while longer and listen to the water flow. Sounds like peace to me, just out of my reach but near enough I crave it. I think of all the nights I sat here crying over Jake Rayburn. To say I loved the fool doesn't begin to explain things. I thought I knew Jake as good as I know Leroy—what foods interfered with his digestion, just where he liked to be scratched, that if the gate wasn't one hundred percent latched he'd sneak out of the corral and party until morning—got that last part right, anyway.

When Jake told me he'd tested positive for the AIDS virus, I thought it was some kind of sick joke he was playing and I slapped him. In horses, they call that the fight-or-flight response, and that was me in fight mode.

30

When he said I should get myself tested, too, I felt blanched, like my skin had been peeled clean off by a pail of scalding water. I could see it in his eyes; Jake wanted me to comfort him, maybe even to give him sex. For once in my life, I couldn't be his everything. I waited until dark, took Leroy, and hightailed it out of there, which is the flight part of fear, when the animal sees its enemy clearly and finally gets smart. By taking his horse, I committed a criminal act that's punishable by fines and maybe even jail. But knowing Jake, once the news settled in that he couldn't have indiscriminate relations with every female who crossed his path, he'd get out the whip and whale on whichever of the horses was handy. He's that way, sometimes, and as much as I hate it I understand where it comes from. Leroy's such a lamb he'd just stand there and take whatever Jake dished out. So I stole Leroy and rode all night, and when I couldn't ride any more I stopped here by Bad Girl Creek and I laid down in my sleeping bag staring up at the night sky and hyperventilating while I listened to Leroy snort around in the weeds. Even at night I could see the water, such a pretty ribbon cutting through the dry hills. I wonder what happened here to give it that name. I wondered a lot of things that night while I set up my camp and cried. After the tears stopped I got quiet and sleepy. Maybe I believed that so long as we were camped here, our lives existed outside any medical diagnosis.

The ranger was pretty nice the first time he

came across my camp. The second time he gave me a talking-to about human waste contaminating the water table, which eventually dumps into the Pacific Ocean, and how there are campsites with restroom facilities in Arroyo Contento twenty miles down the road for ten dollars a night. It doesn't take a ball player to know that three strikes mean you're out, so I started looking for a place. Kind of shocked me how many people said no outright. It's not like I'm the only black person in this valley, either, but I guess all the others must be movie stars. Never expected to be rooming with a white girl, but I guess I can live with anything temporarily.

This Phoebe. On general principle I'm wary of Caucasians. Probably she figures that her being confined to the wheelchair evens us out. But she doesn't know the burden I'm carrying. She doesn't need to know, I tell myself. Keeping my distance is mandatory now. I'll be cheerful, help with chores, find another job, and as soon as I can manage better, move on. I'm thinking maybe Arizona—someplace with a nice, dry climate, clean air, and cowboys in tight jeans.

"LET ME DO THE DISHES," I tell Phoebe that night when we finish eating our supper—a hearty potato soup and whole-wheat muffins she whipped together in under an hour. The soup was so good I helped myself to seconds,

32

and the muffins are perfect for mopping the bowl clean.

"Not on your first night here," she argues. "Go take a hot bath and relax. After camping you deserve some pampering."

"But I love to do dishes. Where do you keep your dishwashing gloves?"

"Fine. Have it your way. They're under the sink," she says, and sits at the table watching me work. "Um, Ness, why are you adding bleach to the dishwater?"

"My Granny Shirley taught me that," I tell her. "To chase away cooties."

"Granny Shirley, huh?"

"Yes, ma'am. The Queen of Clean."

Phoebe lets it go at that.

AFTER SUPPER, she shows me where the laundry is and I throw in my jeans and panties. She wheels along the hallway, opening doors to empty bedrooms. "You can take any room besides this one," she says, coming to the last. It faces the barn and has French doors that open onto the porch. The decorating scheme is gold with black accents—we're talking glossy lacquered furniture, an old Chinese chest of drawers, a silk chaise near the windows, and heavy brocade drapes. Phoebe about swims in the space, so I'm guessing that without changing one thing she moved into her late aunt's digs. The other four bedrooms are spaced around the great room,

kind of like the corners of a castle. Full bath-
rooms connect them, with nice old tile and in
one case, a chin-deep clawfoot tub. I settle on
the room at the opposite corner of the house
from Phoebe's, mostly because it's such a
far cry from a cot in a barn office. Inside
there's an iron bedstead with a double mattress covered with a flowered spread laden with
satiny throw pillows. The dresser and bedside
table are dark oak, antique. I walk into the closet
and pull on the overhead light and stare at the
empty shoe cubbies, the rods with the satin-
covered hangers. It all reminds me of an old-
time hotel, where wealthy guests check in for
the summer season and end up returning for
years.

"Okay if I take this one?" I ask Phoebe.

She nods, hardly looking. "Sure. The bed's
already made up. See you in the morning.
Sleep well."

"Wait a second. You need any help getting to bed?"

The look she gives me could peel the wallpaper right off the walls.

She clutches the arms of her wheelchair, and
in this tiny voice chews me a new one. "Let's
get one thing straight, Ness. I didn't offer
you a room so you'd be my attendant. I can
take care of myself; have been for a long time.
As my roommate, you can come and go as you
please. You're not to worry about me, okay?"

"Not a problem."

She wheels herself down the hall and after
a few minutes, I hear her door click shut.

Well, I guess I touched her itchy spot. I'm as good as alone in this strange place. I hear Leroy neighing from the corral. He's used to snacking on grass and sorry that pastime's ended. I'll go out and say good-night to him after I take a shower. I check out the bathroom and find it fully equipped—shampoo, conditioner, soap, razor, toothbrush, paste, fluffy towels—a fancy product line like you'd find in a spa, not that trial-size stuff from the drugstore. I study the razor and wonder what happens if I cut myself with it. Granny Shirley's drilled it into me that suicide is like slapping God in the face, but does He really want his children to suffer with a disease that wastes them to bones? What happens if I accidentally nick myself, bleed all over the bathroom, and maybe leave a sliver of my skin behind in the blade, and someone like Phoebe uses it? Will she be exposed to what I more than likely have?

I decide to let my armpits and legs grow out, like a hippie girl. Got a good start going in that department anyway. The feeling of hot water hitting my neck is so reassuring and kindly that out of nowhere comes this sob that I try to stifle with a washcloth. I take deep breaths, kneel down there in the shower stall and hug myself hard.

Right about this time of night, Granny Shirley is kneeling, too, on a pillow she keeps at her bedside so she can say her prayers. She never forgets to ask God to bless me. I don't believe in praying for what I haven't earned.

35

The most I can manage is Whoever's responsible, thanks for the shower.

AS I'M COMING IN from the barn, checking on Leroy one last time, I hear Phoebe on the kitchen phone, saying, "Those are just the taxes? Are you sure? But Malcolm, that's almost like paying a mortgage on a house. You know I'm on a limited income. Does this mean I have to sell the property?"

All night my first night, when I should be sleeping like a baby in these soft sheets, I toss and turn and worry about what I heard Phoebe say.

NEXT MORNING when I get up to feed, I come across Florencio tinkering with a small tractor. Leroy's munching on a fatter flake of hay than I would have given him. "Thanks for tending my horse," I say. "You don't have to make a habit of it."

Florencio drops one tool in the dirt and picks up another. *"De nada.* That's a real nice horse. *Por supuesto,* I know horses, and that one, he's a good fellow. You had him long?"

A prickle of alarm travels halfway up my spine. How well does he know horses? Does he bet on them at the track? Could he possibly know Jake? I figure the best approach is to soft-pedal things. "Lots of nice horses in this valley, aren't there? Old Leroy here, he's a plug, but he does have a pretty coat."

"*Si.*"

I stretch my arms out in the sun and change the subject. "So, how big is this place?"

Florencio brushes his arms clean of dust. Lovingly, he pats the tractor seat. "Hop on. I give you a tour of the farm."

He drives me around the fields where all types of plants are growing. The air is hot and dry, but the smell of flowers comes through. The sunflowers' big droopy heads look like they've been looted; the blackbirds are so bent on picking them clean. It's a little spooky how intensely they go at it. And I never knew poppies came in colors besides that yellow-gold, but they do, pink, red, and white. The endless rows of them make the field look as if a pirate hurried through spilling doubloons from his treasure chest.

"Mum, aster, anemone," Florencio says. "They blooming next month."

"Man, that's a mess of flowers. What do you do with them?"

His proud face scans each row. "*Nada.*"

"Nothing?"

"*Señora* Sadie used to sell them to florists. By this time of year, we're usually working hard on Christmas crops."

"We?"

"Well, it's just me now. The others were let go a long time back. Got to wait to see what *Señorita* Phoebe care to do."

"Seems like a waste to let good flowers die on the vine."

37

He touches my arm and I have to remind myself not to flinch, that skin-to-skin contact won't infect anybody. "Flowers never a waste. If nothing else, they feed the *ojo*," and he taps at the corner of one dark eye.

He lets me off at the greenhouses, these massive buildings with cloudy glass windows. Inside the first one are thousands of green plastic pots. What appear to be sticks pop up from the earth inside them, and an intricate watering system overhead feeds each stick. Underfoot, the gravelly floor crunches against my boots. The air feels thick and ripe, as if this is what it must be like to walk around inside somebody's lungs. I touch leaves and wonder who Jake's got his fingers on this very moment, what poor doomed woman is waking up next to him thinking she just hit the lover-man jackpot.

Outside I hear Florencio stop the tractor. "What kind of plants are these?" I say, pointing at the greenhouse contents.

"A few orchid, mostly poinsettia."

"There's about a million of them."

"*Si,* we used to sell them every year. Sadie's poinsettia. People coming from as far away as San Jose to buy. Not the last two years, though. She was too *enferma*. But I keep the cuttings going because it's a crime to lose stock she work thirty *años* to create."

"And what's this flat of dirt?"

He smiles. "Not dirt. My worm castings farm."

"Castings?"

Now he gives me a wink. "What the worms leave behind after dinner."

"Ick. Forget I asked."

He laughs and hands me an orchid in a six-inch pot. It's amazing, this deeply purple-throated thing shaped like a lady's vagina. "The Aztecs believe orchid bring strength to a warrior. Take one up to the house. Put in your room."

I smile. "Do I look like a warrior to you?"

"For a long time Phoebe need a friend like you," he says. "You will cheer her up."

No, I think, no matter how many flowers bloom around here, the longer I stay, the less the possibility is that Phoebe will be cheered up about anything.

I SWEAR THE GIRL READS almost as much as Granny Shirley does, but she goes in for murder mysteries, whereas Granny Shirley reads only one book, the Bible, which I suppose is one big murder mystery, too. Once a week these boxes arrive by UPS to the farmhouse, delivered by this short, buff Latino who hangs around until Phoebe opens the package. His name's Juan, and he looks like an overgrown Boy Scout in his brown shorts and shirt. Juan always says he's worried a book might have gotten damaged in the shipping process, but I think he just likes telling Phoebe jokes and making her laugh. Got to admit, she has a laugh you don't get tired of, high and light, sort of like Tinkerbell. For as long as he stays, Phoebe's happy, engaged in the business of living, but the minute he drives away in the cloud of dust his van kicks up, she stares down the lane for a long while. Then her face closes in on itself like one of the vine flowers along the fence. I've learned that by watching these flowers, which Florencio refers to as weeds, you can tell time, or when it's four o'clock, anyway. So far, those flowers are the only practical things I can see happening around the farm.

If Phoebe's not reading, she's working on the clay sculptures she showed me the first day I met her. Her fingers, like everything else about her, are so small they look like a child's. One of her index fingers is misshapen from arthritis, but doesn't seem to interfere when it comes to the clay. She cranks out the mobiles at the rate of three an hour. When she finishes one, she tallies its type onto a yellow pad and then she begins the next one. On days when I have nothing to do—there are more than a few of them, I hate to admit, looking for shoeing clients is not going as well as I'd hoped—I sit by Phoebe and watch her fingers pinch and prod the clay into shapes.

"Make a horse," I tell her after I've been there three weeks without finding a single steady client.

She pulls off a length of black clay and in a few minutes she holds a miniature Leroy in her palm.

"Wow. That's great."

"You try it," she tells me, offering the clay.

"No thanks, I have no artistic talent whatsoever. I can't even draw a decent circle. Whole thing seems like magic to me."

"It's a little mysterious," Phoebe allows. "At least it keeps me from thinking about my problems."

When she says problems, I hear a door creak open, and I jump in, feet first. "Florencio showed me the greenhouse," I say. "Whole lot of poinsettia plants in there. He said your aunt used to sell them. That true?"

Phoebe nods, then looks away.

"So why don't you keep up the tradition?"

She snorts. "Like I know the first thing about growing poinsettias, let alone selling them."

"Well, shoot. How hard can it be? Florencio does most of the work. You put an ad in the paper, sell plants, take peoples' money, your bills get paid."

Her eyes narrow at me and I force myself not to look away. I can tell she thinks I overheard her on the phone. So what? I'm out of here in a few weeks, max, on my way to sunnier climes. I have a couple hundred saved now, and if in the next few weeks I can double that money, I'll have enough to ship Leroy by transport to Glendale, Arizona, to a ranch that needs farriers and will let me room and board. But I'm a little jealous—Phoebe sitting on this goldmine while I have to practically give my services away to get someone to trust me with their horse. Consider this my parting gift.

"Ness, there's a little more to running a flower farm than positive thinking."

"And that means fear of failure should stop you from trying?"

Delicately, she sets the black clay horse down on the cookie sheet next to the mobiles. "Do you happen to know where the word *poinsettia* comes from?"

Her face is tight. I've probably blown my setup here, but once I get my hackles up, I find it hard to back down. "No, but I can cuss in three languages. Want to hear?"

"Not really. Let me tell you about poinsettias. The word's got Mexican origins, after Dr. Joel Roberts Poinsett, ambassador to Mexico in the 1820s. *Poinsettismo*. He was pushy and intrusive, too."

I lean back in my chair and study this white girl who probably weighs about as much as both my legs. "You're right, this ain't any of my business. What you should do is let those flowers rot on the stem. That would have made your dear departed aunt really happy."

She's bristling now, her neck hair up and twitching. "What gives you, a perfect stranger, the right to presume to know anything about my aunt?"

"Girl, you think black folks don't know squat about grief? Or maybe we're just not welcome at your pity parade."

"It's not a freaking parade!" she hollers, and rolls her chair away a few inches, surprising me with the strength in her small, muscled arms. When she stops, her arms lie flaccid at her sides

42

and her voice grows soft. "I'm lost without her, I swear. I don't even know what to do with myself. Maybe James was right, this is too much for me."

I pick up a piece of the black clay and use my fingers to press it into a cube. I set it down on the table and make another, then stack it on the other one, and continue along, waiting.

Phoebe rolls her chair back. She bends her head down and begins wrapping the remaining clay into cellophane. After the colors are lined up from light to dark, she says, "Sorry. I haven't been getting much sleep lately. I lie there and think about how much work it takes to run this place, and how even if I could walk enough to help Florencio, it still wouldn't be enough to get the plants ready to sell. Why did Sadie leave me the place if I can't afford to run it?" One tear escapes and she scrubs it away.

I've got a real good start on a clay wall going. I expect Phoebe to either mush it all together or begin adding to it, but she just lets it sit there drying out. Part of me thinks I should go indoors before she asks me to, pack my bag, and ride out of here. Last thing I need is another set of problems. But I need to save money. I have to stay unless she kicks me out. Something makes me open my big mouth again. "Mourning takes time, Phoebe. But that doesn't mean you can't get some work done. People been living their lives side by side with sadness for as long as anyone can remember, and the world still manages to spin. I'm telling you, with a little effort, I think you could sell those plants."

She shakes her head. "Sadie had four people to run this farm. I only have Florencio."

"You already got another person—me." Oh, the minute I say that I feel sick with regret.

She smiles gamely. "Thanks, that's a nice idea, but I couldn't afford to pay anyone until the poinsettias were sold, providing we sold enough of them, and Christmas is months away. I'm barely paying Florencio's wages as it is."

"Offer collateral."

"What do I have for collateral? Back issues of *Active Disabled*?"

"What's that?"

"This awful magazine my mother keeps sending me."

"Ugh. Give them to the library. Use them as mulch. What about your place, Phoebe? Odds are I'm not the only homeless girl in this area. Other people need to board horses. Rent out your empty bedrooms. Fill up the barn. You'd have cash in your pockets immediately."

"But what if I chose wrong, and the renters were awful to live with?"

She's so much the doom-and-gloom queen today I could give her a little slap and not feel bad about it. But instead I break my rule about not getting involved. "You think there aren't ways around that? Goodness, girl, you just have to be a little creative. Give me that pad and pencil. We'll write us an ad so that we weed out people who aren't our type." We. What am I saying?

"But Ness," she asks. "Isn't that discrimination?"

And we take good long looks at each other and suddenly it seems like the funniest thing in the world for us to be worrying about. So. One more month here won't kill me, and if it does, well, at least I'll have avoided the bad stuff that comes along with Jake's parting gift. It's not like Arizona's going anyplace.

*Nance*

# 3

## *Macaroni Boy Revelations*

TO ALL THOSE SCIENTISTS out there conducting studies on the effect of stress on middle-aged women, when's my turn to interview? On the way over here, the following things happened:

1. I narrowly missed getting sideswiped by some old geezer in a Cadillac, who just *had* to pass me so that he could drive thirty miles an hour in a forty-five zone,

2. for no reason that I can discern, I was flipped the bird by a kid on a skateboard, and

3. for complete and total humiliation, I was pulled over by a cop who accused me of driving too slow!

"But, Officer," I tried to explain. "I was forced to drive thirty in order not to tailgate the geezer in the Cadillac who passed me."

"Geezer?" he said, curling his mustachioed upper lip as if the minor epithet wasn't part of his vocabulary. "Ma'am, the speed limit on Valley Road is forty-five, and if you can't keep up with the flow of traffic, I suggest you buy yourself a bicycle."

Officer Stern, Badge 99504, made me sign a written warning, which is not the same thing as a ticket, but still has the power to make a woman cry. For about thirty seconds I wished that Duchess, riding shotgun, were a rottweiler instead of the mellowest ten-year-old Labrador retriever on the planet. I didn't want her to break the skin exactly, just show her teeth and make Badge Boy back off. Alas, Duchess only shows her teeth when I come at her with a toothbrush and poultry-flavored toothpaste.

But anyway, I'm an hour early to meet Phoebe DeThomas, the woman who ran the ad in the paper. I'm perennially early for things, which makes me a terrific employee and a bad person to cheat on. The ad said she was conducting "a study of middle-aged women who owned pets and had experienced difficulty locating housing," and that my participation in her survey would "contribute to the great body of women's studies." Her master's thesis, I figured, what a great topic. Why not help out? I certainly met the qualifications. Little did I know the thing itself might compromise my stress... So I called, she sent the questionnaire; I filled it out and sent it back. A few days later, Phoebe phoned me and asked if I would meet her here to go over my answers in person. Good thing I kept a copy.

I parked Rhoda, my four-wheel drive Rodeo, under the restaurant eaves and checked out the sign to make sure this was Katy's Diner. The neon over the newly painted faux wagon wheel swinging doors assured me it was. Today's breakfast special was the $2.99 cow-girl omelet. Four egg whites, cottage cheese, fresh melon, and coffee. I figured I'd eat while I reviewed my copy of the answers. I've filled out some questionnaires in my time, but this ten-page document was something else entirely.

*Question #1. Describe the circumstances under which you began seeking housing.*

Lord, how many pages am I allowed? I lived with Rick Heinrich for three years, but I can't honestly say he lived with me. Sure, he ate the dinners I made and let me fold his laundry. Things weren't always so tacky. In the beginning, I left him photographs in his mail slot at the magazine where we both worked. You know that old saw, a picture is worth a thousand words? I chose images I knew would speak to his soul, like one of a fly fisherman whipping his line above the water, and in another, a field of unrelenting sunflowers, the only kind of flower he didn't deem "girly."

"Don't stop, Nance," he used to beg me. "I live for those pictures."

Well, "live" eventually changed vowels and turned to "love." I moved into his one-bedroom condo that was stuffed with books and more CDs than any one person could ever listen to in a lifetime, not to mention these aging rock music posters on the bedroom walls that should have been my first clue. A man almost fifty ought to be past all that, or at least keep it hidden in a box in the closet.

Rick was big on promises. He said we'd marry, and that before I turned forty we'd have a baby. I'm thirty-nine and the only stretch marks I have are from yo-yo dieting. He insisted he'd pay back the ten thousand dollars he borrowed from me to pay off his delinquent student loan. He did, but he had to borrow ten thousand dollars from his brother in order to do it. Duchess and I spent five out of seven nights a week alone while he covered concerts and interviewed rock stars passing through Portland on their way to fame and glory even though as a part-time photographer for the magazine, at any time he could have asked me to come along.

One morning I woke up and realized that I was going to turn forty no matter what. My viable eggs had a serious shelf-life problem. I had been politely rebuffing perfectly decent men because of a relationship that was committed on one side only. I knew then that if the condo caught fire, and I had only enough time to save Duchess or Rick, Rick would have been the crispy critter. I packed up my suitcase and headed to my mom's in Cannon Beach for a couple of weeks. She was between men herself, and we had a good time for about three days, which is pretty much our limit. She showed me her latest paintings and I pretended to like them. She had too much to drink every night and wailed about being disinherited. Just before she got to the passing-out stage I'd ask her who my real father was, but damn it all, her tongue never got loose enough to tell me.

I figured my absence would give Rick the idea I meant business.

While I was gone, he bought an aqua-blue Barcalounger recliner with, I am not exaggerating, a tiny, built-in refrigerator in the side. The sight of him in that fake leather womb-coffin, his eyes fixed on the television, the beer only an arm's reach away, well, somehow that did it for me.

*Question #2. How long have you had your pet? Describe his/her impact on your life.*

Duchess? Nine glorious years. When I rescued her from the pound, she was skin and bones. She shied every time I so much as lifted my hand to brush her hair. Whoever abused her did a thorough job. Rick was never mean to her, but she could tell he didn't love her. "Give me a big, dumb dog any day," he used to say, right within earshot, and believe me, Duchess is not stupid. She's been with me through good times and bad, including this lousy stretch of housing search. Let's just say the impact she's made on my life has me spending seventy-nine dollars a night to stay in a hotel that allows pets. Thank-you, Visa gold card.

When my cowgirl omelet arrives in high-protein splendor, along with a side of bacon, I set my papers down and call out to the waitress. "Excuse me, not that I'd mind eating it, but I didn't order this bacon."

She's small and dark-skinned, and wears three earrings on her left lobe. "The side of bacon's for your dog," she says, "compliments of Ramon—" and she points her order pad at the cook, who waves from behind the counter. He's flirting all right, just not with me. By his smile it's apparent he has a thing for the waitress, who bends over, causing her skirt to hike up, as she serves Duchess. That's proof there's no end to my dog's magic. My good girl, sitting so quietly waiting for me, is bringing a couple closer and getting a free breakfast in the bargain.

*Question #3. Describe your lowest moment in your housing search. Be honest. Your answers will be kept confidential.*

Gosh, this omelet's wonderful—just the right amount of seasoning—and the cantaloupe's freshly cut, no wilted edges. I set my fork down to reread my longest answer. How could I condense the three most humiliating

50

days of my life onto an 8½-by-11-inch piece of paper? A long time ago, I had aspirations to become a writer. Nothing world shattering, just good old-fashioned books people could check out of the library. The longer I lived with Rick, though, the less I felt like writing. He had a journalist's formula, from which he never varied:

1. Craft your story like a fish hook
2. Pull the reader in
3. Tease him into thinking he's going to get away
4. Then grab him by the gills and get out your cutting knife or
5. Use him as bait for a bigger story

Before I can reread my answer, however, these two women come into the diner. The one in the wheelchair looks like my old Patty Playpal doll, porcelain complexion and big dark eyes. She can't be over four feet five inches. The tall black woman with her is dressed in skin-tight jeans, a tank top, and a belt buckle as big as a saucer. The muscles in her arms are a little frightening. She's wearing scuffed up knee-high English riding boots and looks as if she just stepped out of the Sundance catalog after kicking Robert Redford's butt clear across Montana. They smile at me knowingly. Oh, my sweet Lord in heaven, which one of them is Phoebe? They obviously know me—I described myself to a tee: short blond hair, red leather bolero jacket, and yellow Labrador retriever.

"Hello, there. Won't you have a seat?" I say,

51

my Southern manners rising to the occasion, and then I blush madly because obviously the one in the wheelchair already *has* a seat. The black girl laughs heartily, and I just know she can see up my family tree clear back to my great-great-granddaddy Mattox who used to own slaves.

"Nance?" the one in the wheelchair says. I nod. "Nice to meet you. I'm Phoebe, and this is my housemate, Ness Butler. Your questionnaire intrigued us, particularly the answer to question three. Do you mind if I read it out loud?"

Before I can shake my head no she clears her throat and in that tiny, high-pitched voice, begins reading:

"Why I Despise the Evening Primrose Flower" a *very* short story by N. J. Mattox

The advertisement in the *Messenger* looked too good to be true: *For rent, month-to-month, one-bedroom cottage on Emerald Drive, $850, utilities included.*

The first thing that caught my eye was the lack of a "no pets" caveat. With shaking hands, I dialed the phone number. Three solid weeks of unsuccessful house hunting will do that to anybody. "Bayborough Realty," a woman's voice, thick with a history of cigarettes, answered. "How may I assist?"

Be friendly, I told myself. Don't sound desperate. "Hello. I'm interested in the one-bedroom on Emerald Drive you advertised. Is it still available?"

"Yes, dear. In fact, I'm showing it to several prospective tenants this evening."

Stay cool, be brief, and get to the point. "I'd like to see it. Would it be possible to also make an appointment?"

The craggy voice hesitated. "Why don't you drive by and take a look first? It's very small, dear, and only the one bedroom. If you like what you see, call back and ask to speak to Babs."

Already rented, I told myself, or worse yet, she has a relative who wants it. Still, what could it hurt to look? "Thank you, Babs, I'll do that. Can you give me the address?"

This time the pause on Babs's end was infinitely more telling. I got the feeling that I had somehow sunk my tug without leaving the harbor. "Dear, the houses in Bayborough-by-the-Sea don't have *street addresses,* they're *named.* Look for Evening Primrose; it's seven houses down on the left. Do you think you can find it?"

No, I'm blind and illiterate. Keep your cool, Nance. Just say thank you and hang up, which I did. "I have a feeling about this one," I said to Duchess, who thumped her majestic yellow tail against the nappy motel carpet. "Keep your paws crossed and say a doggie Hail Mary."

Duchess rose elegantly to her feet. We'd been staying at the Sierra Grove hotel for almost a month. At night, she'd curl up on her rug at the foot of my bed and delicately snore, which blended perfectly with the sound of the ocean waves. I'd lie on top of the bed and stare at the ceiling, praying for forgiveness for my most recent wicked thoughts. They're not really that bad— just stuff a woman wishes on a man who didn't work out. Intractable acne, having to go back to work delivering papers instead of writing for Portland's hippest weekly, and with whatever foolish female next occupies his bed, may he forever experience the limpest of willies.

Duchess and I had driven south to this quaint (read expensive) California beach town, looking to start over in a place that would fill our hearts with gladness—and if it wasn't too much trouble, possibly a little more sunshine. I knew I could find work, but I never expected the housing thing would turn out to be such a butt-kicker. Evening Primrose—such a romantic name for a house—naming houses, much preferable to numbers, I thought.

I parked across the narrow street and hooked Duchess to her leash. The house was like something out of the fairy-tale books I used to read as a kid. Small, with a steeply pitched roof, snow-white clapboard, break-your-heart-blue shutters, leaded glass windows, French doors. The roof shingles were arranged in a wavy, gingerbread pattern. On the door someone had painted in cursive script EVENING PRIMROSE. On either side of the door flowers were stenciled in melon pink, Easter basket lilac, and a bridesmaid's seafoam green color that matched the waves, which I reminded myself, were less than six blocks away—a good daily constitutional for Duchess.

I knew this house was just what I needed to get over Rick. Long, thoughtful walks to the sand at sunset. Driftwood fires on the beach. Winter storms outside, Duchess and me cozy in front of the crackling fireplace. When I pulled the iron patio furniture over so I could stand on it and peek in the bedroom window, I saw that there was enough room for my antique double bed and dresser, but not much else. It was a good thing I am only five feet two inches tall, because this place was hobbit-sized—but still perfect. I pulled out my cell phone and punched REDIAL.

"I'd like to put a deposit down on Evening Primrose," I told Babs of Bayborough Realty. "This house is exactly what I am looking for."

"Dear, I'm afraid it isn't that simple.

There is an application process. You'll need to come in and fill out the forms."

"Certainly," I said. "By the way, pets are allowed, aren't they? I have a dog." A very good dog, I thought, and winked at Duchess, who was eyeing the local squirrel population with interest.

"Oh, a dog. How much does he weigh?"

"*She's* a small retriever," I said, "forty-five pounds. And doesn't bark, she's very gentle. She even lets little kids yank on her ears." Shut up, Nance, I warned myself. You're doing it again, offering more information than asked for, and lying, because there are days Duchess barks at shadows and not even a new rawhide chew toy will quiet her.

Babs wasn't there when I filled out the form. I paper-clipped a copy of my TRW to the application—excellent credit, despite Rick—along with a photo of Duchess I took for my sample book. She sported a pink ribbon, and very delicately, in her teeth, she held the handle of a basket of wildflowers. I wondered if there was any evening primrose in the bouquet, because that would be a terrific omen.

One sleepless night passed, slower than the time it takes to heal a broken heart. On Sunday, Babs called. I drove over to meet Emily and Thomas Guinness, a lovely older couple who'd bought

Evening Primrose thirty years ago and used her as a beach house getaway. Emily had been a kindergarten teacher; Thomas sold insurance. I grew up in various places, but I'm the only daughter of a Southern mother who insisted I learn how to mix a martini and deliver small talk in a slight Alabama drawl and to stress good breeding above all else. I was pretty sure I had the Guinnesses won over. We were laughing and talking about all kinds of subjects when they asked to meet Duchess. I brought my best friend in from the Rodeo where she had been napping. Just like a good Southern dog, she offered to shake paws, then laid down in the sunlight so it hit her flanks and lit up her clean, yellow fur. The Guinnesses oohed and ahhed over her, said they had another tenant to interview, and I would be getting a call.

I knew I had the cottage. I just knew it.

Duchess and I celebrated by going to the local nursery and buying plants to fill the empty window boxes. We spent twenty dollars on pony packs of alyssum, baby's tears, and I even figured out which flowers were primrose and bought those, too. I was loading them into the Rodeo when the call came.

"Ms. Mattox? Babs of Bayborough Realty here. I'm so sorry. The Guinnesses have decided to rent Primrose Cottage to another applicant."

Maybe Babs felt sorry for me. Maybe she just didn't want to lose out on another commission. Because after a pause, she whispered confidentially, "They simply felt your dog was too large for the house."

"My dog? Excuse me?"

"Yes, dear. They have imposed a forty-pound limit on indoor pets."

"That's, that's—" I sputtered, trying to come up with the correct discriminatory term. And in the next second I swear, these exact words came out of my mouth, "Would it help if I signed her up with Jenny Craig?"

"I hear how disappointed you are," Babs said, "but you're certainly welcome to try again with another listing."

Was that supposed to cheer me up? Did she think I was not only the owner of a too-large dog but simpleminded, too? Duchess settled herself around the boxes of flowers that I suspected were nonreturnable. I thanked Babs even though I wanted to tell her to shove the primrose up her saggy behind, and punched END on my cell phone. I didn't know whether to call the ACLU or the ASPCA. Neither was going to get me Primrose Cottage. Duchess rode shotgun with me out to Point Anne, where we parked next to a Winnebago. "Maybe

I should get one of those," I told my dog, "and paint it up with hemlock on the sides, give it an apt name like Broken-hearted, Homeless, Overly Polite, Baby-Wanting, Single, Middle-aged Woman inside—approach at your own risk. What do you think?"

She barked, splayed her legs, and spun around in the sand.

I unhooked her leash. Duchess raced down the slight dunes and I followed behind. So far as I knew, watching sea lions was a pastime without a weight limit. Sometimes the Pacific just breaks my heart. The way it pounds the rocky shoreline and never gets a chance to rest. The sea lions dutifully honked out what sounded to me like the mournful anthem of rejected tenants everywhere. I must confess I squirted out a few girly tears.

Phoebe turns the page. "It's a great story. What exactly did you mean by it?"

Ness looks at me expectantly.

"Hearing it read out loud like that, I don't know," I stammer. "I was just playing around, using figurative language, finding just the right adjective. The poetry in words sends chills up my spine, you know? I think that way, too, which is probably a failing."

Phoebe nods. "Go on."

"My old boyfriend Rick would say this *anecdote* is crippled by passive verb construction, riddled with clichés, overly sentimental, and that I used more adjectives than were necessary."

Phoebe smiles sympathetically, and Ness says, "Sounds like a real charmer." She asks the waitress if she can take a look at a menu.

Maybe he was, but I'm just as guilty for hanging around him and pining over his unworthy ass. In my wallet I keep the list of reasons why I left him so I won't run back like I'm dying to every second of the day:

1. Reruns—how can a man with a master's degree watch the same *Seinfeld* episode four times and still find it amusing—more amusing than making love to a real live woman?

2. Refusal to speak to me in the morning—"Too many questions before caffeine are a no-no," he'd say, and that I was supposed to remain silent until he gave me the cue that he felt conversant.

3. One too many recitations of the "Simple Guy" philosophy.

"Nan," he would say softly when I pushed too hard, or said I deserved better than two stinking nights a week shared with Jerry Seinfeld/Tom Waits/Sam Peckinpah DVDs/Super Tetris. "You forget that at my core, I'm a simple guy."

As if what I needed was too complex for his reporter's brain to process. How simple? Rick loved to tell me, "Babe, I'm as simple as my favorite meal, macaroni and cheese."

This one night, I remember making the disgusting dish for him and taking it into the den. I expected we were going to start out eating off the same spoon and end up on the floor kissing each other, but no, it turned out he had the TV muted and was fixated on watching NASCAR racing. Cars going around in a circle! Now *that's* simple, but macaroni sure as hell isn't. It comes from wheat, right? Given that the brand Rick liked was thirty-nine cents a box, the logical female mind deduces that the manufacturer is buying ingredients at a cut rate. Enter third-world economics, where women work themselves to death in the fields, with no time off for giving birth. No, it's up and at 'em, stuff that baby into a sling made out of a really ugly bandanna. For this we'll pay you mere pennies a day! The wheat must be tended, cut, threshed, ground into flour, shaped into elbows, all so it can be made into Rick Heinrich's favorite comfort food, and we haven't even gotten into the fake-cheese-powder element. Now what in the Sam Blazes about that is simple?

Phoebe orders oatmeal; Ness, juice, coffee, and French toast. Phoebe turns the page and continues reading my answers.

" 'Question number four. Exactly what role do men play in your life?' "

Shortest answer: " 'See above response.' " She and Ness are laughing now. "Rick?" Ness says.

"AKA Macaroni Boy, Mr. Recliner, Mr. Waste My Life. Take your pick," I tell her.

"Macaroni Boy?" Ness says. "More about that later, I hope."

"Let's stick to the subject," Phoebe says.

"Nance, you seem like the perfect candidate for what we have in mind."

"And what is it exactly that you have in mind?" I ask, nervous that this simple meeting is about to become some lesbian commune offer where I won't be allowed to shave my armpits or wear leather shoes.

Phoebe takes a photograph from her purse and slides it across the table. It's an old color print of a ranch-style farmhouse made of wooden beams and a slate roof. I bet it was taken with an Instamatic, the only camera Kodak ever made that no matter how you aimed it would not adequately focus. Beside it are fields of flowers, all kinds, one color blending into the next like an artist's palette.

"This is my place," she says. "It has five bedrooms and a working flower farm. I'd like to get it to the point where it can turn a profit, but I can't do it alone. I need rent money for capital, and four hours a day labor, four days a week, from each participant. The work detail will be strenuous from now until Christmas. If all goes as planned, the profits will be divided at that time. Ness is already onboard. Sound interesting?"

I grimace. "Farmwork?"

Ness says, "It's not what you think. It's fun. You have your own private room, and the house is good sized enough you'll have your privacy. Come on and take a ride with us, check out the house, hear our proposition in more detail."

"I have Duchess with me," I stall.

"We *want* you to bring the dog," Phoebe says. "She has to like it, too, and get along with the other animals."

"What other animals? Please tell me I'm not going to have to milk goats."

Ness laughs. "So far just a horse, and he doesn't need milking. Please come with us. There's a pot of gold at the end of this rainbow, you'll see."

Phoebe looks up at me with those doelike eyes and how am I supposed to say no to a crippled girl, that I'm worried you all might be fronting for some animal research outfit? I lay money down on the table to pay for my meal and am about to politely decline when Ness bends down and has a little get-to-know-you chat with Duchess. Phoebe fishes in her purse and brings out a dog biscuit and asks me if it's okay to feed it to my dog. "Sure," I say, and think oh hell, what can it hurt to look?

After Phoebe's folded up her wheelchair and slid it into the backseat next to her, we pile into this gorgeous convertible Jaguar and take off down the highway. Really nice leather seats and polished chrome. I have no idea where I'm going, and commit to memory every landmark we pass in case I have to hoof it back to Katy's. Ness presses a button on the dash and Aretha Franklin begins to testify, one of my all-time favorite songs, "Think."

Well, what do you know? That is something I hope Rick is doing right now. It's ten thirty A.M. on a Wednesday morning, the day his big column is due. On Wednesdays, he's in a bad mood all day until his boss approves his copy and he can cut out early and go to the movies to see a shoot-'em-up. He dislikes his boss, not because she's a woman, he often assured me, but because he's a better writer than she is yet she holds the power of editorial veto. He dislikes his column, too, because it means he has to answer letters from people who don't see the world his way—something he finds utterly shocking. He also dislikes research, editorial staff meetings, and particularly those sensitivity seminars all employees must take to learn how to get along with each other. Seems like the only things Rick doesn't dislike involve very little effort, like the aquablue fridge/recliner and TV shows he's already seen. Why do I still love him?

I reach around the seat to pat Duchess and see that Phoebe DeThomas has her arm around my dog. They're deep in conversation, Phoebe talking, Duchess kissing. Duchess reserves kisses for good people only. I let them be.

"THE FARMWORK'S only four days a week, but if we can make it go, we'll all share in the profits. There's the possibility of thousands of dollars each if things go as planned. Of course, profits might turn out to be a lot less, and in the meanwhile, you have a great place to live, meals included."

I'm still not convinced.

"What the questionnaire was really about is this," Phoebe continues. "I'm offering to rent you a furnished room in this house for whatever you can reasonably afford."

"Excuse me? I get to state the rental amount? How do you know I won't gyp you?"

"From your answers," Ness says.

Phoebe wheels her chair onto the porch and out of the sun. "I had to do it this way, Nance, in order to avoid Fair Housing hassles. I only want women here, really great women, and of course, their pets."

I'm flattered to be included in the really-great-women part, but my omelet turns over in my stomach. Can it really be that I am meant to live with a paraplegic and a black cowgirl? I still hold out a sliver of hope that Rick will call and say he can't live without me. He has my cell phone number; he *could* call. But the house has soul, I can tell. It puts me in mind of pictures of my grandparents' place down in Chapman, Alabama. Every branch of my family uses it as a summer retreat, schedules worked out a year in advance. At some point I'd've been welcome, too, if my mother hadn't borne me out of wedlock and then turned into a drunk and borrowed against her inheritance and lost her share. All my life I've stared at that photograph and imagined my wedding taking place on the huge expanse of lawn with hawks flying overhead, all the trees in a riotous springtime bloom and relatives everywhere wishing me well. My mother says the warped plank pine table in the kitchen dates back to plantation days, back to when the Mattox family, who were cotton growers, owned slaves. If Ness learns about that, I'd hate to think what might happen. But I'm also nearing the limit on my Visa, and another night in the hotel is another seventy-nine dollars plus tax.

"Take a walk around," Phoebe suggests. "We'll be in the kitchen. Let us know what you decide."

Duchess heels without a leash as we walk past the barn and the newly turned fields. I'm thinking hard. Maybe I don't need to be six blocks from the ocean, or live in a house with a flowery name. Maybe the farmwork will turn out to be easier than I imagine, and what the hell, if it sucks I can bail out after one night and go back to my hotel. Out of sight of the house, I sit down on some overturned crates, smelling the rich earth and feeling the sun on my back. It's not Alabama and a family, but it's pretty in a country-French-magazine sort of way.

I slip my binder out of my shoulder bag and open it to look at the last pictures Rick and I took together. There he is, standing on the side of the highway the weekend we drove to the Olympic rainforest. On his right cheek is a big burgundy kiss mark in my shade of lipstick. I was trying to cheer him up because he was pissed off. He was all bent out of shape because I made him come there for summer solstice instead of staying home and watching *Ally McBeal* reruns in the refrigerator chair.

Oh, he is so handsome it makes my lips tingle. I figured that night we'd make love in the rented cabin, but instead, he turned away from me and went to sleep. I just don't understand how it is men can sleep when they're mad at you. I laid there studying the freckles on his back, listening to his breathing, a sound I really miss.

"Come on, Duchess," I say, and we walk back to the farmhouse.

Ness is reading a magazine while she stirs something on the stove. Phoebe sits at the kitchen table, a dozen colors of clay spread out before her.

The phone rings, but she doesn't get it. When it goes to the machine, we all listen.

"Phoebe, it's Stinky again. I'm not trying to pressure you. I just want to talk. Maybe now that you've had some time to think, my ideas about selling make a little more sense. Pick up, dammit. I know you're there. Okay, maybe you're not there. Maybe you're out driving your Mercedes. Maybe the Jag. Maybe you've got them leashed together and are driving both at once, like Monte Montana riding a team of trick horses. Whatever. Call me when you get this. I love you, Wingnut."

The machine clicks off and Phoebe looks up and smiles.

"Wingnut?" I say. "Stinky?"

"It's my brother. He calls every five minutes. Not to worry. Well, did you come to a decision?"

"Here are the things I'm good at," I say

firmly. "I take pictures well enough I get paid for it, and that's something I do on a part-time basis, so I have to be flexible with the farmwork. There're days I have to fly out of town on a moment's notice. I can write fair copy, but I have been known to overuse adjectives. I can arrange flowers and I absolutely slay at small talk. I have this credit card bill that's kind of hanging me up, but I can pay you five hundred a month to start."

Phoebe breathes an audible sigh of relief.

"Told you there was nothing to worry about," Ness says.

"That's because you are the eternal optimist," Phoebe says back.

"Well, somebody around here has to think positive or we'd be hanging crepe instead of pruning flowers. Welcome, Nance."

"Thank you," I say, and sit down to drink some coffee at a plank table heavy with its own secrets and memories.

# 4

## The Andrew Dice Clay of Parrots

"C————!" FLOATS OUT the open window of my studio apartment as I stand in the parking space I don't use arguing with Mr. Shaw, my soon-to-be ex-landlord. He's about to tell me that I'm being evicted because my parrot curses, but really, that's not the reason. I'm being evicted because he's discovered that I served time for a felony, a fact I did not disclose on my rental application.

"The neighbors can't take it anymore," he says. "Before you moved in, this was a quiet little complex, everyone minding his own business. No fighting, no drug deals, rents in on time, everybody happy. Mrs. Benvenuti's Chihuahua—does he bark all hours of the day? No. Mr. McKinney's python—I ask you, do you hear him hissing around the clock, giving everyone insomnia?"

Wait a second. He actually thinks we're happy? With the laundry facilities always broken and half the tenants on welfare, nobody's exactly running the joy meter into the red. A 425-dollar studio that allows pets, on the other hand, even if it is the size of a sardine can, is nothing to let go of without a fight. I figure it can't hurt to offer a bone. "What if I keep the windows shut?"

He takes out a cigarette and flicks his lighter. "I don't think so. Get rid of the bird or move by the end of the week, Beryl."

"I can't."

"Can't what? Move by the end of the week? Take a look at the lease you signed..." And he's off, flipping pages madly, practically foaming at the mouth.

Mr. Shaw reminds me of my husband, J.W. The reason I went to prison is because this one time, out of countless other times when J.W. started screaming at me and hitting, just this once, I stuck a kitchen knife in his chest. Not very far, maybe an inch or so. I don't know why I did it. I was slicing vegetables at the time. Maybe I didn't want any more broken ribs, or to have to explain to the kindergartners I worked with why once again, my eye was black. Delphine, this woman I got to be friends with in prison said, "Girl, what your lawyer should have argued was you figured the son of a bitch was an onion, since the sight of him made you cry." Delphine killed her husband, too, only she ran over him with a Dodge Dakota. Twice.

What happened next was J.W. slipped in spilled beer. It's a logical progression, since this incident began with him throwing the bottle at me and missing. He hit his temple on the corner of the counter, and just like that, he fell to the floor, landing facedown on the knife, which went in up to the hilt, broke off inside severing an artery, and on the way to the hospital he died. I did everything you're supposed to. I put ice on his head, a dishtowel on his chest, and called the paramedics. I guess they notified the police. The coroner's report said it was a toss-up as to what had killed him, the lethal temple blow or the internal bleeding. My court-appointed attorney subpoenaed my own X rays, which offered the story of a twelve-year marriage filled with broken bones, but didn't exactly account for emotional fractures. She argued self-defense, and asked the jury to clear me of all charges. The prosecutor went hard-line. He argued that since I admitted to the stabbing, what other option was there but that I should go to jail? It wasn't me who burst into tears when the verdict came down, it was my attorney. She got in trouble for telling the judge that it was going to be decades before the criminal justice system began to look beyond the surface at battered women defending themselves. He made her pay a fine and promise not to disrupt his courtroom again. I think she believed that this one time, things were going to turn out differently. I was sentenced to five years at Chowchilla Women's Facility for the crime of involuntary manslaughter.

I don't want to stick a knife into Mr. Shaw, but I'd like to see him spend five years in jail, then get out with a prison record and try to mend his life into something halfway decent. His yelling is easy to tune out, just like I used to do the coughing, snoring, and crying of the

71

other inmates as I counted down the months of my sentence. It's a great little device for getting through life's more challenging moments. Just let your mind drift. For example, looking down from this hill in Sierra Grove, I can see the ocean, a blue patch of water covered with fog. When the wind's right, the salt smell fills my nose. Most days that's cheering enough. But when it isn't, I know Verde, bless his twisted little parrot heart, will be glad to see me. When I let him out of his cage, he rubs his head against my chest, sneakily trying to bite the buttons off my blouse. He preens my curly red hair and mutters to his reflection in my one pair of gold earrings. I want to ask Mr. Shaw if he knows that parrots are as intelligent as three-year-olds. That they can live to be over a hundred years old. That a bird's bond with his owner runs deeper and kinder than most marriages. When they're abused or ignored, like Verde was, they develop bad habits, or in a worst-case scenario, go quietly insane. But all I say to dam the tide of his words is, "Mr. Shaw, I can't get rid of my bird."

Which is exactly what he is banking on. Wordlessly, he hands me the eviction notice, then turns on his heels toward his silver Mazda Miata. A man his age should be using Dial-a-Ride, not endangering innocent people with a sportscar. My heart races. Anything official does that to me. I've been out of Chowchilla for a year and a half, but the feeling that I could someday land there again never, ever leaves me. I shouldn't have lied, but if I

72

hadn't, he wouldn't have rented me the apartment.

Obscenities float out of the window again, and I sigh. Verde's what they call a severe macaw. No joke, it's a breed type. When stressed, he won't stop cussing, not even if I feed him peanuts in the shell, his favorite food. And the words he favors are the really bad ones that start with C and deeply insult both sexes. If only he slurred, or had a lisp, but no, I adopted the one parrot in the world with perfect enunciation.

Holding on to the eviction notice, I open my front door to reveal my 12-by-12-foot room. It's mine until the weekend, I guess. When I first rented this place, shabby didn't begin to describe it. An ancient green rug had been flung over the spotted, cracked linoleum. It looked like a Yeti had contracted jaundice, laid down, and expired. The kitchen had no cupboard doors, just skewed hinges from where the doors had been ripped away. No oven, either. A microwave that looked as if it was leaking radiation and a hotplate so old I knew it had some kind of affiliation with asbestos made up my cooking options. First thing, I painted the walls a soft, buttery yellow. Then I tacked secondhand curtains over the open shelves. I found a phony Persian rug at the Goodwill and gave the Yeti a Dumpster burial. My efforts went a long way toward making things human, but the true gem that brightens the place is Verde. I took him home with me from Bayborough Bird Rehabilitation Center where I work for minimum wage cleaning cages and caring for the injured birds. Nobody wanted him. His wings had been pinioned, so he'd never fly again. Agnes and Marty, the elderly couple I work with, have this theory that Verde was smuggled in from South America, given in trade to a drug dealer who had an ongoing fight with his girlfriend—hence, the mutually offensive swearing. All I know is some fool ruined Verde's wings, and he is deathly afraid of men, even Marty, who is as gentle as God makes them.

Right now Verde's sitting on top of his cage, pacing the highest perch of his parrot gym and happily flapping his useless wing stubs now that I am indoors. "Hello, Verde," I say, and he answers back with the F word. "Step up," I say, offering him my arm. With his yellow feet, he grabs hold and climbs up to my right shoulder where, if I bet if he had his parrot druthers, he would spend the rest of his life muttering naughty words into my ear.

When J.W. and I got married and moved into the trailer park, I had this fantasy that all that separated us from the good life was material comforts. Plant us in a two-story town house in a decent neighborhood and our problems would disappear. He'd find a steady job and stop drinking; I'd cook *Good Housekeeping* dinners in my fancy kitchen with the big fridge and one of those automatic hot-water dispensers so you could make tea any old time you felt like it. Together we'd build toward a future even my stepmother would envy. The problem was, I'd come to believe that what J.W. told me was true. That we didn't have a new car with a sunroof, money in the bank, and bliss was my fault. When he raised his hand to me, part of it was because how could he bear to look at the sight of someone who caused him to lose job after job after job? If he hadn't married me, he'd be a manager someplace that gave him stock options and a pension. He'd be living on Easy Street and dressing in sharp suits instead of work shirts and Lee jeans. One good thing about prison is it takes a can opener to that kind of thinking. My wishes for the future now are simple. Someday, I'd like a one-bedroom place with lots of windows, and maybe a yard that looks out over somewhere pretty—a view. I wouldn't mind a few good girlfriends, either, like Delphine, Noel, and Selena. Even though we were in prison, I could tell they were the kind of women who enjoyed making dinner together, going to the dollar matinee, or just talking instead of watching television. As for love, truthfully, if the only man that ever parts these thighs is doing my yearly gyn checkup, that's okay. And Verde has to be a part of the picture. In the year and a half that I've worked at BBR, I've come to understand upholding your end of the bargain with animals. What's a little bird crap on your shoe or a nipped finger now and then compared to companionship? Animals are there for you when people are long gone down the road.

There's a stack of week-old newspapers on

my kitchen table. When I ride my bike home after work, I stop at this coffee place where the kids hang out, Java the Hut. What always strikes me is how callow the young are. I'm forty-five now, and thrilled when I have an extra dollar to buy myself a cup of decaf. I load it up with real cream, granulated sugar, and chocolate sprinkles because that doesn't cost anything. I savor my sips and make every drop last. These kids, maybe nineteen, sit there drinking five-dollar exotic macchiattos they rarely finish, and smoking cigarettes as if each filthy breath they inhale is going to deliver them the wisdom of Solomon. They don't bus their own trash, either, just leave it cluttered on the table when the wastebasket is all of five feet away. The boys behind the counter are good people, though. Once, when I had Verde out for a walk, they invited me in and fed him orange slices. Now they save their old newspapers for me, so I can line Verde's cage. I wonder if where I live next I'll meet anyone that kind.

"Time to check out the classifieds," I tell my bad-mouthed parrot, and in answer, he gives me a string of curses.

"You got that right," I tell him.

He stretches out one stubby wing and begins preening.

"PHOEBE SENT ME," Nance Mattox tells me when I meet her, as agreed upon, at the coffee shop. I have Verde in his harness, and his traveling cage beside me, but I don't like to put him in it until I absolutely have to. "She wants you and the parrot to come out to the farm, so she can go over your answers with you."

I'm instantly leery. This Nance person looks like a society debutante. Perfect blond hairdo, gold jewelry, and I'll bet she buys all her clothes at that Talbot's store in Bayborough-by-the-Sea. She's driving an SUV with Oregon plates, and last time I checked, this was still California. "How do I know this isn't a scam?" I say.

She places a well-manicured hand on mine. "Honey, you'll just have to trust me. Two months ago, I was close to giving up myself. Then I answered Phoebe's ad. Nothing but good is going to come of this for you, you'll see. Now let's go or we'll be late for dinner, and that ticks Ness off."

"Who's Ness, if you don't mind me asking?"

"One of the housemates," Nance explains, and drives me down the twisted streets of Sierra Grove, into the town center, with its restored Victorian houses, numerous bed-and-breakfasts, and my favorite used bookstore, Earl's on Ocean, run by a fellow so nice he almost makes me like men again. From there we take the highway to Valley Road and turn left. Up until then, the traffic's awful. Now Monterey pines and eucalyptus trees, country inns, antique shops, wineries, and farmhouses surround us. It's pretty, all this rural land and the sun just about to start going down. When she turns down a dirt road, I automatically do a checklist of the self-defense tactics I learned from being in jail, because rule number one is at all times watch your back. Then the house comes into sight. Wow—it's so big, and well kept, like some kind of dream grandparents' house where a kid could spend summers, play all day, and go to sleep that wonderful kind of tired. We get out of the car, and Verde, nervous in new situations, tries out a few experimental curses. "Hush up," I tell him.

"It's a beautiful farm, isn't it?" Nance asks, gesturing with her arm.

"Like you'd see in a magazine," I answer, and I mean it. The ranchhouse features a wraparound porch, and the two-story barn is painted that great old dusty-red color that doesn't look right on anything else. There's a corral with a black horse in it, and a yellow dog comes running toward us across fields of flowers.

Nance takes firm hold of the dog's snout, and I tense up, but when she speaks, her voice is all honey and no salt. "Duchess Mattox, what have I told you about running in the herbs?" She plucks some greenery from under the dog's collar and crushes it in her fingers. "Rosemary," she says, inhaling deeply. "Mostly we grow flowers here. The herbs were all overgrown, but I've been tending them, selling some, and I must say, they're going over better than anyone expected. I've already got one local restaurant for a customer. I'm building us a website so we can advertise more, and oh, shoot, there I go again, getting ahead of myself. Why don't we go inside and Phoebe can tell you all about it."

She holds the door for me. I explain to Verde that he only has to be in the cage a little while. There's an end table almost the same size as his cage, so we move it close to where everybody's sitting and that way Verde won't feel left out.

For dinner, we sit at this long wooden table that reminds me of Y summer camp when I was a kid. The room's cavernous, like a hotel lobby, with old leather furniture and decorated with paintings that I bet are the real thing. That Phoebe's in a wheelchair is no big deal to me. All day long I work with birds missing a wing or blind in one eye from some idiot human's gun obsession, and it seems like the birds with the most injuries are the ones with the kindest souls. Ness, the tall black woman who's tearing up lettuce for our salad, handed me a glass of iced tea with lemon and mint in it the minute I walked through the door. I take my napkin—wow, real cloth—unfold it, and spread it across my lap.

"Your questionnaire answers touched my heart," Phoebe says in this soft, small voice. "Especially what you said about your bird and his cursing."

"Well," I tell her. "He can't help what comes out of his beak."

She nods. "And what you said about question seven. 'What puts your teeth on edge—' "

"Cowardliness," Nance interrupts. "Can you believe that I put that down, too?"

"Really?" I say, surprised she'd know what I wrote since the questionnaire said it was confidential. I feel a little squirmy in the ladderback chair and begin worrying the hem of my napkin.

"Of course, I went into a little more detail, naming names, and being gender specific, but that's another story I'll save for later."

"Right," says Phoebe, getting back to business. "I wondered if it might be easier for you to go over the questions you left blank in person."

I thought I had gotten away with leaving them unanswered. I mean, it was only two out of ten, and it's not like they're paying me, but when I look around at their faces, nothing I see reassures me. "I don't know," I say. "Something about this whole thing seems strange. I mean, it said on the questionnaire it was supposed to be private."

Phoebe takes a piece of bread from the plate Nance is holding and butters it. "It is," she insists. "Between you, me, and these women. What you say here will never go beyond this room."

I try to smooth the wrinkles from my napkin. "I guess that's okay."

"You can trust us," Phoebe says. "If, after dinner, you decide you want your responses back, they're yours to take home with you."

I watch her face as she goes over my answers. After working with injured birds, one thing I do know is which animals heal and go on to trust humans again. But for some reason, I can't read Phoebe.

"EVERYBODY THAT NEEDS TO wash her hands," Ness says as she sets down the salad and a small pitcher of dressing.

"Do you do all the cooking?" I ask her.

She shakes her head no. "Only on my night. We rotate the kitchen duties."

"Thank God for small favors," Nance says. "Else I'd turn into a rabbit eating all those vegetables."

"Don't start," Ness warns. "I've been clipping articles from *Vegetarian Times* and I can argue you down point for point, Miss Carnivore."

"You'll never win," Nance snaps back. "My body remains my strongest argument."

"Ladies?" Phoebe says. "It's time to set aside your everlasting bitching and enjoy the food. What do you say to an hour-long ceasefire?"

The women join hands and reach out to me, too.

"Saying grace is usually an individual effort," Phoebe says, before she shuts her eyes. "This is my version, and if it doesn't cover things for you, Beryl, feel free to chime in. Thank you, Heavenly Father, for this food, these good friends, the animals in our presence, and especially for our special guest, Beryl. May she feel as at home here as we do. Amen."

"Amen" choruses around the table. Beneath the table, Duchess thumps her tail. I'm not religious, but I say it, too, grateful that for the moment Verde's holding his tongue. From the open window, the first chill of fall seems to come in and cause the candles to flicker for a moment, and then it's warm again. In a vase at the center of the table, someone's arranged dried flowers in various autumn hues. The sound of clinking silverware and happy laughter fills the room. For the next hour, we fill up our plates and swap animal stories and housing dramas until my cheeks hurt from laughing. I wish this dinner could go on forever.

"Now, about the questions you left blank," Phoebe says, setting down her fork. She looks at me with the big brown doe eyes unblinking.

I know which questions she means. There were two of them. Number five, which was a two-parter: *Looking back from the age you are now, what career do you wish you had attempted* and *What limitation keeps you from pursuing that goal?* I didn't answer because it hurts me to think about it. "I love children," I say. "I wanted to be a kindergarten teacher, but I only got as far as being a teacher's aide."

"Why?" Nance asks.

"I can't get a teaching certificate."

"Why not?" she asks again.

"Because I have a felony record."

Nance gasps. In the silence that follows, Phoebe frowns at me. Ness rushes to the fridge to bring out the dessert, a chocolate icebox cake. She cuts me a piece even though

I haven't yet asked for one. Phoebe pushes her plate aside, leans forward and looks at me. "I have to ask, Beryl. What did you do?"

I figure I'll just say murder, skip the cake, and maybe Nance will be kind enough to drive me as far as the main road and I can walk home from there. "I killed somebody. Inadvertently," I add, and force myself to meet her gaze.

"Did you go to prison?" Ness asks.

"Yes. Central Valley Women's in Chowchilla. Five years."

The silence deepens, and I can tell they don't quite know what to say to me. Now, when I could really use some parrot cussing to break the tension, Verde is maddeningly silent.

"Would you mind taking a walk around outside for a few minutes?" Phoebe asks. "So we can discuss this?"

"That's okay," I tell her. "I'll just take my bird and get going. Thanks for a wonderful meal. I really enjoyed it." I stand up, but suddenly Ness is there behind me, her hands on my shoulders, pushing me back down in the chair.

"Hold on," she says. "Did this somebody deserve killing? Because if so, I have to tell you, Phoebe, the only difference between Beryl and me is about a hair's breadth of restraint."

In my mind's eye I see J.W.'s face, focused in on himself even in our last few moments together, when I was hysterically saying how sorry I was. When the paramedics loaded him into the ambulance, even bleeding to death he tried to hit one of them and they had to tie his arms down. The police wouldn't let me go along with him. That was my last vision of my husband, cussing out and trying to hit the medic who was trying to save his life. It's harder to answer her question than any of the ones on the questionnaire. "He did some awful things, but I don't think anybody has the right to take another person's life. Like I said, it was an accident."

"Why don't you tell us the whole story," Phoebe says. "Maybe if we had a clearer picture..."

And for some reason, I start telling them everything, just spilling out J.W.'s most awful side. The number of broken noses I got from not standing up to him, three. The times he forced me into bed when I didn't want to be there, a hundred is probably too low an estimate. That last horrible day when it happened, and the trial is something I replay in my mind every night before sleeping. It's as if my tongue has broken free of my mouth and is running up and down mountains like some wild mustang. But when I get it all spilled out, I feel so tired I could curl up on the floor and sleep for three days, and I haven't felt that way for almost seven years. Phoebe is looking at her hands, not at me, and this strikes me as a bad sign.

"Let me get this straight," Ness says. "You stabbed him with a *Ginsu* knife? The kind they sell on TV, 'only nineteen ninety-nine and guaranteed for life, but wait—if you order *right* now, we'll throw in a set of steak knives free'?"

"Don't forget the apple corer accessory," Nance says. "Though I doubt it would be as useful as the steak knives, particularly in Beryl's case."

"Watch your mouth, Nancy J.," Ness says. "Beryl spent five years of her life behind bars. Maybe she doesn't think that's funny."

Nance throws up her hands. "Oh, Christ, will you relax? All I meant was, if the booger deserved stabbing, and it sounds like he sure as hell didn't deserve a merit badge, it was a good thing she was cutting with the steak knife instead of coring a damn apple!"

"Ginsu knife," Ness repeats. "Ginsu."

"It's good to know the knife has other applications besides meat," Phoebe says, and a giggle escapes her tiny mouth.

"These women are dyed-in-the-wool vegetarians," Nance explains. "That means they possess this ridiculous case against eating meat and at any opportunity will preach to you. I for one do not freaking understand it. What have carbohydrates ever done for anyone except make her fat?"

"You have to admit they taste good," Phoebe says.

"So does frosting, but no one should make a complete diet of it. I'm telling you, adequate protein is the key to staying slim," she says, and just then Verde lets loose with a string of all his favorite words, in fact, every last one of them, including the one in Spanish I haven't quite figured out. Everybody turns to look at him, which of course, only encourages the beast, and he puffs up his head feathers and does it again.

"Damn, if that parrot doesn't remind me of my ex," Ness says. "Who brought him to the rehab center? It wasn't a handsome black cowboy, by any chance?"

"Nobody knows. Verde was a resident before any of us started working there."

"Too bad you can't get him to do it to tele-marketers when they call during mealtime."

"Or Stinky," Phoebe says. "My brother needs to hear what Verde's saying."

Now that the killing stuff is on the table and no one's run me out the door, I breathe a little easier. "All I know is Trash Mouth got me evicted from my apartment. And I have two days left in which to find a new place."

"Cheer up," Ness soothes. "Something might come up sooner than you imagine. Can I give him some cake?"

"Actually, fruit or vegetables would be better."

"Hear that, Nance?" Ness says. "The animal world understands the perfect diet. Like an apple."

Nance says, "For which the corer would come in handy. I'm sorry, that just slipped out." She and Ness collapse into laughter. "Sorry," Nance says, before succumbing once again. "It's just so damn funny—"

"Why did you want Verde for your own?"

Phoebe asks, trying to interject some dignity into the conversation.

"Because more than anybody, I think, I understand why he cusses," I tell her. "Verde's just repeating the words he's learned. Nobody ever taught him another way. He gets frustrated, and he doesn't know what to do except swear a blue streak. In every other way he's an angel. Why should anyone be punished for the crap someone else dumped on him?"

She smiles at me. "I couldn't agree more. Now, about question eight. What made you leave that one blank?"

*Describe your relationship with your mother.*

I drag the tines of my fork around the icebox cake frosting. It's not just chocolate, it's red devil's food, and with a filling so sweet and creamy I'd like nothing better than to go at it with my fingers. My mom committed suicide when I was seven years old. She was ill with a cancer people didn't recover from in those days. Today, it has one of the highest cure rates. Some people might say that's too young to remember losing someone, but they're wrong. My father remarried in three months, far too quickly for him to not have been having an affair while she was ill. Then he had a heart attack, then another, and then he died, leaving Betty in charge of all his money and me. Every chance she got she reminded me just how lucky I was she didn't put me up for adoption. The last time I saw my stepmother, which was just before I went in to serve my sentence, she was wearing a navy-blue pants suit and a white plastic bangle bracelet. Betty believed in accessories like some people believe in vitamins, so it was pretty fair odds she had its replacement in her jewelry box in case this one got lost. She stood there and told me she was washing her hands of me, that from this day forward I wasn't anything to her anymore. That it was a good thing I had taken J.W.'s name when I married him because that way, no matter what I did next, at least my name wouldn't connect anyone to her or my late father. The guard let her out of the visiting room and then they drove me to Chowchilla. I rode in the back of a white van and couldn't stop thinking how J.W.'s life had ended in the back of a white van and where I was going there was no guarantee mine wouldn't end either. But what weighed on my mind that first night in my cell while I got slowly used to the disinfectant smell and the scratchy uniform and the hard cots was this: How could one unfortunate accident with a knife erase me? For six years of my life, my real mother tied plaid ribbons in my hair, bought me kelly-green knee socks to wear on St. Patrick's Day, had given me baby aspirin, and rocked me to sleep when I spiked a fever—all during a time when someone should have been comforting her. Then she became so sad she felt she had to die, and who could blame her? Enter Betty, the stereotypical wicked stepmother. Exit my dad. All my living blood relatives were gone now. It was just myself and the uniform with the numbers on it.

"I didn't answer that question because I don't like to think about her," I answer, keeping my voice entirely steady. "And that's all there is to say on the subject."

"Oh, cut her some slack, Phoebe. I didn't answer it either," Nance tells me. "But one of these nights, I predict we're going to open a bottle of wine and tell *all*." She goes over to Verde's cage and tells him what a pretty boy he is. He hangs upside down on the perch to let her know he thinks she's foxy.

I excuse myself to use the bathroom, and stay in there longer than I need to, splashing water on my face, running my damp hands through my hair, trying to make it look less frizzy, which is impossible. I'm not exactly a crone at forty-five I don't think, though my body's not like Nance's, all trim and small, but it's served me well and I like it. I'm totally average—five-five, 140 pounds, size eight shoe, and except for the slight bump in my nose from being broken, my face, though covered with freckles, is not bad. Yet I feel decades older than these thirty-something women will ever become. Their house is beautiful. I enjoyed dinner, even though I didn't finish the cake. Yet I can't quite make all this fit together. Nance's reassuring remarks on the way over, Phoebe insisting I answer the questions, this house where they all seem to live, vegetarians and carnivores alike, and add to that the flower farm outside. I head back to the table, intending to come right out and ask.

But Phoebe's not there. Ness asks me will

I help her clear the plates and rinse the dishes, please. "Are you the kind of woman who would share her two best recipes?" she asks while we load up the dishwasher. "I'm praying at least one of them has meat in it for Nance's sake."

Nance sticks out her tongue. "There's all kinds of literature supporting my theory, not to mention the fact that I wear a size four."

"Oh, bite me," Ness says. "Your size four is a direct result of biology, not dead-animal-flesh intake. Look at me—I wear a size fourteen and do I look bad? I get my share of whistles. In fact, I think I look great. Size doesn't matter unless we're talking Mr. Winky and you know it."

Ness and Nance take time out to laugh and tell a few size-does-matter stories. I like these women. How they argue their opinions and don't want to talk about their mothers, and how Nance's dog Duchess is under the table the whole time we're eating, and she doesn't even stay there to beg, it's more like she enjoys the company. They're nice to Verde, and so far no one's complained about his cursing. It's strange to admit, but in a way, they remind me of my prison friends, down to earth, not afraid to talk about their hardships. I feel easy in their presence, except maybe for Phoebe. I think that's because she's the authority figure—she owns the place.

"I can cook pretty much anything," I tell Ness. "Even in mass quantities, since I mostly worked in the prison kitchen. But probably my best meals are drunken chicken, which uses half a bottle of brandy, and fried doughnuts, which takes a half a bottle of oil and as much confectioner's sugar as the oil will sop up."

Nance's squeals of glee seem to rise to the ceiling, and Ness is laughing so hard she has to sit down. "M——f——!" Verde puts in, adding his two cents, and who would believe it's Phoebe, wheeling herself back into the kitchen, who answers him back, matching him word for word and then some.

She has a book on her lap. "I want to read you guys something from my aunt's gardening journal," she says, and flips to a page she has marked with a blue ribbon. " 'Hair of the horse, hair of the dog, soft fur of the rabbit, or your own human hair. If you scatter a little deep into the beds as you mulch, the mineral content will be greatly improved beyond any of the stuff available commercially.' " She shuts the book and looks at us. "What do you think? Should we try it?"

"Why not?" Ness hold up the cake knife and slices off one of her braids. She hands the knife to Nance, who daintily cuts away a lock of blond from underneath her ear where it won't alter her perfect hairstyle. Phoebe lets Nance trim a lock of her dark hair, and Nance holds the knife out to me. It hardly matters with hair like mine; I pull out a curly strand and cut without looking. We each lay the hair onto a plate and I look at it commingled like that, strange communion ready to feed the garden. For some reason, it makes me shiver.

Then Ness starts cutting herself a sliver of cake, and Nance fights her for it, and when I step in and try to take the knife away they feint in mock horror, and Phoebe, who's been quiet for some time now, interrupts.

"Just one more question, Beryl, before we collapse into complete chaos. Do you and that cussing parrot want to come live with us?"

I look down at the cake pan on the counter, the four neat slices missing from its perfect symmetry, and start to cry. The tears wash over my face like I've just been told I've been given a complete pardon. When at last I'm composed enough to raise my head, all three of them are smiling at me, and all at once, they each hand me their napkins—real cloth—wow.

# *Fall*

I never understood why people got melancholy in autumn! Golden leaves, late light, *this* is the season of renewal. How can you have spring without planting bulbs in fall? Think of Persephone, trudging to the underworld, the taste of pomegranate on her tongue. When she returns in spring, the frail blossoms will be lifting their heads. They managed to grow without her there to protect them; they felt her hope underground. They believed and prospered.

—from the gardening journal of
SARAH DeThomas

# 5

## *Pinching Day*

THE WIND BLOWS SO HARD down the neck of my jacket that when I walk from the house to the barn at six in the morning, I no longer stop to exclaim over the pumpkin patch sprawling with brilliant orange, basketball-size fruit. I can't help but glance at the few trees whose leaves have turned that glorious autumn scarlet. Their leaves call out, "Come play," and like schoolchildren, none of us can pass by without picking up a few and bringing them into the house for show and tell. But there's little time for reveling in this fall.

Everyone's too tired. Besides our regular work, there's the farm. And always too much to do, things going wonky that we can't afford to fix. So much depends on the poinsettias that we're babying them like royalty. "I never liked poinsettias" Nance says is her new mantra.

"You don't have to marry them," Beryl replies. "Just make sure the little monsters thrive."

Then Phoebe wheels into the room and we all go silent because if the crop fails, she loses the farm. It's as simple as that.

Meanwhile, I'd like to walk straight into town

to the nearest bar and order up a strong hot toddy, and then when that one's gone, another to keep it company. These days it's as if my thermostat's busted. I cannot get warm. I worry that it's the disease making its presence known, though every winter has me counting the days until spring. From what I've read, people with AIDS shouldn't overdo alcohol. Besides, how can I slack off when as soon as I enter the greenhouse, up before all of us, already working, even with a cold, there's Phoebe.

She ordered Florencio to install a ramp into the greenhouse and lay out boards across the gravel so she can wheel herself around and "do her part." He wanted to do all the work himself, but the man is in his seventies, for crying out loud, and there're four of us. Still, he was furious when she insisted, his male pride puffing him up like a threatened blowfish. Phoebe's stubborn. She won't return her brother's phone calls and she wants to do her share of the work plus keep making those mobiles besides. I can smell her Hall's Mentholyptus lozenges even before I see her. If I'm feeling chilly, chances are that as skinny as she is, she's feeling the shivers that much worse.

"Morning," I say. "Thought it was my turn to have first shift."

"I couldn't sleep." She coughs. "Not when today's the big day."

She says this as if I'd forgotten. I check the temperature gauges to make certain the greenhouse stays between sixty-two and sixty-four degrees. It's sixty-three on two of them, but only sixty-one on another, so I fiddle with the thermostat mechanism until I see the needle start to flicker. "Doesn't mean you have to be insomniac out here in the damp. Why don't you go sit by the fire and get warm?"

She wheels her chair around to face me. In her lap is that journal of her aunt's she's always carrying around. It's like her Twelve Step Program or something. "Listen to this," she says, flipping the pages with her gloved hand.

I lean back against the wooden bench and wait for my daily dose of dear departed Aunt Sadie. Sometimes I swear she's the fifth member of our party, somewhere around the corner just out of sight. I picture her wearing one of those wide-brimmed gardener's hats, her elbows and knees stained dark with earth.

" 'A plant is like a self-willed man, out of whom we can obtain all which we desire, if we will only treat him his own way.' "

"Oh, yeah," I say. "Been there, done that, regretted it big time. Sounds like Sadie had men *all* figured out."

"Sadie didn't say it. Somebody named Goethe did."

"Who's that?"

"I don't know. A writer?"

"Well, bully for Goethe. Why don't we call him up and ask him to come help with the pinching?"

Phoebe laughs. "It's going to go fine, Ness. Stop worrying."

"I will as soon as Florencio shows up. Where is he? I thought he'd be here by now."

Her smile disappears. "Actually, Florencio's in Mexico. He called me last night. His mother passed away. She was ninety-four. He and Rosa drove down to arrange the service. It's just us girls."

And thousands of plants and our thumbs and index fingers. A trickle of cold sweat drips down my back. "You're kidding."

But people don't kid about funerals. We're going to need divine intervention here. I should call Granny Shirley, get the prayer circle going. Trouble is, I think they only pray for people, and once in a while, some truly worthy animal, like a seeing-eye dog.

For the last couple of weeks, we've made certain the poinsettias, shrouded in dark "clothing," have logged their fourteen and one-half hours of darkness with no light leaks whatsoever. According to Florencio, even two foot-candles worth of light can mess them up royal. Over and over we've measured lengths, calculated how much taller each plant might grow after the pinching, and worried over conflicting information Nance downloaded from the Internet. Now today, October tenth, has arrived—"Pinch day." If we figured right, the plants we pinch today will, by Thanksgiving and Christmas, emerge all the same height, the bracts uniform and the colors vibrant. I listen to Phoebe's cough and think if she won't go indoors, she should at least be wearing a muffler.

I hear the door slam, Leroy's whinny, and soon the others have joined us. Beryl yawns hello. She's no morning gal by any stretch of the imagination. Wearing boy's overalls with the legs rolled up over her boots, she looks like a cranky pixie. Nance's work shoes are these fire-engine-red rubber clogs I'm sure she ordered out of a fancy gardener's catalog. Her overalls and barn jacket fit her like a designer outfit. Sure enough, when she bends over to check a plant I spy the little Calvin Klein label on the butt pocket. Like the poinsettias give a rip! My fashion statement is that I've got my braids wrapped in my best headcloth. Beryl's hair is always a wreck, but Miss Nancy Pants has been busy with the curling iron. We bend down to once again examine and measure the plants.

"Around six leaves are supposed to remain below the pinching spot," Phoebe says, reading from the journal, her voice raspy. She takes a time-out to unwrap another Hall's and pop it in her mouth. "When the breaks appear, it says we're supposed to remove the weak ones."

"What the hell are breaks?" Nance asks.

"Spaces maybe?" Beryl offers.

"I don't get it. How can you remove a space?"

" 'Four well-spaced breaks on a six-inch plant,' " Phoebe reads. "Although later in her journal it says five or six is okay, especially on the white varieties, since they root so much more easily. Well, ladies, shall we begin?"

Roots. I can't help but think I'm sending down my own when I promised myself I wouldn't. Arizona feels farther away every day.

It's Nance who makes the first bold pinch. She holds up the stem and leaves and shows us, then drops the plant matter into a trash sack where it will eventually be deposited in the compost. Around here, nothing's wasted. An eggshell, newspaper, coffee grounds, even the rubber band around the newspaper gets used again. Every effort goes toward maintaining plants. It's like an endless cycle of sow, feed, and push to blossom, cut, sell, and reseed. Life, everywhere you turn.

"I SWEAR, THESE BUSINESS CARDS were a waste of money," I complain as I come in the door after shoeing two horses at the most ridiculous discount ever. I slip off my mucky boots and leave them on the mat outside the front door. "The printing cost me fifty dollars! Want to know how many shoeing jobs I've gotten since I started using them? Exactly five. And for the two shoe-trims I did today the chintzy owner only paid me a hundred. His nasty old rat-pony stepped on my foot, too. I don't even have to do the math to know I'm in the hole here. Freaking waste of time!"

Nance looks up from the computer. "Where are you advertising?"

"Feed barn bulletin board."

She scoffs. "With just your card?"

"What else am I supposed to put up? Testimonies from satisfied horses?"

Nance rises wearily and hauls out her camera, which is always near at hand. "Go change into your tan breeches and a red tank top," she tells me.

"It's fifty degrees outside!"

She's loading film and doesn't look up. "It's fifty-five. Don't forget to polish your boots."

I do what she says, and note that I must have put on weight somewhere, because my breeches are way too small. Outside, she poses me eight million different ways with Leroy, who keeps swishing his tail in my face, which really ticks me off.

"I think I've got it," she says after I'm covered with gooseflesh, and she disappears into the bathroom she's using as a darkroom. I take a hot shower in Phoebe's bathroom and wrap up in sweats and slippers. Just before dinner, Nance returns, handing me a stack of five-by-seven prints. They're all the same pose. I'm holding up Leroy's leg, bending forward and smiling into the camera, a hoof trimmer gleaming in my hand. Due to the camera angle, it looks as if I have Wonderbra titties just about to spill out of their cups, I mean, we're talking absolute honkers. "I can't use this to advertise my services," I complain. "Not only do I look like an exotic dancer, the horse is hardly in the picture."

Phoebe wheels over and looks. Laughing,

she says, "If I was a man with horses to shoe, this is the girl I'd call. Give it a try, Ness. What do you have to lose?"

Immediately, I think: Leroy..., if Jake sees the picture. Then I tell myself it's only his leg that shows, and I sure need clients. "How about my good name? Beryl, can I get your opinion on this?" I ask as we sit down to dinner.

She looks at the photo and smiles. "No way am I getting in the middle of that."

"Thanks for the help."

"You're welcome."

"By the way," Nance says as she cuts into a pork chop while Phoebe and I ladle pasta onto our plates. "I'm only charging you for the film."

"You're charging me?" I say.

"Business is business," she says.

OVER THE NEXT FEW WEEKS, the phone keeps on steadily ringing. I raise my prices by five, then ten dollars. I'm working five days a week, sometimes more. Tits or no tits, I shoe the horse's feet same as I ever did. Only now the owners hit on me, and I have to politely fend them off as I go the extra mile with their horses' feet. All this is in hope they'll tell their friends how great I am and eventually I can pack my belongings and ride out on Leroy the way I came in, in the night, my pride and my secret fully intact. It's not that awful here. I mean it's hard to turn down things like clean sheets and good food. I see Phoebe working so hard alongside all of us when we're putting in the hours on the poinsettias and think I really can't complain. But it's not fair to them, me staying here and putting on this false front like I care about the stupid flowers. I can't care. I made a goal to save enough money to leave and go off someplace warm to live out whatever time's left to me. To stick to it I have to earn some money. To earn the money, I have to work.

I LOVE FLORENCIO. He's like the Dalai Lama of the garden. In the mornings, we share a thermos of coffee and talk while we watch the sun come up. Everything that comes out of his mouth sounds wise with double meanings. "Poinsettias," he tells me, "is hardy plant, sure, but must be force to bloom at exact time for sell. When you force something to happen that nature do not have in her plan, always there is loss."

"Really? What loss will it be with the poinsettias?" I ask.

He struggles a long time to come up with the word and finally asks for help. "Like that sheep they make two of? What do they call it?"

"Cloning," I say. "An exact genetic duplicate."

"No such thing," he insists. "The one they make this way age faster, no? Maybe she have less time on earth. A man can trick *madre* nature into certain acts, but he cannot fool her forever."

I gulp my coffee but can't even taste it.

"*Andale*," he says. "We get to work now."

In addition to blankets around the poinsettia pots, Florencio feeds them a chemical concoction made up from a recipe from Sadie's journal. This fools the plants even further. I feel their confusion. It's as if we're playing God here, forcing them into an early spring when they haven't even had their winter naps.

Out of the blue, he says, "Phoebe will miss you if you leave us."

I set my cup down on the ground and Duchess rushes over to investigate. "What makes you think I'm going anywhere?"

He smiles, checking on his worm farms, and I'm left standing alone in the chilly morning weather.

WHEN IT'S BERYL'S TURN to make dinner, she heads to the garden for inspiration. Last night she made pumpkin soup, with a side dish of crumbled bacon topping for the carnivores, cheese bread, and a cabbage slaw. For dessert she baked these brownies so full of nuts and chocolate chunks that none of us could eat more than one. Guess I wasn't alone dreaming about brownies for breakfast, because when I got up this morning, two were already missing.

She and I are on our way to the greenhouses so we can check on the poinsettias and the seedlings. "Your brownies are—" I stop myself before I say "killer." I consider "to die for," but that's just as bad. "Blue ribbon," I say. "And my size-fourteen jeans say thank you."

She smiles briefly. "Thanks."

Beryl's like that—given to one-word answers. No doubt a habit left over from her time in jail. Nance and I are opinionated and upfront. Phoebe's quieter, but believe you me, when James gets to pestering her with phone calls, she's in a bad enough mood that we all share. I try to be patient with Beryl. I know what it's like to feel the odd one out. One of these days, she'll work her way into complex sentences.

Leroy races into his stall as we're walking by and whinnies like the spoiled brat he's quickly becoming, especially with Phoebe's daily visits. Steam juts out of his nostrils.

"Someone forget to feed you?" Beryl calls out to him as we step over Duchess, who's claimed a patch of morning sunlight for as long as it lasts.

"Not likely," I say. "Quiet down, you beggar," I tell my Hoover vacuum cleaner of a horse.

He paws a trough in the cedar shavings. Beryl pulls a carrot from her back pocket and hands it to me. I hand it back to her. "Bear, you're allowed to feed him treats just like I'm allowed to feed cuss-face a snack." Inside the barn's always dim, but I can still make out the flash of the whites of her eyes. "Part of the deal is we all take care of each other's pets. You're not scared of horses, are you?"

"I'm not scared."

By the way she holds the carrot in the flat of her palm I can tell she's had some horse experience. I wonder how much. She pats Leroy on the neck, too, instead of the poll—a horse's forehead—that's the sign of someone who knows that horse skulls sport huge sinuses, and that horses don't appreciate the echo that resonates when you pat them there, which is what most people do. When Beryl blows gently into his nostril that cinches it. That particular move is the equivalent of shaking hands with a horse. Beryl Reilly either owned a horse or worked around them. Hmm. "Too bad we don't have another horse so we could go riding together," I say.

Beryl wipes her palm on the back of her jeans. "That might be fun," she says in a noncommittal, offhanded way.

"The person I'd really like to teach to ride is Phoebe. Phoebe's got some kind of special juju going with animals. You see her down here every afternoon, just sitting and talking to Leroy? I swear he listens. And Verde—it's as if your bird's fallen in love."

"That's partly because of her chair," Beryl says. "All that chrome's like a mirror."

"I never considered that. You think Phoebe could probably ride by herself with a little extra rigging?"

"I suppose."

"The thing is, sometimes Leroy can be kind of a crotch rocket. Otherwise I'd put her on him today."

Beryl laughs out loud, and for just a moment, her face is wide open, a window to who she was as a kid, all red hair and freckles, root beer Popsicles and spinning Beatles forty-fives on her monaural record player. "Crotch rocket. Haven't heard anyone say that since I was sixteen years old."

Which is just enough information for me to file away as interesting and to ask about at a later date. I can't help it—stabbing her abusive husband, may he rot in the underworld for the things he did to her, and the way she clammed up when asked about her mother, and the tears that came when Pheebs said we wanted her to join us—this girl is one nut I intend to crack. "I started working ranches when I was sixteen," I say. "What were you up to then?"

She pulls her jacket closed and rubs her hands together. "Nothing good."

"I didn't even finish high school. Did you?"

She ignores me completely. "Is it true there're owls in this barn? I worked with some baby owls last year at the bird rehab."

"Sure. I'll show you." I shoo Leroy back out to the arena. Being careful not to make too much noise, we climb up on sacks of feed until we can see the pair of owls nesting in the rafters. They look like a couple of tawny cats, lying on their sides in the nest. "See them?" I whisper. "Phoebe told me that as far back as she can remember, owls have nested there, and that her Aunt Sadie said they were here when she got the house in her divorce settlement."

"That's understandable," Beryl says. "A barn's a safe place and a great source of mice. I wouldn't be surprised if the owls had some babies this spring."

"Babies. Phoebe would love that."

Beryl nods, but she doesn't smile. I guess due to her work she has a more unemotional way of looking at birds. To me, what with their singing and flying, birds represent pure joy. Even when Verde's cussing at volume ten, there's something jubilant about it.

We leave the barn and walk down the gravel pathway to the second greenhouse. It's smaller than the poinsettia one, only twenty by thirty feet, and Seedlings Central. Inside, the air is dense and moist, like something mysterious is cooking. Florencio set up a second worm farm in here. I dig a finger in, and all kinds of red earthworms start in wiggling. It no longer grosses me out that their castings go into the plant food if red tomatoes come out of it. There's sphagnum moss, too, not so creepy looking as what hangs from the trees on the scenic drive in Bayborough-by-the-Sea, but green and pretty when tucked into a hanging basket.

Beryl and I split up. I check the long rows of tomatoes and lettuce; she inspects the caulking on the windows she replaced and oils the cranks that open the vents. Greenhouse maintenance is one of our regular tasks, checking what's sprouted, feeding whatever's looking puny, marking with a flag any plants that appear overwatered so they can dry out, and noting any diseases or insect problems, because if you don't nip infestations in the early stages you are just SOL and have to start all over. It usually takes us close to an hour to cover the basics. I don't want to make any mistakes. I want this farm to make Phoebe enough money so that she can go on living here indefinitely. Now that a couple of months have gone by, I see how much the place means to her—she's the kind of person who needs to be growing flowers and cooking dinner, participating in endless debates over dessert. It feeds her spirit. Me, I'm just marking time by driving Miss Phoebe to town in a Jaguar car and getting flattened at Scrabble by Beryl. Still, it beats sleeping down by the creek and peeing in the woods.

Once Beryl gets started on a task, it's like she disappears inside of it. I watch her inspect the automatic watering system for fifteen minutes and she doesn't even notice me looking. It gives me more time to study her. The red, curly hair is natural. She doesn't try to make it lay straight. Her eyes are this intense shade of green, but somedays, when I suspect she's been crying, they can look sort of hazel. Granny Shirley would say that Beryl's an "old soul." All I know is that looking into Bear's eyes it's clear to me that inside of her there's a solid core that nobody's ever touched—not her husband, not what she went through in jail, nobody has been to that particular destination for the longest time. I'd like to tell her about Jake and the AIDS virus, if I was to tell anybody. I get the feeling she, out of everyone, would be all right with it.

When the sprinklers go on, I'm shocked out of my daydream, and Beryl's laughing. "Hey! How about a little warning next time?"

"Sorry," she says. "Sprinklers appear to be working fine, today."

I wipe myself down with an old towel that probably has worm poop on it. "No kidding."

"But this quick fix isn't going to last. The wiring still needs replacing," Beryl tells me. "The reason it shorts out is because it was built when Eisenhower was in the White House."

"Eisen who?"

She gives me a look. "You never heard the saying 'I like Ike'?"

"I've heard it. When was he president again?" The truth is I know, but I want her to keep talking.

She sighs as she resets the sprinkler's timer. "Nineteen fifty-three. He was the first Republican in office in twenty-four years. The Korean War ended, Senator McCarthy ranted his last rant, civil rights really started heating up, the Rosenbergs were executed—all this when I was but one year old—and my mother was diagnosed with a kind of leukemia that's easy to put into remission today."

"But not then?"

"Nope."

"Gosh, Beryl. No wonder you didn't want to talk about her."

She waves her hand and her face is once again unreadable. "I forget that half you guys weren't even born when Kennedy was president."

"Thirty-five's not exactly little league. Anyway, remind me never to play Trivial Pursuit with you. How do you keep all those facts in your head? Half the time, I can barely remember what day of the week it is."

She shrugs and closes the cover to the automatic timer. "There was a lot of time to read in prison so I pretty much read all the books in the library."

I drop the tomato leaves I've been pinching back to the ground. Since the poinsettias, I'm a regular pinching fool. My fingers smell wonderfully tart and spicy, a nice contrast to the cold. "*All* the books? Get out."

She opens the greenhouse door. "Okay, you're right. I skipped over the law books since the law did me no good."

"Romance novels, how-to books, psychology?"

She nods. "A little of everything."

"Well, what did you think of them?"

"Romance novels are dangerous. They make women actually believe in romance, which can lead to accidents with knives." She delivers a brief laugh, and I join in, but I can hear how hers is hard-edged and sorry. "How-to books make for great reading, and

111

you can learn to fix all kinds of stuff, such as ancient wiring. The only grudge I have against psychology books is the vocabulary. Big words or jargon; don't you find that irritating when all you really want to know is the 'why' of something?"

"Yeah, I do. Once I read a book about men being from Mars," I tell her. "A complete load of horse manure if you ask me. It's my personal belief they're all from Ohio, a far less interesting a place than Mars. So, in all, how many books do you figure you read?"

"I didn't keep count, Ness."

"Why not?"

"They weren't going to give me a sticker at the end of summer."

"Say if you were forced to guess."

She sighs. "Probably a thousand."

I whistle between the space in my front teeth. "That's something to be proud of, don't you think?"

"I suppose, if I hadn't been reading in a prison library."

"No matter where you read them, I'm proud of you." I watch her complexion go blotchy with embarrassment. Redheads can't hide anything. She manages a gruff "Thanks."

Just like that, we're back to one-word answers. I swear this girl is a thousand-piece puzzle if ever I saw one. "I'm going to work Leroy now. Stick around. I'll let you ride him when we get all the kinks worked out." I know this is pushing the envelope a little, but if Bear's the horsewoman I think she is, maybe she won't be able to resist. She looks long and hard at Leroy. Legs first, then the rest of him. It's obvious she's dying to say something about his near-perfect conformation.

"I'll take a rain check," she says, and walks back to the house.

Leroy starts in dancing when he hears me getting out his tack. I stick my head outside the barn to check if I need my sunglasses. In the time we were in the greenhouse, maybe an hour, tops, the sun has shifted so that it's no longer directly overhead, and it's cold again. Duchess has moved a foot or so east in order to claim any remaining rays. Her tail wags in time with some wonderful dream she's having, and I envy her. Lately my dreams are filled with crying relatives and funeral music. I rush to the church to tell Granny I'm not dead and when I get to the doors, find they're barred shut, that people with HIV aren't allowed in God's house.

"Come here, you beautiful boy," I force myself to croon to Leroy, and he struts over, his muscles rippling. He slips his head into the halter like an angel. Then he bucks hard and I have to snap the lunge line to let him know I won't tolerate any of that. I work him for half an hour to bleed out the friskiness, and anxious to please me, he finally moves nicely. After we reverse and work in the opposite direction, I think, why not take him out for a short run; maybe it'll do us both good to shake off some dust. So I fasten a bridle on over the halter, hop on bareback, and ride him over to the fields where Florencio and Nance are deep in conversation. Nance is taking notes.

"Fifteen October is official fall planting day," he's saying. "Of course, you can plant until Christmas, but not all variety. Right now, the soil, she still warm enough to get some plants in."

"Which ones? Bulbs? Veggies? I want to put that on our website."

"Website?"

She sighs. "It's like I told you, people log on to the computer, enter in the subject, and our site is in the list."

He shakes his head, not comprehending. "Well, for selling to vendors, I like daisy, delphinium, phlox, stock, and sweet pea. Bulb? All kind. Daffodil, ranunculus, crocus, freesia, Dutch iris, tulip, of course, and amaryllis because we sell a lot of those during the holidays."

He rolls the double *l* in *amaryllis*.

"What in hell is a ranunculus?" Nance asks, laughing. "Sounds like a salsa dance step."

"Oh, *mas* species ranunculus," he says. "Maybe, two hundred or even *mas*. Leaf like a fern, flower in yellow, orange, red, cream, and *blanco*. Popular for basket especially."

"What about the vegetables?" Nance says.

"You caring about vegetables?" I put in. "That's a laugh."

"I don't have to eat them, just sell them. Go ride your horse."

"Artichoke, broccoli, all cruciferous variety," Florencio says. "Sadie favor pea, chard, and

114

carrot. *Duquesa,* she also favor the carrot." He frowns. "I plant, she dig them up. Explain at your dog carrot need to stay in the ground, or we'll be buying the carrot at Albertson, and those taste like nothing, believe you me."

Nance nods her head gravely, still writing. Florencio gives Leroy a pat, and I ride on past them into the hills behind the property. Nance is behaving like that guy on television from *Victory Garden.* Florencio is here rain or shine, his workshirt crisply pressed, his cowboy hat perched on his head of thick silver hair, tending what we've planted. Pheebs says he's been married to Rosa for fifty years, that she looks like his mirror image, only her hair hangs to her waist in a braid. Why do some marriages last and others blow up like a cherry bomb?

Not that Jake Rayburn wanted to marry me. Long before AIDS came into the picture, I suspected that part of his distance was due to my skin color. I'm several shades darker than he is. High yellow, he can pass as a mixed-blood mutt, which these days women find intriguing. I think he thought that a wife would tarnish his image in the horse world. Jake was as type Y as an Arab horse. Big flirt, big temper, even bigger you-know-what. "Love them and leave before the sun comes up," that was Jake's motto. Ran around crowing about his independence. "Nothing comes between me and my horses," he used to say. That was true, not even his rage stayed separate.

In my bed at night, he was as loving as a man in love could be. I can still feel the way he used to curl his body around mine, and the sigh of relief he'd breathe when I told him I loved him.

I loved him hard.

He gave me AIDS.

Whenever I think of that, my knees wobble and I can't catch my breath. I give myself a shake and think, look on the bright side, no more begging him to use a rubber because I wasn't sure who he'd slept with the night before and him refusing. No more of those long, slow, wet kisses, either. You're in this great old house living with three wonderful women, I remind myself, but deep down, there is this howling inside of me, and little by little, I can feel it working its way to the surface.

Shortening the reins, I let Leroy know that he can extend his trot into a lope. I figure with the slight uphill grade he'll get tired before long. He gathers his muscles, tucks his head, and then comes that moment when he lets things rip. We're like a couple of redwing black-birds caught in a wind thermal. We fly. If I have to die, I wish it could be like this, with at least one black man in the world loving me.

WE SLOW TO A WALK NOW. Leroy's spent. I can feel his sides bellow as he drinks in deep draughts of air. When I used to exercise horses for Jake, this cooling-out period was my favorite time. My thoughts were my own. I

116

could take inventory and dream. My list now is simple: I am a terrific cold-shoer. I haul my equipment in a sports bag and don't need a forge. I'm learning all there is to know about flowers and fertilizer, which would make Granny Shirley so happy. She believes the closer one gets to the earth, the better off her soul. Next month's her birthday. I have to make an appearance. If I bring her an armful of flowers that I helped grow she'll be proud.

My mother gave me to Granny Shirley right after I was born. We lived in the projects in a part of Oakland that hasn't gotten much better. She worked as an office cleaner at night, then when I was old enough to stay by myself, she got a job in the San Jose Community College library processing the new books that came in and brought home the old ones being discarded. Shirley is the proudest kind of black woman, but it didn't have a whole lot to do with her station in life, it has to do with God. She's tone deaf, which prevents her from singing in the Baptist choir, but not from mending their robes and baking lemon cakes for the fundraisers, and going to church without fail every Sunday. I think my left ear sticks out farther than my right because she was always yanking on it, making me go with her. Her husband walked out on her, but that didn't stop her from keeping a photograph of him framed on top of the sideboard so that her kids would know they had a father, right next to the one of my mother that looks a little like

Billie Holiday. That picture is proof that somewhere out there in the world, she exists.

Losing her dignity is Shirley's biggest fear, and when my mother left me, I guess Granny felt she had to pass that fierceness onto me. It worked, because the shame I feel that I wasn't smart enough to see the trouble with Jake coming keeps my mouth clamped shut tighter than the lid on my hoof black, which I haven't been able to unscrew since last March.

Leroy and I climb the hills into the oak trees and eucalyptus. Leaves crunch under his hooves, releasing an autumn smell. His black ears prick forward, taking in the sounds of the woods all around him. I've never had a horse that didn't spook at a tree limb until I stole Leroy. He loves the woods. Sunlight dapples the leaves and I spy a red-tailed hawk flying overhead. I keep my eyes peeled for deer and wild turkeys, but don't really expect to see any with all the noise we're making. A mile or so into the forest, I ask Leroy for a halt, and we sit there drinking in the silence, so quiet it throbs. I shut my eyes so I can feel it more intensely, and let my tears spill over my face. All I can hear is Leroy's breathing, occasional faint birdsong, and the beating of my own heart. I lay my head against his neck and inhale the sweaty essence of horse, finest perfume in the world.

Nance goes to church every Sunday, and calls me a heathen pagan because I say that I feel the presence of God best when I'm in the woods. We disagree on nine out of ten things.

She is such the little Southern lady. Granny Shirley would make her cheese straws and lemonade, and feed her fried chicken until she blew up to at least a size six. Then she'd take down the family Bible and commence to tell stories all night.

I let Leroy trot until we get to the hillcrest, where I plan to walk him to cool out. But wise guy Leroy figures out my plan. He stops short when I'm not expecting it, and I lose my balance and fall into the soft, moldy leaf crush all around us. There, like everything good that's supposed to happen, I find a perfectly shaped hawk feather and I tuck it into my shirt pocket like it's a Bible verse, because no matter what Nance says, it is.

*Phoebe*

# 6

## *Stinky on Safari*

"A HORSE? WHAT NEXT, PHOEBE?" my brother says as he closes the door to his gleaming white Jeep and stands in the driveway dressed like Indiana Jones.

I finish writing a check for my physical therapist. We had to quit early today because of my cold. "Check your calendar, Stinky," I say as I wave good-bye to Alice. "Halloween is still a week away. What's with the costume?"

"I don't know why I should tell you since you refuse to return my phone calls, but I will. It's for a theme party at the Fitzwilliamses'. I bought it at After Five. The salesman told me that it makes me look like Gatsby."

"Well, he's probably getting paid a commission. What's the party's theme? Jackets with many pockets?"

"Very funny. This is a genuine safari coat. The Fitzes just got back from Kenya."

I groan. "James, isn't it bad enough to eat meat without celebrating its murder?"

He holds up a hand. "All the animals were shot with a camera. A two-hour slide show with a single-malt scotch-tasting and cigars afterward."

"Sounds like tons of fun. Shouldn't you hurry and get going before they run out of seats?"

James gives me a sour look. "These people own half the Valley, Pheebs. It wouldn't hurt you to be nice to them, considering you're now a part of all that. Why don't you change out of those ugly sweats into something nice and come along with me?"

"Thanks, but I'll pass." Sometimes I look at James and think, God, are you sure we're related? James can waste hours engaging in small talk that doesn't even leave a taste in your mouth. I can think of more nasty comments, but I feel so lousy I save them for later. Today my ninety-minute workout came to a crashing halt after forty minutes. I told Alice I'd hit the wall. She made me drink echinacea tea and listen to a lecture on immune-system-building vitamins. I'm really not up to squabbling with James today, but he appears to be going nowhere. "If you refuse to leave, at least let's go inside and argue," I tell him. "It's cold out here."

But just then Beryl walks out the door with Verde in his parrot harness, perched on her shoulder. "We're going to the library," she says, staring at James, but too polite to say anything. "You want anything?"

"Yes," I say. "I want you to leave Verde with me. It's windy out. He'll freeze and then we'll both have nasty colds. This is my brother, James, and in case you're wondering, he's only dressed this way for a party."

"Very nice to meet you," Beryl says, depositing the parrot on my shoulder, where he immediately begins trying to untie the knot in my black bandanna.

"You, too. Does the horse as well as the parrot belong to you? Are the other occupants of the ark somewhere in hiding?"

"James was just leaving," I tell Beryl, and she heads to her bike looking completely baffled.

"I won't be gone long, Phoebe."

I wonder if she's sending me code—like I can stay if you need me or I, better than anyone, know where the knives are kept.

"Take your time and have fun, Beryl." I turn to my brother. "James, I thought you were in Napa. What brings you into my neck of the woods besides hoping I've changed my mind about the farm, which I haven't?"

"Har de har har, Phoebe. I wanted to know how you were. You don't answer my calls, so I have no choice but to show up, do I?" He looks over at Leroy, running on a lunge line with Ness at the other end. "Aside from acquiring large mammals and feathered friends, you sound like you're getting bronchitis."

"It's a garden-variety cold, Stinky. You don't look so great yourself. I think they make concealer for men now. You might want to try it on those black circles under your eyes."

"Which I only have from worrying about you."

Verde is preening a few strands of my hair he managed to pull out from under the scarf. "Which I didn't ask you to do so you're not making me feel guilty." I extend my arm and Verde crab-walks down it. When he reaches my wrist, he sprays James with curses.

"Nice mouth on the parrot. What does he do for an encore?"

"Bites. Want to hold him?"

"Thanks, maybe later."

"Were you hoping to steal a nice car, perhaps?"

"You always could read my mind." James reaches down and plucks a rock from beneath one of my wheels. "You ought to get the driveway paved before you fall and hurt yourself."

122

"I know. But paving takes money, James."

"It couldn't cost more than a couple grand."

"Fine, you pay for it and I will pave it directly," I say.

He looks up and delivers me a sly smile. "You could sell one of the cars for cash."

I suppress a laugh. "And pray tell, to whom would I sell it?"

Before he can answer, a red BMW pulls up behind the Jeep in the driveway. A woman gets out. She's dressed in a lime-green suit, tight black skirt, and high heels that are going to get wrecked in the dust and gravel. Around her neck she has one of those obnoxious scarves with designer logos printed all over it. She appears to be scrutinizing the ranch-house rather intently, which gives me a bad feeling. Ness is in the corral, scraping horse sweat off Leroy.

James says, "Oh, she's here. Come on, Pheebs, there's the woman I wanted you to meet."

"What woman?"

"Be nice," he hisses under his breath.

James leans down and kisses the lady's cheek. "Barbara, this is my sister, Phoebe."

The woman extends her hand as if to shake mine, but manages to slip me a business card at the same time.

"Babs Smith-Etienne," she says, "of Bayborough Realty. I told James that we usually don't handle properties east of the highway, but that in his case I'd make an exception. And this grand old dame is a charmer, isn't she?

Love the rustic look! How many bedrooms are there—four?"

"There are five bedrooms," I say quietly.

"And of course, the more baths the better. These days everyone wants his own bath, particularly if there's room for a whirlpool tub. Speaking of pools, is there a swimming pool, or perhaps room for a lap pool? What with summer temperatures being considerably higher here in the Valley, a pool can substantially increase the value of your property...and what are these precious cabbage women in the garden?"

She's pointing at my clay ladies in the flower bed. Someone must have scrubbed them clean of moss, probably Beryl, and weeded around them.

"I adore them. You have to tell me where you got them? Are they for sale?"

I just sit there and wait until finally the old gasbag runs dry. I fold her card into an accordion and look up at James like he's sold my chair out from under me. Then I roll down the ramp and hand the bent-to-hell card back to the real estate woman. "James shouldn't have brought you all the way out here when the property isn't for sale."

"Not for sale at this exact moment in time," James says. "Just an appraisal to get a ballpark on the property. You never know what the future might bring, Pheebs. We should be prepared."

Babs gives a little scream when Duchess comes up behind her and nudges her butt. What is this woman's problem, I wonder. Hasn't she ever been kissed by a dog?

James laughs and gives Duchess a pat. "You got a dog, too? Good Lord, Phoebe, you've started a petting zoo."

I'm no longer in the mood for brotherly banter. "Go drink single malts, James."

He waves his arm toward the house. "Come on. Don't get cranky. Give Babs a quick tour. What could it hurt to know what the old place might go for?"

"I've got a pretty good idea what this place is worth since I have to pay the taxes on it. I'm sorry James wasted your time, Ms. Etienne."

"Smith-Etienne," the designer gasbag corrects.

"Dammit all, Phoebe," James says out of the corner of his mouth. "The expenses that go along with this farm are astronomical. You know for a fact that Sadie never once ran it at a profit. Would you rather see it go into foreclosure?"

Ness, who's been working with Leroy, ties him to the rail and marches out of the barn. "Listen here, bully boy. You have a pretty damn nice sister, and plenty capable, so why are you over here acting like she's an invalid?"

He stiffens. "Whoever you are, I'm simply looking out for her interests."

"Which she manages by herself. Knock it off."

Nance comes out of the house to see what's going on. She's wearing her computer glasses, and when the real estate agent makes the mistake of handing her a card and Nance reads it under the magnification of her lenses,

125

it's clear she can't believe her eyes. Duchess is being the perfect Labrador ambassador, wagging her tail, giving big puppy eyes to the realtor, who must be a cat person, and Verde is flapping his wing stubs and cursing enthusiastically. "Duchess," Nance scolds, "Get away from that harpy!" She turns to me. "That's the real estate agent who called my dog fat and gave Primrose Cottage away to someone else."

"This might be a very good time for you to leave," I suggest.

"Certainly." Babs slowly walks to her car, sneaking glances at the barn and the garage. I can hear the calculator in her head ticking up a total with lots of zeroes. She backs up too fast, which sends rooster tails of gravel dust flying and sets me to coughing. I allow myself a brief Isadora Duncan fantasy, only in this version, when Babs's designer scarf gets caught in her car wheel, her face turns the exact same shade of red as the car.

"Who *are* all these people?" James asks.

"My housemates and partners in the flower business," I say, smiling. "With their combined rents and labor, the farm's about two minutes away from turning a profit, James. Ask Florencio if you don't believe me."

James folds his arms across his chest. His many pockets get in the way and he puts his arms down. "Roommates?"

"And full partners."

James says, "I suppose that's one method of acquiring friends."

I guess siblings can probably live to be

eighty and still have to win the chop fight. I tell myself I will not cry, but what with feeling under the weather and what he just said, I can feel the tears building.

"No wonder she calls you Stinky," Ness says loudly. "What's your problem? Won't nobody room with you?"

"I didn't mean it the way it came out. I just—"

"The hell you didn't," Nance puts in. "You're not needed here. Vamoose. And what the hell is up with the jacket?"

He eyes Nance up and down, in her skin-tight blue jeans and knee-high beaded moccasins. She's wearing a sweatshirt up top, but it fails to disguise her pert bosom. "Which one are you?" he asks.

"Which one what?" she fires back. I can see a smile twitching to get out, frustrated by the set of her jaw.

"Well, I'm the big, black mean one," Ness says, stretching up tall so that the five inches she has on James appear more like ten. "Now which part of that sentence do you have a problem with?"

There isn't a white man on the planet that knows how to respond to such a question without appearing racist. Beryl, the Scrabble champ, would say Ness has James in a vocabulary headlock. He takes his keychain out of his pocket and presses the automatic unlock, which bleats twice, and turns to look at me. "I didn't mean it how it sounded, Phoebe. You know that."

"Bye-bye," I say. "Send postcards."

We all stand there and watch him drive away faster than he needs to. Nance squeezes my shoulders, and Verde crawls up her arm to peck at her gold chain. "I'd get a DNA test on that one before I'd buy him a Christmas present," she says.

"Yeah," I chime in, but for some reason, I feel a little annoyed they're attacking my brother, even though they did come to my rescue and he deserves thrashing. Somehow though, if there are insults to be delivered, I want to be the one driving the truck.

"Phoebe," Nance says. "Tell me I was out of line and I'll call him up and apologize."

I don't say anything.

"Then let's go make some fresh coffee. Or hot chocolate. Doesn't that sound good? God, Phoebe, say something."

But I can't speak. Since losing Sadie, I feel my family's dwindling numbers all too painfully. But James actually sent a realtor out here without even asking me if it was okay. In the words of Rodney King, "Why can't we all just get along?"

Ness walks over and squats down so we're eye to eye. "Know what I do when I feel the killin' rage come over me?" She plops a currying brush into my hand and curls her fingers around it. Then, despite my protests that I want to go inside and take a nap, she pushes my chair over to the fence where Leroy is waiting, opens the gate, and steers me inside. "Brush in the direction the hair grows," she says, taking Verde from me. "Leroy prefers a light touch."

She latches the gate behind her and heads over to Nance on the porch. I'm left alone in the arena with Leroy, who I only know well enough to pet with a fence between us.

"What a freak of nature that one is," I hear Nance say as they head indoors.

I don't know whom she's talking about, Babs or James, take your pick. I do wish Verde had pecked his tongue out. I lift the brush and start in on the horse. After a while, we're both sighing, Leroy with pleasure, me with relief that my anger and hurt are finally beginning to lift. Fifteen minutes later, Beryl rides up on her bike. There's a giant book in the basket.

"*Tyto alba,*" she says in this preoccupied voice. "That's the Latin name for our barn owls. They can attain a wingspan of up to forty-five inches, and the male's call is described as largely composed of snoring and hissing."

I laugh.

"What's so funny?"

How can I explain about my brother and hook it up to owls in one sentence? "Tell you what, Beryl. If I'm allowed one request, how about you make some of your famous doughnuts tonight? Is there time for that?"

She nods. "Sure. I'll get started right now."

"Great," I say, and return to Leroy's toilette.

THE UPS TRUCK PULLS UP just as I finish. Grooming Leroy has warmed me up inside and out. It's almost dusk. I can smell the doughnuts, so it's probably time to go inside and grab one before they all get eaten. But I have to watch Juan Nava's athletic leap out of his brown van; it's mortal sin not to. With his knee, he flips a box up into the air, gives it a spin, and then catches it one-handed before depositing it on the porch and whipping out his electronic clipboard. "Phoebe?" he calls out.

"Over here," I say, waving the horse brush and reaching for the gate latch. Leroy is shining like polished marble, and enjoying the drooling stupor that follows a great massage.

"Let me get the gate," Juan says, and he pushes it to the side as I wheel myself out into the driveway. It seems impossible that only an hour ago, the entire realtor-brother debacle was in full swing and I was almost crying. I think my cold must be going away, because all of a sudden, I feel great.

"Really nice horse," he says.

"Isn't he?" I grip the push rims of my chair with a vengeance. "Did you bring me a package?"

"Yes, ma'am, from the Mystery Guild. What did you order this time? The latest Sue Grafton?"

"No way. I always order whatever isn't the main selection. I like giving unknown writers a chance. Never know when you're going to find another Daphne DuMaurier."

"Oh, yeah?" he says, and his smile with all those perfect white teeth just kills me.

Indoors, my roommates are shaking confectioners' sugar over the cooling doughnuts. I imagine how it melts into the doughnut's dark skin, which is roughly the same color as Juan's muscled forearms. So what if he's short, no more than five-two? To me, that's a mountain. His brown shirt's open a button lower than it needs to be. I can't help but strain to see the coil of springy black hair peeking out.

Juan flexes one leg so it's resting on the fence rail. I'm guessing he rides mountain bikes on the weekends, or at least dabbles in rock-climbing.

"Is the horse yours?"

"My roommate's. You can pet him if you want. Or feed him a carrot. There's a bagful in the barn."

"Thanks. I'll do both." He climbs one rung of the fence and talks softly to Leroy. I roll my chair back a few inches and look at his butt. It's still the nicest one I've ever seen, built to make the most of the UPS uniform. I wonder if guys know when women check them out.

Juan brings a handful of carrots back from the barn and hands some to me. We take turns feeding Leroy, laughing at the orange foam that collects on his lips. Juan pats Leroy's neck. I do, too. Our hands are maybe an inch apart and I can feel some invisible energy in that space that makes my heart beat harder, even if his doesn't. Juan steps down from the fence and reaches over and touches my bandanna. "Did you know you look like a pirate in that getup?" he asks me.

"Maybe," I say.

He moves closer toward me and uses his fingers to pluck a piece of straw off my shoulder.

"Are you in a hurry?" I ask.

He smiles. "Why?"

"I was just—well, wondering if you wanted to come inside. For coffee and freshly made doughnuts, I mean. Do you like doughnuts?"

"A man would be crazy to turn that down," he says.

"Race you," I say, and set my wheelchair off as fast as the wheels will spin. Behind me, I hear Juan following along, laughing.

"THANKS, LADIES," HE SAYS, folding his napkin around a doughnut and turning toward the front door. "Believe me, this is one of the nicest things to happen to me all day. I really should get going now."

"Oh, stay for coffee," Nance says, and fills up a mug and thrusts it toward Juan. "It's from Seattle, the coffee capital of the universe."

Juan quickly takes a sip and sets the cup down on the table. "I'd like to, but my shift ends in an hour. I have paperwork, and if I'm late—"

"It's all right, Juan," I tell him. "Thanks for the package. Have a nice weekend, okay?"

He smiles at me. Those dark eyes—I want

132

to believe they're saying something else, but it could be wishful thinking. "You, too, Phoebe."

When he says that, all I hear is gratitude. Somehow all those close feelings we had when we were petting Leroy have faded—if they were there at all. A tickle in my chest erupts into a full-blown coughing fit. Verde tries to imitate me. Beryl brings me a glass of water and pats me on the back.

"You two scared him away," she says, pointing at Nance and Ness. "Next time Juan comes calling, take a hike." She sits down at the table and begins flipping through her bird book.

"That's ridiculous," Nance says. "What in the hell about us is scary?"

"Yeah," Ness says. "Tell us."

Beryl shakes her head as if she can't believe either of them.

I swallow my water and wonder how James is faring at the safari shindig. So long as I keep ordering mysteries, Juan will be back, but just now I'm left with the echo of his van speeding away and this tight feeling in my lungs that can't mean anything good.

WHEN I CAN'T SLEEP, I swig down another dose of Vicks 44, shudder at its licorice flavoring, and open Sadie's journal to the section on poinsettias. There's a dried bloom tucked between the pages. I guess it was red once. Now it's the universal brown of long forgotten leaves. In her dancerly script, I read:

Container plants are the children I never had. Some sleep through the night the first week home, are happily fed, and grow up to be valedictorians. Others continually disturb my sleep with problems I can't figure out. Take this leaf crinkle and distortion business. The leaves I so looked forward to unfurling emerged looking, for all the world, like lizard skin. I sat right down in the gravel and cried, certain the whole crop was ruined. I was afraid to even use them as compost. Then one morning the vent fans failed, and certain of the plants seemed to recover so quickly I had to behave like Miss Marple and ferret out the cause. After a while Florencio and I surmised it was too much air coming on too strong, and we staggered the fans. Then right on its heels came mottled chlorosis— the poinsettia leaves were shaped fine, they just looked as if they had contracted measles. After ruining a good fifty plants trying to correct the color with feeding supplements, I gave up and said Go ahead, bloom ugly, I want nothing more to do with you. So of course the poinsettias I left alone began to make the most brilliant color transformations. Such reds I'd never seen, and that was the first year we developed a true pink.

What have I learned about gardening so far? It's hard to wait, hard not to get in the middle of things and muck them up when you're dealing with something growing, but that's exactly what you have to do—wait. Sometimes patience is the best—maybe the only—medicine.

*Phoebe*

# 7

## *Taking Lester's Advice*

"SURE, I'LL DRIVE YOU to the doctor," Ness says one morning a week later when my cold hasn't improved. "I need to go into town to pick up some horseshoes anyway."

"Um," I say, "he's all the way in Bayborough-by-the-Sea. Is that all right?"

She looks at me seriously. "You want me to drive you into the trendy side of town in a yellow Mercedes."

"Yes."

"Well, hope I don't get pulled over for Driving While Black."

"Forget that," I say, wheezing a little. "Try having a breakdown when you're Driving While Handicapped. Once this cop tried to call the paramedics for me! Prejudice is everywhere, my dear Preciousness. Why do you think I gave up my license?"

"Shh. Don't say that so loud," she begs me. "Last thing I need is Miss Nancy Pants finding out my real name. I didn't know you used to drive."

"Well, I did," I tell her. What I don't tell her is that I quit because one day I got so scared I had to pull over and call James to come and get me.

We get in the Mercedes and secure my chair. As we're pulling out of the driveway, Ness says, "Feel like discussing Mr. UPS?"

"What's today? Harass Cripples with Chest Colds day?"

"Pardon me. I was just asking. We don't have to talk at all." Ness maneuvers the yellow Mercedes down Ocean Boulevard, where a steady stream of tourists in rental cars gawk and poke along, creating a continuous traffic snarl. I know I'm cranky. I should say I'm sorry, but it's hard enough work just keeping my eyes peeled for a parking place. Ness turns right when I point to the minuscule lot outside Lester Ullman's office. My doctor's the salt of the earth, even if he is located in the upscale part of the village. "Should I come in with you?" she asks hesitantly, as if that's the last thing on earth she wants to do.

"Nah. In case you hadn't noticed, I'm horrible company. Go buy horseshoes. Be back in an hour or so, and I'll be waiting curbside."

She looks up at the sky, clouded over and unreadable. Between the Bayborough fog and morning mist, it's hazardous for walking, let alone driving. "Wait inside, Phoebe. Looks like it might rain."

"That, my dear, is decorative fog, an everyday occurrence for which the ritzy Bayborough denizens pay top real estate dollar."

"I don't give a poop what it is. With that chest, you don't want to take chances."

"Fine, I'll stay inside. Honk twice so I'll know it's you."

"And not UPS?"

"Ha ha, very funny." I open my door, and all by myself I get my chair situated on the sidewalk. I push my wheels into the flagstone courtyard where a mossy fountain is dripping. Several birds, despite the weather, are happily bathing.

The first time I saw Juan, he was bent over a stack of boxes he was delivering for Sadie. She belonged to every book club on the planet, and automatically ordered all the main selections. I guess her old UPS driver had died, because why else quit a perky job like delivering in Bayborough? This was just before Sadie went into the hospital; I was in charge of mail and so forth. In Sadie's books, there's this recurring theme of love at first sight, how great it is, and always reciprocal, of course. How else do they sell them? I suppose this sounds tarty, but Juan's butt, well, seeing it that day was enough to make me believe in a benevolent God. Here Sadie was about to be taken from me, and I was feeling plenty resentful, then Juan turned around with this hopeful look on his face and said, "Hi, I don't remember meeting you before."

"I'm Sadie's niece," I told him. "Phoebe."

"She's mentioned you. Aren't you the sculptor?"

"I play with clay," I told him. "I'd hardly call that sculpting."

"Sadie does." The look on his face was genuine. "How's she feeling?"

"Oh, you know," I remember struggling to say. "She has good days and bad. Lately a few more in the bad category, but these books will perk her up. I'll let her pick one and start reading to her this afternoon."

The next time he came out he brought my aunt a potted plant. "What a nice guy," I said, "don't you think, Sadie?"

"Phoebe," she said. "You take that Creeping Charlie and put it in your bedroom."

"But Sadie, he brought the plant for you."

My aunt managed a short laugh. "The hell he did. Now get me a pain pill."

After that, Juan insisted on bringing the boxes indoors and stacking them in ways that made them easy for me to reach. Though those UPS guys usually travel at mach one, Juan found time for a glass of sun tea and conversation.

"How's that plant doing?" he asked one day when Sadie was really having a hard time and the strain must have shown on my face.

"Thriving. I think it likes the sun in my bedroom. Sadie said I should put it there, I hope you don't mind."

"Why would I mind?"

"I don't know. Thanks for bringing it."

We were silent a moment, drinking our tea. Then he said, "You like music, Phoebe?"

"Sure, I love music. Don't you?"

He smiled. "Yeah, I got more CDs than I'll ever listen to. You know what? My cousin's in a jazz band. Sometimes they play local gigs."

"Really? Let me know when they're in town, and maybe I'll go see them. If Sadie's doing okay, I mean."

Juan drank until his glass was empty, and then set it down on the porch rail. "Thanks for the tea. Give Sadie my prayers, won't you?"

I nodded and stared at the glass, watching the condensation that had beaded up on the exterior drip down his palm print. He didn't ask me out, he just mentioned that his cousin played in a band, but the memory of that conversation and what might have been carried me through some long nights.

As soon as the Mercedes's taillights round the corner, I let my shoulders droop and I cough so deep it feels like my lungs are coming up my throat and I have to spit into a Kleenex. When I take it away from my mouth, there're tiny red flecks of blood. Gently I fold the tissue into a square and tuck it in my jacket pocket. My hands are shaking, and I grip the armrests of my chair hard to try to still them. I tell myself that whatever I've got, it's nothing Dr. U with his bag of medicinal tricks can't cure, but then I think how he failed to cure Sadie and I realize I might be in serious trouble here.

Gina, the receptionist, hangs up the phone as I wheel in, and delivers me a broad smile. "Phoebe," she says. "How lovely to see you again. Go on in; he won't be very long."

I roll myself through the door she holds open, and down the hallway I know too well. Lester's examining room is filled with tasteful golf course prints—he's mad for the sport—and a stack of *National Geographic*s that date back five years.

I change into my gown and stare at my now-quiet hands. Normally I'd pick up a *Geographic* and gather facts with which to dazzle my roommates, but all I can do is feel mortified and betrayed. Not because the gown droops on my body so I look like a kid playing dress-up. And not because for the jillionth time I'm sick with a chest cold, and this time, there's the blood in the Kleenex to consider, but because of the ulterior motives that drove me here. Juan Nava, and the possibility of sex. How does a thirty-eight-year-old virgin ask her doctor about birth control?

One time Juan brought a covered dish out to the farm. "I make fair cheese enchiladas," he said. "They wouldn't win any prizes, but I remember Sadie saying she liked authentic Mexican."

Sadie was long past eating at that stage, but I accepted the dish gratefully, and at three in the morning, when Sadie had finally been able to sleep, I ate them myself. He wasn't kidding—they beat every other enchilada I'd ever sampled.

All my life I've been extraordinarily skilled at the look-don't-touch fantasies, so I was fine with this until Sadie, on one of her last good days, pointed out something I'd missed entirely—Juan Nava was looking back.

Does such a timeline of events eventually lead to s-e-x?

Maybe it's easier to leaf through an article on migrating whales. Up to the Kenai Peninsula of Alaska in the summer, down to Mexico's lagoons in the winter where they make love and have babies under the sun. Aunt Sadie once took up an offer to swim with a killer whale at Marine World. She said she thought it would be interesting, and I'm sure it was—for Shamu, as well. His relatives have probably swum through her ashes by now, since it's November, and the cetacean population is making its way to Mexico. Or maybe her ashes have settled to the ocean floor, and lie there glittering between grains of sand like a handful of diamonds, while the whales swim above, their rubbery bodies bathing in what's left of her light.

Lester's taking a long time today. I wonder if he's delivering bad news to another patient like he once had to do with Sadie.

Late autumn was her favorite time of year.

She reveled in the brief warm days, driving the John Deere tractor across her flower fields. She'd whip off her shirt and tool around in a French brassiere, soaking up whatever tan she could in her strong shoulders, embarrassing Florencio to death. Me, I'm wearing a flannel undershirt like some wimpy kindergartner, and I stink of menthol rub. I've gone through a whole bottle of cough medicine trying to tame the tickle in my chest. Autumn makes me melancholy. The leaves look jaundiced on the deciduous trees. Soon the branches will be bare. The fields appear fallow, even though we've been folding mulch and vitamins into the earth, and are about to plant four thousand bulbs. Lately, when the others take off to work in the greenhouses, I've been so chilly I've had to wrap up in a fleece throw and sit by the fire drinking tea. As I sit there, I tell myself I should be doing something—cleaning out Sadie's closets, or being more enthusiastic about Nance's website, which is raking in the hits. Or I could work on my clay ladies, since I'm three weeks behind on my orders, and even sick abed, I can still manage to shape the clay, but I seem to lack the energy for anything but woolgathering and Juan Nava fantasies.

Finally Dr. Ullman comes in, this lean, olive-skinned man with silver streaks glinting in his black hair. He's looked this way since I first started coming here, the year I was twenty-two and had just finished my bachelor's degree. That first visit wasn't for a chest cold, however, it was Sadie's idea—my loving aunt insisted I should be ready for what she called "the inevitable." Lester was such a good sport about my questions. "You were born with a spinal injury," he said, "not a chastity belt." And he checked me out from head to toe so matter-of-factly that I kept coming back for all my medical treatment. I have to laugh. Whereas I was so hopeful thirteen years ago, now I'm not at all ready, and it really, truly might be in the wings—the big event. Or I might be fully nuts and Juan Nava might just feel sorry for the handicapped girl. Probably UPS awards him Brownie points for being extra nice to cases like me.

"I could hear your cough clear down the hall," Dr. Ullman says as he listens to my chest. "And I don't much like the sound of it."

"Me neither, Lester," I tell him. "Usually I come here just for the fun of it, but this time I brought valuable information." I hold up my nearly empty Vicks bottle. "For example, my cough is resistant to this."

"Ever the smart aleck," he notes dryly. "I want you to get an X ray and while we're at it, some blood work. Then let's start you on antibiotics, and a stronger cough suppressant than that over-the-counter crap. Drinking whiskey does about the same amount of good. Why didn't you come in a week ago, Phoebe?"

"Because a week ago it was just a stupid cold," I say. Deep down in my right lung, it feels like there's a storm brewing.

"Bull," he says. "You know better than to

143

wait. With your murmur and valve problem, you can't afford the strain pneumonia would put on your heart."

"I know," I say. "I was hoping it would go away. How's your putting these days?"

"Unfortunately about as good as your chest," he says, tucking his stethoscope into his pocket. He parts my gown so he can tap on my back. I clutch the fabric to my breasts so there's no chance it will slip down. "How's a weekend at CHOP strike you?"

CHOP stands for Community Hospital of the Peninsula, but taken as a verb the acronym is much more appropriate. "Lousy. Lester, I'll do whatever you say so long as I can stay in my own bed." Actually, it's Sadie's bed—a king-size pillow-top number covered with a gold brocade spread so heavy it takes me five minutes to pull it up. "Not the hospital, anything but that." The thought of the bland food and the sick smells and not being around my new friends is disheartening. And they are friends, no matter what Stinky James says. Not that he's called to apologize for the realtor, but I can't stay mad at him.

Dr. Ullman hands me a form for the tests. The lab is right next door, so I can't slither out of it. "I'll have them read the films right away," he says. "And the blood work should be back by tomorrow. Anything else I should know about?"

I hesitate. I know he'll find the specks of blood in my hankie interesting, so I unroll the tissue and show him. "What color would you call

144

that?" I ask him. "A cadmium red or more of a vermilion?"

He shakes his head. This is the way we communicate, Lester and me. He's gruff; I'm silly. That way neither of us has to admit how scared we are. Lester would like me wrapped in cotton, like a butterfly specimen. I'm willing to go so far as cotton panties, but there I draw the line. He'd like me sheltered, too, in the lee of the action under a nice asbestos umbrella, whereas I throb with an unfulfilled desire to stretch my naked body in the sun's most ultraviolet rays. I can hear it starting to rain outside, pounding against the windows that look outside onto the courtyard. I suspect the bathing birds have all gone indoors for thick towels and hot toddies.

"Depending on the X ray, I may want a sputum culture," Dr. U's saying. "Are you hiding anything else from me?"

Thirteen years I've been coming here. If anybody takes the doctor-patient relationship and issues of confidentiality seriously, it's him. "Lester, I've been wondering. Could a person with heart problems like mine get pregnant?"

He cocks his head at me like Duchess sometimes looks at Nance, not comprehending whatever she's patiently explained the dog must never do again.

"Well, could I?"

"Phoebe, your ovaries work just fine. If you're asking me if you could carry a child to term, however, I suppose the answer is yes, with the correct medical support. Whether or not that's advisable is another animal entirely. So. I venture onto the slippery slope of doctorly concern. Are we chatting about a real possibility, or is this maternal speculation?"

I'm a virgin. I think Lester knows that, since I've never asked about this subject before. I can halfway run a flower farm now, so long as I keep my fingers crossed; I just don't know how to ask about birth control. I'm withering away in my chair, a puddle of humiliation with all these as-ifs. "Let me put it this way. Could a person with a heart like mine take birth control pills? Or would that also be inadvisable?"

Lester Ullman leans back in his chair and taps his fingers against my file. It's the size of a world atlas, I swear. "The DeThomas tome," I say. "Gina probably takes it down from the shelf using a forklift."

Lester doesn't smile. "A person with a heart such as yours might consider asking her partner if he'd mind using a condom. Birth control is a fifty-fifty issue, my dear. And someone with a tendency to contract recurrent urinary-tract infections also needs to consider that frequent, vigorous sex may lead to such infections."

"Who said anything about frequent, vigorous sex?"

This makes him smile. "Phoebe, first loves are all about frequency and vigor. Why else do you think the species has persisted as long as it has?"

Frequent, Vigorous. I can't help it. My cheeks grow hot.

Lester looks calmly into a desk drawer. "Heart problems aside, you're too ill to be having any kind of sex at the moment. After you're well, however, with an informed mind and the appropriate precautions, why, you can just go to town in that department. We'll get this birth control matter taken care of in a manner that's pleasing to all parties." He fills a brown sack with condoms, foam, film, and pamphlets. "Look these over, and concentrate on getting over this bug. I meant what I said about the hospital."

Sadie, I think, would have handled this discussion with elegance, with finesse. If possible, I feel stupider than I did before I asked.

Next door there's a new X-ray technician. She gets all bent out of shape that I don't want to stand up so she can shoot two views of my chest. The old technician used to lower the apparatus especially for me, and ask if I was comfortable. This one insists I stand up using a pair of aluminum crutches. I stand all the time at home, but that's in private. I don't miss the concerned look in her eyes that my splayed legs might at any minute go out from under me. She calls in the guy who draws blood, and he dons a lead apron and gloves so he can spot me like a gymnast.

"I'm perfectly fine!" I snap, but not until I'm back in my chair do I feel like myself.

While I grit my teeth for the ritual bloodletting of a CBC, I think about Sadie, whose arms before she died were as pocked with needle marks as any junkie's. She used to turn her face away when the phlebotomist came at her with his syringes, and speak to me of things like physics and the cosmos, and connect them up to the mundane, like planting flowers and doing housework. Not that it's on my mind, but I remember her once saying that making love with a man was proof of the bizarre String Theory concept. Basically, it states that infinitesimal threads of attraction vibrate, call to each other, exchange energy, and entwine. From that brief encounter, the future is forever changed. Somehow when Sadie was talking about sex, I didn't feel embarrassed or hopeless, just interested.

The guy taking my blood is using a Sharpie marker to write my name on the vials of blood. The ink reeks. My blood looks like grape juice. I can't imagine it commingled with Juan's to make anything so magical as a baby. I pick up my films and take them back to Lester's. Gina delivers them to him, I look at the *National Geographic* some more and wonder if there's any chance in the world I will ever see such exotic locales—Alaska, Mexico, or a dozen other places that probably lack wheelchair facilities. Pretty soon I hear my physician's gruff bark, ordering me back into the room so we can look at the chest films together on the light box. Marcus Welby he's not.

"What did I tell you? Pneumonia," he says. "I want you in the hospital, on an IV, closely monitored. Gina will drive you over."

148

I shake my head no. "Not this time, Lester. Give me a shot and load me up with pills. I'm going home. I have a farm to run and women depending on me and the plants have to be watered on schedule and the bills have to be paid or else James will be right and I'm responsible this time, me and nobody else, please, don't throw me in that hospital—"

He pinches the bridge of his nose. "Phoebe, it's—"

"I know, I know. Totally inadvisable. I'll come back tomorrow or daily or whenever you want, Lester. Or you can come out to the farm and charge me triple for making me say ahh. Either way, I'm heading home."

"Only if you promise to call your mother and have her fly up and care for you."

"Honestly, Lester. My mother would turn this illness into an opera."

"Rita loves you, Phoebe."

"And she does it so well from a distance."

"Then I insist we hire you a nurse."

"I'm telling you, I don't need one. I have roommates."

He grumbles, but gives me two shots, one in each butt cheek, and they hurt so badly I have to bite my lip to keep from crying. I wonder if sex is like that the first time, something you know is eventually good for you, but so painful that you just have to grin and bear it. I bet it is. That initial invasion inoculates you for all time against the dreaded disease of elderly virginity. God, I hope so.

RAIN. DAYS OF IT. The thermometer appears
to be frozen at fifty-two degrees.

"One should break into the idea of winter
slowly," Sadie used to say, snuggled up in her
gorgeous hand-knit sweaters, a cup of tea
laced with whiskey in one hand. She and I sat
on the porch and talked for hours. We'd end
the day both a little buzzed off our "mug-ups,"
go indoors, and cook up spicy chili, crumble
Fritos and sharp Cheddar on top, scarf it
down while watching old movies, cry at the love
scenes, share giant Hershey's bars, and fall
asleep on the couch. I dreaded Sundays, when
I had to go back to college, and Sadie always
insisted that day made her fatally lonely, too.
Somehow I doubt the woman had a single
moment in her life where she felt the way I do
right now stuck in her bed. Boredom was
Sadie's excuse to take the commuter plane out
of the Bayborough municipal airport to San
Francisco International. There she'd catch the
red-eye for Anchorage, check into the Alyeska
hotel, and ski Girdwood, with its endless
buckets of snow and relatively uncrowded
season. She loved our forty-ninth state for its
wild heart, she told me, and was a devotee of
the Iditarod dogsled race, so much so that she
once sent Susan Butcher and her sled dogs a
big fat check for kibble and whatnot. The
year Butcher won the race for the first time,
Sadie threw a party down here. Half the guests
had no idea what the fuss was about, but they

wouldn't miss her soirees. The reason I know this anecdote is more than cocktail party banter is because right here, in my feverish hand, I am holding the thank-you letter Susan Butcher sent her.

Dear Ms. DeThomas,

Enclosed please find a photograph of the dogs. They join me in extending a heartfelt thank you for your support...

All this rainy afternoon I've been reading letters Sadie saved. And feeling uniquely sorry for myself. One DeThomas woman's life as viewed through the lens of another's. Sheets in pale colors, an assemblage of picture post-cards. Mail from the famous so real it's like an instant heirloom. She sent me cards, too, so I've traveled vicariously. While I labored in physical therapy and daydreamed about my aunt's adventures, she was embracing them, thumbing her nose at the risks involved. I was being careful, saving my strength—and for what—days like this? I reread those cards until the edges softened under my fingers. I studied the postage stamps as they increased in price when mailing costs rose. Good Lord, am I still doing that? I have lain in her bed an entire week. Ness won't even let me out for dinner. My roommates bring me a tray and sit with me until I've eaten enough to make them happy. And every single one of those days until today it has rained. Only now that the sun's about to set has it finally petered out to drizzling. To add insult to injury, in all that time, *Señor* Nava of UPS fame hasn't stopped by once. Maybe I should switch to FedEx. They're more expensive, but they're always sending me small business coupons. I'm ready to revolt. I'd kill for chocolate, and the way I'd like it best is served warm, painted in thick, swirly brushstrokes across Juan Nava's chest.

"Feel like company?" Nance asks from the doorway. She's dressed in her rain slicker and has mud splatters from her feet to her elbows. I drop the letters I've been reading onto the blanket.

"Well, actually I feel like owl poop, but sure, come on in. Tell me what's going on in the land of the living. I'm so desperate for news I'm about to chat up Verde."

The parrot's on her shoulder as she enters the room. "Slut," he says, as if he's reading my mind.

"Nice to see you, too, Verde. What else am I missing?"

"Well," Nance says. "We're planting the tulips that have been chilling in the fridge for eight weeks. It's butt-cold out there, and the ground is even colder. Why in hell does a bulb need to be cold first, but seeds can go right into the dirt? I don't get that. I wish Beryl were here. She'd know. Somebody didn't show up at the bird rehab and she had to go in and cover the shift. I should call and see if she wants me to pick her up instead of her riding her bike.

It's so soggy out there I hate for her to get all muddy for no good reason, especially when it seems like I am the only one who ever gets out the stinking vacuum. Duchess is still pilfering carrots. Florencio informed me that as soon as the rain stops, I get to help him replant sixteen rows."

"Jeez, Nance," I say. "This is how you cheer the infirm?"

"What do you want, Princess? Bonbons and Fabio? I'm making a big, juicy pot roast for dinner. I'm cooking it with potatoes and green beans and baby carrots simmering in the drippings. That is, for Beryl and me. You and Ness will be dining on miso soup and whole-grain muffins with that phony butter made from soybeans. If you ate red meat, you'd be well by now. I only came in to ask if you wanted company, and since you said yes, here he is."

She pulls Juan by the hand into the bedroom. He's holding a bouquet of peach-colored roses. Oh my. He's dressed in street clothes, not his uniform, but in my mind's eye, I'm still seeing his chest slathered with the chocolate sauce and hearing his whispered invitation to lick it off. If I look half as embarrassed as I feel, I am in deep trouble.

"Kinda redundant, bringing you flowers," he apologizes. "But I didn't want to show up empty-handed."

"Just showing up is pretty nice," I tell him.

Nance smiles wickedly and whisks the roses from his hands. "These will look nice in the Waterford vase," she says, and disappears.

"Make yourself comfortable," I tell him, pointing to a chair. Try as I might to banish the chocolate fantasy, it takes its time in fading. I can almost taste it on my tongue. My face is turning twenty shades of purple, and I quickly decide to fake a fever if Juan happens to notice.

He ignores the chair entirely and perches on the edge of my bed. So close I can see the frayed neck of his T-shirt, this real nice shade of blue under his leather jacket, and notice how well he fills out a pair of Levi's. There's no chocolate on him anywhere, just a faint hint of soap and the right amount of body hair. "You're feeling better, I hope?"

I nod like I'm mute. We look at each other for a while. "How did you know I was sick?"

He smiles. "A little bird told me."

Those wonderful meddlers. I'm going to kill them after I kiss them. "Tell me, Juan. What was this bird named? Ness, Nance, or Beryl?"

He shakes his head. "Florencio. Those girlfriends of yours kinda scare me. Pretty much all girls scare me, I guess, except for you. Are you feeling better?"

"Yes." I point to the cough medicine. "I think there's opium in that, because I'm imagining that Juan Nava is sitting on my bed telling me I don't make him nervous."

He laughs and I can see his teeth, all white with a gold cap on one molar way in the back. "Are you on antibiotics?"

"Horse pills. I have been for a week. Pretty soon I expect to start neighing."

"So you're not contagious, huh?"

"Lord, I don't see how I could be."

"Good," he says, and swoops in and kisses me. On the mouth.

Then he leans back and thoroughly regards me. Juan's eyes are chocolate brown, ordinary in size, but with this kind, steady light reflected in them. My smart mouth has run so completely out of words that I might have to borrow from the parrot if this conversation is going to continue. I'm wearing a clean flannel nightie, but my hair isn't combed. For the last hour, I've been weepy and whiny, missing Sadie because it's easier to dwell on the past than doing anything constructive. Now I've been kissed by my UPS driver whose backside once restored my faith. Utter panic descends. "This isn't what I expected my first kiss to be like," I say aloud, and that verbal confession is something I really can blame on the medicine.

"Your first kiss?" Juan whispers.

I nod.

He's quiet awhile. Then a smile spreads across his face and I can see that he's embarrassed and a little excited about that news. "I'm honored," he says. "Now let's see if I can do better on the second one."

This time the swoop comes in slow motion. He puts his arms around me. His hands pull me close, not crushing me exactly, but tight enough so I can feel my breasts against his chest. Something quickens there, a feeling I've never had up until now, and now that I have the feeling, I can't imagine not having it again—and frequently. Juan's mouth is gentle, warm. He kisses my cheeks and my forehead, too. He takes hold of my chin and tilts my face back and the third time, oh, Sadie, now I know what you were talking about with that String Theory business because am I ever tangled up in this.

After awhile, when Juan is leaning against me, one hand against the headboard, breathing more steadily, I mumble into his neck. "Can I ask you something?"

"Sure."

"There are three able-bodied women living at this house. Good-looking women. You sure it's me you want to kiss and not one of them?"

He takes so long to answer I wonder if maybe this time I was only thinking the words instead of saying them. "Why would you think I wouldn't want to kiss you?"

"Because—"

"Go on," he urges.

What do I say? That I can tell by looking at him he's a jock? That Ness can ride a horse, Nance is a great dancer, and Beryl, well, I'm not sure what her athletic talents are, but I bet they reach further than wheelchair Olympics? "You got those muscles from bike riding, didn't you?" I ask, like I've just been crowned the queen of non sequiturs.

"Sometimes I ride my mountain bike."

I knew it. I sigh hopelessly.

"You're the one I like, Phoebe," he says.

"Long before you got roommates. I been wanting to kiss you for some time now."

And now he's done that, I think, so what happens next? Inside my chest it hurts like I've broken a rib, but I have to say this, for both of us. "You understand I'm not one of those cripples who suddenly stand up and start walking one day, Juan. I'm what you see in this bed, a person prone to infections, with a compromised heart. I have to take care. So if you want to back out of this room and forget what you did—"

He kisses me again. This kiss makes number four—not counting the one on the forehead; only lip-to-lip for the official tally. It's a solid kiss, even a little showy, with a gentle nip of teeth on my lower lip, and it takes the breath clean out of me. "Don't make me try to tell you everything at once," he says, trailing his fingers across my cheek. "Let me tell you a little bit every time I come to see you. With flowers and candy—do you like chocolate?"

On your chest or anywhere else. "Yes, Juan, I like chocolate."

"Good. That way it will be better. Slower is always better, Phoebe. Let's go slow. Dinner and movies, and just sitting around talking."

He could tell me the world was flat and I would offer to build a fence to hold everything in for him. I can't say a word.

"Warm in here, huh?" Juan unzips his jacket.

I need Ness in here ASAP to tell me what I'm supposed to do. Abandon those bulbs; I want to scream from a megaphone, you're needed in room one.

"So, are you going to be well enough to go out with me on Saturday night? I'll bundle you up warm. We don't have to stay long. My cousin's trio's playing at this jazz club in Bayborough-by-the-Sea. It's kinda like a dive, but they make good coffee drinks."

"Probably," I manage to say. And underneath I'm thinking I'm going if I have to eat vitamin C around the clock from now until Saturday, even if it means I spend Sunday on a respirator.

"Sounds good."

Juan's smile just knocks me out. Behind the white teeth I catch a brief glimpse of his tongue. I'm stupid with kisses, and pretty certain my smile telegraphs that.

"Well, I'm going to get out of here and let you rest. You take care, promise?"

I nod. He kisses my forehead and picks up his jacket. He winks at me as he leaves the room. Does he even have my phone number? I guess he must, what with the UPS account.

For a long time I sit there touching my face, feeling my lips, even sliding my index finger inside my mouth to touch the places Juan has been. Sadie's letters are spread around me like the petals of a flower in the old he-loves-me, he-loves-me-not game. I don't have to count to know which petal I landed on. Why this sudden change of luck? Does it mean that God's about to drop the other shoe? Sometime when I'm least expecting it, this four-ton cowboy boot will descend out of the sky and that will be that? "Nance," I call out, a little dizzy with the effort. "Can you come in here? Hurry!"

And as I sit and wait for her, for the first time in a long while, I want legs. Strong ones, so that I could get up out of this bed, whole, and dance how I feel inside.

ON SATURDAY, I WAKE UP determined that I am better. The thermometer concurs, my horse pills have all been swallowed, and last night I didn't need the cough syrup. I call Lester's answering service and ask them to page him. "Listen, I haven't had a fever in four days," I tell him. "My cough's a mere shadow of its former self. Can I please be excused from my sickbed?"

"Hold on a second while I let these morons play through," he tells me.

"Morons? Where are you, Lester? I didn't mean to spoil your Saturday fun."

"On the back nine at Bay Links. It's all right. These guys were boring golfing partners anyway."

"By any chance are you having a lousy game, and using me as a way to save face?"

I can hear him sigh. "I'm not going to dignify that with an answer, Phoebe. So, you've been a good patient for once, finished your prescriptions, and now here you are, calling me on a Saturday. Must mean there are big plans in the offing. I'm your doctor, you can con-

159

fide in me. Does our speculative birth control discussion figure into these big plans?"

"It's an itty-bitty date. I'll probably be home before ten, *virga intacta.*"

"Call me Monday," he says.

"Why, if I'm feeling so much better?"

"You don't think I'm going to miss out on the punch line of this story, do you? Have fun, my dear. Tuck a few of those items I gave you into your handbag, just in case." He hangs up, or whatever it is people do with cellular phones.

I WHEEL INTO THE BATHROOM and start running the tub. I'm going to sit in there and pour sea salt into the scalding water until every shred of illness is leached out of me. I'm adding bubbles, too, if there's a kind in the cupboard that's compatible with salt. I look over Sadie's inventory. How to choose what to smell like? Lily of the Valley? Tangerine and kiwi? Almond and vanilla? I recall reading somewhere that men respond favorably to the smell of pumpkin pie baking. Pies need a pinch of salt. Maybe I should lug one of the pumpkins in from the garden.

"Pheebs?" comes from behind the bathroom door.

It's Ness, no doubt here to monitor my oatmeal intake. "Yes, Preciousness?"

"Hey. You promised that would stay between us."

"I haven't told anyone. What do you want? I'm trying to take a bath here."

"Can I come in?"

"Why? Do you want to take a bath with me? Go ride your horse." I part the curtain and peek out the window. Leroy's prancing around the arena. His left side is caked with something green. "On second thought, go wash your horse. He looks like a cowpie."

Ness lets herself in anyway. She's barefoot, her jeans are soaked, and she isn't wearing a shirt, but she is wearing a red bra that lifts and separates while creating remarkable cleavage. I want some of that, I think, but it's probably too late for implants before my date. "What are you trying to do," I ask, "inherit my pneumonia?"

"I was checking the rows we planted yesterday and got a little wet. You know, Pheebs, I think there might be a problem with the automatic watering system. I pushed the rain button three days ago, but I don't think it shut everything down. It's so soggy out in the first nine rows I sank in up to my ankles. My boots are still out there. And I'm worried the bulbs aren't going to make it."

I turn the taps off. Steam rises from the inviting water I was just about to lower my body into. Instead, I wrap a second towel around my middle so that my legs are covered. "Well, I guess we should be grateful row ten was spared. Did you call Florencio?"

"No."

"Why not? He'll know what to do. The best I can offer is a prayer for sun."

161

"I was hoping you'd call him. He won't yell at you." She picks up the package of sea salt crystals and studies the ingredients. "Sixteen ninety-five for four ounces? How is this crap different from kosher table salt?"

I reach out and take the package from her. "It has flowers on the label. What do you care if Florencio yells? It'll be in Spanish, and you won't know what he's saying."

"It's the way he says it. Please call him, Pheebs. Then I promise I'll let you take your bath and primp all day for your date."

I flick some water at her. "For the record, I was not primping. I do not know the first thing about how to primp. I was planning to take my bath, do some light exercises, and read *The New Yorker*. The cartoons, anyway."

We both smile, and Ness laughs first. "I can show you how to primp, Phoebe. I've had a lot of experience at it."

"Thank God. Put Florencio on the damn speakerphone and let's get this over with. Having never primped before, I want to leave plenty of margin for error."

"*Que?*" Florencio says, as if he can't believe we've gotten this simple thing so wrong. "I coming right over. You tell those girls get the shovel and start digging out a trenches. If we drain the soil good, we can save some plant, maybe." He hangs up.

Ness shakes her head. " 'A trenches' isn't going to undo the overwatering. Still, I'd better go at least make the effort. See you later."

I slide into the tub and the water comes up

to my chin. I feel horrible for missing two weeks of work while they're out there breaking their backs, but what can I do except try to get well. My breasts look like tiny twin islands, floating perkily in the water, the vanilla-almond scent swirling around them. I give them a squeeze and they fill up my fingers. Everything about me is so small. Nobody makes a red brassiere in size 28 AA. My legs are so skinny I have knock-knees. Whatever it is Juan Nava sees in me, it must not be terribly physical. But the kisses, I think, they feel quite physical to me. Who knows? Maybe he'll call and cancel. Maybe my pneumonia will relapse; I'll fall into a coma and die without ever having successfully dated. More likely, Florencio will lock us women indoors until we learn how to properly turn off an automatic watering system in the event of rain. One of his favorite sayings is "The mind of a woman is labyrinthine," at least that is the translation in Sadie's gardening journal.

I shut my eyes and listen as the troops assemble. It seems to me that living with women isn't all that different from men in fraternities. One is apt to encounter wet laundry anywhere there's a flat surface. No cuss word is off limits, depending on the circumstances— a broken nail, a doggie accident, some newsworthy car chase pre-empting a rerun of *Northern Exposure*, Beryl's favorite show. Our resident Catholic, Miss Nancy J., has been known to belch after she finishes her dinner. I consider calling my mother to inform her I'm filing suit for having to cross my ankles all those years, when I hear the troops returning, coming into my room, then opening the door to the bathroom.

"Hey," I tell them. "Ever heard of privacy?"

"Smells like Mrs. Field's cookie parlor in here," Beryl says.

"Oh, that sounds good," Nance says. "Cookies fresh from the oven would be a real pick-me-up. Ness, why don't you bake some?"

"Who do I look like, Aunt Jemima? Drive down to the bakery if you want fresh cookies. I'm tired, I'm cold, and I want that bathtub as soon as Phoebe's done with it."

"Ladies?" I interrupt. "I'm naked here. Can we move the cookie debate elsewhere? And what did Florencio say?"

"He says the first eight rows are history," Ness says. "Fifty bulbs per row, that's over four hundred lost."

"Oh, God," I say. "How many had you planted so far?"

"Only eight hundred," Beryl says.

We're all so quiet I can hear the tap dripping into the tub. Not even Beryl can put a positive spin on that dollar amount.

"I think we should concentrate on the tulip baskets," Nance says. "If we can plant more baskets, sell them for a dollar more than we planned, the bulb loss almost disappears."

But I know how it is with people buying Easter plants—that dollar makes a big difference. "What about raising them fifty cents?"

"No," Nance says. "That's not going to be enough."

"Depending on how the poinsettias do—"

Beryl interrupts me. "You relax, Phoebe. We have everything under control. We only came in here to give you a spa day. Nance'll do your nails and makeup. Ness and I will dress you."

"Thanks, but I usually dress myself. Do I have a choice in the matter?"

"No," they say in unison.

So we order two pizzas, two dozen cookies, and Beryl makes up a monster batch of hot chocolate. I towel off and get in my sweats. Everybody's polite and turns away while I do this, but when they turn around, Beryl's eyes meet mine, and I can tell she's been watching me in the mirror. "Your legs are beautiful, Phoebe," she tells me. "Wear tights and a short skirt." And before I can tell her I don't have one, Ness opens Sadie's closet and starts riffling through hangers. "Look at this stuff!" she calls out, and emerges holding a mulberry-colored beaded dress that looks like something from the roaring twenties.

"Sadie had a fetish for vintage clothing," I say, but I can't stop thinking about the bulb loss and the money that washed away in the rain.

"And cashmere, and Chanel, and oh my gosh, Nance, will you look at this mink coat?"

"Mink? Oh, I always wanted a mink. Then those animal activists came along and I had to settle for wool and that phony rabbit fur around the hood. Nobody loves animals more than me, but fake fur just isn't the same..."

Then it becomes as if we all have this date, not just me. They spread Sadie's things out on the bed, like the mice that helped Cinderella go to the ball, if the mice sported mercenary tendencies and overheated sex drives. Yes, my aunt was petite, but several sizes larger than me. Still, there's a wrap-around black skirt that can wrap another time, and a caramel-colored cashmere sweater set that Ness says "works." They set that aside, and we binge on pizza. Duchess lies on the bed and licks everybody's fingers. I shut my eyes for the makeup and feel totally stupid, as if when all this is finished I am going to resemble one of those awful dolls they sell on the Home Shopping Network. I draw the line at dangling earrings, and insist on one more cookie before I brush my teeth and put on the lipstick.

"Now you're allowed to look," Beryl says, and turns my chair so I'm facing the mirror.

I reach my hand up to touch my hair, the bangs I usually plaster down over my forehead swept to the side. I have acquired cheekbones. My eyes look haunting, intense, and at first I want to wipe the shadow they've painted on away. Then I look down at the lower part of my body, at my legs in the black tights, at my feet in a pair of ankle-high boots my mother gave me last Christmas. This is the first time I've ever worn them. Who is this person? Is Sadie turning over in her watery grave that I'm wearing her things? Does it matter if we run out of money before the poinsettia sale? Will Juan even recognize me? And what if he wants to see the legs underneath the black cotton spandex? "I have to change," I tell them. "I can't go out there advertising a phony package. Give me a pair of khaki slacks and a baggy sweater. He said it was a jazz club, not a five-star restaurant."

Duchess woofs just a nanosecond before we hear the doorbell. Florencio always knocks, so I know it's Juan.

"Too late," Ness says. "Go get him, Tiger."

And this is how I embark on my first date.

JUAN POINTS OUT the members of the band. "That's Puss Pinebluff on the Hammond B-3," he tells me. "Skeeter Hamel on the upright bass, and Hercules Hampton on drums."

The names sound made-up, like something a kid would call his first pet, but I'm not going to say that. "What about the guitar player?" I ask. The man's Latin, wearing a silk shirt, and handsome enough to be related to Juan.

"Joey 'Bighead' Contrearas. Joey's my cousin."

Size wise, his head doesn't look out of the ordinary to me. I wonder if it's something he grew into, or if he had hydrocephalus. I knew some kids at Shriners' who did. The names they got called were much worse than Bighead. "I give up, Juan. Why do you call him 'Big-head'?"

He chuckles and sets his coffee cup down in the saucer. "Let's just say Joey's ego comes from the Big and Tall Shop."

I laugh and sip my drink. There's some kind of alcohol mixed in with the chocolate that makes me feel like I should have worn Sadie's clothes all my life, even the beaded dress, to things like oh, say, breakfast? And over-watered bulbs? Call them water lilies is what I say. Up until this moment, nightclub music struck me as too avant garde to be any fun unless a person was half-schnockered, which is another thing I've never been. Organs were for weepy church hymns, something old ladies in powder-blue pantsuits played for weddings, but this song says otherwise. I have to know its name, so I tug on Juan's sleeve and inter-rupt his quiet concentration one more time.

" 'The Organ Grinder Swing,' " he whispers. "Probably an old Mills Brothers tune, but I'm pretty sure Will Hudson and Mitchell Parish wrote it."

He places his hand over mine and gently rubs it. I can smell his skin, and every time he gives my hand a squeeze my heart does back flips. No wonder Lester worries so much about my heart, because after tonight, I wonder if it might survive another date.

It's like another world—the dark wood walls, the quietness of the people who've come here to listen. And Juan seems per-fectly at home. He points out that Puss

168

Pinebluff's navy-blue jacket has some kind of metallic thread woven in it that catches the light when he shifts his huge body. "Looks like ocean at night, huh?"

"Yes," I whisper back to him. "Like those phosphorescent tides."

"Come summer, when it's warmer, we'll go see the waves," Juan says. "I'll take you swimming at midnight."

He doesn't know this, but I've never been on the beach at night, or much during the day for that matter.

"Ladies and gentlemen, before I announce our last song, I'd like to remind you that next week Club Suva is proud to feature the torrid torch tunes of Lady Lassoulet and the Prime Cuts. Don't miss this band; it really rocks. We sure have enjoyed playing for you and we'd like to close with a special song for my cousin Juan and his pretty lady friend. Boys?" Bighead says, slinging his guitar over his shoulder and belting out "I Cover the Waterfront."

A lump rises in my throat. Juan kisses my cheek. It should be Sadie here in these clothes, next to this handsome gentleman, I think, but unless that opiate cough syrup's affected my brain, it's me.

Juan nods his head ever so slightly to the music. When the waitress comes over to ask if we want refills, I shake my head no and Juan settles the check. Fans, mostly women in slinky cocktail dresses, surround the band and Joey as they finish playing. When it's clear he can't get away, we wave hello and good-bye.

My first ever date ends with a foggy drive home to Sadie's house. All during, I'm quiet in a good way, reliving the music. When Juan cuts the engine in front of the house, I become aware of how dark it is. Every house light is out. The barn's one spotlight is dim, and Leroy must be inside in his stall. But somehow I suspect my roommates, even if they are in bed, aren't sleeping.

"Phoebe?" Juan says, turning to me in the car. "Did you have a good time?"

I laugh. "How can you ask me that? I had a great time. The music was wonderful, and I might be a little buzzed off the drinks, but oh, Juan, it was wonderful fun. Uh-oh. Didn't you?"

He nods. "Oh, yeah."

Now what? I should have asked Ness for more pointers. Made more conversation. Or less. Finished my dessert. Not ordered it in the first place. I wonder if he's going to kiss me good-night. "Am I ever going to see you again?" I blurt out.

He laughs again. "Well, I'm going to Yosemite for a couple days."

Oh, I can picture it in my mind's eye—Juan in those really flattering North Face clothes, popping pitons into crevices, climbing up some sheer rock face while a leggy blond girl feeds him rope. Then they'll check into that hotel Ness told me about, soak in a Jacuzzi tub made for two, and make love in front of a fireplace...

He puts his hand on the back of my seat and

kisses me hard. "But I'll be home by next Sunday. Maybe I could come over then?"

"Sunday?" I say, as if this is archaeology, not a day of the week. "Yes. Sunday is good."

He pulls my coat up higher around my shoulders. "I never met a girl like you before."

"Until you met me," I say. Oh God, oh God, what does he mean?

Juan pulls me close and kisses my neck. Who would have thought the skin there could erupt in gooseflesh? Still, in my brain, way back there in the dark places, a little thought pops up. How long before my legs get in between us? How long before he offhandedly suggests we take a walk, and catches himself, and we try it anyway and the surface underneath us is no longer paved and level?

Shut up, Phoebe, I tell myself. There are roses in your room. A box of See's candy waiting, too, if the girls haven't devoured it and they damn well better not have. Sadie taught me that men have a deep-seated need to hide their real selves for a long while when they first start seeing a woman. I guess the sexes really are different. Aside from not eating everything on my plate and dressing up in a dead woman's clothes, I'm acting perfectly normal.

"Your cousin is really talented, Juan."

"Don't tell him that," he says, nuzzling my neck.

I can feel his fingers at the front of my sweater, where the pearl buttons are. What will I do if he touches my breasts, assuming he can find them? What will he do when he finds out how tiny they are? Ask to see proof of my gender? "I should probably go in now," I say. "What with my recent cold."

"Right," he says. And here is the best part of the evening for me. Juan opens my door, and then he asks if I want any help with my chair. "If you say yes, you'll have to show me what to do," he says, unembarrassed.

"I can do it," I say, "but thanks for asking. It basically folds out like this, and these two levers are brakes."

"I'll remember that."

He walks alongside me to the door. I open it. Then he pulls me to my feet, supporting all my weight, and I cling to his shoulders and feel the length of him against me while he kisses me good-night. I never knew what the planes of a man's body felt like until now. I had ideas, but they didn't even come close to this. When we break apart, he sets me back in my chair and I have to catch my breath just like I did when I finally broke down and took my chest cold/pneumonia to Lester.

"Next Sunday," he says gruffly, and all I can do is nod. Can he see that in the dimness of the porch light? Leroy neighs and then Juan is walking down the ramp, heading to his car. I shut the door and start to roll toward my room, but it's just too quiet. I know they're in there, waiting, expecting details. Sure enough, when I switch on the light, they've rolled out sleeping bags.

"Slumber party," Nance says, her arm

around Duchess. Verde squawks a greeting worthy of a sailor.

Ness and Beryl smile at me, and I know three things for sure: One, if they could manage to get Leroy inside, they'd do it. Two, I'm not going to get any sleep until I've accounted for every minute of this evening. Three, those bad girls have gotten into the See's candy. For this, they will pay dearly. But just for a moment I sit there and savor it all, thanking God and His assistants, and UPS, for every rock and blade of grass in the universe, which feels perfect tonight, and created just for me.

# Winter

Let us love winter, for it is the spring of genius.

—PIETRO ARETINO, 1537
tr. Samuel Putnam

# 8

## *Unpaid Bills*

THE PHONE RINGS for the sixth time this morning and Marty, bless his old man's heart, nods his head for me to answer it. My coworker's got his hands full with Xena, a female red-tailed hawk that wants to tear the glove from his hand. Agnes, his wife, is out sick today with the flu, so it's just the two of us manning BBR, which, on occasion, we joke stands for Birds Beyond Recognition. That's true in the case of the red-tail, who came in with an arrow through her wing. What some people don't dream up in the name of fun.

I coax my wood duck back into his cage and try to wipe the gooey formula off my thumb before I pick up the receiver, but manage to get it all over the phone anyway. When the stuff dries, it's like cement, so the phone feels like it's been stuccoed in several places. "Bayborough Bird Rehab," I say. "Beryl speaking."

What do you know? Once again, there's silence.

"May I help you?" I prod again. I'm used to hearing it all—Somehow I accidentally shot this condor; What's the best food for a crow; How long is the life span of a pigeon?

But nobody says anything, so I just hang up and get back to work.

"Another heavy breather?" Marty says. "Funny how we never get those calls unless it's your shift."

"Hilarious," I say. Marty's sixty-nine years old, a miniature train fanatic, and is hooked on that television program, *Unsolved Mysteries.* He finds intrigue where other people find nothing special. Xena—he named the hawk—has torn a piece of his protective glove away and is now aiming for bare skin. "That bird looks ready to be turned loose, don't you think?"

"I sure as hangnails do. The trouble is, Dr. Llewellyn hasn't signed off on her. Come on, Xena. Let go. You'll be happier in your pen."

Xena has the enclosure all to herself. It's large enough for an adult to walk into without stooping, and features strategically placed branches so she can hop from one to another. As her wing heals, we move them farther apart. When Marty aims her toward a low perch, she stubbornly flies to the uppermost left corner and settles in, then turns and keer-eees at him, her funky, mangled wing stuck out like a shield. "Oh, good girl," he says, and I know without looking there are tears in his eyes that she's made so much progress.

Without speaking, he turns to a cotton-lined shoebox inside which rest two baby brown bats. Not birds, but hey, around here, if it flies, we'll bend the rules. The stronger of the two clutches onto his thumb and opens its mouth, revealing a minute pink tongue. "Feed me, Mama," I say, and we both laugh.

I take a breath and make notes on the records we keep so that everyone who needs meds has gotten them, and nobody gets treatment twice. Right now we're dealing mostly with long-term cases that probably won't be released back into the wild. Our busiest time of the year is spring, when the babies are falling from nests, opportunistic cats are waiting below, and humans acquire this weird notion to shoot at the flying population. Our survival rate is low. I get calls at all hours to come pick up the infirm, the wounded, and try my best not to get too attached, which is how I ended up with Verde. My clothes are usually covered with bird crap and blood and formula. On the days I get to come to work, I wake up before my alarm, anticipating the moment when I walk into the center and am met with the screams and cries of the hungry and wounded. I still can't quite grasp that I earn a paycheck for wrapping gauze around broken legs and feeding droppers full of gunk into gaping mouths—it sure beats working retail and having to be nice to people who want to return clothes they've already worn.

"So, any ideas about the rogue phone caller?" Marty asks me as we sit down to eat our lunch—tiny, homegrown apples some volunteer dropped off, and the cheese sandwiches I made last night and brought in to share.

"Not a one," I say, taking a sip of coffee from my Salvation Army mug. It's heavy white china, with the word ALASKA printed on it upside down.

Marty's face is round, pink, and jowly. I like the way I always see his whiskers, as if he can't ever shave close enough. "It could be a secret admirer. Someone who can't quite muster the courage to tell you how much he likes redheads." He winks one crepey eye at me and grins.

"Or it could be a wrong number, Marty. We're only one digit off from Crown Hardware."

"Did you ever think maybe it's someone from your past?"

"Like the IRS?" I say. "No, thanks. I know, maybe it's a stalker, or the William Tell arrow dude who wants a second chance at Xena." I take a bite of my apple and savor the clean, sharp contrast between flesh and skin.

His smile's gone, replaced with the thin-lipped expression he probably used on his children when they brought home C's. "You know what your problem is, Beryl?"

I laugh, because Marty must say this to me ten times a day. Usually Agnes is here to tell him to stuff it in his craw, but today there's no mercy in sight. "Let's see. I'm distrustful, I like birds more than people, I refuse to look on the sunny side of the street, and what was the other thing? Oh yeah, I remember. I have a chip on my shoulder about the legal system."

Marty sets his apple core down on a paper towel. He's pouting now, and looks about six years old. Agnes has to be in line for sainthood. "Your problem is you won't let go of the past. If you can't do that, how can you have a future?"

The rest of the day's busy enough we don't talk unless it's about a bird. We lose one dove to shock. This tenderhearted busboy brought her in when she flew into a plate-glass window at the River Grill. Then a red-winged blackbird arrives shot so full of pellets a few drop onto the exam table as we spread his ruined wings. A hippie girl brings in a crow her old man's been keeping in a cage because the bird looks "bummed out" and she's decided "all living things should be free," including her, I guess, because she makes us listen to the story of their breakup, too. The crow's starved down to bones, so grateful for the syringe full of formula and chicken baby food I give him he lets me scratch his neck. I get him into a larger cage, slip a heating pad beneath it, and wait for Dr. Llewellyn. Just before quitting time, I check on my wood duck. The cat that attacked him took a lot of his feathers, but otherwise he seems okay. He's drinking water and looks up at me with a quizzical eye. Mostly they stick close to the pond, but this one decided to nest in a tree, where his cat luck ran out. I'd take him home with me to the flower farm if I could, but if Duchess won't stop filching carrots how is she going to leave a duck alone?

Susan Llewellyn, DVM, arrives and does a quick check of everyone. It's still a wait-and-see on Xena's release. We get a hesitant okay to keep working with the bats, but aren't to go spreading word of it around. She shakes her head at the special treatment I've given the crow, and tells me even the scrawniest ones are hard to kill. She agrees the blackbird's a sweetie, but thinks it's hopeless, and readies a syringe to euthanize him. While I stroke the red spot on his black feathers, I apologize to him for mankind's obsession with firearms. I keep touching him until his life ebbs away. Before I put him in the box for incineration, I take one of his wing feathers. Technically, that's against the law, because migratory birds are protected, and all birds, pretty much, are migratory. Not an egg, nest, or feather can legally be disturbed. Given Fish and Game's budget, though, I think I'm safe stealing one blackbird feather.

Here in Birdland, all progress seems infinitesimal. Birds that appear strong right now could do a complete about-face by morning. All I can do is quickly assess the extent of an injury, decide on a plan, clean, patch, feed, and take notes. If anything as endangered as an owl or an eagle comes across the threshhold, I have to call in a specialist, but that's okay. Owls are so regal that I don't think I'd want the responsibility, and eagles, well, as majestic as they are, they make Xena seem downright cuddly.

Just before I leave for the day, the phone rings again. When I pick it up, somebody's playing a guitar into the receiver. It's not rock-and-roll, more like classical, I guess you'd call it, the individual notes plucked with hardly any strumming. It's pretty good, so I listen to the whole song. At the end, when the silence comes back on, I clear my throat and say, "Anyone who can play like that probably has interesting things to say. Next time, try using your voice, why don't you?" And I hang up.

Outside, the wind's blowing. I watch an eddy of brown leaves swirl across the pavement. The sky darkens. I'm hungry for dinner, and tonight is Phoebe's turn to cook. That means later on Nance and I will end up in the kitchen sharing a few slices of baloney, or scrambling eggs for the protein. My bike's wobbly in the wind. Next week's Thanksgiving. Two years ago, I had what passed for turkey in prison and listened to women who missed their families weep themselves to sleep. I wonder what the girls will want to do, if they'll scatter to visit relatives. Phoebe has Juan now, and I'm happy about that, even if it means I'll probably be left home alone. If that's the case, I'll probably spend the day at work. It's the least I can do for the birds while so many people are sitting around a dining-room table eating them.

Finally, reluctantly, I mull over what Marty said.

Some days my past feels like the black-footed albatross, a local shorebird with a seven-foot wingspan whose cry is half-screech, half-groan. Those events weigh me down like bird crap caked on tennis shoes, which incidentally, once dried, remains with you for life. Other days, besides Verde, the past feels like my only anchor to sanity.

"What-cher doin', bitch?" he used to say when I passed by his cage at BBR. At first, his language shocked me. I was afraid of losing this job, so I didn't take time to answer him. Then, on one particularly bad day, when it seemed like everything I touched got sicker or died, I stopped in front of Verde's cage and started to cry. He cocked his head at me and said, "What-cher doin', bitch?"

"What am I doing?" I answered. "You tell me, you foul-mouthed pile of feathers, because I don't have the first clue."

"*Si-es-ta,*" he said, as if he could tell I was ready to drop in my tracks. And the thing is, a nap was exactly what I needed. That settled it. I took the parrot home. In between the cuss fests and the way he imitates the telephone, Verde is simpleminded and frankly honest, the way the little kids I once worked with in kindergarten were, back when I was an aide. I'm certainly ready for a *si-es-ta* today. I wish I had someone to share it with, too. For the first time in a long while, I have a craving for a man's arms to encircle my body. Nothing else beyond that, but, wow, I really miss being held.

A pickup truck stops at the corner, its radio blaring Bruce Springsteen. I don't care where he was born, I think he's a lousy guitar player. I maneuver my bike carefully alongside the truck. It's as if bicyclists are invisible to cars here in Bayborough. Only five miles to go, but I hope I get home before I freeze to death, or worse yet, think any more about what passes for my life.

Here is something that might qualify as looking toward the future Marty thinks I don't believe in. The reason I bought that upside-down-Alaska mug, paid a whole quarter for it at the Sierra Grove Thrift Store, is because every time I fill it, I think how some glitch in the tourist-trinket system led to the cup being made in the first place. Maybe my cup stopped the assembly line, and they shut down the machines in order not to ruin the whole batch. Probably it landed in a discount bin in the airport, someone bought it as a joke, the recipient was not amused, and it was discarded. From Alaska to Sierra Grove, California; that's quite a journey. When I got out of prison, I shopped all the thrift stores, looking for dishes I could afford that weren't too chipped or haunted with domestic history. Here was this rebel mug shouting Alaska, the last frontier! A place where you can find gold in a stream, moose wandering in downtown traffic, long winter nights, longer summer days, and people who happily cohabit with glaciers—all notions of what it means to live comfortably turned on their heads. I don't know. I figure it's got to be a place where if somebody shoots a bird, it's because they need to eat it. I think I'd fit in there, just like the mug fits in my hand. When I tip it to my mouth, the message faces the right way. So yes, Marty, I suppose I do hang on to the past. Maybe that's what happens when a person gets out of the habit of imagining a future with other humans in it, but I've kept the

184

mug. Never underestimate the power of a vessel that holds your morning coffee.

Finally, like the yellow brick road to someplace warm, I see the road to the farm and pedal faster.

NANCE IS WEARING DESIGNER SWEATS and a pout when I see her in the living room furiously flipping the pages of *Cosmopolitan.* Duchess is lying flat on the floor, head on her paws, staring at her mistress with dog worry clouding her eyes. Verde's on Duchess's shoulder, and starts whapping his wing stubs, yelling obscenities the moment he sees me. I offer him my arm. He climbs up my shirt and starts preening my hair. As I sit down on the floor, take off my shoes, and set them on newspaper, I keep an eye on Nance. My shoes look like they should be burned; Nance looks like she could start the fire without a match.

"Wow. What happened while I was at work?" I ask. "Another broken water line? Did Leroy trample your herb garden? Or have we been visited by a plague of bulb-eating locusts?"

"Oh, locusts, journalists, take your pick," she says, and drops the magazine, goes over to her swivel chair, and sits down, staring at the computer screen.

I offer Verde a bite of one of the volunteer's apples, but he's not interested. I don't read newspapers, so if something really bad happened in the world, I missed it. Then it dawns on me. "Hey, you lived with one of those before us, didn't you?"

"Oh, yes, ma'am. I did that. And believe you me, once was enough in that department."

"So, what particular journalist has you all fired up? By the way, your mood's giving your dog colitis."

She pets Duchess and tells her to calm down. "The same smart-ass, know-it-all, egotistical, self-centered brat I lived with."

"Don't hold back on my account."

"I'm sorry, I know I sound like the queen bitch of the universe, but..."

Her voice trails off and I can see she's blinking away tears. "What on earth did he write that's got you so upset?"

"Nothing. Well, it's a story about Lucinda Williams. You know, the singer? Only it's about me, too. Rick does that. He writes between the lines. Not like anybody but me would notice, but he does it all the same."

"Sounds kind of flattering to me."

"Oh, Beryl, you have such a good heart you would think that. Rick's writing used to go through my heart like a rusty fishhook. However, not only does he bend language beautifully, but he also arranges the facts as well so he can exonerate himself. And that, my dear, isn't fair."

With that, she flops down on the floor beside Duchess and strokes her head. Verde clambers down my arm onto the floor. He flips Duchess's dog tags around, playing a little song that amuses him greatly, and we are sitting there, one peaceable if angry kingdom, when Ness comes down the hallway and surprises us all because she is wearing a skirt and a jacket.

"Woo-woo," Nance says. "Isn't it kind of late for a job interview?"

"I have to go see my granny," she says, affixing a silver horse pin to her lapel. "It's her eighty-fourth birthday and I'm taking her out for lobster."

"I want to go, too," Nance says. "I want lobster."

Ness delivers her a look. "Nancy J., hamburger is one thing, disguised in shrink wrap, but I fail to see how you can justify eating a poor sea creature that has been boiled alive."

"Melted butter," she says.

I laugh. "Perfect answer, you have to admit, Ness."

"You're both hopeless. I'm taking the Jag. Tell Phoebe I'll be back by ten, okay?"

"Tell her yourself," Nance says. "And bring me back a doggie bag."

Ness reapplies her lipstick in the downstairs mirror. "I can't tell her myself. She's out in the barn with UPS."

Nance sits up. "In the barn? Oh, my. That's a romantic locale. You think he's *delivering?*"

"Not this early in the game. Maybe if we joined hands and said a prayer."

"And then Phoebe will move Juan in and us out," I say. We're all silent for a moment, contemplating such a thought.

"Beryl, you look like whipped horse pucky,"

Ness says. "Go take a hot bath and a nap or something. There's leftover couscous and some marinated tofu in case Phoebe forgets it's her night to cook."

"Sounds yummy," Nance says.

"Don't you girls dare go to sleep until I get home. I want a full report on any and all barn activities."

When the door closes behind her, Nance and I look at each other in the light of the computer screen. "Can I read what he wrote about you?" I ask Nance.

"Who?"

"The evil journalist."

"Let's go out to dinner first," she suggests. "Leave the lovebirds to cooing, and get a little steak and lobster of our own. I just got paid for doing a high-school-reunion photo shoot which was so awful I need a reward."

I hesitate, performing some math in my head. "I'd love to tag along, but I'm not that hungry."

Nance gets up and moves my shoes to the foyer. She logs off the computer and shoos the animals away, because the minute anyone approaches the door, they think that means a w-a-l-k. "Beryl, I am not leaving you to suffer couscous and marinated tofu. This will be my treat."

I'm getting better at rebounding from my financial guilt plummets—the fact that everyone here has more money than I do—and lobster sounds so good that tonight I refuse to feel sorry for myself. "Thanks. Next time I cook, I'll make that meatloaf you like. Do I have time for a shower?"

"Sure. You freshen up, I'll just sit here and try to stop seething."

ON OUR WAY OUT TO THE CAR, we see Phoebe and Juan coming to the house from the barn. Leroy's glistening; so's Phoebe. Juan leans his head down and says something into her ear, and she laughs. Then, running along behind her chair, he pushes her toward the house, and her hair streaks out behind her. Following our collective encouragement, she's letting it grow longer. What a picture the two of them make, this short, husky guy in a down jacket and Phoebe in her cashmere muffler and Aunt Sadie's mink coat. I try to imagine them in bed together, skin-to-skin, discovering each other that first time. Seems like ages ago that happened to me. Sex is such powerful stuff, like dynamite, I think. Put it in the wrong hands and boom—you can end up in prison. Still, it strikes me that Juan and I, our passions, aren't so different. I push birds toward the sky; he's pushing Phoebe toward the kind of firmament only lovers create. Still, whichever way you view the heavens, they're finite, and feathers or flesh, they only take you so far before you have to come in for a landing. Please, don't let her crash and burn the way the rest of us have. Let one of us in this house experience a happy ending.

189

Nance shouts our dinner plans across the yard and Phoebe nods okay. From the look on her face, I don't think she's entirely thrilled to be rid of us, but Juan is beaming. We wave good-bye and pile into the Rodeo, two single women and a golden dog, heading toward lobster.

HALFWAY THROUGH DINNER, Nance is on her second glass of Chardonnay. She's picking at the shell of her lobster, lining up the plates according to hue. She doesn't eat enough to keep a bird alive. She sighs, looks out toward the Pacific where the waves are barely visible, even though she asked for and we got this great table by the window. The sun goes down so early this time of year it makes me constantly sleepy. I can hear the ocean out there, crashing on the rocks, and I wonder where seabirds go at night, and which ones are hurt and might come into BBR in the morning.

"Rick Heinrich," she says in a voice both determined and wobbly, "writes this muscley, hard-edged prose that just gets to me. I mean, imagine sitting down every day with a deadline, having eight hours to come up with new things to say about musicians who all want to be famous, who all expect him to promote them for free. Think about it. How many times can you describe a drum solo, quote what passes these days for lyrics, elaborate on the latest musical shtick, and say anything of merit? Yet somehow he does that. Over and over and over." She takes a swallow of wine. "Occasionally, he prints a clunker, but not very often."

I'm thinking, so far as I'm concerned it all makes such great cage liner, but I sip my lemon Diet Coke and nod so she'll keep talking.

"Still," she says, looking into her glass where the light bounces on the small amount of golden liquid that's left. "The times he gets it right, he really gets it." She raises her goblet and I see the arc of the glass reflected in the window and this slim, blond Southern girl who is still very much in love with a man who hurt her so badly she moved a whole state away from him. She pulls a folded piece of computer paper from her purse and begins to read. " 'Comets streak across our sky so infrequently their arrival is just cause for us to stop and bear witness. Occasionally music can be like that, too. We who have the power to recognize such singularity reward it with applause and Grammys. However, awards rarely delve to the bedrock—to what inspires such innovation, to that which originates in the human heart. Many times it's found in the people we don't begin to miss until they're gone. If the absence is our fault, and we're particularly lucky, we come to realize that without them, what we're left with is a sky empty of the possibilities of stars. Nothing can hope to fill such a void, which is why Lucinda Williams's latest CD strikes so deep in the heart....' "

She folds up the paper and tucks it into her wallet. "*After-hours Magazine, Portland Herald,* November issue."

"He definitely has a flair for language," I admit. "And it sounds like maybe he misses you."

She rubs her fingertip on the edge of her glass, making it whistle. "When the sex was really good, he used to call me his Supernova. I know that sounds stupid, but it made me so damned happy I could burst. Trouble is, he's a proud, angry man who couldn't say he was sorry if Satan held a pitchfork to his heart. Most days I wish I'd never met him."

"So what's to miss?"

She lifts a fork and sets it down again. "Everything, nothing, and I'd crawl back to him right this second if I wasn't here with you, Beryl. Thanks for going to dinner with me."

"Thanks for buying my tortured shell-fish."

She frowns. "That stuff about boiling the lobsters alive. Is Ness telling the truth? I can't believe she is. Surely there's some kind of lobster Valium they give them before they plop them into the pot. Let's not think about it. Instead, let's split a dessert. I was thinking that mocha mousse sounded pretty good."

We dip spoons into the rich ganache. "J.W. couldn't write his way out of a paper sack," I tell her. "But he could dance the Texas two-step so well you could just tell he would be great in bed. He was, until I married him. Then, hello alcohol, good-bye any sort of dancing except to get out of the way of his fists. I miss him, too, sometimes."

"You miss a man who beat you?"

"In this dreamy way where if I could go back to a moment frozen in time, move forward, and this time get it right, yes."

Nance pays the check and we walk along the shoreline for a while, Duchess on her leash. There's moonlight on the water, and I can feel my hair kinking up into an unholy knotted mess.

"Look," I say. "I'm no one to give advice. But maybe you should write Rick a letter. Tell him how much you liked the article. Just to open a channel. What could that hurt?"

"And rip the scabs off my heart? I don't think so. If Rick Heinrich wants to hear from me, he can write me a damn letter."

"But Nance, he did sort of write you a letter, with the article."

She shakes her head no. "I want a real letter, not a few lines he got paid for."

"But you moved out of state. How would he know where to send it?"

She takes out her key chain and separates the car key from the others. "He has my mother's address. Plus, these days, what with the Internet, you can find anybody with the click of a key. If you wanted to."

"Well," I offer, as I loop my backpack onto my shoulders, "just so you don't dismiss the idea entirely."

We drive home looking at the lights in other people's houses, the early Christmas decorations of those who can't wait for the holiday, and then traverse the darkness of Valley Road toward our own abode. I think about my mystery phone caller and wonder what he's doing tonight—watching television, looking over his unpaid bills, wondering how he can juggle the money this month and make his creditors happy. Or maybe he doesn't have any—though I can't imagine what life without owing something to somebody would be like. It doesn't have to be money, either. I feel beholden to Phoebe just by staying in the house. I don't know how to repay her except for working hard on the poinsettias. But what happens if nobody buys them? Oh, I wish I had a guitar to play the blues on like my mystery caller does, but the most I could do would be to send him an injured bird. I find myself looking forward to his next call, even though it's disconcerting that he seems to know which days I work and the days I'm off. Duchess rests her head in my lap and I stroke her velvety soft ears. In my purse I have the packet of oyster crackers that came with my chowder. I'll give some to Verde tomorrow.

Juan's car is still there when we pull in. Phoebe's window is dimly lit, as if by candlelight. Nance and I grasp hands. We creep into the house and tiptoe down the hallway to Phoebe's room, where we stand as shamelessly near as we dare to the closed door, listening. Inside, soft music's playing, but we can't hear anything else. I fix a pot of hot chocolate and take it to my room.

Nance follows, giggling softly. "I can't wait for Ness to get home," she says.

"Me neither."

Nance fetches a box of photos and dumps them out on my bed. We spend the rest of the night together looking at pictures she's taken of the Oregon coastline where her mother still lives. The monolithic rocks jut up from wet sand like dinosaurs. The water's not blue like it is here, but churned into a gray, rumpled sheet. There's a rainforest, too, with impossibly green trees and hiking trails that I'm sure lead somewhere interesting. After I press, she shows me a photo of Rick of the article fame, and I study his craggy face and the smirk on his mouth. "Do you think he's sexy?" she asks.

"I don't know if I trust anyone who doesn't show his teeth when he smiles."

"That's Rick, all right. The stifled smile. Like it would be giving away too much to let one peep of joy out."

"He's sexy," I say. And he is, about as sexy as they make them, but deep down, to me anyway, this man looks deathly insecure, just like Nance is, at her core. What a delightful combination they must have made. I can picture them in a passionate liplock, then two seconds later, fighting over something really important like ice cream flavors and going to bed utterly furious, sweet tooth still aching. Nance falls asleep on my bed, the photo of the journalist clutched in her hand. I cover her with a blanket and invite Duchess up on the bed, too.

I hug myself tight, but it doesn't help much. The trouble is that they're my own arms. I always know what they're going to do.

# 9

## *Such Confidences We Keep*

WHAT I FAILED TO TELL THE OTHERS was that I'm also driving to see Granny to borrow enough money to finally hit the road. It wasn't easy, but I screwed up the courage to ask her for five hundred and she said yes. After tonight, I'm on my way. It's time to bail out. Florencio keeps asking me questions about Leroy, and I know it's only a matter of time before somebody puts the pieces together. My plan is a good one—in Glendale, Arizona, there's this warmblood horse farm, a big money operation, and supposedly they're always looking for good help. When I tell them they can have my services in return for board and a hundred dollars a week, they can't say no. Pretty soon, I'll be in a warm climate and away from all these flowers. It's not that I don't like them, or my roommates. But shoot, some nights I dream about bulbs coming up before Easter and I have to run through the garden smacking them with a frying pan like that Whack-a-Mole game for children in the pizza parlor. And don't even mention poinsettias, because if I ever see another one I might be sick. Lord, I think I hate poinsettias more than I hate the sight of blood. Yes, just get through this dinner, take the money, call the horse transport people, and give them the phony papers I have that make Leroy look like my own.

To Granny Shirley, Red Lobster is living the high life. She answers the door dressed in her purple polyester pantsuit, not one but two natty rhinestone pins affixed to her left lapel. I hug her gently, and we take off for the restaurant. "Nice automobile, Precious," she remarks.

"Isn't it something?" I say.

"Kind of Phoebe to let you borry it to take me to supper."

"Phoebe's like that, Granny. Very generous." I don't tell her she's in a wheelchair or any of that, because why complicate things when I'm leaving?

Granny studies on the menu like it's last Sunday's sermon notes. I have to admire how she squeezes the most out of every experience. Her loud jewelry, sharing opinions, the way she tells the waiter he's such a nice-looking boy it's a shame he had to go and punch holes in his ear like that.

"My girlfriend thinks they're cool," he tells her.

"Cool is a breeze just passing through," she says. "You wait until you're my age."

"Better humor her," I explain. "It's her birthday."

He smiles, and she orders her lobster with all the trimmings. I ask for a salad and a baked potato. With that out of the way, we commence to talk about the flower farm, which she thinks is a "much better profession for a colored woman than shoeing horses."

"Tell me what the place looks like, Preciousness. Paint a picture for me in my mind."

Thanks to macular degeneration, her vision has blind spots. "Well, there's not a lot of color going on at the present, Granny, but everything's growing. We have golden mums and tons of herbs, and of course, the potted poinsettias, which will be sold starting next week and throughout December. I never knew they came in so many colors. I'm in charge of the greenhouse seedlings. It's really something the way those tiny sprouts grow big enough to transplant."

"When things start in blooming, I'm going to take the bus down so I can see for myself. I always did love a real nice farm. Now, how's your horse?"

I told her Leroy was mine; it was easier than making up a story. "Leroy couldn't be happier. Florencio, the farm manager, dotes on him."

"Well, child, it sounds like your cup is full up with blessings. Are you going to church?"

I sigh. "In my own way, Granny."

She sets her water glass down using two hands. "What's that supposed to mean?"

"One of my roommates is Catholic. She makes sure we say grace every night. I keep constant with my prayers."

Slowly she butters a slice of bread, smoothing the creamy spread to the very edges. "Visit the Lord's house once in a while, Preciousness."

"To me the whole earth is His house," I tell her, getting sucked into the argument I promised myself I'd sidestep.

"Then look at church as His parlor," she says, biting into her bread. "And Sunday services as a standing invitation to tea. I'm telling you, girl, you'd better go inside once in a while or there will come a day you won't be able to find it."

I wish I could convince her that my soul's gone elsewhere, that somehow since Jake told me the news, inside I feel lost with a capital *L*. I know Granny Shirley better than that, though, so I move us along to a different subject. "I brought you a gift," I say, and slide the wrapped box across the tabletop. "Open it."

"You shouldn't have, what with needing to borry money."

"It's all right, Granny. It didn't cost me anything. I traded Phoebe some chores for it."

"Barter, huh? What a clever idea." Granny Shirley's gnarled fingers slowly untie the ribbon and smooth the paper flat. She lifts the lid and takes out the mobile I had Phoebe make especially for her. She scrutinizes it intently. "Preciousness? Are my eyes done in for good, or are these women buck naked?"

I laugh. "They're wearing God's clothes, Granny, their birthday suits. Do you like it?"

Her face crinkles up in delight. "I love it, child. I think I'll hang it in my powder room, in the window. It will positively shock Sister Anne."

"Wherever you want," I say, and lean across the table to kiss her on the forehead. I keep my lips pressed tightly together.

"Cool mobile," our waiter says when he returns with the entrees.

"You look here," she tells him. "The only holes pierced in them are for the fishing line what hangs them."

He points to his one ear, which as yet remains intact. "Tell you what, in honor of your birthday, I'll leave this side alone."

"Quit trying to butter me up for a big tip," she says.

And I know he'll get fifteen percent, not a penny more, unless he takes out the earrings. Granny taught me money lessons beginning when I was age five. My mother was gone for good, it seemed, and I was a kid, so full of want I ached from it. Saturday mornings she deposited two nickels in my grubby palm, one I was supposed to put in the church collection basket, and the other was to save. She walked me to the five-and-dime and bought me one of those glass piggy banks that don't have a stopper, just a slot to drop the money into. She also got me a bag of popcorn, its yellow kernels a heavenly fragrance to my tiny nose. Jesus got his nickel; the clear glass belly of the pig gobbled the remaining coin. For a while, that was interesting, then I learned how to cross the street and walk to the store on my own. I discovered that a nail file inserted just so would dislodge a nickel from the pig. This I secretly spent on penny candy and gum, and soon I was flush with friends, who wanted to help me with the candy.

*I'll be your best friend,* they'd say.

It only took a few of these encouragements until I smashed the bank and spent it all on one memorable day where I was popular for about thirty minutes.

"What's got you so quiet this evening?" Granny had said to me that night at dinner. She'd fixed me artichokes, pricey on our budget, but my favorite meal. I sat there too sick and sad to dip a single leaf in the melted margarine.

"I did a bad," I told her.

"Oh, my goodness," she said. "Better confess."

"I busted my pig and bought candy with my nickels."

"Preciousness, why would you do that? There's a candy dish in the living room. You can take a piece whenever you want one."

"They said they'd be my friends," I explained. In a rush, it came back to me, how I felt like a queen marching into the store, how I let them choose Pixy Stix and SweeTarts and Sugar Babies, and how cold I felt in my belly when I counted out the seventy-five cents and the clerk put it in the till and the drawer shut. What I didn't tell her was how they ran from me, the bag clutched in their hands, and how alone I felt crossing the street, more alone than I'd ever been in my life.

"Important lessons are always the hardest," she said as she covered my choke with Saran Wrap and stowed it in her tiny fridge. "Thank the Lord, good things keep. You can enjoy this another night. Let's go read a story, and tomorrow, we'll get you a new bank."

From the beginning, Granny Shirley understood about my not liking meat. She never forced it down my throat, or made me eat half-cooked liver to get to the artichoke. When junior high school came around, and I wanted to be around horses instead of the boys, she let me take a job mucking stalls so that I could afford riding lessons. I wish I could say her firm but gentle hand led me to greatness in life, but all I have to show for my thirty-five years is my trade—shoeing horses.

AFTER GRANNY SHIRLEY'S blown out her candle on the cupcake I brought her, we sit in her living room with our decaf coffee. I can hear the next-door neighbors' television and it makes me realize how quiet the flower farm is, even with all the animals. "Granny? You ever give a thought to moving to a warmer climate?"

"How could I move? I have my church, my grocery nearby, and you. I still miss Oakland, but I like San Jose just fine."

"You could have sun all year round in a place like, say, Arizona. There's Baptist churches in every town."

Her dark eyes sparkle behind the cataract glasses. "What are you planning, Precious?"

I cross my fingers where she can't see them. "Nothing. Just dreading the rainy season."

She sets her china cup down on the doily on top of the coffee table. "Tempting, but if we moved, how would your mother know where to find us?"

"She's not coming back, Granny. Sooner or later you have to accept it."

She frowns, and I start worrying that her blood pressure will go up if we turn down this road, but it seems we already have.

"Uh-oh. You've got that look on your face. What happened? You didn't fall again, did you? You're supposed to call me when anything like that happens."

"I didn't fall."

She totters upright, goes into the kitchen, and I hear her open a cupboard, take something out, and shut it. She returns with a quart-size glass Ball jar. Inside it old worn green dollar bills cover up a pile of change. She sets it down on the coffee table, next to her Bible and a carnival glass candy dish filled with Meltaway mints. "What's that?" I ask.

"Three hundred twenty-four dollars and eighty-six cents." She beams. "I took up a collection at church for you. It's not five hundred, but maybe you can pay some toward that bill what was troubling you."

I stare at the jar and want to die. The thought of old women like her saving their dimes for me, parting with dollars they might have tucked away for a Hallmark card to send a grandchild makes me feel like the devil incarnate. "Oh, Granny," I say as blithely as possible. "I clean forgot to mention, I don't need that money after all. Will it be too much of a problem to return it to everyone? I'll definitely write them a thank-you letter."

She smiles. "I don't think it will be any trouble. Everyone knows how much he or she put in. If there's any left over, we'll just save for the next crisis. No shortage of those, it seems."

"I'm glad. Not about the crises, but returning the money." Why don't I just open my mouth and stick my feet in?

"I'd like to watch my stories now. Will you stay with me?"

"Sure, I will."

She sets the jar down next to her Bible. All through *Jeopardy!*, *Wheel of Fortune,* and the rerun of *Everybody Loves Raymond,* I catch glimpses of it. When it's nine o'clock, I get up to use the powder room, and dry my hands on a fingertip towel embroidered with blue flowers. I peek in her medicine chest to make sure all the prescriptions are current, and that she's not mixing up medications. When I kiss her good-bye at the front door, she tries to slip a twenty-dollar bill into my purse. "Take that back," I tell her. "I told you, I don't need any money."

"You're in my prayers, Precious," she says. "Every Sunday I ask Brother Fowler to pray that you'll find a good husband."

For somebody whose husband left her, she can't wait to see me married. "That's too much to expect," I say. "Lately I haven't met any men worth praying for."

"That's because you're not looking in the right places," she tells me.

"Yes, Granny," I say. And after I hear her lock the deadbolt, I make my escape, thoroughly shamed.

IT'S HARD TO TELL who likes the quiet drive along the coast more, the Jag or me. I turn the radio to a jazz station and listen to Monterey Jack on Sierra Grove's public station. He's spinning the disks of the late, great Miles Davis. It's foggy out, and I'm glad I started home before the highway got completely socked in. It's nice to have this time to pull myself together, and to contemplate another month at Phoebe's without going crazy. Maybe I should return Leroy to the ranch, or try to buy him legally. Jake would never sell him to me, not that I have the money. Thank God Granny didn't change all that money into a check, or I might have never known how she came by it. Old ladies have such big hearts. They're bait to magazine subscription salesmen, phone scams, boys selling candy that they insist will keep them off drugs and out of gangs. Guess if I can't get to Arizona just yet I'll have to start coming up here weekly, keeping on top of things.

At the Bayborough Shell station, I stop to fill the Jag's tank, and when I reach into my purse to get some money, there's the twenty-dollar bill. I finger it as I wait for the pump to click off. The sea air is so moist it feels like I'm taking each breath into my lungs through cheesecloth.

"WAKE UP," NANCE WHISPERS as she kneels next to my bed. I have my arm around Duchess and could kill Nance for interrupting me before Denzel Washington can finish ravishing my body.

"This better be good. You just interrupted the best dream I've had in ten years."

"UPS," she says. "He spent the night!"

"He did? Well, go make them breakfast in bed and ruin everything, you nosy roommate." Duchess and I sink back into the mattress. Then I think of Leroy, wanting his breakfast, so I groan and start to get up.

Nance stands at the doorway and grins stupidly. "Don't you want to know what happened?"

"Not before I've had a chance to drink my coffee and pee. You're all dressed and bushy-tailed, go feed my horse and don't forget his vitamins. I'm going to take a shower."

"The only reason I'll do it is there's a better view of Phoebe's room from outdoors," she says. "Duchess, come."

206

Her dog looks at her, then at me, then hops back into my bed and snuffles her head under the covers.

"Am I the only one around here who realizes the significance of what happened last night?" Nance wails.

"Maybe they just slept in the same bed, Miss Filthy Mind."

"And maybe Verde's stopped cussing," she says before she stomps off.

I stand under the shower and think about Phoebe getting some loving. Nance is only putting a voice to the ache we're all feeling—our collective lack of a sex life makes us too interested in poor Phoebe's. I soap up and rinse, and wonder if Jake Rayburn ever thinks about me at all. We used to take showers together, and then lie down wet on the bed, plastering ourselves into one hungry body. What with the remnants of my Denzel dream and this recollecting, I am not doing myself much good. I blindly reach one hand out of the shower curtain for a towel and Beryl hands it to me.

"Let's go out to breakfast," she says, "and give them some time alone. Come on, we'll go to Katy's and drink high-test coffee. Bring Duchess. There's nothing worse than being interrupted during sex by a wet dog nose."

Apparently everyone except Phoebe and Don Juan are in my room. I step out of the shower and Nance is in my bed, under the covers. "You think they're doing it again?" she says.

Beryl and I just look at her. "Duh," we say in unison.

KATY'S IS HOPPING. We wait ten minutes for a table, and then are seated in the corner where we first interviewed Nance. The walls are covered with photographs of local people, past parades, and various horse folk. I spy one of Jake, easily ten years old. He's wearing fringed red leather chaps, an embroidered cowboy shirt, and a black Stetson. I tap the glass and tell the girls who he is.

Nance takes her time looking, but right away, Beryl says, "Handsome."

"I won't disagree with you there."

"I think he looks dangerous," Nance says.

"Oh, you got that right," I admit. "Lamb on the outside, but inside, all teeth."

"Just my type," Beryl says.

"Me, too," Nance sighs. "How sad is that? We should stop at the bookstore on the way home and stock up on self-help stuff so we can acquire new tastes."

"I have to work," Beryl says. "But if you're looking for books, I highly recommend Earl's on Ocean in Sierra Grove."

"We'll remember that," I tell her. "You want us to drop you off at work?"

"Sure."

We're eating toast and working our way through omelets when Sam Patrini walks in the saloon doors. He looks directly at me and

I just about drop my fork. "That's the son of the man I used to work for," I whisper.

"Oh," says Nance. "Are you going to ask him to join us?"

"No. We weren't that great of friends. I'll just go say hi."

Beryl stirs her coffee and says, "Go, we'll save your seat."

"Be right back," I say, and get up from my chair, walk to the counter where Sam's sitting, and say hello.

"Ness," he says, regarding me evenly. "How you doing?"

"Can't complain, Sam. And you?"

He takes a sip of his coffee. "Oh, you know winter. I guess I just keep on holding out hope that spring's on the way."

Winter's a tough time of year for horse people. You end up doing things you never thought you'd say yes to—teaching riding to rich kids, giving phony-baloney seminars on training, selling feed in tack stores, gambling on the same horses you sold. I nod.

"Imagine you heard about Jake."

"Heard what?"

Sam shakes his head. "Maybe it's better if I don't tell you." He takes off his hat and runs his fingers through his thinning hair. "Somebody stole his favorite horse, and if that wasn't bad enough, well," he looks around the café, filled to capacity. "Maybe we ought to step outside a moment."

Something goes cold inside of me, deep down in the pit of my belly. It feels like a rock dropped down a wishing well landing in dry earth. Sam tells the waitress he'll be right back and we walk out onto the porch where a dozen people are waiting for tables. Despite the brightness of the morning sun, it's just plain wintry.

"Jake's in the hospital, Ness."

I bite my lip. "Did he have another wreck?"

"Not exactly. God, I wish he'd contacted you. It ain't fair, making me the bearer of bad news."

"I promise not to kill the messenger, Sam. Just tell me and let's go finish our breakfasts. Katy's food is too good to waste."

"Well, all right. Jake got a real bad cold a couple months back, coughing and a fever. When it didn't go away, Pop dragged him to the doctor and they ran some tests. Turns out he's got that disease Magic Johnson's got."

"You mean AIDS."

"Yeah. Damn, I'm sorry to have to tell you. You look great, by the way. Close call, huh? Guess what they say about wrapping the rascal ain't no joke."

"Yeah." White noise is rushing through my head. I can't hear anything, the cars passing by me, what's coming out of Sam's mouth, the birds nesting in the rafters above me. It's with me again, my invisible burden. Every ache and pain I feel on a daily basis— does it mean my disease or that I'm getting old? I think hard, when was the last time I nicked myself in the greenhouse? Made dinner for the girls and scraped my knuckle as I shredded the tofu? Kissed Granny Shirley on the lips? I feel like I'm going to upchuck, then it occurs to me that if I did, and somebody touched it, I could hurt him or her without even meaning to. I hear Duchess whining from the Jag.

"Thanks for the update, Sam," I manage to say. "I'll send Jake a card."

Sam looks at me, worried. "You okay, Nessie? Didn't mean to dump this on you..."

"Sure. Fine."

"You hang in there."

"You, too, Sam. Winter won't last forever."

"That's what I keep telling myself." He leans over, kisses my cheek, and then returns to the counter, to his plate of steaming hot-cakes and eggs, and his appetite.

I weave through the crowd back to the table where Nance and Beryl are holding up crispy slices of bacon like they're cigars, mugging, teasing me. I can't explain how now, more than ever, cooked flesh smells like death to me. I force a smile and fix my shaking hands around my coffee cup.

WE DROP BERYL AT WORK, and get stuck in Monday traffic. "I want a baby so bad I can taste it," Nance says as we watch school-children being shepherded to safety by the crossing guard. They look like puffins, swelled up in colorful winter jackets and hats I know they'll shed the minute their mothers' backs are turned.

"Maybe I'll get artificial insemination from one of those genius sperm banks," Nance says. "But then if she's too brilliant, kids will tease her. Tell me, Ness. Why is there no easy way to procreate?"

I'm never going to have a child, I realize. No baby nursing at my breast, any chance to make up for the way my mother did me wrong, gone. I won't even get to be a granny like the woman who raised me. "Because it's an awesome responsibility," I say. "Children are precious. They're the future."

Nance insists, "All I ever wanted was a yellow Labrador retriever, a house with a white picket fence, and a baby girl."

"Count your blessings, you got two out of three," I tell her, though our fence isn't white.

She eyes me strangely. "Something the matter?"

"No. I'm fine."

"The hell you are. Ever since you got back from Granny's birthday, you're quieter than Beryl. My photo shoot doesn't start for an hour yet. Let's go walk on the beach and let Duchess have a run."

"Love to, but I have a shoeing job in the Valley," I say, keeping my eyes on the road. "Six horses, full sets of shoes, lots of cash. I really should get going now or I won't be home before dark."

"You are *not* off the hook," Nance tells me as she leashes her dog. "We will talk later, when I get home, okay?"

"Go to work, Nance. There's nothing to talk about here. Phoebe, on the other hand..."

She grins. "I know. It's killing me that I have to wait all day to hear the juicy details. I guess I'll live, though."

At the last minute, I reach out for the leash. "Okay if I keep Duchess with me today?"

"Sure. She loves adventure, don't you, girl? Later, 'gators." She kisses her dog and bounds out of the car at the Sierra Grove studio. In a little while, she and a photographer will take off for Santa Cruz to shoot a fiftieth anniversary party, which is something else I'm probably not going to have. I fake a toothy smile, wave good-bye, and drive out to the Valley as slowly as I can without getting pulled over. The trees have mostly dropped their leaves, but the stark limbs are beautiful against the piercing blue of the sky in a brittle kind of way. The road winds deeper into the Valley, and when the space between houses grows in distance, I can hear my heart beating. I wonder if the blood that courses through my valves is so tainted that before long the whole system will revolt.

"Damn," I tell Duchess. "We missed the turn." I make a U-turn at a scenic lookout and the Jag doesn't even flinch. This is my first visit to the home of David Snow. All I know about him is that he's a private horse owner, and that Juan told me he's "kinda fruity, but he writes good checks." Duchess and I are so deep in the Valley that the trees are dense and spooky. The barn is brand new. He's built it so the horses' stalls are in complete shade, there's frost on the ground, and the mist from the horses' breath is visible and pungent. That's the first thing that puts me off. The second is the Eddie Bauer Ford Expedition in the driveway, polished to a forest-green sheen. Mr. Snow's third strike is the cow skull he's nailed over his front door. That's yuppie BS for decorating, because I'm sure the horses don't find the reminder of death entertaining. Still, money is money, and I try to put Jake's legacy out of my mind as I set up my equipment.

What I love best about cold shoeing is the methodical measuring and trimming of each hoof, without which there can be no horse. Early man knew this; evidence of horseshoes can be found way, way back in history. *For the want of a nail, the war was lost—all for the want of a horseshoe nail.* I pay particular attention to the soles of their feet, because standing in damp, the thrush ailment is almost a given.

Mr. Snow brings me a cup of coffee. He's thin, but muscular, like he works out, but he doesn't look healthy. "I grind this blend myself," he informs me. "Arabica, Italian roast, and a pinch of nutmeg." He says he's a mostly retired Hollywood screenwriter, and I believe it, because nobody else in the Valley but a screenwriter would be dressed in ironed jeans, a preppy argyle pink-and-navy-blue sweater, and loafers with tassels. The macho hands that work the Patrini ranch would beat this man up and steal his horses without a second thought. Jake would throw the first punch.

"So long as it's hot," I say when I accept the china cup. It's so thin that through the side I can see the coffee's shadow.

"Not a whole lot of people of color in this town, are there?"

I give him a look. "What's that matter to you?"

He shrugs. "It's just something I noticed. Makes for a rather bland community."

"Maybe you should have moved to San Francisco."

He tries another tack. "That's brutal work, shoeing horses. Hell on your nails, I imagine."

I've never had a manicure in my life, but I'll bet Mr. Snow has. "It's an honest living."

"Honesty in work! Now there's a concept the world could use more of."

I won't disagree with him there.

"You mind if I sit here and talk while you work?"

I shake my head no. He can dance pirouettes so long as he remembers to pay me.

"You ever heard of Dogstar?"

"Nope."

"That's Keanu Reeves's rock band. They play at the Viper Club, the same place where River Phoenix bought the big one. Well, this one night, some studio suits were..."

All morning he entertains me with Hollywood stories, name-dropping like a starstruck teenager while I discern the idiosyncrasies of his animals' hooves. Who cares who is taking what drug, or whether or not Jim Carrey still pines away for Lauren Holly? All

I want is to get so lost in my work I forget I have AIDS and that Jake is dying of it. But I don't tell him to shut his mouth, because at the end of this day I will have enough money to pay my December rent, buy hay, and still save fifty dollars toward my Arizona dream. Mr. Snow sits on a low wall, petting Duchess, chatting happily, and Duchess seems to think he's good people even if he is annoying the crap out of me.

"Everything you hear about the madness in movies is true," he insists. "Twenty-two-year-olds making executive decisions, starlets sleeping their way into good roles, the bodyguard marrying the celebrity, nose candy everywhere, and way too much money. Which allowed me to buy this house, so what the hell am I complaining about?"

My thoughts exactly. Since Sam's news, it's as if this once-shut door inside of me has opened, and all these nasty thoughts are emerging, sometimes right out of my mouth. "Really?" I say, and then I get brave, and point with my trimming knife toward the stalls. "Mr. Snow, you have some real nice horses here. Why in God's name don't you cut back the trees so they can get a little sunshine? They're growing mold on their backsides and the bay's feet are so thrushy I'm going to have to pack them. You got pruning shears in that barn?"

"I think so."

"Good. Get them out and I'll help you."

"Right this moment?" he says, his second

cup of coffee steaming, and to me it looks as if he's wondering which outfit he should change into for this endeavor.

"After I'm done with the horses. I've got no more clients today, and I don't particularly feel like going home."

"Okay. Then you have to let me feed you lunch. I make a wonderful pesto..."

I sense this is one way to get rid of him, so I say, "Sure, pesto or whatever; sounds real nice."

I CLIMB THE TREE and Mr. Hollywood, who has donned overalls and a flannel shirt for the effort, nods when I point to the offending branches. I cut; he catches what falls. It's both power and relief, sawing those oaks back into submission. Together we split them into firewood and stack them near his bungalow. He gets sawdust on his sleeves, but doesn't seem to freak out. The sight of the chestnut and bay horses, muzzles raised to the sun, is worth the brief sweat I popped. When I leap down from the tree, I feel better than I have since breakfast. Duchess barks and nudges my hand.

"My goodness, you're bleeding," David Snow says. "In a half-dozen places." He reaches out to touch my hands and I pull away so fast that the look that passes between us tells him what I fear without using words.

"You don't want my blood on you," I say.

We both pause.

"Me, too," he says, softly.

"Oh, God," I say, and sit down hard in the dirt. Every time I look up at him I say it again and sigh. Finally, I get to my feet and manage to look him in the eye. "How long?"

"Five years. If you're not on the cocktail you should get on it as soon as possible. Who's your doctor?"

"I haven't been tested yet. I just heard that my ex is in the hospital."

"Get the test," he tells me. "It's always better to know. I can give you some numbers to call." And he goes into his house, coming back with a first-aid kit, and when he returns, his hands are sheathed in latex gloves. "This is for your protection," he says. "You still might be okay." And he gently dresses my cuts.

I don't cry. The stone in my gut that landed there when Sam told me about Jake has grown to the size of a boulder. The only thing I can ingest is yuppie coffee. Not even the foccaccia and sun-dried tomatoes David offers will go down my throat. I watch him eat his lunch, peel a tangerine, and feed Duchess a biscuit. There are vitamin and pill bottles lined up on his counter. Books on boosting the immune system and cookbooks from fancy restaurants, like Chez Panisse and Green's at Fort Mason. "It's nice to have someone to talk to over lunch," he says. "I get a little sick of my own voice, you know?"

"Mr. Snow, what happened to your friends?"

He smiles. "Call me David, please."

"David."

"When I told them I was HIV-positive, some of them couldn't handle it. That's the chance you take, and it's something you need to do, for their peace of mind, but the others understood. We get together now and then, when they come up from L.A."

Right. This man is alone. No wonder he needs six horses to take his mind off things.

He pays me five hundred in cash for shoeing his six horses, and throws in another fifty for the tree trimming. When I stand up to leave, he puts his arms around me and hugs me tight, and fruity or not, I'm not in the least offended. Instead, I feel like I've joined this secret club, which is horrifying but somehow a comfort all at the same time.

"Here's my number," he says. "Anytime you need to talk, call. Or come by. We can listen to some classical music and watch the horses. Get tested, and don't isolate, no matter what the results are. Trust me when I tell you you'll need friends if you're going to get through this."

But he's alone. I pocket my money and say thanks. I look back at the horses, taking note of their unmistakable relationships. The big bay gelding is king here and commands the spot nearest the mineral block. His stooge is a spirited little chestnut. With a quick, well-placed bite, he keeps everyone else in line. The other four are content to meander by themselves, but there's a dappled gray that has "human" eyes, the whites revealing the depth of his intelligence. It wouldn't surprise me if he organized the others and one day soon, toppled the hierarchy.

I honk the Jag's horn and wave to David. Driving back toward the DeThomas farm, I admit to myself that I love this valley. The winding esses of G16, the few cattle ranches, the comical signs that dot the road saying NEWTS CROSSING, the occasional wild turkey strutting across the tarmac like he owns it. It's hard to imagine not being here, not being able to claim my square foot of earth. I pull over at the bird preserve and shut off the engine. Duchess and I watch a field of maybe four hundred Canada geese that have stopped to feed. There's a swampy stream running through the field, and they're drinking from it, tilting their long necks and guzzling. Their calls to one another are hoarse and throaty, but somehow within the community they find each other. Beryl would eat this up, I think. I intend to drive her back here before the birds move on, but right now, I can't do anything except bear witness to a species that seems to have it all over humans. Mating for life—imagine. What if we humans weren't so proud and bullheaded? Is that even a lesson we could learn?

I PASS THE BAPTIST CHURCH near the farm with its white steeple piercing the sky and pull into the driveway of the farm. Phoebe's in the barn. I'm so glad to see her. She pushes herself up on her wheelchair's arms, waving me over. Leroy whinnies out a greeting, too. Duchess bounds across the field, returns with a stubby carrot in her mouth, and I can hear Florencio yelling, *Bandito!* along with a string of mild Spanish curses. I take the contraband vegetable away and feed it to Leroy so there won't be any evidence in case he comes after her.

I lean down and press my cheek to Phoebe's, carefully avoiding eye contact. I'd miss moments like this if I left. "So, Miss Moony, you got something you want to tell me, huh? Maybe you should wait for dinner, because I have a feeling you're going to be asked to tell this story more than once."

Her skin's glowing, and her cheeks are flushed like she's sunburned. "Oh, Ness."

I laugh. "That good? Hmm. Usually the first time's kind of awful. Guess waiting paid off." But deep down, I'm thinking how it's always good in the beginning stages, and how that's part of what makes sex so dangerous. Leroy steps between us, irritated that there're no more carrots coming his way. Part of me wants him to stay there forever, so I don't have to look Phoebe in the face. Things would be so much easier that way. But he moves aside and wanders over to the waterer. "How about we take a ride, and you can tell me all about it?"

"Sure," Phoebe says, though up until now I haven't been able to convince her that Leroy's safe.

I tack Leroy up in my Western saddle, pad it with sheepskin. "I thought you meant a ride in the car," she says, balking.

"Sorry. There's no escape." I scoop my hands under her armpits and lift Phoebe up until she grasps hold of the saddle horn. "Use your legs," I tell her. "You do all that work with Alice, let's put those muscles to some practical use." She grimaces at the stretch her legs make. "Excuse me, how different is this from what you did last night in bed?" I joke. "Not a whole hell of a lot, so shut up and give it a try."

I switch the stirrups from the usual leather pieces to these breakaway ones I use on green horses who like to throw me. "Just hold on to the horn," I say. "I'll lead him with the reins."

"I'm so far away from you," she says. "Everything looks so different."

I know what she means. And it seems to me that if my body is going to deteriorate, grow decrepit at an early age, maybe I can do something here to help make hers more whole. Something for these women who are so nice to me, like stay at least through poinsettia season. "Get used to it, sweetie. I've just decided riding lessons are part of your daily therapy."

"Daily?"

"Oh, yeah. You can't take any time off or you'll get sore. Plus, this builds up your leg muscles, which you need to wow UPS in the boudoir."

"Very funny."

"I'm just being practical."

"Does it really build muscles?"

"Take a look at my calves, Phoebe. I wasn't born this way." I'm also planning for the future. If I die, when I die, Leroy will have a bond with someone else.

Florencio takes off his hat as we stroll by and gives Duchess a dark look. "Even without the dog I having trouble with the carrot," he says. "All that water spill last month, the root they are splitting. Also, maybe some disease coming."

"We'll have a farm meeting tomorrow at noon," Phoebe says.

"Someday I like to ride that horse," he says, staring with admiration at Leroy.

"Sure," I tell him. "You can ride him anytime you want."

"*Verdad?*" he says.

"*Absolutamente,*" I answer. Florencio will be my Plan B, I think, and immediately I hear David Snow's voice in my head, *Get the test.* I imagine how it would feel to spend a quiet afternoon in the company of someone who accepts me fully, letting him brew me his imported coffee, and listening to music I won't have time to learn to appreciate. For no reason at all I remember Jake's body, his hardness entering me, and how at the time, that moment of surrender felt like the most important thing in the world. Now I can't help but think of his penis as a weapon, and how each time he came inside me, he was infecting me. I don't want to get the test, but I can't stay in this limbo forever.

"We did it," Phoebe is saying, her normally small voice bold and sure of itself. "Not that first night, Ness. That was mostly about all the baby steps, then. But oh, what steps. And in the morning, Juan woke me up, carried me to the bathroom, we brushed our teeth, and then he brought me back to bed and took me to the moon. I'm still all tingly. I can't believe it. Why didn't you tell me it was going to be like that? Sure, it hurt a little bit, but he went slowly, and pretty soon it didn't hurt at all. Afterwards, I felt like one of the plants out here, firmly rooted in good earth. Like my feet were on the ground for the first time ever. I can't wait for next time. I hope there's a next time. Maybe this was one of those conquest-the-cripple-and-move-on kind of things. God, I hope not. I'd hate to have all this awakened and then spend the rest of my life living like a nun..."

She reaches down to squeeze my hand. I wince a little under my Band-Aids.

"Why are you still wearing your work gloves?"

"My hands are chapped from shoeing horses," I say. "Okay, sit up straight, and try to sink your sexy bottom into the seat like all your weight's there. Now, here are the reins. Hold them in your left fist, like the knot's a double scoop of Ben & Jerry's Chunky Monkey. Whatever you do, don't let it spill, 'cause there ain't no more left in the freezer, thanks to Nance's sweet tooth. Lay the reins on the left side of his neck. See how he turns away? Now try the right. That's

224

it. You want to stop, shift your weight back and say 'Whoa.' "

"Whoa? I thought that was only in cowboy movies."

"Movies aren't so different from real life. 'Whoa' is real live horse language. Try it."

She does, and as I suspected, Phoebe catches on fast. I lead her up the hill past the creek where I slept last summer, dozing off to the sound of crickets and water spilling over rocks, so secure in my health I drank from the creek without a second thought as to the bugs swimming in it. I want to ask her where the creek got its name—Bad Girl—especially now that the water's practically roaring, but Leroy's getting snorty at the complex winter scents— deer, raccoon, the occasional coyote—it's all wildly exciting perfume to him, and the moment is lost. He starts pawing his front feet in the water, and then bends his head down for a drink. The leather sings through Phoebe's hands and she cries out. "Yank him back up," I say. "Let the spoiled brat know he needs to ask permission."

"Really? That doesn't seem very nice."

"Trust me, Phoebe. You do not want anything male, even gelded, thinking it can get away with such crap."

"Can I tell you some more about Juan?" she asks. "Or does this gross you out, hearing the details of how I lost my virginity? What a stupid way of putting it, 'lost,' like I forgot it in the car or something."

Her brown eyes are brimming with wonder.

She's clearly overwhelmed by this new bend in the road. I know how that feels and I want to cry. But I smile and listen, because that, more than anything, is what friends are for.

# 10

## A Brief Thanksgiving

IT'S A SHOCK TO DISCOVER there are so many nerve endings in my ankles, the same weak joints that so often refuse to support me, but Juan's tongue is convincing. If physical therapy had been like this, I might have learned to walk a whole lot better. Sex has its downside, however. Like the flu, once it hits, you might as well lie there and let the illness run its course. Me, I'm wallowing in it, hoping I never recover, when I hear my beloved whispering my name.

"Phoebe," he says working his way up my leg to the bend of my hips, which are so small he easily cups one in each hand.

Reluctantly, I open my eyes to look down at the top of his head of thick, dark hair. "What?"

"Okay if I do this?" And without waiting for

226

my answer, he moves his mouth *there,* where it feels as if a candle's been lit, its heat spreading through my limbs like melting wax. He wants permission to make me feel this good? Sorry, I have no words for that, no possible language, just the wet heat of his mouth against my body and the cries my skin seems to be making all on its own. I'm happily riding this wave of sensation, trying to feel secure that his wanting me's apparently not a one-time thing. My hands in my lover's hair, I pull him close until there's no clear definition between where he starts and I end. I can smell the heat of our bodies, the finest perfume in the world. Juan pulls my legs up so that they slip right over his shoulders. I never knew they could do that, but somehow it seems wickedly right. Two days from now is Thanksgiving, but I don't think I could feel any more grateful than this. Saturday is the poinsettia sale, on which so much depends. What's any of that matter while the heat's rising in my body, barreling upward and out at the same time, charging up my spine, through the scar tissue from my surgeries, all the way to my fingertips, flooding my toes, culminating in *oh,* which I am discovering, is probably the most eloquent syllable in the world...

"Ah, the universal yes," Juan says, laughing. He swipes his damp fingers across my mouth, making me taste myself, and then he moves inside me, and I hold on tight, thinking of nothing at all except how I want to stay forever in this, the best dream I've ever had, because it's real.

"FORGET THE PEST-CONTROL ISSUES for a moment, we have to discuss the poinsettia sale," Nance says, her notepad and pen at her side. "While it costs practically nothing to put an ad in the *Blue Jay,* that's a only weekly paper. I think our money would be better spent in the *Herald.*"

"Fifteen hundred dollars!" Beryl says. "I can tack up flyers around Sierra Grove and outside the supermarkets. That won't cost anything except shoe leather."

"No offense," Nance says, "but we want to attract the Bayborough-by-the-Sea crowd. How many of them walk anywhere, including on the golf course?"

"Well, pardon me," Beryl says, clearly offended. "I guess ordinary people don't decorate for the holidays."

"Oh, Beryl, will you stop with the poverty mindset already? You live in the Valley now. Do you still buy your clothes at the thrift store?"

"As a matter of fact, I do. You have a problem with that?"

This only stops Nance for a second. "Well, the Bayborough Thrift Store stock has designer labels, so you can't deny you look the part. Ness, can we have your opinion, please?"

Ness doesn't say anything, just holds on to her glass of ice tea and looks out the window where the wind is blowing through the oaks next to the barn.

Nance and Beryl look to me for a solution. I'm sitting here in a daze, too, not really hearing the logic in anybody's argument. Lately my brain is just plain checked out except for things like breathing and interesting sexual positions for which we can blame UPS. But it's true, inside the greenhouse and overflowing into the barn we have five thousand poinsettias, white, pink, and red to sell, and some kind of ad needs to be placed—tonight. Florencio's cousin Segundo is coming over to help out the day of the sale. Most of the pots are priced at ten dollars. The wimpier ones are five. If we sell them all, after covering the costs, DeThomas Farms will pay its bills, distribute dividend checks to the workers, and we will have a nice fat cushion to sit on until spring. If we don't, we'll have the most decorated property in the Valley, and should Babs Smith-Etienne drive by, she could sell it in a heartbeat, which we would need to do with that much inventory. Aside from the *Wall Street Journal*, the *Herald* is the most-read paper among the B-b-t-S crowd. They're not going to cut us a break on the ad at this late date—unless I make a phone call to James, who knows the editor-in-chief personally—he's a wine-and-cheese partymonster, too.

"Nance has a point," I say. "I think the ad should go in the *Herald*. Yes, fifteen hundred is a bundle of money, but as my brother Stinky says, you have to spend money to make it. Actually, I think we should ask him to place the ad."

229

"I'm perfectly capable of getting into bed with the advertising people," Nance says.

"I know that, Nance. As does everybody at this table. But James drinks *wine* with these people. If he pours some Château de Snob down their throats, he can cut us a better deal."

"Screw James and his freaking expensive wine. I suppose sleeping with a journalist for three years doesn't count squat for learning the fine art of negotiation?"

Beryl laughs; Verde cusses from his cage. Ness stands up, all six feet of her, and starts in. "All you people think about is sex. I for one am a little tired of the innuendoes, the jokes; even the parrot's got a filthy mind. Did you ever stop to think that maybe sex is not funny to some people? No, you all say whatever comes to mind, no matter how dirty." Then she leaves the room.

"What? What did I say?" Nance says, and looks at me stricken.

"I'll go to her," I say. "Nance, you call James and invite him for supper."

"Ew, do I have to?"

"Yes, you have to. And be nice, we can't afford to piss Stinky off at this late date."

"What if he brings the realtor?"

"Tell him to come alone. We need that deal on the ad. Jeez Louise, look at Beryl. Make her breathe into a paper sack. It isn't anything either of you said, I'm sure. I can get Ness to talk to me. Just give me ten minutes alone with her and try to behave yourselves."

I wheel outdoors, stopping long enough to

put on a hat and throw Sadie's mink over my shoulders. Wearing this coat is horribly politically incorrect, but I didn't kill the minks, and at least they have a good home here on my shoulders. Love it I do, not just because it smells of my aunt's perfume, but because it makes me feel like some mobster's girlfriend, living the dangerous life. Am I? Oh, you betcha. Every month I juggle money as if it's beanbags. If I pay the farm bills when they're due, things get squinchy with the flowers. I have to pay the utilities, that's a given, but then there's the farm equipment insurance, and those people are not fond of waiting. When things break down, I can't believe what it costs to fix them. I hated going to Florencio to ask him if I could withhold a small portion of his salary with the promise that in the spring I'd pay him back with interest.

"*Calmate,* Phoebe," he said, bless his heart. "Sadie, she do that every *año.* "

When I do manage enough cash flow to pay everything, I end up staring at the twenty-five-dollar balance in the checkbook, terrified some new crisis will occur before I can find a way to pay for it. If it weren't for my Social Security and disability checks, I worry there would be days we'd have to talk about eating instead of doing it. Fifteen hundred dollars. That's fourteen hundred dollars more than I currently have in my bank account. Of course, the girls have no idea. At night, before I go to sleep, I'll make twelve of the mobiles that sell the best. I'm tired of them, and they leave my arthritic fingers aching, but I figure that's why God invented Ibuprofen, and in thirty days, they'll translate to a check. As far as making real art—forget it. I have the cabbage ladies in the garden to remind me that once upon a time I dabbled. James wasn't lying when he said Sadie never showed a profit from the farm. In her journal she occasionally mentions the investments she left to my brother and I could strangle her for not dividing everything fifty-fifty. This poinsettia sale is a larger gamble than anyone but me needs to know.

Ness, predictably, is in the barn with Leroy. I swear this horse is groomed and petted so often he's beginning to look like he belongs to Prince Charles. The poinsettia plants are wrapped in green foil and cellophane, ready to go. As far as Christmas flowers go, I've never much cared for them, but I'm praying my view is in the minority. "Hi there, Leroy," I say. "Who's this sad sack who won't leave you to eat your hay in peace?"

He doesn't whinny for his usual handout. Ness keeps her face turned so I can't see it.

"So. Neither of you are speaking to me, huh?"

She gives me a weary sigh.

"Dammit all, Preciousness, you're walking around here in a permanent state of PMS. Beryl's so convinced it's her fault that she's about to pass out. Nance thinks you can't stand living with her because she comes from the South and her ancestors owned slaves."

Ness turns to face me. Her black face is shiny

with tears and the gleam in her eyes dares me to say more. Then she breaks her silence. "They owned actual slaves?"

"Well, I'm just guessing. But they probably did. I mean, look how she dresses. Unless she came from oil or organized crime, they had to make their money someplace. Alabama—cotton—you do the math."

"And you, Phoebe? What do you think?"

For a second I think she's talking about slavery, which is a no-brainer, and then I realize we're back to the first subject. "Well," I say, turning my chair so she can't escape me, "if you want the truth, at first I thought you were jealous of Juan."

"That's ridiculous!"

"Hey, you can't blame me for trying to figure this out when you won't give me a clue. Whatever's eating you up, I'm sure it's much, much more than my sex life. I figure when you're good and ready you'll fill me in, so I'm trying to be patient. If I let you give me another riding lesson will you tell me what's wrong?"

She shakes her head. "It's too cold out for you to ride. Me, though, it just might help if I galloped a little ways in the dark, like say, off a cliff."

"We're pretty much fresh out of cliffs here in the Valley. If it's cliffs you're looking for, you'd have to head south to Big Sur. Thanksgiving wouldn't be the same without you sharing my Tofurky. Plus we really need you for the poinsettia sale. I mean it, Ness. If this thing flops, we're all going belly-up. *Hasta la vista,* farm. And if you let on to the others about what I just said, I'll tell them you were lying."

She looks at me gravely, and then begins to rearrange Leroy's tack into neater stacks, straightening his bridles and reins where they reside on various hooks. "I'm just not ready to talk about it, Phoebe."

This isn't what I want to hear. In fact, I'm almost ready to tell her that the prima donna act doesn't play well at my house, but I hold my tongue. "Fine, you tell Beryl and Nance that and we'll all wait patiently together."

She frowns. "It's not that I don't want to talk, it's complicated—"

"Horse manure, Ness! We're four women living together so closely our menstrual cycles have synchronized. When one of us stubs her toe, the others say 'ow.' Secrets fester unless you share them. I think you're making a big mistake here, but I love you so much I'll respect your wishes, even if they are completely lame."

The wind is kicking up, and I can feel myself getting chilled. Lord, I don't relish another round with pneumonia. Ness takes a horse blanket down from the shelves and fastens it around Leroy. I want her to give me one, too. For months now I've watched her tend that animal more lovingly than any mother tends a child. It's a beautiful sight, except when I see her treating herself so shabbily. My mind is taking all kinds of wacky leaps—she's got a gambling addiction, she's sick with cancer, that client she has deep in the Valley raped her... What do you do when somebody you love gets like this? "Come on inside. It's freezing out here. Let's go make dinner and get you a jumbo glass of wine. Thrill for the week, I invited James over."

"What makes you think he'll come?"

"My brother never turns down a free meal, especially when it gives him a chance to check out the property he so desperately wants for his own. He'll be here in half an hour, napkin tucked into his shirtfront. Beryl can make him her honey-and-mustard spareribs. He loves sweet, greasy animal fat almost as much as he loves day-trading."

BERYL SHOWS ME THE NOTE she found tucked inside Aunt Sadie's *Best All-Time Southern Cookbook*. Wilton B's North Carolina Sweet Potato Pie:

> *Make as you would ordinary pumpkin pie, however, for all liquids, substitute the richest eggnog you can find. Halve the sugar and add exactly that much molasses. Crumble pecans and peanuts in a fry pan, throw in a stick of unsalted butter and more molasses, and cook until dark brown and thickened. During last fifteen minutes of baking, top pie with this mixture so it forms a crust. Serve with*

*homemade whipped cream liberally doused
with whiskey. Trust me, Sadie, one bite of
this recipe will make any man forget why
he was mad at you in the first place—*

The rest of the paper is torn, so we'll never
know what Wilton B said after that.

"Perfect," I say. "Only let's serve James
his whiskey in a glass."

"Was your aunt Southern?" Beryl asks me,
as she dumps the pared sweet potatoes into
the boiling water.

"Goodness, no. If she'd been Southern on
top of everything else she was, she probably
would have found a practical use for kudzu.
Nope, she was a native Californian through and
through." For a moment I get that strange feeling again, the one that sometimes wakes me up
in the middle of the night. Here I am holding
on to her kitchen utensils, the ghosts of dozens
of meals she prepared rearing up, demanding
to be remembered. If I let my mind wander, I
can almost smell the fleeting aromas. A lovers'
quarrel over steaks crusty with peppercorns.
Business deals carefully negotiated over beef
Wellington and asparagus drenched in hol-
landaise sauce. Those singular bowls of chicken
soup stirred and restirred and ultimately ignored
in times of great sorrow, when she stood alone
at the sink and wondered if she had made all
bad choices, or if it was too late to fix maybe a
few things. "Sadie was a mutt, Beryl. She was
a little bit of everything. Maybe that's what gave
her such strength, that hybrid vigor."

"Wish I'd known her."

"Me, too," I say, thinking there are so many stories of Sadie's I've never heard, so many secrets I don't know, that I can't really speak for her. All I can do is gather clues from the house and the gardening journal. She's dead, and I'm learning to learn to live with that, but Ness, who is very much alive, isn't going to get off so easily. In the beginning, all Beryl ever let us know was the bare minimum, but she's warmed up so much there are days she's downright chatty.

"Ness, get your butt in here and lend a hand with the potatoes," I tell her.

Without arguing, she trudges into the kitchen and picks up a fork.

"I apologize if what I said about Rick upset you," Nance says as she uncorks the wine for the table. "Sometimes my jokes are awful."

One by one, Ness stabs the cooking potatoes, until they are all pierced through, then again, a little more fiercely.

"I don't think that's going to make them cook any faster," Beryl offers.

Nance sighs. "If it makes her feel better, where's the harm?"

Beryl gives her a hard look, and I can smell the fight these two have been working toward all day. "Don't you two start bickering. Ness has something she wants to tell us," I say. "She's just about ready, I think, so why don't you pour her some of that wine, Nance?"

Ness glares at me and drinks her glassful down. She lays the potato fork on the counter.

For the fifth time tonight, she washes her hands with gardener's soap and dries them on a paper towel and throws it away. When she looks up at all of us, I can feel the love we have for her surrounding her. Why can't she? It's the same as the sun shining in a certain window on a winter day, that warm ray you can almost touch. Once you know it's there, all you want to do is bask for hours, soaking the warmth in and holding it close like a quilt.

"Jake's terminally ill," she says in a matter-of-fact voice. "I'm just having a hard time accepting it. I apologize for worrying all of you. That's all, nothing more."

Beryl goes to her and puts an arm around her shoulders. She lays her head against Ness's shoulder, and doesn't say a word. Ness doesn't reach out to hug her back.

Nance takes off her reading glasses and they slide down the silver chain she wears until they rest against her breasts. "Ordinarily, I'd advise against you seeing him again, Ness. But in this case, I think you'd better say good-bye. For men, things just end, or they switch the channel and when the sun comes up it's a brand-new day complete with the possibility of football. Women, on the other hand, need all the friggin' closure they can get."

"Closure?" Ness repeats, as if this is the first time she's heard the term. "Sounds so formal. Like shutting some big old door forever."

And she gets this sad look on her face, so far from us that Nance elbows me. "Ness," I say, but before we can take this very interesting line of thought any further, my brother breezes in the door.

"Greetings, Wingnut," he says affectionately, and hands me a CD. It's some saxophone player I've never heard of, but Nance has, and she puts it on the stereo.

"Hello, Schmoozer," I say. "Haven't seen you since your ill-fated date with Babs of Bayborough Realty. Hopefully you've expanded your social circle."

He takes off his leather blazer and folds it across the back of the couch. His face is wary, but I can tell I've struck a nerve. "Like you care."

"But I do care, James. Why would you think I don't want you to be happy?"

He sniffs the air. "Hmm. Thought I was invited for a home-cooked meal. Why does it smell like baloney in here?"

I give his hand a squeeze. "Can't a sister be nice?"

"Well, that would be a pleasant change. So, what are we having? Please don't tell me no animals were harmed to fill my stomach."

Nance brings him the glass of scotch. She brushes a piece of lint from his shoulder. "Nice shirt," she says in a voice that comes out just above a whisper. "You should wear blue more often."

James turns, surprised. "Maybe I will."

"You didn't really get off to a good start with the parrot," I say. "So we cooked up one of his relatives for you."

"What?"

"Phoebe, stop teasing the poor man," Beryl says. "I made you spareribs, James."

"Yeah, tell the pig those ribs were spare," I say. "Drink up, James, and tuck your napkin into your shirt. We have some business to discuss."

He pulls out a chair and takes a seat. "It's true what they say. No such thing as a free lunch."

Nance lays out the ads she's designed and explains the cost of the *Herald,* and how the deadline is tomorrow morning. James looks them over, clearly impressed. "You took these photos?" he says. "Nice work."

She shrugs. "I have my moments."

"You ever think of going professional?"

Nance laughs. "Now who's trying to schmooze who?"

"No, I'm serious. People would pay money for these."

She scoffs. "Doesn't everyone in Bayborough fancy himself to be the next up-and-coming Edward Weston?"

"Your work may not be Weston, but it is commercial," James argues.

Sounds to me like James spots more than a financial opportunity. "Yeah, yeah, she's the next Imogen Cunningham," I say. "You can pose naked for her in Pfeiffer State Park sometime. Will you help us get a break on the ad or not?"

He leans back in his chair and sips his scotch. "What's in this for me?"

"Excellent karma, getting in good with Saint Nick just before the holidays, both viable options, I should think."

He grins. "Pheebs, it's probably going to take a little more than that. Can somebody refill my glass?"

"Happily," Nance says, and does.

James drinks deeply, and smiles when he comes up for air. "I can't believe you ladies would break open Sadie's Glenfiddich for little old me. Is it insulting for me to tell you that I feel as if I've fallen into a harem?"

Nance cocks her head. "Depends. Did you ever go to journalism school?"

At this, Ness finally smiles. "James?"

"Yes, tall one? Tell me what I can do for you. Anything at all. At the moment I'm feeling both lubricated and generous, so ask away."

When Ness wants to, she can pull off positively regal with so little effort it's criminal. All she has to do is turn her head just so; stretch out that racehorse neck and smile like a Mona Lisa with a past not even Jesus could forgive. Her voice comes out smoky; she works every syllable like she's singing it. "Tell me something. Does everything in the world have to have a good financial reason underwriting it?"

James stands up and paces the room, touching a few of Sadie's baubles. The dragonfly Tiffany lamp, which I worry he would sell; a shell box from Morocco that Sadie kept matches in; a silver Navajo teapot inlaid with spiderweb turquoise from mine number eight. He's beyond flustered, and the scotch has kicked him in the head far harder than Leroy could have. "Well, I don't know, Ness. Sometimes it sure seems that way." He waves his glass, which again is empty. "Phoebe? Would you sell me one of the cars?" he says without emotion, and it takes a sister's ear to hear the truth of what's under that tone of voice. Desperation.

My brother wants to polish his image with the patina of an aging, well-kept Mercedes.

I think a while before I answer. This is a tactic I learned from James. "I might."

He sighs. "Any time in the near future?"

"If you could find it in your heart to finagle me a really good deal on a replacement vehicle."

"Come on. What do you need two cars for?"

"We need two cars because there are four of us here and only two automobiles if I sell you one. And don't think I'm unaware of the blue book on the Mercedes, James. It's a collector's car. I've had other offers." I cross my fingers at this small but effective lie.

"Pheebs," he says, setting the silver teapot down on the mantel with a clunk. "I'm willing to pay you the full value, less the cost of the *Herald* ad, which by the way, I think I can get up to a quarter-page size for not too much more money."

"Like how much is not too much more?"

"Maybe another thousand. Running it in two sections is always better than one. Talk it

242

over with the ladies while I go, you know, inspect the facilities."

Off he shambles, his glass in hand. One of us is going to have to drive him home.

"What's the car worth?" Nance asks me. "Should I look it up on the Internet?"

"That beautiful yellow Mercedes," Beryl says. "How could you part with it?"

"Or the Jag..." Ness says, before she walks to the window and stares out into the darkness at God knows what.

"They're only cars, you guys. Sadie left them to me. If we can use the money to keep the farm going, why not?"

"Ultimately it's your decision," Nance says. "And the advertisement will be a good thing. It's just a shame to sell off any of your aunt's things. It's like disturbing the most beautiful tableau."

Now I feel guilty. But without the money, it won't be just me who'd lose this home. I feel responsible for these women. I made them a promise when I ran that ad. Sadie, what would you do?

In her journal she quotes a great deal from this Beston fellow: "The adventure of the sun is the great natural drama by which we live, and not to have joy in it and awe of it, not to share in it, is to close a dull door on nature's sustaining and poetic spirit."

Whenever I read that, I see her so clearly, standing up after spending the day planting tulips, her knees covered with dirt. Oblivious, she stretches her arms above her head and ends in the yoga posture salute to the sun. She turns. Her profile appears etched in the afternoon sunlight. So many options to choose from, so many directions she could take. Will she dine tonight with a handsome gentleman art collector, or will she slip on the red cowboy boots and go dancing at a roadhouse?

"I'm going to check on dinner," Beryl says, and exits the room in search of my brother.

We pick at our food while James stuffs himself, dropping the scraped-clean bones in his plate long enough to groan and grab another. "This is so good," he says, several times. Beryl switches his scotch to water and in the background I can smell the coffee brewing. Ness cuts the sweet potato pie and spoons whipped cream over the top.

James chortles at the nut topping. "You're not very subtle, are you, ladies? Fattening me up for the slaughter."

"What are your Thanksgiving plans?" Nance asks him. "Big date?"

"Ha. Lately I and my hand are going steady."

Oh, Stinky. He has to be half-crocked to say something like that out loud.

"That's a shame," Nance says and leans in her chair closer to him. "You want to have dinner with us?"

He takes a drink of water and looks at the glass, perplexed. "Can't. Big party. Dinner with some people out on the Links."

"Business or pleasure?" Nance presses.

"If it isn't always both, it's a waste of time, Ms. Mattox."

244

She laughs. "What an intelligent way to look at things. I applaud that. Surely you need a date. I have a little black dress that never fails to impress. And really, doesn't it increase your value a notch to be seen with a woman who can hold her own with the money crowd?"

My smart-mouthed brother is actually blushing. "I-I-I assumed you and the coven were probably holding a girls-only ceremony here. Broom, tofu, voodoo, something along those lines."

This amuses Nance greatly. "I'll have you know I'm a good little Catholic girl. I never miss Mass."

I assumed broom and tofu, too. Whatever Nance is up to, I have a feeling it doesn't fall under the category of Good Samaritan acts. "We witches will eat early," I say. "After all, we have a lot of work to do to get ready for the plant sale."

"Oh, yeah," he says. "For a second I forgot."

Nance flashes her best smile. While not as transforming as Ness, she runs a close second.

James probably has a boner the size of Tallahassee, and dares not get up from the table lest we all notice. As if Nance can sense this, she snakes her arm around his shoulder.

"Then is it a date?" she asks. "Or do you want me to haul out my dress and model it for you?"

"That's not necessary." He laughs nervously. "Sure, come along. Bring your camera."

She clinks her glass with his. "I was planning to."

"I'll be here at seven," he tells her. "Can we use the Mercedes?"

"I think that can be arranged," I tell him. "So long as you bring her back in one piece."

"Nance or the car?"

Now he's back, the obnoxious brother who once hid my tennis shoes in the toilet tank where the bleach tablets my mother was so fond of using rendered them from a glorious purple to a horrible salmon color. "Ha ha, very amusing, James. Now about the ad?"

"What about the car?"

He's definitely sobering up, but I'm still not letting him drive. "It's yours, if you get us a really sweet deal on a SUV with four-wheel drive."

"Done before Christmas. Somebody want to bring me the phone?"

Beryl does. Mr. Bluster discusses golf scores, Tiger Woods's magic, choice technology stocks, and rumored mergers, and some upcoming wine-tasting event that is supposed to be star-studded and sounds like a journalist's wet dream. This takes approximately fifteen minutes, during which time we pick at the leftover salad until only the wilted lettuce remains. Then he logs on to Nance's computer, sends over the ad artwork, waits for the confirmation, and tells us it's a go for Saturday's paper, page two of the Home Living section, page twelve of Metro. Nance gives him a little hug, and I watch her walk my brother toward the door. There's more bounce in his step than when he was nine years old and used to score some mediocre baseball card he could trade to a dumb kid for a better one. *Why don't you take the gum, too?* Generous James used to say.

"What is the name of this particular game?" I ask Nance when she's dumped James into a cab and is back at the table, clearing the dinner plates.

Her face is dead serious. "Nothing. Right now, I just want a shot at those rich people to talk up our sale, nosh on imported goodies, and take pictures."

"Really?" Beryl says from her place at the table. "I thought maybe you were after embarrassing the realtor who gypped you out of Morning Glory cottage again."

Her back stiffens. "It was named Evening Primrose. And gravy on that particular turkey, my dear Bear," she says with a wicked glint in her eye, "would be the ultimate Thanksgiving treat."

ON THANKSGIVING MORNING James and a buddy show up to get his Jeep. He sniffs around the house, generally making a pest of himself until I take absolute pity. "Nance isn't here, Stinky. She took Duchess for a walk down on the beach in Bayborough-by-the-Sea. Now either light someplace, help me with the dinner, or go after her like the lovestruck basset hound you are."

At first he tries to pretend otherwise, but I

wag a finger in his face, and before long, he gives up and pushes my chair toward the front door. "Could a girl that beautiful go for a clod like me, Pheebs? Or is this another one of your jokes?"

He looks about as embarrassed as a dog dressed up in a Halloween costume. I reach up and touch his cheek. "Stranger things have happened."

"Yeah, Florencio told me about UPS," he says. "I hope that guy is treating you right."

"No worries there."

James looks at me like I've just told him I joined a terrorist organization. "Phoebe! Don't tell me you went to bed with him."

"Fine, I won't."

On the porch, he paces and rubs his chin. "I just—" he begins. "The only reason—" he tries next. "Shouldn't you—" doesn't pan out any better. Finally he sits down in the swing and says the F word. Twice.

"I'm all grown up, James. Just because I can't walk straight doesn't mean I can't enjoy a little sex. Why should the able-bodied have all the fun?"

He turns and looks at me with a most peculiar expression. Then he kisses me on the cheek and gets into his Jeep and drives away. I feel the wind cool the skin where his lips touched me and I'm sad. Not just because Ness is freaking me out, or that we might go belly up with the poinsettias, but that things ever have to change in the world of our childhood. That we grow out of the game of telephone and chop fights and come to see our parents for the vulnerable humans they are—widows lonely for arms to hold them, fathers who worked themselves to death because the idea of being in debt was inconceivable. No matter the size of our brains, it seems like we learn nothing from their mistakes until we make the same damn ones ourselves, in the name of happiness. Freaking holidays. I wonder if all this sex is making me get my period early. If so, the girls will be right behind me. Mood swings and the upcoming holidays—sounds like a girl punk band. It strikes me that Sadie would have seized such an opportunity to invest in Midol stock.

AROUND NOON, NESS GETS A WILD HAIR that we have to roast chestnuts. It's a culinary must. Apparently Granny Shirley never let a single Thanksgiving pass without this foodstuff on the table.

"I'm sorry," Beryl says. "I hate them. They're all grainy and mushy, like prison oatmeal."

"I agree," Nance says. "Plus they're a pain in the butt to peel."

"Fine, I'll do it all myself," Ness says, stomping off, and we hear the front door slam.

We hear the Jag peel out on the gravel, go about our business, and are astonished when, having found some foolish gourmet market still open, she returns with five pounds of the ugly brown rocks. God knows how much they cost.

"How much did you pay for those?" Beryl asks.

"I used my own money, so why does it matter?"

"I was just curious."

"No, you weren't. You wanted to act all shocked that I'd squander money when we're all so broke and make me feel like crap on a national holiday."

"Honestly, Ness, I didn't."

Ness begins cutting X's into the shells and tossing them into a baking dish like she's slam-dunking two-pointers for the Lakers. There's a manic quality about her prep work, like a chef on methamphetamine.

Beryl's tight-lipped, basting the small roast she and Nance will share, having put her foot down on the turkey issue—citing Verde's civil rights—and Nance is only adamant that she make creamed onions and that green bean casserole with the crunchy topping. But not even this simple menu can go smoothly. Somebody—no one will 'fess up—has eaten the freeze-dried onions, and we are left with two options: go without or use Cap'n Crunch cereal.

"Enough arguing!" Beryl says, halting the discussion by crushing the cereal into a brief approximation of breadcrumbs and dumping it on the beans. "Settled," she says, to this madhouse in my aunt's kitchen, when we'd all sworn that for once we'd keep Thanksgiving simple.

250

I miss my boyfriend, who is spending the day with his mother in Salinas. He might as well be in Antarctica versus an hour away. Then I remember something just awful. "You guys? I think Juan ate the onions. He gets hungry late at night after we, you know—"

"Will you shut up about your precious stud puppy?" Nance says.

"Why should she?" Beryl puts in. "You have a date tonight, even if you did ask the guy out."

"My so-called date is purely business," Nance sniffs. "I am not in the least attracted to James DeThomas, and if he tries to kiss me, I'll smack him with my evening bag."

"Just admit you like him," Beryl says.

Then Ness butts in. "It's totally obvious, Nance. You just can't say it because that would mean you were over Rotten Rick. And not entirely in control of the situation, which is a mortal sin, right?"

"That tears it." Nance throws the casserole into the oven. She flings the hot pad at Ness, who catches it and laughs, a little too hysterically for my taste. Nance huffs off to her room, Duchess in tow. We don't see her until things are ready to serve, and when she does show up, her face is painted ice blue with some kind of strange mask that no doubt will make her already great complexion shine even more lustrously. "Nobody say a single word," she admonishes us. "If you make this thing crack I'll whup every one of you with the ugly stick."

There's a loud bang from the kitchen, then another, and Ness screams.

"What happened?" I say, rolling toward the sound as fast as I can.

"My chestnuts are blowing up," she says, crying. "One of them hit me in the face." She rubs at a welt on her cheek and I can't help but start laughing.

"Why's that so damned funny, Phoebe? My one contribution to our first holiday meal, and I can't even get it right."

I haul her to the table and we sit down together. I raise my glass of sparkling cider and say "Happy damn Thanksgiving. Here's to proof that holidays bring out the worst in total strangers as well as family."

"Hold on a second," Beryl says. She clears her throat and puts her hand on Nance's to stop her from serving herself the creamed onions. "I want to say a prayer."

"That's what this group needs," Nance says stiffly. "A big old prayer. One that will remind us to do unto others and so forth."

Beryl looks uncertainly around the table. "I didn't mean a religious prayer, just to say thanks. You know, on behalf of all birds everywhere, not just the maligned turkey. I know Verde's grateful. And I wanted to take a moment to tell you all, even though we're kind of fighting right now, that you're my friends. And that this has been the best couple of months of my life. I wish every one of us at this table the happiest of holidays. That's it."

We're quiet, chagrined, and not just at what Beryl says, but that it always seems to take her, who's had the hardest time of all of us, to remind us how lucky we are.

"I wish that too," Nance says. "Especially for Phoebe and Juan. Lord Jesus, let at least one of us get things right in the man department. And that we sell the poinsettias, every last one of the ugly sons of bitches, even if just so I don't have to water them anymore. And for Ness in particular, I hope saying good-bye to Jake gives her some peace. I don't mean to be disrespectful of a dying man, God knows, but it sure would be nice to start having some fun around here again."

Ness's tears segue into sobs.

This is what tears it for me. "All right. This is how it's going to be," I say. "Nobody is lifting a fork until Ness tells us the truth of what's bothering her. I mean it. I will personally stab the first person who moves a utensil."

And we wait. The food that smelled so great in the kitchen grows tepid. There's a latent pop from one of the chestnuts. Duchess lays her head down on her paws. Verde is silent. The cube of butter somebody pressed a sprig of rosemary into is starting to melt. Every time Ness tries to leave the table, Beryl and Nance tackle her. This greatly upsets Duchess, who starts baying like a bloodhound. Verde begins imitating the telephone; a short but accurate trill that tricks us at first, then pisses everyone off. Ness sits there peeling her chestnuts, one by one, but she doesn't eat them. She throws each one into her plate with a ping that echoes in my ears. Finally, they're all peeled.

"Jake's got AIDS," she says. "I'm pretty sure he's given it to me."

"Oh, God. That's what Sam Patrini told you at Katy's, isn't it?" Nance says. "I knew something major was wrong."

"Maybe it's just a rumor," Beryl offers. "You know how these things get started—"

"It's no rumor, Beryl," Ness says. "I knew it before Sam. Why else do you think I ran away from the best job I ever had? So I could camp by Bad Girl Creek?" She puts her face into her hands. From behind her fingers she says, "Might as well confess that I stole Leroy, too. He belongs to Jake. Generally I don't hold with stealing, but if I hadn't of taken him, Jake would have beat him senseless."

Now our quiet is earned and leagues deeper. I'm sick. No one will look up from her plate. Nance's face mask may not have cracked, but the salty tears streaking down her cheek probably aren't doing it any good either. I can't get past the fact that Ness knew she'd been exposed—that she kept the truth from all of us—that right from the start, she kept it from me.

Beryl looks to me. "Phoebe, you have to do something."

All I can think of to do is call Lester, who no doubt is sitting down to his own family madness, and how fair is that? He never should have given me his home number. I wheel out of the room and make the call.

"Hi Lester," I say when he picks up. "One quick question, then I'll let you go. Can you perform HIV tests in your office, or is it necessary to go to one of those confidential clinics?"

"Lord, Phoebe, what have you gotten yourself into? It hasn't even been a month since I saw you last. We haven't even gotten through the birth control controversy."

"Can you do it or not?"

"Of course I can do it. Now tell me you're not worried about having this disease or I won't be able to finish my pie."

"It's for my friend. Honest. The rest of us want tests to give her moral support."

He sighs. "The older I get the less I understand women."

"WE'LL ALL GO GET TESTED ON MONDAY," I say when I return. "Lester says it takes a week to get the results. Whatever happens, we'll deal with the outcome the same way we've faced any of our problems here on the farm. Together."

Let those poinsettias sell.

"I think this is a little more serious than overwatering asters," Ness says, her voice jagged.

By now Nance has picked half her face mask off and the chunks lie on her napkin, blue as the shell of a robin's egg.

"Yeah? So what? Things like this happen. My aunt didn't ask for colon cancer, did she? I didn't ask for a bent spine, or rheumatic fever, either. There're great drugs for HIV now,

255

and we can afford them if we sell the poinsettias and whatever else we have growing out there. We're smart women, intelligent enough to know how to take the proper precautions if you test positive, which you aren't sure you are just yet. God, Ness. Every single one of us is at risk for something. We're all going to die someday. My heart's a ticking time bomb. Now we'll eat this great dinner, sell the plants, and on Monday, we'll get our blood tests and go from there, okay?"

They look at me like I've just torn off my clothes and begun speaking in tongues. "Eat the damn food, you guys. I am not letting this holiday descend into utter pathos. We were happy up until this happened. We will be happy no matter how it turns out. Happy, do you hear me?"

I pick up a chestnut and pop it into my mouth to make my point. It tastes like library paste. Try as I might, I cannot swallow the thing. I spit it into my napkin. "Ness, honey. I gotta ask. What do you see in these things? They're ghastly."

"Family," she says.

Beryl reaches across the table and takes her hand. "You get to see that in us every day," she says. "And none of us is planning to blow up and slap you in the cheek. Here, have some Tofurky. Look how realistic the fake skin is. How do they do that, Phoebe? Get the pores just right?"

"Damned if I know."

"Have some cranberry sauce, too. Please,

Ness. I love you. Nance loves you. Leroy loves you. I'm glad you stole him. We all love you."

We raise our forks and we eat, not tasting a thing. We are as festive as four women can be with the sword of Damocles hanging over their heads. When Beryl mutters something about dessert, Nance excuses herself and dresses for her dinner with James. She emerges from the bedroom looking like a blond Audrey Hepburn, but her face is so sad. "I should cancel."

"No way," I tell her. "Wait until Babs Smith-Etienne gets a load of you."

"Screw Babs," she says. "I want to stay here with Ness."

"Go," Ness tells her. "I'll still be here when you get back."

Nance sighs. "Fine, but it's not going to be any fun. Pheebs, can I borrow the mink?"

"Borrow away."

In it, she looks unstoppably beautiful, but those concerns are nothing compared to the cloud of uncertainty descending into my gut. Ness is sitting by the fire, wrapped in a fleece throw. Verde is on her shoulder plucking her braids. Duchess lies across her feet. I don't understand how any of this can be happening when we've only just found each other. What fresh hell it will be if she is taken away.

"Scrabble?" Beryl suggests.

"For pity's sake," I say. The next three days will not only kick our collective butts nonstop, but the nights that come along with it will be unending. "Get the other bottle of wine and three water glasses. We'll drink our way through this." And we join hands, hang on tight, only letting go when our glasses need refilling.

*Nance*

# 11

## *The Ugly Bug Ball*

EMBARRASSING AS IT IS to admit, my mother's real name is Bunny. She can slap on a thrift store sweater, khaki pants from Target, K-mart loafers and walk into a complete stranger's party with utter confidence. Even between marriages, Bunny drank gourmet blend out of a Limoges cup. She had to, with all those hangovers. She wasn't stingy with her coffee, and always offered me some, but all I could think about was the Brazilian economy and subsequent rain-forest dilemmas involved in her precious beans, so I developed a taste for tea. I told myself small protests were better than none. Now I can't live without caffeine. I worry I'm becoming more like my mother every day. No matter where we lived, my mother planted flowers, daffodil bulbs, geraniums, and that rank-smelling paperwhite that always fools me with its prettiness. So in that way, it's as if I've come full circle as her daughter. But in every other way, we remain polar opposites.

Take for example the period when Bunny was still enjoying first-wife status. Even disinherited, she did the proper Southern thing, marrying a neurosurgeon. We lived in an historic Victorian house in Sacramento, where I attended kindergarten through third grade. I'm sure that gorgeous old lady cost as much as any one of the countless multi-million-dollar mansions lining the fifteen-mile scenic drive James is taking to deliver us to the very important party. But for reasons I never quite heard explained to my satisfaction, the neurosurgeon wasn't good enough for us, and one day she bought us matching luggage and we packed them to the gills and left. Bunny didn't get the house in the divorce settlement; she barely got alimony. She sure didn't get child support since the neurosurgeon wasn't my father. Neither was Daddy number two, a stockbroker who made and lost a fortune, or the man she lived with, Dennis, the one decent guy I wished was my father. He taught linguistics at the University of Oregon, Eugene, and when they broke up, he made sure Bunny got a house to live in, the Cannon Beach home where she still resides to this day.

The subject of my father is rarely broached unless encouraged with copious amounts of alcohol. No matter how looped I get her, though, Bunny stops short of the information that interests me most. Her bottom line is that I was the one decent by-product that came out of that weak moment that ruined her life and permanently estranged her from the Mattox clan.

It's hard growing up hearing that every day, but even after witnessing all those awful breakups, I'd still like to get married—once. I'd be good at it, I know, taking care of a man, making nice dinners—I even enjoy folding laundry. But where I'd shine most is motherhood. With no effort at all, I could slide right into the role of a mama who stays home and plays blocks with her babies, who reads them picture books and sings along with that poor misunderstood, clubfooted Barney. When my hair starts going gray and my wrinkles no longer react favorably to Nivea, I imagine myself giving up gracefully—in theory—not undergoing "procedures," like my mother alludes to, but that doesn't mean I won't remain Clinique's best customer. Tonight I'm wearing their fawn eyeshadow, a smoky liquid eyeliner, oil-free base makeup, and shimmer blush that has minuscule specks of mica in it. You could have knocked James over with a feather when he saw me in my little black dress. It's seven years old, cost two hundred dollars when I bought it, and I think of it as the old warhorse. I don't believe James expected me to wear my jeans and red sweatshirt, exactly, but up until now, that's all he's seen me in. And for some reason, I feel as jittery as Leroy when the hay truck delivers.

We stop at the gate leading to the fifteen-mile drive because unless you're a resident, it costs ten dollars for the privilege of putting your tires to the tarmac. James, however, waves at the guard and we're ushered right through.

"I guess you rate," I tell him, and he turns to me.

"There's a sticker in my window for the party. The guy doesn't know me from Adam."

"Oh." The street's narrow, winding, lined with twisted Monterey pines and tall eucalyptus. A couple of times he slows the Mercedes to stop to let deer cross. This, I like, a guy who flips on his emergency blinkers for Bambi and company. After Ness's news, however, I'm not exactly in a party mood, but I'm determined to go on a damn date and leave Rick Heinrich in the past.

James is so quiet that I can tell the drive borders on religious for him. He turns the radio from the oldies station we usually sing along with to soft, seductive jazz. I touch my forehead against the Mercedes's window and strain to see the Pacific, nothing more than a dark expanse of gray this time of night.

"You haven't said a word since I explained my windshield sticker," James says. "Something bothering you?"

I turn to look at this man Phoebe so tactfully refers to as Stinky. He's dressed in a very nice suit, a dark blue silk shirt, and he smells faintly of something spicy. His hair is auburn, unlike Phoebe's, and brushed back from his face so that his profile is strong and sure of itself. He's so not my type, but if he were my boyfriend, the first thing I'd do is make him ditch the diamond pinky ring, even if it is an heirloom. Next, adios to the tasseled loafers. Other than that, he's handsome in a JFK Jr. kind of way—a little horsey, but clean cut.

"James? I have a question. Do the residents of Bayborough Links stand on their patios once a day and listen to the ocean for which they so dearly pay to live near? Or are they so busy making the money they need to afford to live here, they forget it's there?"

He chuckles. "Don't know the answer to that one. You'll have to take a survey at the party."

"Don't you live here?"

"No, ma'am. I just get asked to some of the parties."

"Really? That's not the impression I got."

He smirks. "You think these parties are fun, Nancy? This is business. Let's talk about something more entertaining than how much behind I kiss in the name of being an investment counselor, okay? I've been to college and Europe. I can hold my own on any subject from New Age medicine to quantum physics."

"Impressive."

"Well, I can fake it."

I don't hesitate with my answer, because I want to get a feel for the true James, who he is when Phoebe isn't in the room. "That's refreshing," I say. "Most men who take me out just want to talk about movies with lots of sex in them, whether or not the actresses wore panties, what do I think of that, and will I go to bed with them later?"

He laughs heartily, and I like how his laugh sounds like Phoebe's. "Then I guess you'd better thank your lucky stars I'm not most men."

Okay. We've established his gentleman status. Next thing I do is shut off the radio. James doesn't say anything. Rick would have argued with me, said how he *needed* the music; the silence was just too oppressive. When I'd ask him to talk to me instead, he'd just turn the radio up to a higher volume and start singing along to punk songs I never even knew existed. James serenely keeps driving. Outside the wind is kicking up, and the trees are swaying, which provides its own lovely kind of jazz. I crack the window and we listen for a while. When the road's straight enough for him to look away, I catch him watching me. "Are you coming to the plant sale tomorrow?"

He frowns. "Hadn't planned on it."

This causes me to sit up straighter in the caramel-colored leather. "Shame on you. You'd better show up and buy a hundred poinsettias if you know what's good for you. They make the perfect gift for snotty realtors, don't you think?"

"I'm truly sorry about Babs," he says, taking his hands from the steering wheel to gesture helplessly. "I had no idea you two had a history."

"Make it up to me by getting her the wimp-iest plant you can find. I'll have Florencio inject it with some contagious plant disease."

"And if I pass on the plant sale?"

"Not a good idea, James. For one thing, I won't ever be your faux date again."

He looks at me. "Is that what you are? In that little black dress you don't look faux any-thing from where I sit, madam."

Okay, so maybe his thoughts are not exactly one hundred percent gentlemanlike. "I was joking. Forgive me."

"What's to forgive? Incidentally, I'm plan-ning on being there, Nance. I was just yanking your chain."

"Whatever for? Is that some bizarre California pastime?"

"No, but it's hard not to when you make it so available."

I examine my manicure, which is pretty good, considering I did it myself. The polish is called Mother Earth, which makes me pic-ture Duchess, her snout covered with dirt when she lets herself play with major abandon. I let an entire mile pass before I respond to James's remark. "Prepare to get yours yanked back, then."

"Oh? And will this yanking be taking place anytime soon?"

I smile. "When you least expect it." Ahead of us a long line of cars is being valet parked on an estate with a circular driveway. Appar-ently we're here. "Good Lord, look at the cars. There must be enough money tied up in those automobiles to feed a small country. I'll try my best not to belch on anyone important."

"I want you to be yourself," James says, taking my arm and tucking it through his, then giving a little flex of biceps to let me know he likes us touching, even if it is for show. Oh, I like this, too, being on the arm of someone who seems steady and treats me like a lady for a change. Nervously, I apply my finishing-school smile and follow the glittering white Christmas lights wound through the trees up to the front door of the palace. It's so chilly and beautiful. *Call me Bunny,* I want to say, because being my mother with all her matrimonial mistakes would be easier than being Nancy Jane Nobody with a life like chopped salad. Surely none of these people have friends facing down a possible HIV diagnosis. Do I talk of decorating schemes and Windjammer cruises? The last Martha Stewart show, which Beryl and I watched one night when we couldn't sleep, and I swear, where a caller phoned in and asked where exactly it was gourds came from?

I hand Sadie's mink to the coat girl at the door. In a dark corner of my heart, I think what good fortune it would be were I seated next to Babs, I mean just so we could chat about just any old thing that happened to come to mind.

"Canapés?" a passing waiter asks, and James spears up two fried artichoke hearts and three stuffed mushrooms while I shake my head no. I'll say one thing for Phoebe's brother, he has a healthy appetite.

"You okay to mingle by yourself?" he asks.

The old Nance, pre-Ness's news, would have flung back a smart remark, something along the lines of: *Not only that, I can mambo, buddy,* but the new version feels as naked and afraid as somebody standing before God. "So long as you bring me some wine first," I say.

He squeezes my hand. "I won't be long. Just have to kiss a little wealthy heinie, then I'll spend the rest of the night with you, I promise."

I watch James's broad back as he makes his way through the crowd. No slouch in his shoulders. No permanent bad mood. He's as charming as Rick was pessimistic. James is determined to work this party and he's doing it. What would it be like to have such a man in my life full-time, I wonder. Somebody who'd show up on time, turn off the television, and stand up the minute I came into the room. The thing is, whatever passion I felt for Rick undid me every time I tried to break things off. *Babe,* he'd say, *please don't cut me off just because I screwed up this one time. You're a fixture in my life,* and I would tip over backward into his bed. I think the trouble was, deep down, we weren't best friends. Not that I didn't try to be his. But Rick had this abrasive way of keeping people distant, maybe from the fear of getting hurt, I don't know. In the process, all those roadblocks caused me to feel like some dirty old penny thrown on the ground, kicked away rather than picked up and polished, counted as good luck.

I HAVEN'T BEEN TO EUROPE, but last time I checked, that wasn't an arrestable offense. I did take art history in college, and if I'm not mistaken, the walls of this house are lined with Picassos, Diebenkorns, and the sculpture outside by the pool with drinks set atop it is a genuine Henry Moore. The man who owns all this is predictably as squat as a toad, richer than Croesus, and what Rick would call a "flamer," and what I guess I call out of the closet. When James introduces me, the art collector is interested only in him. It's unnerving to James, who tries to no avail to fend off the affectionate squeeze our host attempts to deliver.

"Aren't you lucky," I say, pulling Mr. Toad back to a safe distance, "to be surrounded by so much beauty? Come take me on a tour of all this art, won't you, sir?" And I take his arm and direct him to a very ugly Lichtenstein that is probably worth more than I will earn in my entire lifetime. It's personalized to Saul and Carl, from Roy. "Tell me the story behind this one, please?"

Saul the mauler whips out a cigar and uses it to gesture to the frame. He's telling me about his last foolish relationship, and how this print was a present to both of them, and honest, I was listening at first, but now I am in the peripheral mode, where the things happening around me are all I'm taking in. The skinny women in their beaded black dresses;

the balding men who tote the skinny women; the painted matriarchs dripping in pearls; the social climbers and the wheeler-dealers like James, who move from gathering to gathering, dispensing a joke, pressing a glass of wine, introducing people to one another, discussing local politics and whether or not Clint Eastwood will show up at this party.

Here is one thing I know. Rick Heinrich of *After-Hours Magazine* would have done some impressive gathering of his own by now—quotes to drop in articles, little bon mots that border on slander—Rick had a thing for authority, and it wasn't respect. I take it as a bad sign that I'm looking at the people at this party only to seek out his features. The craggy jaw of the waiter—his. The way the man playing the piano has his hair blocked at the nape of his neck—Rick always kept his cut like that. And how when I pressed my face to his hairline he always smelled of this strange but comforting combination of soap and artichokes, yes, artichokes—summer and youth and heat—that kind of smell found nowhere else in the universe.

"Which artists do you collect?" Mr. Toad is asking me as his hand hovers at the small of my back. "Anybody up and coming you recommend?"

"Oh, definitely Phoebe DeThomas," I say. "Her sculptures are small but terribly amusing. If she got her hands on some grant money she could be a name."

"DeThomas," he mutters. "It's a familiar

name, but I can't put the work to the artist. Who shows her?"

And I press the flyer for the plant sale into his hand, at the same time admiring his watch. "This is her home address," I explain. "Direct sales avoid the commission fee, you know. You should come by and see the plants as well. Talk about impressive. Why, I believe this particular strain of poinsettias goes back almost fifty years. Actually, to be entirely frank, I do their PR."

"PR, huh?" Mr. Toad folds the flyer into his jacket pocket and leers at me. He has jowls like Minnie Driver, but on her they're sexy. "And will cute little Nancy be there?"

"Nancy will. Taking many publicity photos which I am sure the *Herald* will print."

James shows up with my camera. "Thought you might want this."

"Take a picture of us together," Mr. Toad asks me, and I set the f-stop to the proper setting. The look James gives me before I press the shutter is pure Help.

Which is how I come to spend the schmoozing portion of the party shooting pictures and taking names—and in the process, dispensing invites to the plant sale. Half these people won't show up—but they might send their household help to buy poinsettias for their Christmas decorating.

"I get a kick out of how brazen you are with that camera," James says when we sit down to dinner, crown roasts, smoked geese, and baby vegetables.

"Thanks." I'm not hungry but I can't resist the meat so I pile my plate high.

"And quite the hungry girl, it appears," he says as I lift the silver fork to my mouth.

I set it back down on the plate. That was a Rick remark if ever I heard one. I never knew what to say when he'd make a crack like that before, but now I do. "Did you ever consider that comments like that breed anorexia in pretty girls, James?"

He blushes a little. "Sorry. You work this room better than I do. And you're beautiful; no, let me rephrase that. You're exquisite. Very scary package, Ms. Mattox."

I pat my mouth with my napkin. "I am not beautiful," I tell him, "I am an alpha female, also known as an ocelot. Me, your sister, Ness, too, when she wants to be, we're all ocelots. Alpha males all desire us. We're lovely, we can hold our own in most every situation, but the thing is, we don't take well to choke collars. Once the alpha male discovers this, he runs for the hills when, if he stuck around, he could be part of an unstoppable team. Tell me, James, why do you suppose that is?"

He butters a roll and sets it on his plate. "Holy Mother of God. Maybe we're afraid you'll neuter us while we're sleeping."

"We'd never do that." I squeeze his knee under the table because I know how crazy it will make him. The touch of my fingers causes him to cough, and he has to take several sips of water in order to recover.

I just smile.

Dessert is a chocolate castle, intricately molded, sitting atop a spun sugar landscape. Inside, there's mousse, and some kind of coffee, I think. Beryl would know. I wish I could take mine home for her to see. I wish all the girls were here with me, too, but Phoebe the most. I'd love to watch the seas part when she rolled her chair over the Aubusson carpets and examined the dollar-sign-dripping artwork. In the powder room are a series of Weston photos that the Toad told me Carl loved. I can imagine the breakup, filled with histrionics and Saul insisting he keep the one series Carl loved. If they'd fit under the mink, I'd swipe them, have James find his whereabouts, and deliver them to his doorstep.

As James takes a fork to his castle, he leans over and asks me, "What do you plan to do with the film you shot tonight?"

"I thought I'd give it to you so you could plaster the walls of your house with Bayborough's rich and famous."

"I live in a condo," he says. "And I know what you and the flower farm ladies think of me."

"Oh? And what is it we supposedly think?"

"That I'm nothing but a climber. A real shit. That I want Phoebe's farm so I can turn it into a strip mall."

"Well, do you?"

"No, Nancy. I'll admit I do want what's best for my sister. Would it surprise you to know that the only art I own is Phoebe's?"

The look in his eyes makes me almost

believe him. "That's something I'll have to see for myself."

He stops dismantling the dessert. Slowly his mouth changes into a smirk that badly wants to be a smile but is perpetually afraid of rejection. Under his breath he says, "When?"

"Tonight." I pat his hand. "Eat your castle, James. This is an important party, and your place will be there after it's over."

But he doesn't eat it. Just lets it sit there on his plate, half-toppled, melting, the kingdom of a monarch undone by his lust.

CLINT NEVER SHOWS, but it is Thanksgiving. He has a new baby girl now, the woman next to me says, and probably he's spending the night with her. Seems like everyone on earth has a baby but me. People begin leaving. James steers me by Babs of realty fame and I deliver her a smile that's pure ice. I don't care about Primrose Cottage anymore, but neither do I want her to repeat this error. Surprisingly, she places a hand on my shoulder. "Those sculptures in the garden," she says. "Could you find out what catalog they came from?"

It takes me a moment to figure out what she's talking about. Phoebe's sculptures. "They didn't come from a catalog at all." I hand her a flyer for the poinsettia sale. "If you're interested in them, you'll have to call this number."

"Very ladylike of you," James says as he fetches the mink and helps me put it on.

"Business is business," I say.

Outside the air is clear and cold. Overhead, a few stars peek through the treetops, but the typical Bayborough fog is rolling in. The valet brings the Mercedes around and I ask for the keys so I can drive us to James's house, where I plan to stay only fifteen minutes because I have to know about that artwork.

He directs me through the maze of streets until we come to the dollhouse oceanfront of Bayborough-by-the-Sea. They're tiny old beach houses, carefully maintained, with gingerbread roofs and brick walkways. None of them is under a million dollars because of their relative proximity to the water. Bunny would be very comfortable here, drinking her G & T's and passing out in the foyer. "You live *here?*" I manage to squawk.

"No, but I will someday," James says. "For now, I have a condo in Sierra Grove. It's nothing special, but it's a good investment and it has a great view."

"Well, then," I tell him. "Let's go see it."

It's a guy place—beige carpet kept pristine by the housecleaning service, leather couches with no discernible butt impressions, angular, modern furniture that looks like it came from Ikea, miniblinds he never closes. There's a moderate-size stereo, no DVD player, and a Mac computer humming on a desk in the corner. Being a Mac girl myself, I react favorably. The walls are stark white, not a nail pounded into any of them. I'm about to say, *You phony, you promised me art,* when James

273

flips a light switch and illuminates an antique oak cabinet with glass doors. Inside, clay sculptures that range from a child's first experimental squeeze of clay to fully formed men and women are set on clear acrylic bases. There must be a hundred of them. He reaches in and takes out a female figure. "Pheebs did this when she was living at Shriners'," he says. "It's my favorite."

He places it in my hand. It's heavy, fired brown clay, the crackle glaze sloppy and thick, not at all like the Fimo she currently works with. The figure reclines, her arms well modeled, but the legs blend into that solid wedge shape Phoebe favors. What's remarkable about it is the face. Somehow Phoebe managed to capture her expression—equal parts ennui and amusement—in just a few simple gestures. "Sadie," I say with certainty.

His face grows solemn. After a moment, he says, "Yes."

"Were you two close?"

"Not like she was with Phoebe, but I always wanted to be. They had some strange kind of bond, those two. She was the best aunt on earth, Nance, a genuine angel with a mouth like a truck driver. In some ways, you remind me of her."

"Thanks. I'll take that as a pretty high compliment."

"You should." He sets the sculpture back into the case and shows me others—Phoebe's childhood attempt at a duck, a carved shell with a hinge, a fairy peeking over a rock wall. "I don't understand. Why do you have them and not Phoebe?"

"She'd throw them away," he says, shrugging. "And there's a chance that someday she's going to be famous, and people would like to see her early work, I'll bet. But even if all that weren't true, I'd still have to keep them."

"Because?"

He shrugs. "Because our mother didn't."

I let this heartbreaking information sit a minute. "Maybe that's part of it, James, but I think there's more."

He walks over to the plate-glass doors and opens them. The dampness of the Pacific streams in and even inside the mink I shiver. "Oh, hell," he says. "Hers is the only art I understand."

Which is why I put my palm to his face and turn it toward me, looking directly into his blue eyes until it dawns on him that I want him to kiss me. I feel the moisture frizzing my hair, but I don't care one hoot. This man deserves a kiss, and I want it to come from me.

He's a good kisser, thankfully not a show off, and I kiss him back before we break apart. A strange little hum persists between us and that surprises me. James shakes his head as if to clear it. "Was that the yank of my chain?"

"Only if you wanted it to be."

He sticks his hands in his pockets and stares out at the water. "God, no."

I rub his shoulders while he thinks that over.

Finally he yanks me inside and shuts the door. "Enough driving me crazy, Ms. Mattox. Let's get you home."

In the car, he buckles up and locks the doors. Then, before he starts the engine, he turns to me and says, "Nance? Do you see this ever happening again, or was it a one-time thing?"

"Oh, that all depends," I say, "on how many poinsettias you and your friends buy."

ALL NIGHT I TOSS AND TURN, which I tell myself is a natural by-product of not sleeping with Duchess. Just as I fall asleep, I have this really crazy dream where I am making love to the stud of the universe on a patio chaise lounge, under the most wonderful sun, like we used to get once every three years in Portland. This man knows how to work a woman's body. He believes in foreplay. When he takes me to the river for the third time, I push him up off my breasts so I can kiss his mouth, and it's James. I sit up in bed and feel my heart beating like it's going to leap right out of my chest.

Immediately I reach for the telephone and punch in Rick's number at the magazine. All I want is to hear his voice, and know that it's really him in my dream, that I haven't gone round the bend after one stupid party.

"*You've reached Rick Heinrich, editor of* After-Hours Magazine. *Either I'm not at my desk right now or I'm on assignment, but your call is important, so please leave a message..."*

I think about what I might say. That it still hurts to hear his voice, that I'd rather eat rocks than say I'm not over him, that I just don't understand why something so full of potential had to go so incredibly wrong.

I had fun with James. Kissing him was nice, but it wasn't kissing Rick. When I finally hit my sheets, I tried to conjure up a little fantasy about him, but it wouldn't knit together. Sometimes women's hearts are as senseless as men's penises. We're both so anxious to wander off into dangerous territory we don't even think about the consequences. Rick's message beeps for the part where normal people leave a message. Ashamed, I hang up the phone and tiptoe out of my room to see if anyone else is awake.

Beryl is sleeping on her side, one hand clutching the pillow. Ness is in a fetal position, and my errant dog is lying nearby, next to the one who needs her the most. At least Duchess thumps her tail lightly to acknowledge me. Phoebe, however, is not only awake, but is also working at the computer. I smell coffee in the kitchen so I pour myself a cup and wander out to see what my date's sister is up to.

"So, did you kiss him?" she wants to know.

"Yeah. But then I made him drive me home."

"Why?"

"Why did I make him drive me home? Because I live here. Do I need a better reason?"

277

She turns and gives me a look. "Why'd you kiss him?"

What do I say? Because I saw your sculptures, Pheebs. Because James really loves you. Because I felt this overwhelming notion that it was the right thing to do and now I'm not so sure? "Your brother is a decent person, Phoebe. He just likes to dress up like a jerk on occasion. What are you looking up?"

"Stuff on AIDS. There's only about five million websites."

"You have to narrow the search." I show her the engines I use and we sit there reading over the information regarding drug regimens together. The news is not all bad, but it is expensive. "You think she's positive, don't you?" I say.

"Well, the odds don't lean in her favor. I just want to be armed with as much as I can if the news is bad." She hits print and starts gathering up pages of information.

"I think I'll make breakfast," I say. "You hungry?"

"I wouldn't kick a plate of tofu scrambler out of bed."

The name alone makes me shudder, but I heat up two skillets and in one I crumble the tofu and in the other I murder six eggs. Then I toast half a loaf of bread, butter it, and get out the jam. I uncover Verde and let him walk around on the newspaper for a while. Soon enough, we'll be outdoors selling plants and he'll have to be caged. The sun is just starting to come up.

Phoebe rubs her neck and sips another cup of coffee. "Why are we up so damn early?"

"Because so much rides on this plant sale," I answer.

"Have you been snooping in my files, Nance?"

"It doesn't take a genius to read your face. Don't worry, Pheebs, we're going to sell them all. I kissed enough rich heinie last night at the party, we'll probably run out before noon. Go wake up the others, this food is getting cold."

Ness chooses that moment to walk into the kitchen. "Morning," she says sleepily. Duchess goes straight to her dish, which I've already filled with kibble. "What are you up to, Pheebs?" she says, and picks up the pages that the printer is starting to spill on the floor. Her face grows tight. "What in the hell do you think you're doing?"

"Just trying to help," Phoebe says, setting the jam jars on the table.

"Dammit all, this *my* problem, not yours! I knew I should have kept it to myself. If I want information from the stupid Internet I'll get it myself!" She runs out the door, presumably to Leroy.

Phoebe looks like she's been slugged in the gut. I put her plate of tofu down on the table. "That was a mood swing," I say. "Nothing personal. Eat your breakfast and don't give it another thought."

But she can't any more than I can, and the words hang over us like Spanish moss on the trees on that impossibly beautiful, expensive fifteen-mile drive. I get the feeling today's going to be a long day. I run upstairs to change into clothes for church. If I hurry, I can be back a half hour before the sale begins.

UNDER A CLEAR BLUE SKY and relatively warm day, we sell a dozen plants before noon, a measly dozen. Our customers are the cooks from the Wagon Wheel, the lady who runs the copy shop, some winery employees, and a few strangers probably on their way home from church. Florencio and his cousin Segundo set aside ten each for themselves, and this self-sacrifice moves me close to tears. Beryl comes up with the great idea of lining the driveway with plants, and this does indeed look festive, but it doesn't sell that many more plants. Ness is working the cash box, and she keeps counting up the bills like they might have multiplied in the last ten minutes. "Stop touching the money," I tell her. "You'll wear off the numbers."

James isn't anywhere to be found, and when I call his place, I get the machine. I blow a raspberry into the tape. "Hope you enjoyed that kiss, buster, because you'll never get another one from me or any other women on the planet unless you tear yourself away from brunch or golf or whatever you're doing and shag your cute behind over here and bring your wallet."

Phoebe overhears me.

"That's not necessary, Nance," she says with great dignity. "If we fail, we fail."

Over my dead body. Failure is not in my vocabulary.

"Know what? You need a sandwich," I tell her. "I made a bunch. Let's bring them out and take a break. Things'll pick up."

"I don't know," says our Phoebe. "Not even peanut butter and marshmallow is going to get rid of these ugly old plants. What the hell was my aunt thinking?" She wheels herself back out to the porch.

"How about if we offered free pony rides?" Beryl suggests when I come out with the tray.

Ness gives her a snotty laugh, which irritates me. "Leroy look like a pony to you? Plus, he has his moods."

And she doesn't?

"What if someone got hurt and sued us?"

Beryl picks the crust off her sandwich and feeds it to Duchess. "So it was a dumb idea. At least I had one. Hey, do you suppose one of the other farms is having a sale, and that's why we're not getting any business?"

"The nearest flower farm is in Salinas," Phoebe says. "If the rich people aren't going to drive ten minutes into the Valley, they're sure as snot not going to drive a half hour to Salinas. Face it, the Christmas poinsettia is passé."

"No, no," Segundo insists. "Wait until late afternoon. The rich people's hangovers will all be gone and they will come buy. You'll see."

I pray he's right, but I take a Tagamet anyway and wash it down with Diet Coke.

"I think it's going to rain," Ness says an hour later when nobody else has come to buy a plant, ask for directions, or even want to know if there's real estate for sale.

Captain Bringdown speaks. The sky is certainly grayer, but I don't see any clouds. "Why don't you go ride your horse," I tell her. "You're making Phoebe nervous."

"I am not," Ness says, her hackles just itching to rise.

"Yes, you are," Phoebe tells her. "Ride out to the highway and flag in some customers. Lord, this brings back such awful memories. Failed lemonade stands, the humiliation of Girl Scout cookies. The only reason I ever sold anything was my chair. I know, how about I wheel out onto the highway, and Nance, you can make me a sign that says 'Buy a plant or we'll repossess this woman's wheelchair.' "

Florencio and Segundo exchange grave looks and go off to work in the fields.

"That's right, you cowards, go pick bugs off vines," Phoebe yells after them. "Has to beat hanging around the happiness girls."

She's almost in tears.

Beryl throws the ball for Duchess, and Duchess, always a good sport, brings it back, but the look on her face is one of pure Labrador incredulity: *Lady, can we stop this already? There are more important concerns on the agenda.*

At two-thirty, six cars pull up. I recognize one of the faces from last night's party. I snap a picture and sell her twenty plants, which she has her buff young driver load into her trunk. "Check okay?" she asks.

"Actually, we'd prefer cash. If you have it."

I don't know what makes me say this, but she unfolds the bills from a wad as thick as the white pages. Then she looks into her trunk, and this completely undecided expression settles on her face. "Paul," she calls to her driver. "Do you think twenty will be enough to cover the front steps, or should we get thirty?"

He winks at me. "Ma'am, if you want my honest opinion, I think you should probably get forty. That is, if you're going for a lush look. If not, the twenty will probably be just fine."

She buys *fifty*.

And the next carload takes thirty. I was right, the household help of nearly everyone I chatted up at Mr. Toad's party is here, and clearly worried the others are going to outdo them on decorating. Hurray! Soon we are down a good three hundred plants, and the cars in the driveway are honking because there's no place to park.

Beryl takes over the cash box, Florencio and Segundo shoot me the I-told-you-so looks I deserve, and Phoebe is busy showing Mr. Toad her sculptures. I run to load plants and hurry back to rearrange the remaining stock, trying to catch a glimpse of Phoebe and Saul whenever I can. Florencio and Segundo return the plants they'd set aside to the regular stock. After two hours of this frenetic pace, our stock has a significant dent in it. Then things are slow again, but I'm still pumped up on the earlier rush.

Then it happens again, fancy cars, including a Hummer, and everybody jostling to fill up the trunks and hatchbacks. "Put some of this money inside your bra," I tell Beryl, "until we can get a moment to hide it in the house."

Late in the day, James arrives, hoofing it down the long driveway. I stand there making change and watching him draw closer. He's dressed in a Santa Claus outfit, and looks perfectly happy, as if the lateness of the hour doesn't matter.

"Glad you could make it, Santa," I tell him, coolly.

He looks at me curiously. "What did I do?"

I count out change from a hundred for a young woman who is giving James the eye before I answer. "Buddy, if you can't figure it out you're more hopeless than I thought."

He groans. "What now? Did I screw up in your dreams? I once dated a girl who used to get all cranky if I misbehaved in a dream. I hope you're not of that ilk."

"Ilk schmilk," I say when the girl has finally given up and driven her BMW away. "Didn't you get my message?"

He takes an armful of white poinsettias to a lady in a red van with three kids and a barking springer spaniel that has decided Duchess is the devil's spawn. I want her life. She probably lives on enough acreage that she has a barn and a decorative cow and enough time off to read even the books that don't make the bestseller list. "No, I did not. It's been a busy day, Nance. I had an appointment this morning, I needed to do some banking, a client called who wanted reassuring, and then I promised to be Santa for the Y kids—"

"That's very noble of you. All I'm saying is we could have used your hands around here earlier..."

"Where's Ness?"

"She's off riding Leroy, thank God." I hold up my hand. "Don't ask, okay? It was the best course of action, under the circumstances."

Florencio signals for James to come help him load plants into a pickup truck. The logo painted on its side reads: SIERRA MAR WINERY, VINTNERS OF FINE WINE SINCE 1986. They fill it up with several hundred plants, and as soon as it pulls away, another two trucks come to take its place. Soon we have five hundred or so plants left—surely we can sell five hundred of these ugly plants by Christmas. Beryl is making change like a carhop, wishing everyone a happy holiday season and grinning. James disappears from view, good riddance, and I get busy with the arrival of some elderly women who only want a few plants, but spend a long time exclaiming over them to make up for it. Between them they buy twenty plants.

"The church was decorated with poinsettias when I married my William," one tells me. "December twenty-third, 1942. I sent him off to the war and planted poinsettias in my yard that Christmas. Bush grew up four feet tall and produced every year until we moved to the retirement community."

"And William?" I ask.

She wrinkles her nose. "He started out about five-ten, but shrank some in the long run. Now that I'm old enough to have learned a thing or two, I much prefer a nice, colorful garden to marriage. Here's my money. I believe I get six dollars back, honey."

Ness returns and lets some little kids feed Leroy apple slices. They hurry to James and he hands them candy canes before he waves good-bye. I bring Verde's cage outside and show him to them, too. Before long, we are down to two hundred and ten plants, all red, and that's all she wrote.

"Did the poinsettia bandits hit when I was out riding?" Ness asks as the children wave good-bye to Leroy.

Beryl yanks the wad of cash from her bra and lets it float through her fingers. Ness whistles. Phoebe comes out of the house with Mr. Toad. I wave heartily. "Hey, Saul. What did you think? I'm right, aren't I?"

He gives me an oily smile. "Poinsettias?" he says, as if this is the first time he's seen them. "I suppose I could use a few. How many are left?"

"What you see here," I tell him. "We had a bit of a run while you were inside."

"I'll take them, then."

"How many?"

"All of them that will fit into the car, dear heart."

He nods, and Florencio and Segundo fill up his Range Rover, which is so shiny I'm sure it's never actually roved. He gives them twenty-dollar tips and asks for my telephone number. I give him most of it. When he drives away, we girls look at each other for a moment before we start whooping. Beryl does a little dance in the few plants that remain. Phoebe is quiet.

"Did that old buzzard try to cop a feel?" I ask.

She shakes her head no. "He wants me to make larger sculptures. Maybe some time down the line, sponsor a show in a gallery. He gave me a check. Look at all the zeroes on it." A tear runs down her face.

"Well, smile, dammit. That's wonderful news."

"I'm trying. It's just hard to believe the way the day went, that's all."

"Believe it," Beryl tells her. "And tomorrow is going to go all right, too."

A seasoned but classic tan Toyota Land Cruiser pulls up, and for a moment, I experience a pang of envy. This is my dream car, and it would be mine if I'd followed my mother's path and married for material things instead of holding out for love. I could drive Duchess to the veterinarian in it, or drop in on a sale at a trendy dress shop in Bayborough-by-the-Sea, or even motor down to Big Sur once in a while for a botanical facial at the Post Ranch

Inn spa. Instead, I have Rhoda, four more years of car payments, and my dignity intact, but oh, for a moment there, I am sorely tempted to trade it all in. I turn to tell the driver that we're closed for the day, but strangely, it's Santa James behind the wheel.

He rolls down the window. "It has low miles, four-wheel drive, and it's been gone over with a fine-tooth comb. Now can I have my Mercedes?"

"Yes," I say, "among other things." And that's when I give him his second kiss.

*Ness*

# 12

## *So Now I Know*

"WE CALL THIS A BUTTERFLY NEEDLE," the nurse explains as she pierces my skin with a shaft of metal so thin I can hardly feel it go in. The needle's attached to green plastic wings and a length of tubing. Guess that's to keep my blood even farther from hers than usual. Her hands are double-gloved. Her face, on the other hand, is as calm and kindly as if she is performing any old run-of-the-mill cell count instead of my probable death sentence.

Together we watch my garnet blood travel the plastic loop and pool in the test tube. Everything looks so normal. Knowing however she answers that I'm still going to feel coldness in the pit of my belly, I forge ahead. "How long before you know?"

"No longer than a week."

"Do you get the results quicker if you pay more?"

She pats my arm. "Ms. Butler, a week is how long it takes for everybody. Dr. Ullman will do his best to see it's done promptly."

"What happens when it's, you know, positive?"

She affixes a sticker with my name on it to the now-full tube and begins filling a second vial. "If we get a positive Elisa, then we perform a Western Blot test and go from there."

Western Blot—sounds like a country-and-western headshrinker's exam. I'm so scared I nearly giggle, but manage to keep my mouth shut, just sit there soberly when it occurs to me that she's now filling her third test tube. "Hey? You trying to drain the virus out of me or what?"

Her expression is kindly. "If it were that simple, I'd open my own clinic and work twenty-four hours a day. Dr. Ullman thought it would be a good idea to give you all physicals since you're here."

"Please, if you'd call me Ness, I wouldn't be so nervous."

"Certainly." She sets the tubes onto a tray and zips the needle out of my arm, neatly pressing a cotton ball on a Band-Aid onto the puncture site. "If you'll call me Gina."

"Um, Gina? How much does the physical cost?"

"I believe Phoebe and the doctor came to a consensus, a fleet discount if you will. Think of it this way—in one visit we're covering all the bases, from Pap smears to chest X rays. Such a bargain."

That Phoebe. Her determination to keep us all well and whole will be her own undoing. It's like when I caught her surfing the Internet looking for AIDS drug information. What—isn't her fight to stay healthy exhausting enough? Her caring like that when I had been trying to borrow off my granny so I could leave, well, it rankled me so much that I was pissy the entire day of the flower sale. I even snapped at a few customers, I couldn't stop myself. It was as if Verde had bit me and suddenly I had come down with Tourette's of the heart. Aside from the virus, what the devil is wrong with me? I live with three great women and sleep in a real bed every night. Okay, so it's not my bed, and I may not have much in my suitcases, but my jeans and boots are all paid for. How am I going to get through this? I just want to hang on to my self-respect, if only I knew were it's gotten to.

Gina hands me a paper gown and tells me to get undressed and put it on. I do, and sit on the examining table, shaking. When I get frightened, I always think I have to pee. If I get up and go to the bathroom now, I know the doctor will walk in. Worse, I might run into one of the others, and right now sympathy would tip me over. I fix in my mind the picture of my roommates dancing after we shut down the poinsettia sale. Little Phoebe waving her arms in her chair like she was doing the Jerk; Beryl dancing some primal Irish jig; Nance kissing James through the window of our new-old car which Phoebe let me drive over here. First time I jumped a four-foot fence and managed to stay on the horse I felt like that. Christmas mornings at Granny Shirley's, when I caught sight of my stocking bulging with treasure, I flat out cried with the wonder and goodness in the world.

All that seems so far away.

Even though I stood a little ways off to the side of the poinsettia dance recital, the whooping and hollering and counting the cash meant something to me. The day had its moments. On my ride with Leroy we saw three hawks, this ratty old turkey that managed to outwit the holiday hunters, and a pheasant so brightly plumed it appeared Granny Shirley's Sunday hat had grown legs and gone for a walk. I ran Leroy up the hillside, down the trails, through the trees, and came to a stop at the edge of Bad Girl Creek. When I saw Leroy's and my reflection in the water, for a moment I didn't know who we were. His gleaming black sides heaved from the workout, and he's filled out so since living at the farm, he looked like a champion. And me—no matter what viral agents are traveling my veins, the woman staring back was strong, whole, and happy, at least until she started thinking again.

I suppose that was the moment I knew I was going to test positive, no matter what Phoebe keeps on telling me, or how normally Dr. Ullman's nurse speaks to me. HIV positive: It's a fact as much as my dark brown eyes or the scar on my palm where I wasn't careful once with a hoof trimmer. My days on this earth are numbered, far less than the women I live with in that old farmhouse. Beryl would say all this means is that from sunup to sunset I have to wring more out of each day than I did previously. Beryl talks all sunny but I have my suspicions that deep down she's walking in the shadows more often than not.

Even though strong emotion makes Leroy nervous, I cried a little bit then, and got more snot on my sleeve than I thought humanly possible. So I shook myself out and then I prayed, yes, *prayed*, to Whatever Gods May Be— Nance's patriarchal pope in the gold lamé robes, Granny Shirley's Jesus, and my own roving higher power that most closely resembles a stand of strong trees. I dismounted from Leroy, picked up a smooth rock that had been winking at me from the creekbed, and, instead of skipping it across the creek, I stuck it in my pocket and rode back to the farm a little bit lighter in heart.

But I left the damn rock in my blue jeans, which are draped over the chair next to the desk. Should have brought it with me when I put on the gown for something to hold on to. Instead, I sit here feeling my clammy palms and studying their darkly pigmented creases. The door opens, and Dr. Ullman stands there smiling, holding a folder and a pen. "Your real name is Preciousness?" he says.

Damn that Phoebe. It's clear that before I ever got up the nerve to kill myself, first I'd have to do her in.

ON TUESDAY I HAVE SIX HORSES to shoe, four privately owned and well tended, and two newcomers that I decide to do first. I suppose I shouldn't be working at all after what Dr. Ullman said. The same way pregnant women aren't supposed to change cat litter boxes those who are HIV positive shouldn't be around horse manure. Then he said I had better not feed Verde. Duchess was okay, so long as I didn't pick up after her. But the way I see it, if I cut those things out of my life, it isn't much of a life. So until the test says for certain, I'm going to keep working.

These horses are Percherons, a draft breed, massive and docile. They're stabled on the grounds of the winery that bought so many of our poinsettias. Much like the plants, which are now clustered around the buildings looking very festive, the horses are decorative, too. They're palominos, with masses of curly manes and tails that brush the ground. The foreman tells me the long-term plan is to train them to pull a tour wagon, but for now, they're just getting used to things. I love draft horses, the gentle giants with feet the size of pizzas. These two, however, shipped north from Southern California, are green to regular foot care. Their hooves curl up like Shriners' slippers, and my farrier's eye tells me they'll need several trimming sessions before the idea of shoes can even be broached. They're certain of one thing: A black woman with a knife in her hand can in no way be good news. With them weighing in at twenty-eight hundred pounds each, I'm inclined to introduce myself slowly. It takes me three hours, but I'm able to trim all four feet of the gelding and the front feet of the mare before she lets loose with a kick that if I wasn't experienced at ducking, could have split my skull. For a second I think that might not be a bad way to die, working my trade, in the presence of horses, but not just yet. I find the foreman and explain to him I'll come back in a few days to finish up the mare. Even though I say it can wait, he pays me anyway.

I can't help but wonder what David Snow's doing on a day like today. The air's chill, but the sky is clear. If I had his life, would I ride one of my six horses, or sit watching them, just so I could be looking at something beautiful? He has no friends to go with him to the doctor, to make sure he eats enough, to give him a hug for no reason at all, yet he's grateful. Me, I'm bitchy, but the girls seem to put up with me anyway.

It's when I'm doing the easy horses at this family ranch that the plan comes to me. Say I try things Beryl's way, work hard at making each minute count. That could work for a while, but what about if I have to quit shoeing? Who's going to pay my share of the rent? Or the first day I can't get out of bed, and I lie there thinking about all those wasted hours? No, that's not the way it's going to be.

I finish up the shoe-trim on the second horse and turn him back into the arena. I lead the third horse over to the wash rack where I have my equipment set up, and tie her to the rail. She's a stubby, mouse-colored mare, thirty-two years of age, the owner told me. A family horse, no doubt she's taught a couple dozen children to ride. She looks up at me with nothing but utter trust in her eyes, lifts her rear foot the moment I touch it. High-grade hay, fresh carrots, love, and kind-ness have come her way all these years. I stroke her neck and listen to the contented nickers she gives me in return.

I've been around when horses died. Some deaths are as easy as the vet's needle finding the vein on the first try and the horse lying down in clean hay. Other times there's a blind terror in the animal's eyes I wouldn't wish on Idi Amin. With horses, things don't always go like you want them to. The biggest problem is that most owners can't look past what'll hurt them least and see what's best for the animal. Right then and there, I make a pact with this old girl. If she goes, I'll come be with her, hold a hoof, and bear witness. And maybe, later that same day, after things are cleaned up and the knacker's come for her, I'll go, too.

The mare's feet come out perfect. It might be the last shoeing job I ever do, and I'm glad it came out good.

I look out over the orchard of trees behind the house and think that there's no reason I can't plan for my time, choose it myself. I've met enough drug addicts I should be able to score the right kind of pills for a nice, painless suicide. Failing that, there's always carbon monoxide poisoning, but I'd never do it in any of Phoebe's cars, no sir. I'm pretty sure David Snow would help me. He seems like the perfect source to ask. I saw a book in his shelves about suicide. He said I could borrow it. I've had him on my mind for days now.

I sweep up the hoof shavings and put them in the trash. There's nothing like the feeling of finishing a good job. I clean off my tools and replace them in the carrying box and load it into the Jag. The burden rises off my shoulders and I take a breath, only to feel it replaced with the hammer blows of selfishness. No matter what happens, Granny Shirley will blame herself. When she looks at me and fiddles with her brooch, I know she sees the last glimmer of hope for the Butler women, the mending of every mistake she made with my mother. AIDS is a shameful illness. Her church will certainly see it that way. How can I lay this burden on her when what's responsible are my bad choices and Jake Rayburn's wandering penis?

When the owner hands me my cash, I smile a big false smile, then shove the bills in my pocket without bothering to count them.

ON WEDNESDAY, I DRIVE GRANNY SHIRLEY to evening prayer meeting. Like always, she asks me to come in, and this time I shock the hell out of her and say yes. She usually sits in the second row, but doesn't have a problem when I say I'd rather stay in the back, and places a hymnal in my hands. The deacons are present, the only men in the pews, and their children, no doubt guilted into coming, are the only people under fifty.

"In the New Testament," Granny Shirley whispers to me, "whenever Jesus spoke, the women listened and believed. Men, on the other hand, had to be hit over the head to get His message."

Sister Elvia stands at the altar and leads a song. Her voice reminds me of Etta James, with a warble on the high notes. On the second verse of "Wade in the Water," a hymn that supposedly was written by Harriet Tubman, she is moved by the spirit and cuts loose. Elvia puts her whole throat into it, and her hands fly into the air like beautiful black birds let out of a cage. Several of the other church ladies give her approving nods, and Granny Shirley's pheasant hat is bobbing in time. She elbows me to get with it, and I try tapping my foot.

Granny Shirley takes hold of both my wrists

and makes me hold up my hands palms out.

Okay, so there's something there, maybe a faint electric current. Is this supposed to convince me that it's God's will I end up with this disease? Granny Shirley must see the doubt on my face, because she starts grinning, and singing louder. "That's the spirit of the Lord, Preciousness," she says. "Embrace Him."

The singing buzzes so pleasantly through my skin I'm getting goosebumps, but when I open my mouth to join in, no words come.

After the hymns, prayer requests are taken, and Granny Shirley stands up and asks the congregation to pray for me. Sixty women and four children join hands and talk to God. It's not a plea for miracles, which I could use; they simply ask for my burdens to be lightened and my soul to be drenched in goodness and light. And though my cynical heart is resistant, the rest of my body feels as if it's being lifted out of this wooden pew and into some kind of massive candleglow. It makes me gasp.

"Sugar, this is one of life's jeweled moments," Granny Shirley says. "Hold it to your breast and let it seep inside your heart."

My throat narrows with joy, something I haven't felt for a long time. I know I couldn't possibly nor would I want to swallow it, so I let the tears come. I try to believe that Granny Shirley will get through my suicide a whole lot easier than watching me waste away to skin and bones.

After services end, we go to the Pie Factory, where my granny orders lemon meringue.

"Have some pie, child," she says to me. "You can afford the calories."

"The crust's made with lard, Granny. You know how I feel about eating animal products."

She calls the waitress over. "Tanya Marie, you got any vegetarian desserts back there? My grandbaby won't eat nothing animal, the fool."

Tanya thinks a minute. "Um, banana pudding? It's made with milk, though."

"I can do milk," I tell her.

My grandmother is pleased. "Good. Now whatever's bothering you, Preciousness, you just lay those bananas on top it and smother it with sweetness."

"Yes, ma'am, I'll try. How are you doing on your new blood pressure medicine?"

"Fine, fine. I got no complaints. Wasn't tonight's singing lovely?"

I nod.

"Maybe you'll come back next week. You got a birthday coming up, don't you?"

Always pushing, my granny. "Yes, my birthday's soon, but if you promise not to make a big deal of it, I'll think about coming back to church another time."

Her face crinkles in delight, and she signals Tanya Marie to refill her decaf so she can talk me all the way into it.

THURSDAY MORNING, the phone wakes everyone early. I pick it up at the same time Beryl does, on a different extension. We both say hello and

299

are met with silence. "Must be a wrong number," I say, and am halfway to hanging up when I hear Beryl speaking softly into the receiver. "How did you get this number?" Somebody starts playing guitar and I can tell she is listening. I hang the phone up quietly and I'm sure enough fully awake now.

Nance and Duchess are downstairs starting the coffee when I stumble into the kitchen. "What kind of imbecile calls this early?" she asks.

"Check this out. It was for Beryl. He didn't say anything, just started playing guitar. I have to get to the bottom of this. Hey, you're not making decaf, are you?"

Nance fixes me with what I call her librarian look. She hasn't put her contacts in yet so she has on these plastic-framed tortoiseshell glasses that make her look like an old lady. "You should be having herbal tea."

I groan. "Nancy Jane, please, don't start treating me like I'm going to fall over dead any minute, and don't take away the only vice I have left. If you won't make me real coffee, I'll drive down to the diner and buy some. "

"Fine." She dumps out the grounds and pours in French Roast from Trader Joe's. The rich aroma fills the room and I inhale gratefully. Duchess wanders over to her dish and gives it a nudge with her nose.

"Your dog's hungry."

"So? Am I the only one who knows where the kibble is?"

"My, my. Look who woke up on the wrong side of the bed."

"It's always the wrong side of the bed if it's before nine A.M."

I fill up Duchess's dish and, ignoring Dr. Ullman's warning, I uncover Verde, who calls me that Spanish curse no one can figure out. He hangs upside down and bites at the door latch, so I take this to mean he wants out. Once freed, he scuttles over to his parrot gym and starts ringing all the brightly colored bells. When he knocks his ceramic food cup on the floor and it smashes to bits, Nance and I both jump, and Verde says, "Ooh," which is just what Beryl says when she knocks something over.

I sweep up the mess. Nance cuts up an orange and sets the sections on a paper towel on his parrot gym floor. "Eat your breakfast," she tells him. Verde cocks his head and looks at her, clearly not pleased.

"Well, if you wanted it in the dish, you shouldn't have broken it," she says and turns away.

Verde calls her the C word and we both crack up because telling him to stop it makes him do it all the more.

"All this racket and no sign of Phoebe," Nance says.

"Take a peek out the window, Nancy Drew. UPS's car's here. He spent the night again."

We exchange smiles. "He's averaging three nights a week," Nance says.

"Keeping track, are we?" I tease.

Beryl comes down fully dressed and Verde goes nuts. He flaps his wing stubs and squawks until she extends her arm and tells him to "Step up."

He rubs his beak against her cheek and she ruffles his neck feathers. Madonna and parrot—here's a subject for Nance's camera if ever I saw one, so I'm hardly surprised when I hear the shutter click.

"Stop that," Beryl says. "I'm not awake yet."

"Who was on the phone, Beryl?" Nance asks, still snapping pictures.

Beryl's face flushes. She sets Verde on his parrot ladder, pours herself a cup of coffee, and sighs. "It was a wrong number."

"Since when do wrong numbers come with background guitar music?" I ask. "Confess, Beryl. What's going on?"

She stirs milk into her coffee. "Did you hear from the doctor yet?"

"No, and stop trying to change the subject. Jeez, if you don't want to talk about your mystery caller, just say so. But don't act like we're brain dead."

Beryl runs her hand through her curly hair. Behind her, Verde is working the flesh out of his orange slice, and Duchess is waiting below in case he drops any. Nance takes one more picture, and the kitchen clock ticks loudly. "What do I have to do to get you to stop photographing me?"

"Start talking."

"Okay. Fine. You two have to know everything, don't you?"

We nod.

"Apparently this person just likes to call me. I don't know if it's a man or a woman, a geezer or a kid. Generally, the calls come when I'm at work. He—or she—doesn't say anything, just sits there until I get bored and hang up."

"And plays a little guitar."

"Well, the music part's new. As is getting a call here at the farm."

Nance gives a little shriek. "But that means it's escalating! He could show up here and kidnap you!"

"That kind of pessimistic thinking is what you get for living with a journalist," I tell her. "Think, Beryl, who have you given your home phone number to since you moved here?"

She sips her coffee. "Guys, what is the big deal? If I ignore it, he—or she—will get bored and stop."

"Humor me," Nance says. "I bet we can solve this mystery if we just give it a little thought."

Beryl sets her cup down and picks up the pencil Nance always leaves on the table to do her crossword puzzle. She makes a list and then reads it out loud. "Work; my old landlord, may his Mazda Miata blow a head gasket; the feed store where I get Verde's chow; and Dr. Ullman. The thing with work is, our home numbers are on a rotating list. That way if somebody finds an injured bird when we're closed, whoever's next on the list gets the call."

"Anybody weird brought in a bird lately?" I ask.

Beryl shoots me a look. "Define normal. The birds they bring in *somehow* got shot to bits or were nesting in their mailboxes that just happened to get run over and it's either their own guilt that compels them to bring them to me for healing or some odd obsession with avian suffering, I'd really rather not know. I meet more than my fair share of the strange ones. I couldn't even remember the last time somebody normal walked through the doors of BBR, and certainly none of them were playing guitar."

"It's simply a matter of logical deduction," Nance says as she starts cooking a pot of oatmeal. "One by one you eliminate the potential suspects, and then you zero in on the likely candidates."

"Or you could just hit star sixty-nine and call them back," I say.

"Like I haven't thought of that?" Beryl says.

"Or get Caller ID."

"Whoever it is, Ness," Nance says, "they have a blocked number if she can't star sixty-nine them, which means it wouldn't show up on Caller ID, either. Let's not waste time going there."

"How is this wasting time?" I say. "I don't have anything to do today after I finish in the greenhouse."

"Let's go browse the feed store," Nance suggests.

"This is ridiculous," Beryl says. "The people who work there are nice."

"Maybe they're nice; maybe they're serial killers," I say. "Remember Ted Bundy?"

"I'm going to the feed store with or without you," Nance says. "You coming along is only a factor in the level of embarrassment you may suffer when I start asking questions."

"Go, Nance!" I say.

Beryl sighs. "It's my day off. I planned to loaf around here. I was going to read."

Nance's expression doesn't change. "You can read in the car."

"Let's go," I say. "We need an adventure."

"Fine. Far be it from me to deprive you two. But I'm only going if we can drive all the way out to the feed place in Sierra Grove, too. They have the best bargains on bird toys. And Verde gets to pick his own toys, so he'll have to come along."

"That's a terrific idea, Beryl," I say. "Whoever he is, this guy probably got all fixated on you because of the parrot."

"What makes you so sure it's a he?"

"Because if it was a woman, she'd come right out and say she liked you."

Beryl chews on this a while, and Nance serves up our porridge. I notice she's given me a bowl that's twice the size of Beryl's. In front of it, she sets a jar of wheat germ, organic honey, heavy cream, an assortment of dried fruits, and a bottle of megavitamins that look suspiciously like Leroy's. I decide not to say anything, just to eat until I blow up, because with Nance, it's like arguing with a rottweiler.

Phoebe rolls out from her bedroom with the look of fevered delirium we've all come to expect. Cheeks all pink, that eternal smile, she looks like a chipmunk that just found out the nut people are building a new factory next to his tree. "Good morning," she says. "You guys are up early."

"Where's Juan?" Nance says. "Did you shove him out a window?"

"Ha ha. Very funny. He's taking a shower."

Beryl gets Phoebe a cup of coffee. "Is he staying for breakfast?"

"I don't think so."

"Is he afraid of us or something?"

Phoebe stirs in cream. "Yes, Beryl, I think he is."

She looks stunned. "Well, that's not right. Tell me. How are we scary?"

I give her a look, like she of the mysterious-admirer fame has any say-so in how Phoebe runs her love life.

Phoebe says, "Hey, anybody able to go pick up Alice for me? Her car broke down."

Nance and I stare at each other. I owe her for the poinsettia sale, the extra chores last week when I was too upset to work, and we both know that of the two of us, she is the better detective. But I don't want to miss one second of this drama, especially when concentrating on it takes me so far from my own. Still. "Not a problem," I say. "I can go."

PHOEBE DOESN'T NEED ME to go right this second, so after Nance and Beryl leave, I wander outside where Florencio is pruning rose-bushes. He's got on his hat, a pair of leather gloves, kneepads, chaps, high boots, and is armed with loppers, shears, pruning tape, and a tank sprayer with a pump handle. Tucked in his belt are several old shirtsleeves. When I ask him what they're for, he explains, "Sometimes the roses? They fight back. I put these over my shirt *para* sacrifice. The rose doesn't know from sleeves, I get pruning done, and Rosa, she don't yell at me for ruining my clothes."

"Good idea. Can I wear a pair?"

"You want to help me?"

"Sure."

He gets me outfitted and we set out into the rows of brambles that bracket the side of the house. It's a mess and then some. They look as if they finished blooming twenty years ago. "Hey, Florencio. You kept the poinsettias going when Sadie was gone, so how come it looks as if nobody has worked in here in the rose garden for decades?"

"Because nobody has."

"And the reason we're changing all that?"

He points his loppers toward the main house, where Juan and Phoebe are on the front porch, kissing good-bye, rather passionately. Oh, the way the UPS man lifts her out of her chair and holds her to him just takes my breath away. It's as if one of these days he's going to take her up out of all that chrome, kick it away with his foot, and it will be *adios* chair for good. What a feeling it must be, being loved like that. I could bask in this kind of glow all day.

"Sooner or later, a wedding, no? *Por supuesto,* we gonna need the rose garden to look real good."

A wedding? I suppose it's possible. And suddenly more than anything, I want to be there if and when it happens. Surely my suicide plan can keep that long. "Show me what to do," I tell him. "Let's shape these babies up so they'll bloom in June."

Florencio should have been a teacher, I think. He's so happy when we listen. He seems to understand that knowledge is best absorbed through stories, not lectures. "Most gardener will tell you wait until *Enero* to prune, because frost, she sometime sneak in like a cat and touch everything, but just before Christmas is *muy* much better. Everything clean, ready for company. Like tidying up the stable for the *bambino,* no?"

He winks.

"First, cut away dead matter, place where diseases likes to hide. See branches thinner than pencil? Cut. You trim back to where bush end up maybe one-third original size. On old girl like this, all tangles must to go. Like haircut. Crossed branch invite pest. No, no, not like that. *Mira,* watch me."

I do. When I come across a few green leaves,

308

I ask what to do. "Strip them," Florencio says. "And don't drop leaf or cane to ground. They go in tarp, and after we finish, we burn."

Disease, I presume. It seems to lurk everywhere.

LATER THAT AFTERNOON, Alice is in working with Phoebe, and Nance and Beryl still haven't returned. I've finished all my duties and done theirs, as well. Here I thought manual labor—and I have the scratches and sore muscles to prove it—would erase my anxiety, but all it's done is heighten my nerves to the point where I'm feeling lightheaded. I lift the phone to call Dr. Ullman before I realize how silly that is. I take the keys to the Jag and go for what I tell myself is a drive, meandering around the highway, thinking maybe a walk on the beach will help me see there is a larger picture. Instead, I drive up the coast and inland, and before I know it, I've taken the turnoff to the hospital Sam Patrini told me Jake's in.

The lobby's decorated for Christmas. A tree in the corner is covered with white teddy bears and red ribbons, and a nearby sign on an easel urges visitors to donate toys for the needy. The clear lights in the branches blink on and off in a rhythm that makes my head ache, and I'm suddenly on fire with wanting to tell Jake Rayburn what I think of him. I ask at the information desk for his room, and an elderly woman in a striped uniform directs me to the elevator. I take the hallway at a march, each step filling my throat with invective. In the elevator, I ride up with an elderly black gentleman in a wheelchair who smiles and says, "Hello, Sister," in a feeble voice. I say hello back. I can't help but check his wheels against Phoebe's. Blocky and utilitarian, his chair seems to be standard hospital issue. Pheebs's is more technologically advanced, cut down, slanted, almost cute. For the first time, I wonder what it must have cost, and like smoke, some of the anger in me wisps away.

Jake's floor is quiet. I circle it twice, but if there's a room 7E, I sure as hell can't find it. Finally I stop at the nurse's station and ask him where to go.

"Oh, you want the hospice unit," he explains. "Go back to the elevator and make a left."

"Hospice? Are you sure it's okay to visit?"

"Sure," the young man tells me, his face amazed. "What makes you think the dying don't welcome visitors?"

What's left of my anger turns to cold sweat. I don't feel ready for this. I peek in the rooms I pass, and in one, I swear, I see myself lying in the bed. My legs feel like somebody has poleaxed them at the knees. I grab onto the doorframe for support, and the woman turns to me. She stares blankly. Okay, she's not me, she's just another black woman who hit some real bad luck. I smile and move along, not at all sure how it is I cannot go into that room and hear her story. Tell her mine. Make my stupid legs work. All those years I took for granted

310

that the world would keep on spinning on its axis and now every single day is out of whack.

At the door of room 7, I stand for a while and look in. There are four beds, made up with colorful spreads. Jake's bed has the flannel log cabin quilt I made out of his old shirts. How I ruined my thumbs with the needle stitching that thing. There are men in two of the beds, one reclining and the other sitting up, reading. The remaining beds look ready for immediate occupation. It must be hard to take your place on the mattress, knowing you're probably not getting out of here alive. The green canisters of oxygen, the lack of life-saving machinery; this is God's waiting room if ever I saw it. The television is set to ESPN, the volume low. Jake's bed is nearest the window, but he doesn't have a view of anything except the parking lot. That's a mighty big change for a man who lived his whole life within a few steps of horseflesh, which he used to say was the finest landscape on earth. There's a framed photo of Leroy on his nightstand. I have to at least tell him his horse is okay.

Jake's asleep. I pull up a plastic chair and sit by his side, studying his face. He's on oxygen, not a mask, though, the kind that goes through little tubes directly into his nose. His cheeks are sunken, his skin dry and dusty-looking; he appears older than the old man in the elevator who called me Sister. The IV in his hand is taped down with paper adhesive and I remember how allergic he was to regular tape, and I'm glad whoever is taking care of him knows this. There are warning labels everywhere, those red boxes for infectious trash at the head and foot of his bed. His roommate who's reading a book thoughtfully keeps his gaze averted, but I draw the striped curtain around us anyway, and take Jake's hand in mine. It's warm, but somehow feels lighter, as if he's dropped all his muscle tone, which from a man who could pull a cast horse out from under a fence rail and haul her to her feet with his bare hands is tough to imagine. I clasp the fingers that used to flick over my skin just so, raising shivers, making me cry out with a passion so large it somehow made me forget that he'd likely been with another woman the night before, or would be tomorrow. On my way up here, I wanted to break his fingers one by one, slap his face, chew his ass out until the anger inside me landed on him and sank in its talons. Now, I lift each finger to my mouth and lightly kiss them, because I see there isn't anything Jake can give me that he hasn't already given himself. They taste like ashes. I want to say good-bye with kindness and grace, but I don't know how. When I kiss his cheek, Jake opens his eyes, and pulls at the oxygen tubes until they come out.

"Nessie?" he wheezes.

I nod. "Sam told me you were here. Thought I'd drop by."

His eyes fill with tears. Mine do, too. "I'm real sorry, girl."

"Yeah, me, too, Jake."

"I should have known better."

"Guess we both should have." I slide the tubes back into his nose and watch his breathing, clear and short, doubling occasionally, like sick horses sometimes do. We look into each other's eyes for a long while. I dab a tissue to his tears, which slide down toward his ears and puddle at his neck. He turns his face away, embarrassed. I sit there patiently until he screws up the courage to turn back. "There's something I want to tell you," I begin.

He interrupts me. "After how I did you, why would you come here? You want to say I told you so? To kick my black ass from here to hell? Won't take much to do that. I can't even stand up to take a leak."

"I loved you, you miserable horse trader," I say. "Even if it didn't mean nothing to you, it meant the world to me."

He tries to push my hand away, but I won't let him. "I don't deserve anybody's love."

"Oh, Jake. Who does?"

He cries like the weanlings when they're separated from the mares. The pitiful call-and-response goes on for days, and sounds so cruel that I have to believe it is. I hold his hand throughout, and when it loosens against mine, I can see the crying has worn him out so bad he can hardly keep his eyes open.

Sleepily, he asks, "You taking good care of Leroy?"

He knew all along. "The best," I say. I kiss him on the forehead and leave the curtain drawn when I go. Jake, for all his philandering, always did appreciate his privacy.

WHEN I GET HOME, I go straight to Leroy and feed him his evening flake. He mutters over the best parts, noses the hay until he gets it just the way he likes it. I hold on to the fence and watch him eat. When I stole him, I really needed the company. I mean, I always had my granny, but I don't think I could have left Patrini's alone. And maybe, admit it, it was a last jab at Jake, but it's funny how it ended up the best thing for everyone.

"Your old master misses you something fierce," I tell my horse. "He told me to tell you he loved you, and that he was sorry he ever once lifted a whip to you."

Leroy stops eating to slurp up a drink of water. Then he shakes his huge head, splattering me with green bits and slobber.

Finally I take the apples out of my pockets that Granny Shirley gave me and feed them to Leroy. I had to go straight from Jake's hospital bedside and tell her right then or never tell her at all. She listened without saying anything, then she got down on her knees in her kitchen on that hard linoleum and said the Lord's Prayer. Afterward, she tipped her fruit basket out onto the table and gave me the apples to take home. She smoothed my hair back from my forehead and kissed my cheeks. "You'll always be precious to me," she said, and walked me to the car like it was any old day of the week I'd come visiting.

"THE GUY AT THE FEED STORE in the Valley definitely gave Beryl a suspicious look," Nance says, her fork poised over whole-wheat spaghetti and homemade garlic bread. Garlic, the carnivore informed me as she assembled our supper, is a natural blood cleanser, and should be ingested on a daily basis. I resign myself to breath that will scare away Leroy.

"He thought I was shoplifting," Beryl says.

"Not true," Nance says. "In particular, he was checking out her butt. So I just happened to ask if in addition to liking redheads if he played the guitar by any chance, and get this—he asks me what my problem is, if I'm writing a book. Now don't you find that rude?"

"I found it rude that you asked him so many questions," Beryl says.

Phoebe laughs and passes me the salad she made—romaine, mandarin oranges, and kiwi fruit—because she wants me to have seconds and kiwi fruit is apparently so chock-full of vitamins she thinks we should now have it every day. So much for apples. "You do have this rather interrogative style, Nance. That journalist rubbed off on you more than you like to admit."

"The hell I do! This is a genuine mystery we have on our hands here. All I want is to make sure it isn't some psycho after our Beryl Anne. Which is why the next time the phone rings, I think we should press Record on the answering machine."

"Don't ask me how I know this, but tape recording without the speaker's consent happens to be illegal in fifteen states," Beryl points out.

"And pestering you with phone calls isn't?"

"Actually, I don't think it is," I say. "The definition of annoying phone calls is kind of vague. You should call the phone company, get them to tap the line."

"And tap BBR as well? Maybe I should just get myself a Kevlar vest and carry pepper spray."

"Well, if it isn't against the law to call up and not say who it is, somebody should introduce legislation to make it illegal." Nance eats her spaghetti by twisting it with her fork against the spoon, no doubt something she learned from dining with the Bayborough elite she photographs. "And I find mysteries plenty annoying, so I think that justifies the recording."

Me, I don't care. I just chop the noodles up and fork them into my mouth. I think I've forgotten how to be hungry. I take the seconds on the salad, too, and eat kiwi without tasting it. My roommates have a running tally of what food goes into my mouth and how many megavitamins are left in the bottle. I suspect they count them, and each day a different person is assigned the task of reminding me to take them.

"I haven't had a call in two days," Beryl points out. "Maybe he or she got bored, fixated on someone else."

"Ha," Nance says. "This ain't over, not by a long shot."

"Do you know how fake it sounds when you say 'ain't'?" I say.

There's a silence and suddenly AIDS is right back there on the table, a withered centerpiece that has overstayed its welcome, in a vase of smelly, green standing water. What is my problem? Everything was easy for a little while there. I have to protect those moments, revel in them, and not dump on them.

"You know what I think?" Phoebe says. "We should take a weekend away when we get the rest of the summer bulbs planted. A girls' weekend someplace with a spa. We have the bucks thanks to the poinsettia sale. And it shouldn't cost a lot, it being the Christmas season, and everyone out shopping the malls. Wouldn't a healthy getaway just fit the ticket right now?"

Healthy being the key word. There is much excitement over this idea, and Nance is pushing for Napa, Phoebe for Esalen, when the phone rings and we all put down our forks and look at each other expectantly. It's six P.M. on a Monday night, the telemarketer's favorite hour. Or Beryl's mystery guitar man.

"It's him," Nance says. "Let me get it."

"It could be anybody," Beryl points out, "even James."

"I already talked to James twice today."

"Twice?" Phoebe says. "Things must be heating up. It's kind of early, but Juan likes to call to say good-night." She starts to wheel herself over to the phone stand, and Verde squawks at the sight of her chrome.

"Or Granny Shirley could have fallen and broken a hip. I'm answering it," I say, and leave the table and catch it on the third ring. "Hello?"

"Oh, is this Ness?"

"Yes, who's this?"

"It's Gina from Dr. Ullman's office. We need you to come in for that second test we discussed," she tells me. "Would tomorrow morning be convenient?"

"Sure," I say. My heart seems to stop beating. I hang up the phone and turn back to the table, where everyone appears to be suspended in time, frozen between lighthearted conversation and this grim future we all knew was coming and now has arrived.

I know they mean well with the vitamins and good food and general attempts at assuring me there is a future. I can't help it. The only person I want to see right now is David Snow. I manage to make it to the bathroom before I throw up my dinner. I tell myself I will not cry, but the tears run so hot and steady I think they might never stop. Outside the door, I hear Beryl knocking softly. "Ness?" she says. "Can I come in?"

"Not yet." I rinse my mouth, and then I clean the bathroom from top to bottom, with bleach.

# 13

## *Rescue Remedy*

WHEN I OPEN THE DOOR, Ness is there on her knees, wiping the floor like some deranged Shakespearean actor. She holds up a hand in warning. "Don't come any closer," she sobs. "I don't want you to die."

"Oh, Ness." I want to tell her that everybody dies of something, that this initial terror will pass, but instead I go back to the kitchen and put on the plastic dishwashing gloves. They're elbow high, pickle-juice green, and so ugly they should be outlawed. My stepmother used to wear gloves like these for every household chore, including placing my dirty clothes into the washing machine. "Did you really think we were going to let you clean up your own barf? That's why you have roommates. Now go change into your jammies."

"You're not my mother, Beryl. I can mop up my own—"

"*Go*, Ness," I say, and boy, do I mean it.

She gives me one last belly-wrenching sob, I hand her the tissue box, shove her toward the door, and she heads off in the direction of her bedroom. I haul in a bucket and clean the place again; top to bottom, finishing up with a disinfectant spray that doesn't smell quite so gnarly as straight bleach. Cleaning up vomit is nothing to me. In prison, a mess was something you put your shoulder to and erased ASAP because things were already bad enough.

When everything's shining, I dump my sponge and towels into the bucket and take it outside to the trash. All of it goes into a plastic sack, including the gloves. I wrap a red twist tie around it so everybody will know this is Ness's trash and place it in the new red garbage can Nance and I bought on our way home from looking for Buckethead. That's what we're calling my mysterious phone call man, after that crazy guitar player we've heard on the Sierra Grove public radio station. According to Monterey Jack, the evening drive time DJ, Buckethead is an enigmatic virtuoso. Unlike every other rock star wanna-be, Buckethead makes no attempts at promotion, gives no interviews, *nada*. Supposedly he wears a KFC chicken bucket and a mask so nobody can see his face when he does play in public—I assume it's a clean bucket. How you find out about his gigs is word of mouth, and apparently he plays up here a lot. Monterey Jack's pet theory is that Buckethead's really Pat Metheny, playing solo.

"Isn't Pat Metheny already famous enough?" I asked Nance when we heard that part.

"Indeed, he is," she said. "I guess even being pigeonholed as a jazz-fusion legend can feel stifling."

"I don't know," I said. "If I was any kind

of legend, I think it would take me a long time to feel stifled."

"What would you do if your phone caller turned out to be Buckethead?" Nance asked.

I told her, "Look. If Antonio Banderas turns out to be my phone caller, I really don't care. All I want is some peace and quiet around the farm, a chance to read my books, and for Ness to be all right."

Nance didn't say anything, but I could tell she felt that way, too.

Seeing that red tie on the white bag breaks my heart. Red is the color of Christmas Santas and Valentine's Day hearts. It's the color of the best-tasting candy, and cardinals, and Macintosh apples. Red is Phoebe's socks in the laundry, so tiny they look like they should belong to a ten-year-old, not a woman in her mid-thirties who is having sex almost every night of the week. Red is the color of good, strong blood, not its opposite, but red is the color we all agreed would be easiest to remember, so the twist ties are red and the trash can is red, and I'm seeing red because dammit all, I don't want any of this to be true and apparently it is.

EVERYBODY WANTS TO GO ALONG with Ness to the doctor in the morning, but it turns out only I can. Nance gets a call from James about taking pictures for the new winery, and Phoebe, who overslept, is having lunch with Rebecca

321

Roth, a Sierra Grove gallery owner who wants to host a spring show of her clay ladies. Everyone's prospects sound interesting, but given the choice, I'd still rather accompany Ness. As we cross over the highway and wind our way into Bayborough-by-the-Sea, she asks me, "Girl, how come you don't drive?"

It's a sunny day, the tourists are out in force, there isn't a parking place to be found. "What's so wrong with riding my bike and hitching rides?"

"It slows you down."

"Sometimes slowing down is exactly what a person needs."

"Yeah, listen to me," Ness says, "talking like I own this car. Six months ago I rode my horse places. Thanks for last night. Sorry I went all rubber-room on you. It won't happen again."

"That's okay. So this test today, what's it going to determine?"

She stiffens, like I'm not supposed to ask that question. "How sick I am, I guess. Any calls from Mystery Guy today?"

"Nope. Just like me, I don't think he's a morning person."

"So who do you think it could be? The feed store clerk, or is it somebody from your deeply cryptic past you never want to talk about?"

"I haven't a clue. Maybe it's somebody from *your* cryptic past."

This merits an immediate pout, complete with jutting chin and a moment of deeply offended silence. It doesn't take Einstein to figure out that she's about to deliver me a lecture. I hold on to my hat.

"The way I see it, Beryl, now that I'm positive, my real life's over. Ain't no reason to dig up bones, and there's no mystery about that."

I mull this around in my head for five minutes, watching the scenery pass outside my window. With Ness, you have to go slowly, because she gets offended so easily. "You know," I say, "when I was in prison, they had this program where you could read books out loud to be recorded on tape, for schools and so forth. We all signed up to do it, just for the chance to sit in a soundproof booth for a couple of hours, because to be quiet and alone was heaven. Only problem was, about a quarter of the women in there couldn't read well enough to do the taping."

"Well, that's depressing as hell. Why are you telling me this?"

I shrug. "You asked about my past."

Ness is quiet a moment. "So, what kind of stuff did you read?"

"The Bible, John Grisham, poetry, mysteries. Sometimes I got special permission to read to the patients in the infirmary, too. Didn't matter if I read Emily Dickinson or a comic book, those women sure liked to hear the sound of a human voice telling them a story. Of course, once it got popular, some bigwig made us stop. But while it lasted, it was really something."

Ness stops at the crosswalk, and she stares out the window. Two old ladies make their way along the tarmac, Nieman-Marcus bags in their hands. They're both frail, and they link arms to make this trek, which is at times perilous due to the large number of SUVs in Bayborough-by-the-Sea.

I put my hand on Ness's shoulder, which is rigid with tension. I'd give her a neck rub if she'd let me. She hits the steering wheel with her palm. She smacks it again, and then a third time. "You shouldn't have gone to prison. That was a travesty. So much unfairness in this stinking world."

"How can you say the world stinks, Ness? This is paradise."

She gives me a look. "How can you sit there and say that to me knowing I'm going to die of this awful disease?"

I shake my head. "I'm sorry. That's the way I look at my life. I always assume everyone else does, too."

"Even with prison?"

"Maybe especially there."

"Give me a break! Who are you—Polly-freakin'-Anna?"

A car honks at us to move, but to do so would scare the old ladies. Ness stays put. The person in the car leans on the horn, but not until the ladies reach the curb do we move along. "The first year and a half I was in prison I was terrified some stupid fight somebody picked just because they were going stir-crazy would extend my sentence. I lost weight, my hair started falling out, and I wasn't sleeping. Then it occurred to me, I had better find some good somewhere inside that place or flip completely out. So I spent my spare time in Chowchilla reading books, sketching, even though I was lousy at it, and going to AA meetings, even though I didn't have a drinking problem. I went wherever I could go to learn how to make it through each day. I learned how to repair faulty electrical wiring, put together a meal for five hundred, and work an industrial laundry machine. I survived. When I got out, I realized that if I live every day that way, if I press the sucker flat like I've ironed all the good stuff out just for me, I sleep like a baby. So I pester Florencio to show me stuff, and I try to treat each bird I deal with at BBR like it's the most important one on earth. Guess if I had AIDS, I'd want to read everything ever written about it."

"Ah, but you're not me," she says.

And indeed, that is the bottom line.

"BERYL," GINA SAYS when we check Ness in at the desk. "How nice to see you again. So long as you're here, Doctor can go over your test results with you if you like."

"Okay." I leave Ness in one exam room and go into another. I get halfway through an article on the oil spill in Valdez, Alaska, when Dr. Ullman enters with my file in his hand. "Am I going to live?"

"Appears that way. Disappointed?"

I smile. "No, sir, not at all."

"Glad to hear it." He pumps up the blood pressure cuff on my arm and reads the numbers.

"Um, Gina already did that."

"I know. I wanted to see if it would come down any after you rested a while. Your blood pressure runs a little high, are you aware of that?"

"Guess I am now."

"Anybody in your family have hypertension?"

"My dad died of a heart attack."

"And your mother?"

I swallow. I don't have to say suicide so I don't. "She had leukemia."

"Well, you don't have either, but I'd like to start you on a beta blocker to see if we can't ease your numbers down into a more normal range." He flashes a penlight into my eyes. "Do you ever get headaches?"

"No more than the usual amount. Why?"

"One of your pupils is slightly larger than the other."

I laugh. "Oh, that. My dad had it, too. We used to joke about it, call each other Popeye. It's nothing, really."

Dr. Ullman makes a note in his chart. "You should get an eye exam every year, just in case you need glasses."

"I see fine. I don't even need glasses for reading yet. I understand that's great for somebody over forty. My eyes are the same as they've ever been."

"Good. Now get yourself an eye exam and make me happy."

"Wow, you don't give up, do you?"

"I'm Phoebe's doctor. Where on earth would she be if I showed my belly every time she questioned my advice?"

"Touché. I'll get the exam."

He writes out a prescription for the beta blocker, and I wonder how much it will cost for me to get it filled. "I know you can't talk to me about Ness's condition," I say. "Doctor-patient confidentiality and so forth."

He scribbles with his pen poised onto the white prescription pad. "That's correct."

"But I want to ask you something anyway."

He sits back in his chair. "Proceed."

"Well, this morning I found this book by Ness's bed. It's about suicide methods. I know I'm ratting her out by telling you this."

"Sounds to me as if you're behaving like a friend. Perhaps we need to intervene."

"No, no, not at all. I mean, I'm not saying she needs to be slapped in the loony bin, and even if she did we could take care of her better than they could. I think she's exploring all aspects, and who can blame her for that? I guess what I'm looking for here is for you to tell us how best to help."

Dr. Ullman rubs his neck and sits back in his chair. "I'm an internist, Beryl. The thing about HIV is, the primary doctor generally ends up being expert mostly at making referrals. Here's the number to call for medication trials. This is the night the support groups meet. Somewhere along the way, the patient needs to unload, or more crudely put, to periodically 'lose it.' That's what friends and families are for. You might call her mother, let her in on the situation."

Mothers, I think. If only he knew. Ours are dead, crazy, or they abandoned us—who among us at the farm has one decent specimen we could call on?

He straightens the stack of magazines and then seems to once more slip into his aloof physician's posture. "It's rare, but there is such a thing as false positives. The second test will tell us what we need to know. Nevertheless, you keep me posted on that particular concern you mentioned. That's not violating any code of ethics I subscribe to."

"Thank you. I will." He leaves the room. I take the magazine with me to the waiting room. Ness's situation isn't going away, and I plan to be there for her. Right now, though, I want to know how the clean-up people in Valdez managed to save any of the seabirds. Oil is such nasty stuff. Nine times out of ten, the bird suffocates. In lost causes, what I do is place a drop of this homeopathic stuff Agnes and Marty swear by, Rescue Remedy, inside their beaks. I figure it can't hurt, and sometimes it even works.

ON THE WAY HOME, I basically force Ness to take us to Earl's on Ocean. When it comes to used bookstores, Earl's is like a box of expensive chocolates, everything's neatly shelved, alphabetized, the price written inside the cover in pencil in case you want to give the book as a present, but my favorite aspect of shopping here is Earl takes trade-ins, and gives you credit toward another purchase. I haven't been to Earl's since I moved into the farmhouse and now that I realize how near we are, I'm having a jones for it.

"All I want is an entire box of Entenmann's doughnuts, the chocolate variety," Ness whines, "and to go home, take them to bed with me, and not have to share."

"I promise, we'll get some later. Right now you're coming with me to the bookstore and getting something to read."

"Beryl, I don't even like to read."

I think of the suicide book and almost say something. "Stop your whining. I'll even pay for the books. Now turn left here and find a parking spot."

"This is Sierra Grove beachfront. There is no such thing as parking."

"Keep looking. Somebody will pull out."

She gives me the evil eye and says, "Wish Jake Rayburn had."

I haven't been here in so long that Earl looks shocked when I open the door. His mouth actually drops open a little. Ness, meanwhile, is circling the block, trying to park the car, no doubt cussing me up one side and down the other, using Verde's best vocabulary words.

"Beryl," he says, pushing his wire-rim glasses up his hawklike nose. Earl's dressed in his usual faded flannel shirt and blue jeans. His gray hair's pulled back into a neat ponytail that is secured with a beaded leather thong. He's about fifty, cute, in an intellectual-hippie sort of way. "Thought when you moved away you'd forgotten about this place."

"What? All I did was relocate to the Valley part of town, Earl. Nothing else about me has changed, I swear."

When Earl wants to smile, his nostrils flare, like they are right now. I look at him and wonder what woman did so much harm to him that he can't just cut loose and grin. The most he ever manages is a smirk, which most people misunderstand as smugness. He dusts off the counter with his sleeve and moves aside a stack of books. "Must be nice to win the lottery."

"Yeah, I guess it must, but how would I know? I got a job on a farm, and the living situation came along with, Earl."

His nostrils retract back to normal. "How's your bird?"

"Verde's doing great. He's even learning some new words, other than cussing, I mean. He just got a new toy, so you know; it's basically bird nirvana until he breaks it, which should take about a week. How's your cat?"

"Hester's good. Last I saw her was over in Historical Fiction."

"I'll be sure to say hello." I lean on the counter, just above the signed first editions Earl has locked in the glass case. One of them is Edgar Rice Burroughs's *Tarzan,* priced at fifteen hundred dollars. One day when it was rainy and nobody else was in the store, he took it out and let me see the illustrations. Then he read to me, with different voices for all the characters. At that moment, I thought to myself, Earl was so good he could have been an actor. "How's business?"

"Last month I sold that leather-bound set of Rudyard Kipling. I managed to score two estate sale libraries, one of which had some valuable Steinbecks and the other a signed first edition of *Leaving Cheyenne,* so I can't complain. Listen, I set aside some books, you know, on birds and wilderness, all that stuff you like." He hauls up a crate with my name on it. "In case you ever came back."

"That was really thoughtful of you, Earl." I start to rummage through them and I'm totally absorbed when Ness comes in.

"This better be worth it, Beryl. I had to park clear around the block."

"Earl, meet my friend and roommate, Ness Butler. She's deeply in need of some comfort reads. Got any suggestions?"

He steps out from behind the counter and leads her to the children's books. They have their heads bent over fairy tales and so forth, so I return to my pile of reads and savor each page. There's an older book on owls, with some fine pen and ink illustrations. It's three bucks. Also, a barely used hardcover on the mind of the raven, not even a year old, and Earl's marked it ten, which is fair, but out of my price range. There's a picture book on Alaska, too,

which makes me remember the article in Dr.
U's office, and I sit down on the floor near the
register and pretty soon I'm lost in color
photographs of the aurora borealis and snow-
drifts so deep they topple over and close
down highways. Sure, the first thing that
crosses my mind when I see pictures of our
forty-ninth state is the cold, but the second
thing that I think of is how clean and pure all
that snow looks. Clear water, inaccessible
beaches, humpback whales; spruce trees and
glaciers and grizzly bears. I guess if I could travel
one place in my life, Alaska would be where
I'd choose to go—if I were to win the lottery.

Ness comes to the register with a paperback
of Kate Seredy's folktales, a lavishly illustrated hardcover Persian story collection,
and a fairly new *Misty of Chincoteague*. "Earl
says I can't leave the store without these."

"That's right," he says. "Kids' books are
better than penicillin."

I laugh. "How much are they?"

We perform some addition and for fifteen
dollars, we can walk out of Earl's with everything but the raven book. I could put back the
Alaska book, it's mostly photographs, but
I'm torn. In the raven book, the author insists
ravens are more like wolves than birds. He's
raised them himself, and spent so much time
in the wild he probably has tail feathers under
his jeans. I want to go along with him, even
if only in the pages. Still, ten dollars. And it
doesn't transport me the way the Alaska book
does, though it comes close. "Earl?" I ask as

I reach for my wallet. "I can't live without the Alaska book. But can you keep the raven book on hold until I get my next paycheck?"

"I guess," he says, frowning. "Hey, don't forget to take a look at the new paperback shelf while I bag these. We got in some great new mysteries. Only a quarter each."

"Oh yeah, Beryl loves a good mystery, don't you," Ness says, laughing.

I haul her away before she starts in on the Buckethead conspiracy. We add one more book to our bunch. Initially the cover is what attracts us because of the embossed quilt pattern, but then we discover it's set on the Central Coast. "Granny Shirley used to quilt before her arthritis got bad," Ness says. "After Phoebe reads this, can I pass it on to my grandma? Or does it have bad words in it?"

"That book's clean enough to eat off of," Earl says as he hands over the bag. "Perfect for grannies. Plus she writes better than P. D. James, I'd say."

"Earl is the only person I know who reads more than I do," I tell Ness. "And his recommendations you can take to the bank. Too bad it doesn't buy groceries, huh, Earl?"

He nods and the smile almost emerges. "Don't worry, I made a profit off you ladies. Now don't be such a stranger, Beryl. Bring Verde by sometime."

"I'll be back for that raven book in a week," I promise.

"That's not the first time I've heard someone say that," he says.

333

"Yeah, but this someone means it."

Ness trips on the clutter behind the register counter on her way to the door, catches herself, and laughs. "Just call me gazelle girl," she says.

"See you later, gazelle girl," Earl says.

On the walk to the car, it's overcast again, and feeling wintry and chilly. "Look at the sky," Ness says, where gray clouds are clumping up like the lint in a dryer trap. "Rain tonight for sure."

"Which means we better check to make certain the sprinklers are shut off."

"And start a fire in the fireplace, and buy those doughnuts." Ness stops for the third time to rub her toe.

"Now what's the matter?"

"My toe. I wonder if I broke the skin."

"Let me look."

"No!" Her face is wide open with concern.

"These days people live a long time with this disease, Ness. There're new drugs being invented every day."

The wind whips her braids across her face and Ness pushes them away with her hand. She's breathing hard. "You didn't see Jake in that hospice place, Beryl. You didn't have to sit there and watch him work for every breath. You didn't taste ash in your mouth when you kissed him, either."

"No, I sure didn't."

"So where do you get off telling me to look at this any different?"

Apparently it's providence that I came

today instead of Nance or Phoebe. By now, Nance would be all defensive and yelling and Ness would have brought up slavery. Phoebe, on the other hand, would be so hurt she'd try to manage Ness into seeing things her way, which would make Ness go even more ballistic and break Phoebe's heart. I'm thicker skinned. Still, we take all this punishment in the name of loving her, and it's not easy. I figure what do I have to lose if I hand her attitude right back to her, so I say, "Prison," and then I wait for the strafing of bullets.

Ness's face softens. "Guess I deserved that."

"Sweetie," I say, touching her shoulder and squeezing lightly. "What will you worry about if you live?"

WE STOP FOR COFFEE at Java the Hut. I order mondo lattes, three shots each, with a shot of cinnamon syrup and don't spare the foam. It's almost enough just to sit there and smell the coffee; that is until we take our first sips and sigh with pleasure. One by one, we take our books out of the grocery sack to examine them. "I have no clue what you see in Alaska," she says and shudders. "All that snow. Brrr."

"How about it's the last American frontier?"

"So is the newest shopping mall. Your point?"

How can I explain why it appeals to me? "Well, everybody there has a past."

"As do most folks here."

"Yes, but up there, nobody cares. It's almost respected. You can really, truly start over. Become a fisherman, sell crafts, and maybe even teach school way out in some distant village where they're glad for a teacher no matter what her past is. And my goodness, springtime— imagine, after all the snow melts, and the flowers start coming up. Or those endless summer nights when the sun refuses to set? That has to be a pretty great reward. I mean, where else do you see moose walking around downtown?"

Ness laughs. "In Bayborough-by-the-Sea. Only here they're disguised as tourists."

"Okay, bald eagles?"

"Fine, Beryl, you win. Alaska's a paradise so long as you're dressed in a million layers of long underwear ten months out of the year. Now Hawaii, there's a state I wouldn't mind seeing...give me a bikini, a beach towel, and a trashy paperback novel with lots of sex in it."

I reach down to the bottom of the bag and discover the raven book. I know I didn't pay for it. Earl must have stuck it in there on purpose, or else it would be on the top. Why would he do that? Because it's almost Christmas? I told him I was coming back next week to pay for it. Then it hits me, Ness stubbing her toe on the clutter behind the counter, which included an amplifier, and Earl's black telephone sitting right there on top. There are probably whole days nobody comes in, and the place is so quiet, even when people are shopping, he could make private calls. How great it would sound to play guitar in an echoey building on a rainy afternoon, when you're all alone with your cat and you start thinking of how your life might have gone if you'd made a big right turn instead of that righteously stupid left. But can Earl really be Buckethead? No, that's a crazy idea. I let Ness chatter on, bagging on the state of Alaska. What do I care? I don't have to argue to know I'm right.

I'M HELPING PHOEBE wrap up clay ladies in bubble wrap for shipment to Little People when the phone rings again. It's an ordinary Saturday morning, Ness is out riding Leroy, thank God, and Nance is on a breakfast date with James, but she'll be back soon because we're going to stuff sachets for our Christmas boutique sale day after tomorrow. Phoebe, who seems to be coming down with a head cold, looks at me with concern. "Want me to get it?"

Earl—or Buckethead—hasn't called me in days, not since I visited the bookstore, and I kind of miss him. "No, it's all right." I pick up the phone and say hello, and am met with the usual quiet. "Listen, I have a pretty good idea who this is," I start to say, but a woman's voice interrupts me.

"Why, this isn't Phoebe."

I'm startled. "No, ma'am, you're speaking to Beryl. May I tell Phoebe who's calling?"

There's another silence, and this one's icy. "You certainly may. This is her mother."

"Hold on, please." I hand the phone over, whispering, "Your mother."

Phoebe sighs as she takes the receiver. I leave the room to go sit in the living room on one of the couches in front of the fireplace so Phoebe can have a little privacy. The logs are piled high, and it only takes a single match to get the fire going all nice and toasty. This is the way to start a morning, I think.

Whenever I sit by myself in this room, it's as if I can feel Sadie, as real and right here as any of us. She walks in the door just back from traveling all over the globe, drops her luggage on the floor, and bends down to start a fire before doing anything else—kicking off her traveling shoes, checking her mail, seeing what the garden's been up to while she was away, telling us with whom she had a mad affair. Nothing but that homey warmth takes precedence. Or it's three in the morning, and she's returning from a party with friends who have the kinds of names people love to drop. Her hair is coming down from her fancy, upswept bun, but on her it looks sexy. She's holding her glittery high heels in her hand, a seasoned Cinderella who told the prince to take a hike. The fire blazes up, she has the room to herself, and it's like steeping in a cocktail that's equal parts independence and loneliness. Bittersweet. I want to ask her if the last twenty years of her life were full enough without a man to share them. If she accomplished all the things she wanted to, and died satisfied with her life. What, on her deathbed, did she regret, besides leaving?

I think solitude is a tough thing for women to wrap their hearts around. I mean, who wants to end up dying alone? But is that any reason to have babies, or marry somebody you don't really love the way you know you should? When Sadie was dying, she had Phoebe by her side. That's got to be pretty wonderful, one woman taking care of another, each feeling nothing but love in her heart. I tell myself that love doesn't always have to be about a man and sex, but lately I ache for some. I'm trying to come up with what Earl—if it's him—got out of the conversation when he listened to me say hello over and over, and what he was trying to say when he played me songs on his guitar. Even though I'm anxious to know, somehow it doesn't seem polite to just come out and accuse him.

The blazing fire just isn't enough. I light the squat, ivory-colored candles on the coffee table to keep it company. I set a match to the wicks of the tapers in the candelabra, too. Duchess trots in from the dog door Juan installed, shakes herself once, and lies down on the hearth with a contented doggy groan. Verde's quietly pouting. Yesterday I clipped his claws and he always responds by getting miffed at such unjust treatment. He sticks his head under his wing stub for a day and won't talk to anybody, even for a peanut. Phoebe and Nance and I all got our HIV tests back with happy-face negatives. Ness still hasn't heard from Dr. Ullman about the Western Blot thing. I'm worried that it's taking so long. Phoebe's cough sounds deeper to me than it did yesterday, but I know if I say that she'll deny it. I can't figure out which concerns me more, the possibility of her pneumonia returning so quickly or the way she blithely pretends she's just fine. One thing I know for sure, Ness shouldn't be around anyone contagious.

Mornings I pour myself a cup of coffee and stir in way too much cream. Worse yet, I dip toast in like an utter slob, afraid to think about anything more strenuous than flowers and farm chores. On my workdays, I go off to bird rehab where I fret silently about what the future holds. Nance spends whole days on the Internet, bettering our website and secretly researching AIDS treatments Ness refuses to discuss. Lucky Nance has photo shoots and James for escape; Phoebe has Juan. I have my books, and they don't disappoint. In the raven book, I learned that scout birds are sent out to look for food, and how they learn just when certain restaurants dump their garbage. They take this information back to their buddies—the smorgasbord is now open— and then they dive in, the avian version of *Babette's Feast*. It's suggested that they particularly enjoy Thai food, which I'd like to learn to cook, because it sounds like it might please carnivore and vegetarian alike. I think of how people with AIDS can live ten years or be quickly felled by one single opportunistic illness. How will we deal with it if that happens? Oh, maybe this living together was too good a thing to last.

Phoebe wheels herself into the living room and stops before the Christmas tree we bought last weekend, a nine-foot balsam fir. Its branches are utterly bare; its scent is deeply fragrant, like the woods it probably came from. Last night I found a frog in the tree well and set it loose in the herb garden. Phoebe reaches out and takes hold of a branch, then lets go. It springs back at her touch, strong, it will last. We haven't got around to decorating it yet, but there are twenty boxes of lights and ornaments on the floor that I found in the barn rafters when last I spied on the owls. The look on Phoebe's face is not what I'd call joyful, triumphant, or eager for the season.

"Why do mothers always make you feel like you're five years old and have just crayoned on the wall?"

"I give up, why do they?"

"Because they can, ha ha," Phoebe says, coughs, and reaches into her robe pocket for a lozenge. Around the bulk of it in her mouth she says, "All I did was ask her if she was planning to come up here for Christmas, a perfectly innocent question if you ask me, and she gives me a ten-minute lecture."

"So I take it she's not coming."

"Of course not. Since Father died, Mother likes to spend Christmas flying somewhere tropical. She's got a date for every evening from now until New Year's. She says I should send

341

pictures of the flowers and the farm and myself, pictures. That at her age she has enough soap and powder and monogrammed stationery so those are out for the present ideas."

"Maybe you could fly down south and see her," I suggest.

She looks at me aghast. "Are you serious? She'd sabotage my chair, Beryl, feed me until I burst, and I'd never see the light of day again. No, thanks. I won't die if I don't see her for Christmas. I just kind of wanted to show off the farm is all. God, how can I be tired at ten in the morning? Maybe I should take a nap."

"Go ahead, Pheebs," I say.

"I can't. I promised Nance I'd sew the casings for the lavender sachets and I told that Roth woman I'd work on stuff for the gallery show in the spring."

"Ness and I will do the casings. Spring's a ways off yet. Go sleep. You're not one hundred percent and you know it. I'll wake you up if we need you."

For a moment she sits there, her hands on her push rims. "Okay, you talked me into it."

She wheels herself down the hallway and I drag the sewing machine into the great room, close to the fireplace so I can enjoy it while I sew the tiny satin pillows. We were listening to Phoebe read from Sadie's journal when Nance came up with the idea for the sachets.

Lavender: the name comes from the Latin, *lavare*, to wash, but some say the plant itself originated in India. That I can believe. It loves the sun, and lavender's so wonderful that the British would typically steal it and claim it as their own. So much can be done with this herb. Scatter flowers in a dresser drawer for scent. Make a tisane of lavender water for splashing on your wrists in hot weather. Grow a hedge of it by strawberry plants and the crows will let them alone. It's simply wonderful stuff! I read in my herb book that true oil of lavender—a thousand pounds are required to net a mere ten pounds of essence—is the only remedy for the 'panting passion of the human heart,' thank you John Gerard. Ha! I confess I haven't tried that. Not entirely sure I want mine cured! Oh, what does it matter, so long as you can stand with your eyes shut and smell it on the wind?

Indeed.
The colors Nance chose for the sachets are regal—bronze, copper, silver, magenta, emerald green. She bought an entire spool of gold cord to tie them shut. As soon as I finish one pillow, I drop it into a basket and start the next one. It's easy work, but the bad thing about that is you can't stop thinking. Phoebe's mother not coming for Christmas—I can't get it off my mind. Of course it makes me think

of my mother, my stepmother, and wonder if there's any way in the world for us to ever make peace. Here is the one area in my life where books have utterly failed me. In stories, the mothers and daughters get along, share a kinship, maybe even save each other. I guess that's why they call it fiction. In real life, they go on cruises or write you off when you need them most.

The door shuts and Ness comes into the room smelling of horses and cold weather. "Hey, Bear. Need help?"

"Sure. You can fill up the little sacks with lavender and tie them shut."

She measures out flowers in a scoop. After completing five and spilling half that much on the floor, she looks up at me, bored. "Jeez, I'd almost rather weed than do this. Where's Nance? Wasn't this her big idea?"

The door shuts again and Nance and James come into the room. Nance's cheeks are bright and James is smiling that besotted smile men get when they're in the presence of something they long to hold on to. He takes off his jacket, drinks a cup of coffee, fixes a wobbly hinge on a cupboard door, admires the Christmas tree, and generally hangs around so long that Nance puts him to work stuffing the pillows while she ties the bows.

"No fuller than two-thirds, remember," Nance instructs him. "And leave room so I can make the bow."

"Yes, ma'am," he says.

I'm sewing as fast as I can. Ness stands

behind me and cuts the thread so each finished pillow drops into the basket and I don't have to stop each time I get to the hem.

"Assembly line," James says, "just like the poinsettias. You ladies amaze me. Where's Pheebs? Out with her lover boy?"

"Your mother called," I tell James, and he looks up, questioning.

"Oh, God. What happened?"

"Phoebe invited her to come up for Christmas. After she said no, Phoebe decided she wanted a nap."

James frowns. "Let me explain something about Rita. She spent sixteen years pushing her handicapped daughter into an independent life, never dreaming she'd succeed at it. After Phoebe moved to Bayborough, I don't think Rita knew what to do with herself. So she maintains this busy life in order to forget that her children can survive without her daily help."

"Oh, that makes wonderful sense," Nance says sarcastically. "My mother's just the opposite. She needs me the way a remora needs a shark." She laughs, but it's forced, and James is looking at her a little cockeyed, like this is a new piece to the puzzle.

"When Phoebe wakes up, let's decorate the hell out of this tree," Ness says. "Just stuff the branches so full of cheer they sag under the weight of it."

"A task like that calls for reinforcements," James says, standing up and pulling his keys from his pocket. "I'll be back in no time."

345

When he leaves, Ness pounces on Nance. "So?" she says. "What's happening between you two? Horizontal mambo?"

Nance grins. "Wouldn't you like to know?"

"That means she hasn't slept with him yet," I say. "No way she could keep information like that to herself."

"Hush your dirty mouth," Nance says, but I can tell I'm right.

"How many of these sachets do we have to make?" I ask.

"Count how many we have now. I think we should get a couple hundred done at least. I picked up three hundred bars of soap at Pic 'n Save for mere pennies. If we color-coordinate them along with the sachets, and for the packaging include some notecards with photos or pressed flowers on them, people will snap them up. You'll see, they make a great gift item, and not just for Christmas, but all year round..."

Right away Ness starts complaining. It's what she does. When it comes to the clinches, she will stay up all night tying ribbons, if that's what it takes to keep us solvent. The back of my neck aches, but I keep sewing anyway. I think of Sadie again, imagine her hovering around the room, happy that we four have made this a home where something good is always happening. Angels, I think, if they exist at all, have to be somewhat weary creatures. First of all, the wings look heavy. Not only that, but angels are sort of wedged between the world of the living and the reward of heaven, aren't they? Keeping track of everybody, reporting to the Boss, guarding those among us who most need it. I still hesitate to call myself a believer, but this much I know for sure: Should they exist, Sadie is among the ranks. She might even be the one angel the Boss trusts will tell him how things really are, with no BS. I glance over at her portrait and miss a woman I never knew.

Phoebe rolls out of her room, yawning, still in her robe. James arrives a while later with three bottles of Dry Sack, imported cheeses, nuts, fruit and mistletoe, and chocolate, lots of good, glorious chocolate. "Merry Christmas early," he says, and takes turns holding the mistletoe above our heads, kissing each of us. I notice he saves Nance for last, and the kiss he gives her is on the lips and lasts twice as long. That's okay, no, it's better than okay. It's exactly what we need, a reminder that during the holidays, all things are possible.

Everybody's talking and eating and the crackle of the fire is companionable. Duchess quietly begs for cheese and gets some. The candles I lit this morning have burned down to deep pools of aromatic wax. The tree casts giant shadows on the wall. "Let's trim that mother," James says, and begins opening boxes.

"How did your aunt decorate?" Nance asks.

Phoebe looks pensive. She coughs twice, and I see that she's close to tears. "Every season it was something different, wasn't it, James?"

He nods. "Remember that year you had the thing for purple, and she covered the tree in violet bulbs?"

"How about your cowboy-and-Indian tree? That was the year you made everyone call you Hopalong Cassidy."

"Really?" Nance says.

"A complete and total fabrication," James says. "Want to see my six-shooter?"

Nance laughs. "I'm afraid we don't know each other well enough yet."

"Damn," James says.

"How do you follow tradition like that?" Ness asks.

"By making it a reflection of ourselves?" I offer.

Phoebe laughs. "Let's see—what would that include? My birth control pills, Ness's blood tests, a whole truckload of poinsettias, and maybe some peanut shells from old Trash Mouth?"

"All of that," I say. "Something as memorable as it is hopeful."

James fills everyone's glass and we set aside the sachets to trim the tree.

On Sunday afternoon I'm awakened by a phone call from the BBR hotline. Somebody has found an owl on her property, clinging to a fence. The bird will not budge and her dog, a blue heeler, is worrying it to death. The owl's obviously sick, but the rancher finds him too testy to get near enough to move. I ask Nance to drive me out and we tromp a quarter mile through boggy cow pasture to find this beautiful bundle of brown feathers, white stripes on his breast, and the most staring yellow eyes I've ever seen. Lacking ear tufts, he's squat and smaller than a screech owl, so I deduce that what we've got on our hands is a saw-whet owl, usually a fairly friendly guy, found in parks and wherever there are oak groves. Ness has probably ridden Leroy right by this fellow's cousins. I put on heavy gloves and wrestle him into a box I cover with an empty feed sack. He's emaciated under all that plumage, but clearly not happy to be rescued. Nance is madly snapping pictures during this whole process. The rancher who made the call has one hand on her dog's collar and the other clasped around her snout. The owl's pitiful cries sound like "too, too, too," as in this is too much for any living creature to bear.

"Will he live?" she asks.

"He'll probably be all right," I say, because he might and why depress anyone this close to Christmas? We drive to BBR where I'll call the veterinarian who will check him out and then, if he looks salvageable, she'll hand him over to the owl lady in Santa Cruz.

Nance goes around taking pictures of the birds we have in house at the moment. She checks out the bats. They're getting so fat and sassy they're almost ready to be released, even if we aren't emotionally able just yet to set them free. Marty checks on them first thing every morning, and Agnes confided in me that he comes down at night, too, just to tuck in "his babies."

Before I place the owl in his cage, I dribble a drop of Rescue Remedy onto his tongue. He shuts his eyes and grabs onto the perch. I cover the sides of the cage with flannel and page Dr. Llewellyn.

"What should we make for Christmas dinner?" Nance asks.

"What's James's favorite?"

Nance smiles. "That man will eat anything set in front of him. Such an appetite. How about we do a crown roast, Yorkshire pudding, and horseradish?"

"Fine by me. What about our vegetarians?"

"Oh, green bean casserole. Potatoes. Squash. Lots of salad. It's not my fault if they don't recognize good food when it's set before them."

"Do you love him, Nance?"

She smiles. "He's fun to be with, and so far he hasn't critiqued one single sentence of mine, which earns him major points. You think Phoebe minds us seeing each other?"

"Why should she? She likes seeing James happy."

"Me, too," she says, and snaps one last photo of a cedar waxwing, such a sweet bird, who trills a faint song and is terribly grateful when I feed him a piece of grape.

"Good," I say. "Now say a prayer for Mr. Owl, and tell him nighty-night."

Nance peeks into his cage and he opens his eyes. "They look like suns, they're that yellow," she says.

Like so many unknowns we're living with lately, I pray they'll come up tomorrow.

NESS AND PHOEBE are setting up the tables for the boutique, covering them with tablecloths and clear plastic tarp. They keep arguing over the hem that hangs over the edge being even, bumping into and swearing at each other. Nance has had a bad hair morning with the curling iron and she's whining about it. I'm in the kitchen unseating my blackberry and champagne Jell-O mold cups, remembering that I forgot to make the wassail we were going to sell for a dollar a cup and trying to imagine how I can get that ready in time when there's a knock at the door. Verde squawks out his all-time favorite curse, and Phoebe calls out, "People are here already? The sign says we don't open for another hour."

She's still in her jammies, red long johns, the kind with the button-butt. My mother dressed me in them when I was small. I can still remember her settling me in bed, reading me "The Night Before Christmas" every evening the week before the holiday arrived, never getting tired of it. How wide her eyes would go when she got to the part, "When all at once, there arose such a clatter. . ." I can't help it; I love everything about the Yuletide, sugar cookies, the dime-store wrapping paper, the dopey carols, and little kids believing in Santa Claus.

I hear Juan call out, "Oh, Lucy, I'm home!" and he comes into the kitchen balancing the clipboard on top of his head, performing a little mambo that makes the most of his very admirable butt. He lays a bouquet of roses down on the counter and a huge box. The roses in his hand aren't part of UPS's regular delivery service, they're for Phoebe. The box he scoots along the floor is not. "For you, madam," he says, and imagine that, the big brown box has my name on the label.

"Well, open it," Phoebe says. "We're all dying of curiosity."

Juan lends me his pocketknife and I split the tape and open the box. Under the packing material is a huge gift basket wrapped in red and green cellophane. It's filled with Alaska Wildberry chocolates, caribou sausage, birch bark syrup, fireweed candy, a videotape on Alaska birds, and a plain white envelope. Inside the envelope is a round-trip plane ticket to Anchorage and back again. The flight time's left open. "Who sent this?" I ask Juan.

He shakes his head and shows me the clipboard. "It doesn't say anything except where to deliver it. Phoebe, come over here and give me a kiss, I gotta go spread more Christmas cheer. You want to go out to dinner tonight?"

"Absolutely," she says, and her voice is so hoarse she sounds froggy.

Juan stops in his tracks. "*Cara,* you sound worse than you did last night. Call your doctor and make him squeeze you in. I'll bring some soup over. You stay in bed, you hear me?"

"I hear you," she says, but I can see her fingers crossed behind her back.

"I mean it," he says. "I'm coming back here tonight and I want to see proof you went to the doctor."

"How Latino," Phoebe says. "You're getting me all riled up. Go to work."

When Juan leaves, she wheels inside to take her shower.

The rest of us continue setting up the yard for the sale—tables of sachets and soaps, plants varying from Christmas ivy to rosemary wreaths to the last fifty or sixty poinsettias, which we've marked down to half price. The same people who came to the poinsettia sale show up and it appears they've told their friends. We sell steadily all day, and when it starts to drizzle, they open their umbrellas and keep on spending. I smile, take the money, and all the while try to figure out who would send me such an extravagant gift basket. Agnes and Marty usually give me a ten-dollar gift certificate to Bay Books in Bayborough-by-the-Sea. They're on Social Security. Dr. Llewellyn gives us all the same thing, a bird ornament from the National Wildlife foundation and a card saying she's made a donation in each of our names. I can't think of anyone else who would do this besides Phoebe, and she swears she didn't. Then it strikes me, maybe it's Buckethead. But how could he know my address, or my interest in Alaska, for that matter? Earl knows. But like me, Earl dresses in thrift-store clothing. He couldn't afford this—

besides, it's not his style. Maybe there is a Santa.

We sell our wares and collect the cash. People keep asking if there's going to be an after-Christmas sale, and will we have a Valentine's Day event and lilies for Easter. Phoebe sucks Hall's Mentholyptus and assures everyone there will be a sale every month or so, and instructs Nance to take names for a mailing list.

It's almost Christmas. The season when even the curmudgeonliest folks smile on their fellow man. I think of my stepmother and wish her well. All around us are the acres Sadie let go fallow, mulched, planted, watered, and fertilized with Florencio's special blend. Underneath that dirt, things are growing. In the spring, with luck, thousands of bulbs will sprout. Crocus, lilies, ranunculus, hyacinth, iris, tulip, and more. How can I be sure? Because I planted about three thousand of them myself and I have the calluses and aching knees to show for it.

# 14

## *Mothers and Other Strangers*

"OH, WOW, WILL YOU GUYS LOOK at these dessert forks," Beryl says as she hauls them out of the silver chest and holds them up in the candlelight, the evening of day two of the Christmas boutique. "They're probably a hundred years old! If I had silverware like this, I'd use it every day." She cuts a piece of the leftover chocolate cake James brought and lifts it to her mouth. "This is just what I need after today," she announces. "It's manna from heaven."

"To Sadie every day was some kind of holiday," Phoebe says, tipping her wineglass, shocked when she sees it's empty. "Hey, who's hogging the wine?"

"Here," Ness says, holding up an empty bottle. "Whoops. We need reinforcements if we're going to toast to my semi-good news. James?"

James has been coming over every night, bearing gifts like he's one of Santa's elves. Tonight he brought smoked salmon—my favorite—and some ugly brown almond-and-mushroom pâté for the leaf eaters. He opens bottle number two of Sadie's private reserve and begins pouring. "What good news would that be, Tall One?"

She looks him straight in the eye. "My Western Blot came back negative."

"Western what?"

"Western Blot. It's an HIV test. I'm positive, but I have yet to sero-convert."

"Oh. I had no idea you were..." his voice drops off as he gathers his composure. He leans over and kisses Ness on the forehead. "Well, may it remain negative for years to come."

"Thank you, James."

"That's wonderful," Beryl says, sighing. "Now you can relax."

Ness pets my dog, who doesn't know from tests and loves everyone equally. "Beryl, sweetie, the virus isn't going away. It's a real thing and it's with me for life. The doctor wants me to interview for some study group on investigational medication."

"It's still good news," Beryl says, but now her voice is less convincing. "We're going to take care of you, Ness. You'll see, it'll be like having three mothers." She looks at James. "And one very generous uncle. Thanks for bringing all these goodies, James. It's really starting to feel like Christmas."

"You are most welcome, Beryl Anne. I'll even sing some Christmas carols if you like."

"Um, that's okay," she says.

Beryl just cracks me up—she always thinks everyone is telling her the absolute truth. I give James a pinch.

"Well, all you mothers listen up," Ness says. "I like bananas in milk when I'm feeling blue, sometimes I like to watch the soaps, and chocolate, dear James, no matter what form it arrives in, will never be turned away."

Everybody laughs, but it's a weary sound. We're tired from the last few days—selling the Christmas goodies, planting bulbs, continually trimming the tree, and I must say, this tree is just about decorated to death. All the ornaments are on it. I mean, every last one that was in the box. Cowboys and Indians segue into the land of purple bulbs; enormous glass stars twirl among a myriad of various era Santas; and hand-carved farm animals race in and out of glittery snowflakes like they're fleeing a Wyoming snowstorm. If Sadie could see this, she would double over with laughter.

James passes me my refilled glass. In his eyes I see sentimental, snuggly feelings—and a vein of something else that runs deeper. Ness's news didn't freak him out, which is another point in his favor. He lifts his glass and says, "To good news everywhere, yes, Nancy?"

I know what he wants. I just don't know if I'm ready to give him that present.

Then he turns his back to me and begins rebuilding the fire. Suddenly I want to get in Rhoda and drive straight back to Rick. I'm sitting here in a jewel-red Calvin Klein sweater set and imported French jeans I paid a hundred and eighty dollars for on sale. I have my legs crossed very ladylike at the ankles, and I'm sipping my wine instead of gulping it the way Phoebe is doing. Inside, though, I feel as muddled as our tree. I can hear Rick singing "Merry Christmas, Baby," as he bends low to kiss my neck. Ness is HIV positive; no going back on that score. James is falling for me, and I suspect it's not the kind of falling that means one night of physical merriment and then all parties move on, sated and single. Add to all that, next week, just in time for a *really* merry Christmas, I will turn forty. The halfway mark. Middle-freaking-age.

There won't be a party, and not simply because I haven't told anyone when my birthday is. I quit trying to make birthdays a festive occasion a long time ago. Nothing could ever live up to the Barbie doll with the frosting skirt and the sterling silver charm bracelet I got when I was five. Too many birthdays after that my mother got drunk and dropped the cake or forgot entirely. Believe it or not, Rick was kind of sentimental about birthdays. He sent me flowers and sweet e-mail and once he even bought me a stereo for Rhoda. Included were several CDs he wanted, but they were wrapped. Forty. Where is my real estate, the career I went to college for, my golf-playing husband, my blond-headed babies? It's hard to shake the feeling they've been doled out by God to other people.

"Walk me to my car?" James asks me, holding his hand out.

"Sure," I say. "Duchess, come."

It's one of those starry Valley nights, so cold that any minute I expect to feel snowflakes on my face, but this part of California doesn't get snow. James's Mercedes is parked in front of the garage. When he opens his car door, Duchess hops in.

"Get out of there, you crazy dog," I tell her.

"Your dog wants to come home with me," James says. "How about you?"

I back away, and if I had a cigarette, I'd light it to have something to do. "My dog would lie down for the first guy who came along with a piece of baloney," I tell James.

He grins. "Her mother's holding out for steak, is that it?"

"Oh, my God. Enough food metaphors," I say, and step into the circle of his arms and let him kiss me. I hate being intelligent. My mind is analyzing my body's every reaction, warning my heart to be cautious.

James loosens his hold on me. He nestles his chin on top of my head, and sighs. It's amazing how well we fit. "What do you want for Christmas, Nancy?"

"That's simple. World peace."

"Let's see. In a size six?"

"Hey, do I look like a six to you?"

"God, a size four then. And if the store is out of world peace?"

"Oh, just pick me up a cure for AIDS, whatever color it comes in."

"Would if I could, dear heart. How long have you known about Ness's being HIV positive?"

"Only a couple of weeks. I guess she's known a long time. She kept it to herself, though. It's a damn shame. She doesn't deserve that."

"No one does."

We're quiet for a while, holding on to each other while Duchess whines at our feet. The fields look empty, but under the dirt, it's a regular soap opera. Florencio's worm castings, fertilizer, and those chilled-to-perfection bulbs eating it all up. It's hard to be merry what with Ness's news.

"Listen," James says. "Lots of parties going on this time of year. Want to be my date for all of them?"

"I'll have to wear the black dress. It's the only good one I've got."

"Fine with me. I rather like that black dress."

I squeeze his arm. "That's good."

"You know," he says, brushing my hair with his lips. "You're starting to really grow on me, Ms. Mattox."

"Hmm. How so? Like mold on a shower curtain?"

"Not exactly. More like new skin. I wonder how you feel about that."

"Well, I feel the way I feel, I guess. Sometimes I like it and other times it makes me nervous."

He lets go and holds me at arm's length. "I'm asking you seriously now. Would you like to come home with me tonight?"

Oh, God. Of course I would. What woman on the eve of her fortieth birthday doesn't want to tangle her legs in a new man's? Press her breasts to his hairy chest and feel all that magic, struggle to make it to the mountaintop along with him and not have any mess-ups along the way? But first sex is always so awkward. And it's as if he's moving faster than I am. If I add this stress to my birthday week I will come apart at the seams. "James," I say, and before I can utter another word he kisses me on the forehead, gets in his car, and turns the key in the ignition.

"I'll call you," he says.

I hold on to Duchess's collar and watch him drive away. I've probably just blown the greatest thing that ever came into my life, but I can't lie. Not to Phoebe's brother.

"AND THAT'S THE REALLY IRONIC PART of mothers," Phoebe is saying when I come back into the house.

"Oh, not mothers again, please," I say, settling myself on the floor where they are all lying propped up on pillows or snuggled under afghans. "Okay, I'll bite. What is the really ironic part, if not all of it?"

"Not being able to talk to them," she says, gesturing with her glass. "I mean, here's my mother, mourning a dead husband, and me with my first boyfriend, terrified, and we can't even discuss how love feels. How important it is, how awful it is when it gets yanked away from you. Nope, it's wheelchair Olympics or nothing with Rita. The tragedy of mothers and daughters is how much time is spent reminding each other of the rules instead of sharing information."

"My mother was easy to talk to," Beryl says. "At least what I remember of her."

"What do you remember, sweetie?" Ness says. "Tell us. We could all use a happy story tonight."

Beryl takes the throw pillows from the couch and arranges them around herself on the floor. She smiles, a sight so rare it's as if someone has lit her wick, causing her to glow from the inside out. "She read me poetry. 'The Highwayman came riding,' I remember that much. The sound of her voice put me right up alongside him on horseback through the woods. And she brushed my hair with her fingers, gently working out the knots, and never once told me it was ugly for being so red and curly. She said that redheads ruled the world, and for a long time, I believed her."

"She sounds like a dream," Phoebe says, fishing a lozenge out of her pocket.

Beryl takes a breath. "She is."

"How do you mean?" I ask.

"She killed herself when I was seven and away at Y camp. Guess so that I wouldn't have to deal with it up close, you know? Then my stepmother came on the scene and told me that having red hair predisposed a girl to round heels and pregnancy out of wedlock."

"What in the hell are round heels?" Ness asks.

"It's a euphemism. Means you tip—" She has to stop for an outbreak of hiccups. "Over easy. You know, for boys."

"That's a charming thing to say to a daughter," Phoebe says. "Can I go run over her with my wheelchair?"

"If you can find her. What about your mother, Nance?" Beryl asks. "Don't you have two cents to add?"

"Oh, you don't want to hear about Bunny," I say. "She's boring."

"The hell we don't," Ness says. "She must have had some good qualities; she certainly taught you high-tone taste in clothes."

"Fine," I say. "You want a story, I'll tell you one. Then that's it, subject closed. Somebody pass me the wine."

"Can't," Phoebe says, giggling. "I drank it all."

"You little piglet!"

"Here, I've had too much already," Beryl says, and hands me her half-finished glass.

I take a sip, but I've had so much it doesn't really register on my taste buds. I've always stuck to a two-glass limit, but somehow tonight, I'm forgetting that rule. "Well, this happened when we first moved to Cannon Beach. My mother just had to leave Decent Dennis because he was boring. Translation: he worked regular hours, saved money instead of spending every dime, and liked to eat at home instead of out every night..." I close my eyes and remember how it felt the first time I walked into that beach house. "Dennis gave it to us probably because he thought Bunny might one day come back to him. Ha! One thing she never did was look back. So, I'm thirteen years old, hauling a cardboard box of my things up the front steps of a summer cottage with graying cedar shingles and creaky wooden floors. It's so romantic, I think, you know, like a house from a gothic novel. Until the November nights when I realize the wall heater is meant for August. My mother finds me a lime-green dresser at the Salvation Army and cons some man into helping her lug it home. 'Look baby, with a little paint, this thing will be perfect for your room,' she says and the man puts his arm around her like he's sure he's going to score. I cover the dresser with a scarf and sit on my bed reading *To Kill a Mockingbird*. When Bunny's asleep, I sneak looks at photographs of my grandparents and imagine my grandfather is Atticus Finch. On the nights I hear her partying in the living room with people she meets downtown I organize my dresser drawers. Panties folded on the left. Socks in the middle. On the right side, I lay my two bras flat. When I wash one, I wear the other. Only problem is, it's so damp by the ocean they never completely dry.

"When Bunny starts having men spend the night, I sneak out my window and walk on the beach so I don't have to hear them. It's like I showed you in those pictures, Beryl, these amazing craggy rocks that jut up out of the sand like the hands of God. The coastline is cold and windy, clean, not filled with leftover flotsam from tourists like in Bayborough-by-the-Sea. One night I find a green glass fishing float with a cradle of twine knotted around it. I stand there holding it in my hands and imagine the direction it came from, Japan. Some fisherman's net got away from him, probably, and he lost his catch and had to return to port with an empty hold, but that was okay, his wife made him hot tea and rubbed his shoulders. I comb the beaches and collect agates by flashlight. My teacher calls my mother to let her know that I need more sleep, not to mention a winter coat. I'm resourceful; I steal one from the school lost and found. When all the other kids are collecting canned goods at Christmas for the needy, my teacher quietly gives me a bag of them to take home. And you know what? I take the cans because I'm that hungry. The day Social Services come to ask me questions, I give them Dennis's telephone number, and he tries to get them to let me go to him, but they won't because he isn't my real father; he wasn't even married to my mother. But whatever he says to Bunny works, because she pulls herself together for a while, and by then I've learned how to work the system. I baby-sit. I stay after school and help my teachers. I get straight A's in everything, and O's in citizenship, which is how I got my scholarship to college and learned to dress so well. Holy Mother of God, why am I dredging up this crap? I think I'll go to bed now. Goodnight, ladies."

"Wait," Phoebe says.

"I meant what I said, Pheebs, the subject is now closed."

"I just wanted to ask you something."

"Ask," I say impatiently.

365

"Do you—" She laughs, and I can tell she's more than a little buzzed. "Do you think *any* woman has a decent relationship with her mother? Or is that a myth? I mean, books, movies, the nonsense you read in women's magazines, is it all just one big fairy tale?"

"Well," I say, "they didn't call them the Grimm Brothers for nothing."

"Amen," Ness says, and shuts her eyes. In the next moment, she's snoring.

Beryl shakes her head, and reaches a hand up to pull the afghan higher.

For a while, nobody says anything. It's as if we've knitted ourselves together with our private thoughts. I study the twinkle lights illuminating the twisted branches of the crazily decorated tree and try not to think about my birthday, when a very strange thing happens.

Phoebe gets up out of her chair and walks to the table for the bottle of wine.

Ness is asleep, but Beryl and I aren't. We glance at one another and lie there open-mouthed as Phoebe fills her glass and makes her way back to her chair. It's only a few steps, but they were real. We've never really gotten to the brass tacks of her walking. I assumed she was in the chair because she had to be. But walk she did. I saw her thrust her legs forward with an awkward bowlegged pitch and make her way to the wine. I know it happened, because I can see it reflected in Beryl's eyes. And all of a sudden, I am stone cold sober.

"Bed," Phoebe says, like the word is a ten-pound weight, and wheels out of the room, her glass balanced between her knees.

WE CRASH RIGHT THERE ON THE RUG and that's where James finds us in the morning, when he lets himself in the doorway all bushy-tailed and amnesiac that I wouldn't go home with him last night. "What in the hell happened here?" he says in a whisper when I tell him to be quiet. "Even your dog looks hungover."

"Shh," I say. "Don't wake Ness and Beryl." I drag him to my room where the bed is still made. Duchess leaps onto the comforter as if to establish clear boundaries.

"Wait here," I say, as I grab my robe and trudge off to the bathroom Beryl and I share. "I have to take a shower and brush my teeth. My mouth feels like the inside of Verde's cage. And don't you dare turn on the radio. I need utter silence if I'm going to live through the noise of the shower."

"I'm not going anywhere until I hear the end of this story," James says, and settles down next to Duchess on my bed.

I RETURN WITH WET HAIR, minty breath, and a vow never to drink red wine again. James sits up on the bed and stares at me until I want to slap him. "Hey, I know what I look like without makeup," I tell him. "So stop reminding me already."

"You don't look so bad."

"I look a hundred."

"Give or take sixty years."

I give him a little smack on the arm.

"What happened after I left?"

"We talked and got thirsty. You saw the results."

"Where's Pheebs?"

"She went to her own bed, which was smart, because let me tell you, my back is killing me from sleeping on the floor." I reach around and try to massage the small of my back.

"Let me rub it for you."

"Ha. I'll just bet that's not all you'd try to rub."

"Can you blame me, Nance, what with you standing here all fresh and clean from the shower? I hardly slept a wink last night."

"Talk like that nets you a smile, buddy, nothing more."

"Nice smile."

"Stop it, James."

"No can do."

The smile leads to his stroking my face, and me leaning into his hand. We kiss for a while and sigh. Beneath us, the bed feels ready even if I do not. James urges me down on the pillows and rubs my back. I stifle the groan of relief I want to let out lest he misunderstand as men are wont to do. After five minutes, I reach back and stop his hand, pull it around me and we nestle like polite spoons, not touching anywhere too intimate. "Why wouldn't your mother come up here for Christmas?"

I can feel him shrug. "Probably because it pisses her off to see Pheebs living an adult life."

"But James, that's perfectly crazy. All you have to do is look at Phoebe to see how incredibly happy she is. How being in love with Juan has made her stronger. Last night, Beryl and I saw her walk."

James sits up and turns me over. He holds onto my shoulders. "She got out of the chair and walked?"

I nod. "Why? Is that against the rules?"

He reaches down and pulls the halves of my robe together so that they more adequately cover my breasts. Such a good boy it makes me want to rip the robe wide open and shimmy like a belly dancer. "I haven't seen her walk in fifteen years. Not that she can't do it, it's just that it embarrasses her."

"Must have been all the wine. We drank four bottles."

"And you look this good with a hangover? Jesus, I'm a lucky man, or at least I hope to be."

He has his hand on my neck, stroking. I slide it down a few inches until it's resting on my collarbone. "This might be a good time to press your luck," I say.

James does not need to be encouraged twice.

It is one thing to kiss a new man, and to feel his interest in my body, and another thing entirely to unlearn the man who was there before him. It's unbearably sad in some ways, how James's touch smears away Rick's, but I'm guessing all growth has to hurt, and suddenly I feel sorry for the flowers in our fields having to work so hard to push up out of the earth. Rick has short, skinny fingers; James's are longer, and thick. Rick is a masterful kisser, and he knows it; James likes to let me kiss him until he's all revved up and can't hold it in any longer and runs after me determined to race his own engine. Rick used to make me sit up and take off my clothes myself, which always made me feel strange, like I had to convince him to make love to me, but James's fingers hesitating on the tie of my robe are shaking with a definite urgency.

He runs his hand across my belly and stops just below my navel. I wait to see if he will move any farther. Then, with a deep breath, he takes his hand away and sits up. "What's wrong, James?"

"I'd prefer to continue this someplace else, where I don't have to be quiet or worry about my sister walking in on me."

I laugh. "Phoebe's not going to do that."

"One never knows, apparently." His stomach growls.

I tousle his hair and kiss his cheek. "Let's go eat breakfast."

"Then can we go to my place?"

"We'll see."

On the way to the kitchen, we stop at Phoebe's room, and I softly knock. "Ness?" I hear her say faintly.

I peek in the door. "No, it's Nancy and James. How's your head this morning?"

Phoebe is lying back against the bedclothes. She looks flushed, like maybe she has a fever again. She's breathing ragged, and I wonder if our knocking woke her from a dream. "Not too bad. But I think I have heartburn. It's the oddest thing, my fingers are numb, but only on this side." She tries to hold up her left hand, but doesn't get it two inches off the bed-spread and she's trembling.

"You need some antacid?"

"I guess I do."

James sits down on the bed and takes Phoebe's left wrist in his hand. "Any pain in your shoulders?"

"Maybe a little. It's the strangest thing, James, but the edges of my vision are blurry."

"How about chest pain?"

She looks away. "I don't know. Maybe there was earlier. I think I need to pee. Can you help me into my chair?"

James frowns at me and inclines his head toward the phone. "Call Lester," he says.

"James, she's got a hangover. All she needs is aspirin and rest."

"Bring me the aspirin and call Lester," he says. "Tell him I think Phoebe's having a heart attack."

# 15

## *Dr. Foxglove Pays a Visit*

*On Garden Failures*
*When a plant is ailing, consider planting foxglove nearby. Often called fairy bells or lady's thimbles, foxgloves were so named because the flowers resemble the fingers of a glove. Where they flourish, you can often find foxes' burrows. The cottage farmers of old knew what they were doing when they planted* Scrophulariaceae dig-italis. *Nothing stimulates growth and discourages disease like the common foxglove.*

SADIE'S JOURNAL HAS A CHAPTER on everything except letting go. Seems to me that whenever you crave shade, odds are the day will be so sunny you'll be drenched in sweat before ten A.M., as if God enjoys playing jokes. I suppose it's one way to keep a person tethered to the planet. Something along the lines of: Sorry, you can't go now, you haven't finished your work.

"Where's the complaint department?" I ask the orderly who straps me down to the bed in the ER while his fellow gangboy pumps up my blood pressure cuff so tight I'm sure it's going to sever my arm. He acts as if he doesn't hear me, and a nurse cuts away my nightie and begins plastering my chest with nitroglycerin cream. Now she's attaching those awful octopus suckers to my skin so she can wire me for an EKG. "Excuse me," I tell her, "I was rather fond of that nightgown. What's the replacement policy at this hospital?"

For that I get a stick in my hand and an IV, an oxygen mask, and two doctors arguing over the heart monitor report. Six medical people in all, dedicated to working on little old me.

Must be a full moon, because everybody and his brother seems to be having a medical crisis here in CHOP's state-of-the-art, open twenty-four-hours emergency room. Of course all the cardiac patients are in the back with me, but every once in a while I hear the nurses yelling at each other and that's how I find out what's going on. *Get X rays stat; call somebody down from Ortho; four units typed and cross-matched; pump this guy's stomach*...will Lester ever be pissed off that I got him out of bed at this hour. Right now, Juan is beginning his daily route. What with Christmas nearly upon us, his van's probably loaded up to the gills. He's got his cup of Starbucks on the seat beside him; he loves to whisper in my ear that his blood type is latte—I shiver when he rolls the *l*. I haven't decided what to give him for Christmas. Is a leather jacket too much? I think we've moved beyond CDs and gift certificates. He's singing along to the carols on the radio, because winter be dammed, Juan Nava is one sunny dude. That man with the perfect butt for some strange reason loves me. Last time we were in bed together, I confessed my chocolate sauce fantasy and he got this look on his face that let me know it sure as shoelaces wasn't going to remain a fantasy much longer.

That's right, Phoebe, concentrate on sex at a time like this.

I wonder if I can blame sex for getting me into this trouble. But Lester said I could. He used the words "frequent and vigorous." He said there was no reason...

"Phoebe?"

James is standing by my bed, looking so worried I want to get up and let him lie down for a while, but it's as if my limbs are made of lead. So handsome, that brother of mine, if only I could erase that frown line between his eyes. I want to tell him how it makes him look like an owl, and that he should leave now to avoid the carnage, but now that my heart's settled down to a calmer rhythm, the nurse is giving me a sedative. The nitro is making my heart beat hard and precise, like one of Hercules Hampton's drum solos, but everything else seems to be moving in slow motion. My lips are dry and stick together when I try to form words. Has James seen Sadie's owls in the barn? *Tyto alba,* Beryl calls them. Every year when the conditions are right, they make babies. Well, if anyone asks me, it seems like conditions are as right as they are going to get. Have yourself some merry little babies, James. Make

Nance's dreams come true. From now on, your sister will be out of sight... I'm pretty sure that's how the words go.

"If this were a blockage or an uncompromising attack, we'd do an immediate bypass," the ER doctor tells James. "But things look relatively stable, and her enzymes aren't so elevated that I'm eager to cut. The infarction is one thing, and the arrhythmia we've gotten under control with meds. It's the sound of her lungs that has me concerned. After the ultrasound and X rays, I'll be able to tell you more. She'll definitely be staying with us for a while..."

A headache descends courtesy the nitro cream. All I can do is retreat far behind my closed eyes. Like a movie screen, on the backs of my eyelids I see all kinds of drama. There's Beryl with her stack of books, her curly red hair falling into her too-serious face, Verde pinned to her shoulder like an X-rated Girl Scout sash. Who can blame him for cussing out the world? Beryl with the saddest mother story of all. If I were a doctor, I'd revive her mom, give Ness a total body blood transfusion, and hypnotize Nance so she could forget the TV-addicted unworthy journalist. Then I'd sprinkle my heart with Florencio's special fertilizer mix so overnight it could grow new chambers so instead of spilling things out, it could hold my wonderful, amazing life in.

"Double pneumonia," I hear somebody say.

Now the screen shows my brother James, looking exhausted. He should go home. And Lester. Where have you been, Les? I want to ask. How's the crappiest golfer on the peninsula doing today? When he peels my hospital-issue gown back, James doesn't turn away. I feel faint with the smells in this place—so much alcohol. Cold on my breasts. Oh, who cares who sees the soft pink pads of flesh that drive Juan Nava crazy with lust? They're skin; that's all they are. Behind my breast is the most important concern, my heart, tapping out its nitro-assisted rhythm. I feel so tired; I'm surprised it's still got the energy to beat.

"Dammit, Pheebs," is all James says, over and over. Is this some kind of code? Damn what, exactly? That alcohol smell for one.

I'd like my chair. I need to go to the bathroom.

*Use one of the chairs here.*

But they're too big. I like my chair. I'm used to it.

*Then get up and walk. Heard you did that the other night.*

Okay, fine, I'll shut up about the chair. Nice way to talk to the wounded, whoever you are. See, I'm resting quietly. I just have one more question. James, are you sleeping with Nancy? Please say yes and I can die happy.

My brother takes my hand in his and pets it. I feel his fingers rubbing my palm. Winter skin, tight and dry. He says nothing. Doesn't have to. But I think I hear a voice tell me *not yet, but soon, I hope. And pray he doesn't blow this one, Phoebe, because he's finally met a woman he wouldn't mind sleeping with for the rest of his life.*

I must really be out of it because I know I'm alone.

"Phoebe," James says. "I called Juan."

Oh, no. I don't want that. Yes, I love him, and yes, if I'm on my way out his is the face I want to remember seeing last, but it's wrong to put him through this right now. Besides, he has to work. Bring me Duchess—smelly old carrot-breath. With her solid Labrador warmth under my hand, I know I won't get any more needle-crazy bloodhounds. And let's put Verde on the PA system. Four-star cussing would be a vast improvement from the mysterious doctor codes and pages. By the way, in case anyone cares about what I think, if I'm going to die, I'd prefer to do it at home, like Sadie did. If anybody's listening.

"Go to sleep now, Phoebe. Rest."

I can't. I'm afraid if I do, I'll stop breathing.

"PHOEBE. WAKE UP, PHOEBE. We need you to wake up, wake up, wake up."

I'm ignoring James. He's lied to me before. Saying he heard Santa on the roof or that one time he got into my Easter candy and ate the ears off the bunnies. Besides, he's a grown man. What earthshaking reason requires my immediate participation? They've got me peeing into a bag, attached to a machine so I don't even have to breathe for myself, and on top of all that, I'm sedated deep enough to float away at any given moment. Later, buddy.

I remember making the mermaid mobile, the ladies with their legs tucked into fish bottoms. How my fingers knew to shape them. How my tears dripped onto the clay. Sadie, floating away on the tide a little more each time she woke. I cried so hard when she wasn't looking. Did God send me Juan to make up for losing Sadie? Sadie and I used to read poetry out loud. Emerson. She made me memorize poems.

> *Though thou loved her as thyself*
> *As a self of purer clay*
> *Though her parting dims the day*
> *Stealing grace from all alive*
> *Heartily know*
> *When half-gods go,*
> *The gods arrive.*

I thought that was so beautiful. Now each word stabs me in the heart. Bleeding heart. *Dicentra spectabilis.* The flower looks like a bleeding heart until you turn it upside down, then, no joke, you'd swear it's a woman sitting in her bathtub.

Sadie. I idolized her. Was she only a half-god in my life? I'd like to join her, but I'd lay odds she won't let me. I can just hear her now: *You have far too much to live for. Juan and the girls. My flower farm. You have to watch out for your brother, too, because he's going to marry Nancy and you know how headstrong she can be. Yes, they'll be happy eventually, but things are going to get off to a stormy start. All really great love affairs do, you know. We're all so afraid of letting others see the true us. We hide under makeup and droll stories and wheelchairs and too much alcohol—ahem—what exactly did you think you were doing drinking all my Ravenswood?*

What a crappy daughter I've been to my mother. I should be arrested. Whoops. Guess my heart already did that for me.

If my heart's not the problem, then what is?

My attitude.

Speaking of false gods. Sadie never should have married Ken in the first place. He was a playboy with a fat little wallet and a wandering penis and absolutely no idea what to do with his life. He certainly did not approve of her having her own. What she should have done is had an affair, and waited for Howard, who was the right man for her, even if he died too young.

Get a grip, Phoebe. This sad tale is supposed to make you want to live?

The great thing about dying is you get to see everybody again. Fences get mended. I'd see my father happy instead of overworked. Maybe he's taken up tennis, plays with Arthur Ashe, who also died too young of AIDS. Please don't let Ness die. I should be nicer to my mother. Who knows how much time she has left? Maybe that's what makes mothers so nudgy when it comes to their daughters' lives, the enormous fear of leaving them behind.

I may be immobile, but I'm not brain-dead.

Maybe it's time I got up out of that chair like I did the other night and started walking full time. Would that heal my heart? Do I want it healed? There's a whole big world out there, Juan's always telling me. He has such plans! Maybe he won't care how it is my legs move. Maybe he'll leave. In heaven, I imagine dancing is how everybody motors around. You need practice to be a really good dancer. Juan wants a dance partner. We all do.

"YOU LOOK SO MUCH BETTER," Beryl says as she sits in the chair near my bed. I know it's her—she smells like soap. Always taking a shower, Beryl is. Says birds are dirty business. She says, "Your face isn't so puffy today. And you have color in your cheeks. I just wish you'd wake up. Open your eyes, Phoebe. Look at me."

Into my hand she presses something—oh, I get it. A feather. If I wasn't on a respirator, I could say thank you. If I try to move, one or the other of the monitors sounds an alarm, and that in turn affects my heart rate. Then she's gone, and it's the whoosh whoosh of the respirator. On my movie screen, I see a stack of library books with feathers for bookmarks. I should have told Beryl thank you, not just for the feather, but also for everything. Without her, our house is lopsided, out of whack, like bad *feng shui*.

OPIUM PERFUME. The sound of good Italian heels on linoleum. Nance. "Phoebe, I've taken care of the garden chores, so don't worry. Florencio has got us all set with a schedule and I'm planning our February sale, Valentine's Day, potted ferns, ivy trained over wire hearts, the whole nine yards. Rosa sends her best. James is covering expenses until you're well enough to sign checks. Maybe when you get home you should consider having him put on the account, just to be on the safe side. Mr. Colburn thinks it's a wise idea. He sent flowers last week, but they wilted so I put them in to compost. Rebecca Roth sent a card. She says don't stress about the show idea, just get well. Duchess sends her love, as does Leroy. He's missing your brushing him something fierce. Phoebe, I'm sorry we let you drink so much that night. I knew you weren't feeling a hundred percent and I should have said something because you were scaring me. I don't know why I didn't. I'll regret it until the day I die. Jesus, have mercy. I haven't asked for much and I take back every awful thing I ever thought about Rick Heinrich if you will please make Phoebe wake up."

Movie-screen Nance: She's wearing her glasses instead of her contacts, going after life with her usual clipboard efficiency, walking her faith like a tightrope—she would make me laugh if I could remember how to.

NESS SITS BY THE BED for a long while without speaking. I know it's her because of how her fingers feel against my arm. Latex instead of her usual warm, moist skin. "It's supposed to be me lying there, not you," she whispers from behind a face mask. "Lester says your immune system is more compromised than mine. Did I give you some bug just by living with you? God, I'm so sorry. I have everybody from here to San Jose praying for you. I'm going to church every single day. Granny Shirley says any minute she expects to see pigs fly across the sky. I'll sprout wings myself if that's what it takes to get you back here. By the way, I've started my meds. Lester got me into a drug study so I get a lot of stuff free. So far my only side effects are loose caboose, if you know what I mean. Phoebe? Please don't leave me. I'm scared to be sick without you. Wake up and check out these flowers, will you? David Snow sent them. You can always count on a gay guy to pick out really incredible blooms. We're getting to be good friends, David and me. Imagine—a black cowgirl and a gay Hollywood dude. Guess HIV levels all the playing fields."

The tall black cowgirl transformed into the little girl who got rooked out of her candy money by a gang of kids who didn't mean to be cruel, just wanted sweetness in their meat-and-potato lives. I'll never forget that Ness is the one who cracked open the door of my heart by showing me hers. Hearts being the stupid, fallible muscles that they are. Oh, is she gone already? Was she really here? There was something I needed to tell her. I can almost remember. It was something from Sadie's journal, something about the creek...

JAMES STANDS IN THE DOORWAY for hours, it seems like. He doesn't have to speak; I hear his thoughts. *I'm sorry I put your shoes in the toilet tank all those times and for tearing the heads off your Barbies and I apologize for being such a shit about the realtor and you can have the Mercedes back because I feel like an idiot every time I drive it, like people are saying, Hey, everybody take a gander at the big chubby nerd in the yellow Mercedes, pretending to have class along with his newly inherited money. I suppose a Mercedes is less ridiculous than the Jeep, but I'll donate it to charity if it means I get you back, Phoebe. I want my sister to be okay more than anything in the world, even more than I want Nance, but I've got to admit I want Nance pretty bad. Pheebs? If I take a real job, like, say the hardware department at Home Depot, will you believe me? If I don plaid golf pants and do a soft shoe in the hallway, will you agree to come back?*

James, I wish I knew how to answer that question.

AT NIGHT, when I'm supposed to be sleeping, Sadie comes to visit. I don't know if all ghosts wear green mermaid tails and hover like mist, but my aunt does. She touches down on my bed and plays with the mechanism that self-adjusts every fifteen minutes, so I get adequate blood flow and won't develop bedsores and never manage any real restful sleep. She weaves columbines into my hair and sings songs about unfaithful crows. She bitches that these motorized contraptions aren't any more comfortable than regular beds, so where is all this supposed twenty-first century technology?

One night, we play a card game called Spite and Malice. *It's very old,* she tells me, *and the rules are apt to change at any time. You have to pay attention, Phoebe. You have to think two moves ahead of you, and remember what cards have been played. The jack is worth extra points, but only when he faces right...*

I don't want to concentrate anymore. I'd rather sleep.

*Sleeping is for babies,* she informs me. And leaves without telling me a story that night.

*UP, OUT OF THIS BED and on your feet. Now.*

Sadie? Don't be mad. I'm tired is all. Let me take a nap, okay? I'll walk tomorrow. I promise.

*I don't believe you, Phoebe. I can tell when you're lying. And by the way, who said you could borrow my mink?*

Excuse me, who left it in the closet?

*You should have asked.*

You shouldn't have left it behind if you didn't want it worn. Doesn't it look terrific on Nancy?

*I suppose. But I think it's really going to be smashing on your daughter. They'll be back in style then. Collector's pieces. No more of this fur controversy.*

You mean *Nance's* daughter.

*No, sweetie, I don't.*

SPRUCE AFTERSHAVE. Coffee breath. I want to rise up and meet it, but I'm trapped here in a body that only wants to perform the basic functions. "I want you to wake up, Phoebe," Juan says firmly. "Come back to me. I can't sleep, I can't eat, I drop boxes, and my boss keeps threatening me with a desk job. All I do is kneel in the church and pray for your heart to grow strong and the pneumonia to take a hike. I'm making bargains with God, Phoebe. I'm just about ready to join the priesthood. Don't make me spend Christmas by myself, or worse yet, with your roommates. All their crying, I can't believe it. Those women must be ninety percent saltwater. My mother's praying for you, too. Please Phoebe, I got you a ring. It's not a very big diamond, but it's a nice one, clear, with no flaws. I want to slide it on your finger and ask you to be my wife. Wake up, okay?"

This concept of rings intrigues me. A circle of precious metal with no end. Diamonds, on the other hand? I suppose some other species could rightly call them rocks. And Christmas, well, it shouldn't be unimportant, but how many people share the holiday with God is what I'm wondering. What it's about is the birth of the baby Jesus; what *everything's* about is babies. One after another, they arrive clean and perfect in this dirty world, and simply by doing so, they make tiny alterations to the infinite plan. Sadie said a daughter—Juan's and mine. Lester said *Maybe* not advisable but certainly possible. Do I really want to go all the way back for that big an if?

"I love you," Juan says. "*Madre de Dios*, I don't know what else to say."

WHERE HAVE YOU BEEN, I ask Sadie when I feel her hovering by my pillow.

*Steeplechasing.*

So, how was it? I send out into the constant dark, night, day, I don't know. The nurses check my vitals every four hours. Worth blowing me off after your big announcement?

*It was glorious, Phoebe. I rode Nijinsky and Howard chose Misty of Chincoteague. The horse clears the fence and you're literally flying.*

You're insane, Sadie. Misty was an Island

pony. She couldn't jump a two-foot fence let alone an eight-foot one.

*Ah, but this is Heaven, where all things are possible.*

Like fibbing to your niece about her impending daughter?

*Well, you see, that's the one annoying thing up here. We're not allowed to lie. Remember the Ten Commandments?*

Most of them.

*Turns out She meant them.*

She?

*He, She; it pleases me to think of God as a She, but God can just as easily be a He. Imagine a union beyond opposites, that's what God's most like. His vision reaches beyond both sides to see* all *sides. Nothing to stress yourself over, but remember God's there, and that God is love.*

Listen, I need to know a little bit more about this daughter, Sadie. See, the way I look at it, if I die while I'm having her, or early in her life like Beryl's mother did to her, there's no real point in returning. If I get to be a mother, I want the whole nine yards of it. That's only fair—to her.

*Listen to you, greedy-guts. Maybe you should try making peace with your own mother before worrying about something that hasn't happened yet.*

That's not the subject at hand.

*Baloney, it isn't. Always have to have the guarantee in front of you, don't you? Nothing's set in cement, my dear. When it's your time to go, you go.*

Can you tell me at least if I live through the

birth? I don't want Juan saddled alone with a daughter. Not that he'd do a bad job; it's just that a girl needs a mother.

*And an aunt?*

Yes.

*Well, yours will have a mother and three aunts. Actually, four, but we haven't met her yet.*

Now what are you talking about?

*Your new roommate. Now don't ask me any more questions. Just trust me that she's on her way. And she's bringing the strangest animals with her. They'll fit in nicely with Duchess and Leroy. This woman and her pets—they've had such a hard time, it's very sad. It's terrible what people do to one another, don't you think? I mean, I lined my walls with good art, I traveled all over the world, I slept with some great men, I ate five-star meals and skied the black diamond trails, and the sad still outweighed the happy in the long run. Not that I'm complaining. It's just that looking at it from over here I can't help but shake my head at how far we go out of our way to unnecessarily mess it all up.*

Where is "here," exactly?

Sadie laughs, and silver clouds fill the room. *I thought you knew.*

Well, I don't. So far as I'm concerned, you're a voice, and sometimes this shimmering green ghost at the end of my uncomfortable and expensive bed.

*Oh, the mermaid tail. I wear it especially for you. But I have to tell you, Phoebe, it makes Howard so frisky sometimes I wear it for him, too.*

Sadie, stop joking around. Where are you?

*In your blood, you goose. Pushing up through the fields you girls so lovingly tend. In the shake of Leroy's tail every time he bucks, bless his horse-size heart. Traveling the waters of Bad Girl Creek, which, by the sound of your mouth lately, you've been drinking from a little too often. Don't get too comfortable there.*

That's what I've been trying to remember. The creek. I have to know—how did it get the name?

*Oh, you want me to tell you that story, do you? You think that just because you asked, I should just give it to you?*

Well, how did you learn it?

*When he thought I'd earned the right to know, Florencio sat me down and told me. You want to know the story, ask him yourself.*

Damm it, Sadie, tell me now.

*I will not. So what's it going to be, my love? Are you going to take Juan's ring? Get up? Walk down the aisle? Develop stretch marks? Be the maid of honor at James and Nancy's wedding?*

I'm thinking about it.

*Don't think too long, Phoebe.*

Sadie? Will you still visit me if I decide to go back?

The respirator whooshes in and out like the tide. My heart beats. From somewhere far away, I can hear a person coughing painfully, choking on the very ordeal of breathing. That breath—it's faint, but it's got a melody, almost like a Christmas carol, a song of faith. Whose, I wonder?

"CHRISTMAS IS OVER, Phoebe," James tells me in my fog. "Your packages are gathering dust. Those roommates of yours won't let me put them in the closet and they refuse to take down the tree. They spend every day in the garden, transplanting, weeding, culling, making hanging baskets. The greenhouses are overflowing with ferns and ivy, thanks to Nance's plan for the February sale. Me? Mostly I wander around feeling useless. Oh, I'm doing your books, and I've made some choice investments for you. Maybe that's my role here, to keep moving, because you know how it is if one person stops in the middle of a crisis. The bottom falls out of everything and the tears won't stop."

Crying. The movie-screen James is able-bodied, a teensy bit overweight, impossibly handsome, with the kind of lines in his face that make me want to reach out and trace them with my fingers. Back in the real world, I used to see old people on the street and feel this moment of panic that each one of them was our future, come to fetch us right that moment when I hadn't the chance yet to live out the present. James. It's an old-fashioned name, like a guy who wears suspenders might have. But he never was a Jimmy, not even a Jimbo. James sits in the chair next to my bed and folds a white handkerchief with his initials embroidered on it into my hand. "Feel that?" he says. "J.D.T. I'm your brother and

I need you here in the real world." Sometimes he changes the channel on my television set, watches a talk show for ten minutes, or turns the sound down low and lets the news pass over us, quick and hard, like a hailstorm. This is the first time in our lives we've spent so much time together without getting into a fight. I listen to him say the numbers out loud as he balances his checkbook. I hear the click of the Chapstick lid as he pops it off to swipe my dry mouth and smell its waxy no-scent. I feel him squaring up the corners of my bed. Where did he learn to get them so perfect? How kind he is to the nurses who tend my intake and output, going so far as to bring them pastries some mornings. But the nurses who take too long to see to my needs he bullies like he's prodding extremely slow cattle.

"Those EKG pads need to be changed every six to eight hours, I'm telling you. If they stay on any longer, when you go to remove them, a layer of skin comes off. I'm setting my watch now. I'll remind you in an hour."

Yes, Mr. DeThomas. Yes, Every brother.

He hovers over me, making sure everything within the realm of his control is done right. Funny that I never noticed how fierce and fighterly he could be. We were always feuding about something or another. I think he didn't know how to grieve for Daddy, and I know he was jealous of Sadie because I wanted to spend all my free time up there instead of with him. I relive the last few steps I took before I ended up here tethered to the machines, and then I feel it, moving in the wind. Someone has hung one of my clay ladies mobiles to my IV pole. Movie screen of all their faces. For the first time, I see that my model for the ladies isn't Sadie, or even me, as James suggests. It's our mother.

IF I THOUGHT LOSING MY AUNT the first time around was hard, I'm living the lesson that things can always get worse. The emptiness Sadie leaves behind is cavernous. I figure she bailed out on me on purpose. How else do you provide a concrete example of the only possible solution to fill the void—which is going back, finding the courage to face my future?

The only trouble is, I'm not entirely sure which direction that is anymore. It's very weird to have missed Christmas. *Waking up is hard to do,*—oh, this is another song. So much of my brain is wasted on memorizing songs I never danced to.

Sadie once said that expectation was the only intelligent reason to embark upon a garden in the first place. The desire to know what will bloom next was indeed good enough reason to put spade to earth. But the flowers don't need us. They don't really console people who've lost loved ones. They remind us that life goes on, that's all. Ness, Nance, Beryl, and me, we've irrigated Sadie's dreams with our sweat. We've sold the poinsettias she used to tend, planted new bulbs in her old shoe-mulched earth. No matter what, they'll give the coming spring color and life. We've siphoned the water of Bad Girl Creek, irrigated herbs and vegetables. What a terrible waste not to see it all the way to harvest. This is what finally convinces me to wake up, I think. I may have given up Christmas, but I'm not letting the sickness gods take my spring. I want the scent of roses in my nose in the morning, and hot purple irises waving like flags in the fields at midday. I need the afternoon anthem of Florencio's whistle as he bends to the earth to correct whatever latest mistake we've made trying to help. I want the heady scent of orange blossoms on nights so clear stars poke through the firmament showing the undercarriage of heaven. I want my life back, so I begin to push my way through the fog and start scrabbling up through the dirt toward something. Dammit all, I want to see tulips.

"WELL, HELLO," LESTER ULLMAN SAYS as he sits on my bed and taps a bubble from the IV line. It's late afternoon, and the room is dim, just when I'd like it to be bright. "Nice to see your eyes open for a change. If your throat's still sore from the tube I can order you a painkiller."

"Don't you dare," I rasp. "I want my pain, and the awful hospital broth and the scratchy ten-dollars-a-box Kleenex I'm paying for."

Lester clasps my hand. My gruff physician,

393

who never shows emotion except on the golf course, has watery eyes. Allergies? "You scared the life out of me, Phoebe."

"Scared myself a little, too."

"We're going to have to make some changes, if you want me to keep on being your doctor."

"Like what, exactly?"

He sighs. "Devise a better exercise program for one, change your diet, for another. And no more alcohol, and more sleep."

"Whatever you say, Lester, so long as I still get to have sex."

He stands up and crosses to my window, which holds a view I have yet to see. "I couldn't get you to give that up?"

"Not a chance."

He opens the blinds and the room is filled with the colors of the approaching sunset filtered through the twisted pine trees common to the peninsula. Never have I seen anything so beautiful. I feel the warmth in every cell of my body. "We'll make sure that sex is a part of things," he says. And then, distractedly, "It's stopped raining."

I have the feeling I'll never bitch about rain again. "Lester?"

He turns. "Yes, Phoebe?"

"How close did I come to not coming back?"

He shoves his hands into the pockets of his white coat. "You're here now. Why be morbid?"

I move one arm experimentally, and crinkle my fingers. It makes me tired. "I had the oddest dreams."

"You were comatose."

"Wow. In a real coma?"

"Real enough to keep me awake too many nights to be any good for my golf game."

"Don't blame your rotten golf game on me. So you're saying it was pretty close?"

"Close enough, Phoebe."

I'm still so weak that just looking at his white coat and bushy eyebrows feels like an assault on the senses. Good, but tiring. And making words hurts, too, but it's the kind of pain that lets you know you have muscles. Later on, there will be time to tell him about my dreams and visitors, to get confirmation on all that strange stuff floating around my skull. I know what Lester will say—the effects of chemistry on the brain, forget about it, but I won't. I turn my head and see a feather on a stack of unopened cards. It's cussing-parrot green. And someone has brought me Sadie's gardening journal.

"There're a lot of people who are going to want to see you, Phoebe. Of course, I'm for limiting visitors to begin with, and this time you're going to follow my rules, right? You get one visitor today. So. Anyone in particular at the top of your list?"

I don't have to think this over. It's got to be my brother. But for one second, I have this burning desire to say Florencio. "James," I say. "Then the girls, then Juan. Juan is patient, but I know that once I see him, I won't be able to let him go. Thank you, Lester."

"Thank God," he says, and like a dad, kisses me on the forehead.

When he leaves, I use all my effort to lug Sadie's journal off the table and to my chest. I hold it tight, this amulet full of quotes and stories and nonsense and practical wisdom of flowers. For the time being, it's as near as I can get to the farm, my farm.

*Ness*

# 16

## *Waiting to Sero-Convert*

WHEN PHOEBE COMES HOME from the hospital, she's supposed to take it easy, rest in bed, get her strength back. Instead she gets all fired up to talk to Florencio, convinced that only he knows the story of where the creek got its name, that Sadie has told her this when she was in the coma. I take her hands in mine and stare her straight in the eye, but it doesn't seem to be crazy talk, more like determined little Phoebe trying to get to the truth of something that is bugging her no end. "It'll keep," I say, over and over, but she won't let up. So as soon as the weather seems warm enough, I wheel her down to the greenhouse where Florencio is working and she asks him straight out.

"Tell me the story, Florencio. Sadie said only you knew."

He sets down his wrenches and pile of machinery. "You supposed to be out of bed?" he says, looking kindly and old, but underneath it all, fearful, like any minute someone in uniform is going to ask for his immigration card.

"Please. I have to know."

He gets to his feet and I can hear his bones creak. Why the man doesn't retire is beyond me. Surely after all these years he'd rather be in Mexico, where there's sun instead of this endless fog, not to mention his relatives. "*Si*, I tell you, but only if you promise to go back up to the house."

"Deal."

I push her chair up the gravel walkway and into the front room, get her settled on the couch with a comforter, and put a pan of milk on to heat for Mexican-style hot chocolate. Pretty soon, Florencio knocks at the door, kicks the dirt from his boots, and comes inside. He takes off his hat and sits on the edge of a wingback chair and looks around the room while Phoebe waits. I add the cinnamon to the chocolate and bring it to him in a china cup and saucer. *"Gracias,"* he says, and takes a deep breath of the steam rising from the cocoa's surface, a forced smile playing across his face.

As poor as my Spanish is—mostly I picked it up around horse people—this is what he tells us.

"What is water but life itself? Men come and go on earth, but water, she continues. This creek

of ours, the Bad Girl, she's not even big
enough to make the map, but she has her
seasons, *verdad?* Like a girl growing into her
adolescence," he says, and it's the oddest
thing, but he stops to take out his handkerchief and wipe a tear from his cheek.

Phoebe and I look at each other, and I
wonder if we've opened some awful kind of hor-
nets' nest by forcing Florencio's hand this way.

"Sometimes she gets too big for her britches,"
he continues.

It is strange then, how Florencio's face
lights up, like he's telling a folktale to a flock
of rapt children, like it's mandatory that he
keep us listening, or maybe that's the only way
he can get through the telling. His calloused
hands spread out in front of him, and the
cocoa sits in the cup on the table, cooling. His
lined face is so animated it's like he's an actor
in a play.

"One hot summer day this headstrong girl
didn't want to stay at home and grind corn into
meal for her mother. No, the work was necessary, but the day was sweltering, and the creek
was always a cool place to go. In summer the
water was shallow and pleasant, so the girl ran
quickly to the creek's edge. She hid in the tall
horsetails where no one would ever think to
look for her. So clever, that young one! Such
hopes her parents had for her. Pretty soon
though, the rocks on the bottom of the creek
looked so pretty, shining there like golden pennies, that she had to lie on the bank and take
a closer look at them. Then, creeping closer

still, toward the surface of the cool, clear water. Oh, this was nice, certainly better than grinding dusty cornmeal, but then as the sun drew higher overhead, the brave little girl decided she wanted to drink from the creek, and so understandably, she had to put her face into the water. Just a little, then a little deeper. And then presently, she opened her eyes underwater and what do you know, the pretty stones weren't shiny pennies at all, but the tiny faces of many other girls, all beckoning her to join them. You see, they, too, were bad girls who had betrayed their mothers, and it was lonely there, in the shadowy life on the other side of the water. 'You're already one of us,' they told her, 'you've already come halfway here. Why not slide all the way under the water and become one of us forever?' And so she did.

"Now you might wonder how it is the mother of this girl knew the creek had taken her daughter. Well, it's not because she found her daughter's clothing on the bank, or a special doll, or any particular token left behind, but because when the creek swelled in winter, when the water ran especially high, she could hear her daughter's crying, begging to come home and help to grind the corn. And in the summer, when the water was so low that the animals came to drink, she swore she could hear her daughter laughing, teasing her mother to come find her."

Florencio stopped then, took hold of the edges of his hat and gripped it. He looked up

399

at Phoebe. "So you see, Phoebe, this is why Rosa and I chose to stay in the Valley, even when Sadie passed away, and we could have gone back to Mexico to be near my *madre*. Better to be near Bad Girl Creek, to be near to our daughter, near her memory. *Comprende?*"

Our eyes meet for a moment, and I decide right then and there to leave Leroy to Florencio now, not when I die. He sets down his hat and goes to Phoebe, who's crying, and he makes her drink the cocoa.

LATE AT NIGHT when I can't settle down, I design my square for the AIDS quilt. First off, I stitch a black satin horse racing across a field of embroidered flowers—no poinsettias, poppies mostly, and one purple orchid. Then, with thimbles on both thumbs, I appliqué a green patchwork parrot in the corner. Above him are the typographical symbols for swear words in some kind of metallic thread that shimmers and a gold lamé dog. Along the borders, in red letters, I sew Jake's name first, then my own, and next to that, David Snow's. With silver thread as fine as a spider's web, I fashion the chrome spokes of a wheelchair wheel spinning out of sight. Last, in blues and browns, I piece the winding, wet path that connects everything together, Bad Girl Creek, because now that I know how she got her name, I see that it can't be any other way.

FLORENCIO'S COURAGE gives me my own to say things I used to swallow down, like what I'm about to tell David.

"Mr. Snow," I say as I stand in the doorway to his house, fumbling with my hoof pick. "I'm not saying you're a lousy horse owner, it just seems crazy to have me out every six weeks to shoe animals that are sitting idle and growing flabbier by the day. Look at that bay. He used to have muscles, now his butt's sunk into his bones."

David looks up from his computer. In the light of the monitor, his face appears drawn. I can tell that what I've just said is contributing to his bad day, but hell, somebody needed to say it. "You're right. I should sell them."

"For Pete's sake, who said anything about selling your horses? All you need to do is ride them once in a while."

He taps his hand against the mouse. "And what happens if I fall and break something? Will you take care of the horses then?"

"You know I would."

He rubs his hand over his handsome face. "All the same, I'd prefer just to look at them. Aren't they beautiful enough without saddles on their backs?"

A few weeks after Phoebe got out of the hospital, David came down with shingles, which he informed me more than once was "Dante's eighth circle of hell." During the worst of it, the most he would allow me to do for him was feed the horses. I brought homemade soup over anyway, and fresh vegetables from the greenhouse, because even when you don't feel like eating, the sight of a ripe tomato or a green pepper in your fruit basket can be cheerful. When the pain got so he couldn't lie down comfortably, I telephoned Lester. Lester explained how acupuncture was proven to be effective in such cases so I called Alice, Phoebe's physical therapist, and she knew of one fellow who made house calls and was okay with HIV. After only three treatments David's up and around now, starting back to work. He's still snippy about my butting in, but he said thank you for the acupuncturist. Friends have the right to nudge.

"Horses are beautiful to look at, I'll grant you that, David, but riding them's even more fun. No matter what your HIV status, a person needs to have fun."

He smiles wearily. "Oh, I see. Now I get to hear all my lectures repeated back to me."

"Something like that."

"What if I pay you to exercise them? Will you go away and let me work?"

I sigh. "Mr. Snow, it's a good thing I'm a Christian woman, or I could take advantage of you flapping open your wallet every ten minutes. Sorry, you're not gonna get me to play that game. If you wanted equine art, you should have bought yourself some paintings. Live animals require a daily relationship. Come on, now. Out of the dumps and into the barn. I brought along an extra saddle I think will fit you just fine."

He ventures as far as the doorway, and then shoves his hands in his pockets. "Looks cold out. And I have to finish this script. People in Hollywood are waiting."

"There's plenty of stuff for them to do down there to amuse themselves. They can have a power lunch, or maybe for a real thrill, stop off in an oxygen bar. It's fifty-five degrees, sunny, and clear. That doesn't happen too often. I know, why don't you put on your fancy leather jacket? You paid all that money to look like a cowboy, might as well scuff it up."

He returns to the computer and clicks save on his file. I pocket my hoof pick. This whole past year it seems like everyone I met was deciding whether or not to leave the cocoon. Yes, it's admirable how much a person can accomplish from inside one—order flowers for the sick, get groceries delivered, write entire movie scripts, but cell phones and faxes and take-out food isn't real life. Getting up every day is. Doing your work, even if it means risking your health, going to bed good and tired, and in between times, doing for your friends, that's what matters. What with blood tests, Phoebe's illnesses, and losing Jake, I've had more experience at waiting lately than I care to. Those weeks Pheebs was in the hospital I didn't think about my blood; I watered flowers, cleaned the house, and sat by her bed. This one night I remember standing in the parking lot gulping in air, and Nance there next to me saying, "Today's my birthday. I'm forty years old and everything I ever thought I wanted was complete and utter bullshit. Lord help me, Ness. I can't take this vigil business one more second."

We were all pretty much living on Snickers bars and cafeteria coffee. Nance doesn't eat enough anyway, and here she was, forty, no cake, no kind wishes. What good was it doing Phoebe, all of us falling apart? I told her, "What do you say we go out to dinner someplace fancy? We'll enjoy every bite of food, get seconds if we want to, and after that, we'll get down on our knees and give thanks. Then we'll go home and sleep eight full hours. The hospital will call us if there's any change." The maître d' was very understanding about three women kneeling in the restaurant foyer, but I'm sure he had his doubts whether Nance's credit card was going to clear.

The next morning Lester pulled the breathing tube and Phoebe turned over in her sleep and sighed. Nance said, "Best belated birthday present I ever got." A week later, James phoned and we rushed into her room and held on to each other, grateful for second chances, while she blinked those big brown eyes and looked confused at our making such a fuss. And then, like God dropping the other shoe, I got the call that Jake had died. It could have been any one of a dozen opportunistic infections, but the bottom line is, when he passed, his suffering stopped. Lester says I'm

404

a long way from all that, and though he's not in favor of my shoeing horses, there's no way he can stop me. I take precautions. Latex gloves under my work gloves. I get someone to help me if the horse is thrushy. When my watch timer goes off I take my pills and vitamins, and I say a little prayer for myself. In the drug study I'm part of, I'm one of ten "women of color who have yet to sero-convert." What that means is my immune system hasn't yet met a compromise it couldn't fight. Damn straight, I say. Every week when we meet with the research study people, we report on our various side effects and have our T-cells counted. My labs remain just this side of normal and steady. Nice to be first at something for as long as it lasts; it kind of makes up for elementary school. When the study ends, some company honcho will crunch his numbers, sort out the percentages, and race to release the newest medicine in record time for the big fight. Then these pills will cost more money than I can afford, but like Lester says, we will cross that bridge when we come to it.

"A short ride," David insists when he returns to the living room in his jeans and jacket, his scarf wrapped around his neck. "On flat ground. Promise."

"Sure." I boost him up onto the gentle gray gelding. When he's got his feet in the stirrups, I pull myself up on the enormous bay. I can feel the horse shifting from hoof to hoof, shaking the dust from his unused muscles; this sucker wants to *move*. We cross the road and lean into the saddles the same way Jake and I used to on the Patrini ranch, back in the days when I squandered my laughter and didn't know the meaning of caution. David and I wind our way up the gradual hill and the wind bites at my cheeks. For a moment, I shut my eyes and feel the kind of peace that knows no bounds. At the hilltop, we turn the horses and look out over the Valley. While I can't see all the way to the farm, I do recognize some landmarks—the neon of the sign for Katy's Diner, the steeple of the church where I pray. Just beyond the rise, that stand of trees where I once saw the overwintering Canada geese and thought my life was over. Where are those birds now? What do they do in spring? Make love, have babies, Beryl would say. She'd know all the details of their life's path. All around us, the first brave soldiers of springtime are starting to leaf out. I love that shade of green, pale and new, that baby green. Back at the farm, one thing or another's always in bloom, from the seedlings in the greenhouse to the pansies near the front porch, so I get to see it a lot. I am so lucky I live there. I can't believe I ever wanted to leave for Arizona.

"I want you to come for dinner," I tell David Snow. "Phoebe wants to meet you. And her brother James." I have to laugh. "You two'll probably get along like oil and vinegar. Gay men make him nervous."

David shakes his head. "Ness, you're my friend. I have no desire to break bread with this James character. He sounds like a real prince, if you ask me."

"Oh, for crying out loud. You both stand up to pee. You'll find something to talk about. If James makes a snotty remark, I'll be surprised."

"Fine," he says. "You be surprised all by yourself."

"Why, David Snow, you're not hiding, are you?"

He adjusts his reins and leans forward to pat his horse. "Preferring solitude is not the same thing as hiding."

"It's only one meal. You know I'm not going to let up until you say yes."

"Okay, dinner someday, just not today. Can we go back now?"

"Soon, my friend."

I lead him down the backside of his property, leaf-strewn from the last rain, the trampled trail long and flat. "Your reins are looking a little loose there," I tell him. "Why don't you shorten up?"

The minute he does, I leg the bay into a bristling trot. David's horse whinnies with excitement and follows suit. "You tricked me," he says, and that's when I ask the gray for a canter.

"YOO-HOO! PRECIOUSNESS!" I hear from down the driveway. Beryl and Nance shoot me a stunned look as Granny Shirley and her friends advance. I guess they took the bus down from San Jose to Salinas, and then shared a taxi. Phoebe sits in her chair, quietly wrapping flower stems in cellophane, stapling them shut. A brief smile crosses her face, but my true-blue friend who kept my secret reins it in fairly quickly.

"Childhood nickname," I say to the others.

Nance starts laughing. "That is *so* not true! And you're always after Beryl for keeping secrets, for shame! Preciousness, Preciousness, Preciousness," she chants.

Beryl takes an armful of newly cut irises from me. "I'm going to start calling you Precious. It suits her, don't you think so, Florencio?"

*"Si. Precioso,"* he says, wagging a finger. "I always have a suspect about this."

"Oh, horse pucky on the whole lot of you!" I say and abandon the tulips and daffodils that lay in a pile waiting to be sorted and arranged. Now that our bulbs are coming up in force, we're so overloaded we sell them to whoever wants fresh cut flowers, including the supermarkets. Florencio stacks the cello wraps into white plastic buckets to load in the back of his pickup. Then he makes the deliveries and comes back with his pockets full of checks that have made us more than solvent; we're actually banking money each week.

Just look at my granny, all dressed up in her traveling clothes. A brown polyester suit and polka-dot scarf, orthopedic stockings, low-heeled shoes with a brass buckle, and a tidy velvet hat with black netting across the front.

When I move toward her, Leroy whinnies, worried I'm going someplace interesting without him. Duchess rouses herself from her sunny spot in front of the barn and accompanies me down the gravel road. She spins her tail like a pinwheel, happy for company. "Granny," I say and hold my arms open for the hug I know so well. "What a nice surprise."

"I brought Sister Anne and Sister Mabel along, Preciousness. They wanted to see your flowers. How about a glass of tea before we take the tour? That taxi ride about done us in. Very spare on the seat padding, those taxis."

Bayborough is too snobby to have a public bus system. "You should have called me to come pick you up."

"Yes," Sister Anne says, "that's what I said. But does anyone listen to an old woman? No."

I take them into the house and get them their drinks.

"This is a right fancy home," Sister Mabel says, smoothing her hand on the couch and eyeing the artwork. "Spacious."

"It once belonged to that woman in the portrait," I tell them, pointing to Sadie's likeness, which I've come to see as impish, never the same expression twice. "She won it in a divorce from a man who beat her."

"Oh, divorce," Sister Anne says, "how immoral."

Sister Mabel winks. "Reckon she deserved the house for putting up with a brute like that, Sister Anne?"

"Only the Lord could say for sure, Sister Mabel."

Granny Shirley hasn't weighed in with her two cents. I know that look on her face, though, like a juror taking her civic responsibility seriously. Once she makes up her mind, it's carved in marble. "Preciousness?" she says. "Where's the cussing parrot? I want to meet that scoundrel."

"Are you sure? He's got a pretty trashy mouth."

"Doubt he can say anything I haven't heard."

I give her my arm and we walk through the kitchen, still messy from breakfast. Nance's computer is on, and the screen saver is swirling in a wash of bright colors. The dishes are soaking, because it's best to get the flowers cut before the sun's overhead and tend to indoor chores later. We wind through the mess to the back porch where, in a sunny alcove, Verde is working out on his parrot gym. Bells ring, wooden blocks are being splintered; he's a feathered Arnold Schwarzenegger, committed to keeping the world safe from avenging parrot toys. Verde greets us with an enthusiastic C word, and then he says the Spanish curse. Granny Shirley says, "Oh, my goodness gracious. I never did hear that before, but it don't sound nice."

"I warned you."

"He doesn't mean it," she says, and offers the arm of her nice brown suit for him to step up. Verde does, and immediately begins chattering to her silver brooch, in awe of his reflection. "There's a pretty boy," she tells him, and slips a cookie from her handbag to his gaping beak. Beryl won't like it, but I'm not going to bust my own grandmother for wanting to succor the world.

Granny smiles. She sets a package of cookies down on an end table. "For later, when the pretty boy gets a sweet tooth."

I leave it there, not about to argue that parrots don't have teeth. "Shouldn't we get back to your friends?"

"In a minute. Come sit down and talk to me for a moment, girl. You're so busy all the time."

I lean against a chair. "You saw the flowers out there. Can't hardly cut them fast enough to sell."

She nods. "Quite a bounty."

"It's really something, Granny. They never stop blooming, they just change color."

We're quiet a minute, and the warm breeze blows through an open window, ruffling Verde's feathers. Beyond the window, eucalyptus trees sway. Deciding he wants my arm now, Verde negotiates a successful leap, and begins arranging my braids.

"Pastor Fowler sends his regards."

"How nice. You give him mine, too."

"You know, Precious, it makes me so happy that you've decided to return to God's house."

"I know," I say.

"I wanted to say this one thing, however."

"Aw, Granny."

"I'll just make the one comment and then

I'll hold my tongue still. There may come a time when you'll want your mother with you. No one understands you like the woman who brought you into the world."

Our eyes meet for a minute, and I know what she's saying. She's telling me she'll take care of me to my dying breath, her own health be damned, but that my mother would, too, if I told her I needed her. "Yes, Granny," I say, but I still don't believe that contacting her would help. I have friends now. I don't need a woman I don't remember.

I watch her cast her gaze out past the trees to an empty parcel of land that is too uneven for farming. The other day I saw Phoebe and James out there, walking around and talking. Phoebe was using her crutches, which she uses about fifty percent of the time now, except in front of Juan because she's chicken.

"This place where you live," my grandmother says. "It's downright lovely."

I pat my grandmother's hand. I'd love for her to meet David Snow. I return Verde to his perch and stand up to face the formidable woman who raised me, bent now in age, but still moving with purpose to wherever it is she needs to go.

"HEY, PRECIOUS," Beryl asks me over breakfast. "Can I get a ride to BBR, so long as you're headed that way?"

I sip my mint tea and spread jam on my toast.

"When you stop calling me that you can get a ride anywhere I'm going."

Beryl smirks. "Then I guess I'll have to hitchhike."

"Ha ha, very amusing. When are you all going to get over my name?"

"As soon as you do," Nance says, serving up Phoebe's tofu scramble.

Phoebe sips her juice and smiles. She swallows down her vitamins and the heart medications Lester prescribed. We are the pill-taking twins these days. "If you can tear yourselves away from the name debate for a moment, I have something I'd like to discuss."

My heart isn't the only one that sinks, I'm sure. Since Phoebe's illness, we're continually on tenterhooks. Will she sell the farm and move into a condo nearer the hospital? Is her mother pressuring her to relocate south? And the burning question that nags me: Is running the farm too much for her? She still insists on doing her share of the chores. I set down my toast, no longer hungry. "We're listening."

"This month we're so far ahead in the profit margin I'm able to give Florencio all the back pay he's due, plus a bonus."

"Great," Beryl says.

"I wasn't finished," Phoebe continues. "I think we should hire Segundo full time. We have the money coming in, and there's so much for us to do in terms of the monthly sales that we could use the help outside. Florencio's getting old. He'll always have a job here, but he can use the help."

"Oh no," Nance says. "Does this mean I never get to drive the tractor?"

Phoebe smiles. "If you're really good, we'll see. In addition to your regular pay this month, I'm giving everyone at this table a check for a thousand dollars."

"Phoebe," Beryl says. "Maybe you should put it in the bank in case we have a problem."

"No, Bear. You guys earned this money. Pay your rent; buy baubles or AT&T stock. And take a vacation. This is a quiet time. We could all use some R & R. Beryl, use your mystery plane ticket. And guys? Thanks for taking such good care of the farm while I was sick. I don't know what I would have done without you."

"Well," Nance says. "I can finally pay off my Visa."

"And run it back up again," I say.

She sticks her tongue out at me. "Not without a good reason, Precious."

I hold up my hand and tick off on my fingers, "Yes, like a sale on Cole-Haan shoes, or a new suede jacket—"

But Phoebe isn't through speaking. "And I've decided to sell the adjoining land."

"Why?" Nance asks. "On the spreadsheet, everything looks terrific."

"It's not that," Phoebe says, shaking her head. She winds a piece of hair around her finger. It reaches the tops of her shoulders now, the same length as Sadie's in the portrait. "The land's lying there idle, and with the break of trees between the house and the property, I

414

think a house could be built and still maintain a feeling of privacy."

Someone like her and Juan, I think. I guess it would be all right having them next door, but it wouldn't be the same as having her under the roof. I hate change; I just hate it to pieces, but even more than that I hate that I'm good at surviving it.

"Did somebody make you an offer?" Beryl asks.

Phoebe nods. "The same somebody who's wanted it all along. James."

Nance walks to the sink and begins filling it with noisy water, lots of suds, which translate to, Count me out, I only date the fellow.

"It's your land, Pheebs," I say. "You can do with it what you want."

"This is *our* farm," she says, her dark eyes flashing. "We made it work together. If you guys say no, I won't sell the land to him. It's as simple as that."

Nance scrubs frying pans furiously and drops more than the usual amount of flatware. There's no way she can vote on this.

"Can we finish this discussion later?" I say. "Beryl and I have to go or we're going to be late."

"Dinner," Phoebe says. "We'll talk about it then."

"WHAT'S UP WITH THAT," I ask Beryl when we are in the Land Cruiser. "Phoebe and James living within walking distance?"

"He's family," Beryl says.

"I don't think it's that simple," I say. "Other forces are at work."

"That's because you think everything's covert," Beryl tells me.

I smile. "Like your phone calls?"

Beryl frowns. "Like whichever way the wind blows is more like it."

"How is old Buckethead these days?"

"His guitar playing's improved."

"Do you know who he is yet?"

"I have an idea," she says, and looks out the window where the passing traffic is starting to thicken—nice weather equals more tourists. We can't complain when it means more business for us.

"Gonna let me in on your guess?"

"When it's time," she says.

We pull up to the entrance of Bayborough Bird Rehabilitation, with its feathered inhabitants behind the wooden gates.

Beryl steps outside the car and tilts her head up to the sky. She takes a deep breath and grins. "Smell that?"

"Smell what?"

"It's spring! Just about time for all hell to break loose. Every day I look up in the sky and tell the birds, 'Don't have sex yet!' I'm the Tipper Gore of the bird world. But if Verde doesn't listen, why should I expect any of the others to?"

Her words strike a chord within me, but it no longer stings to remember how once upon a time, I threw the sheets back without a second thought. "You need a February vacation, girl. If you're going to Alaska, better pack your long johns."

Beryl laughs. "I have a thousand dollars! I can go anywhere. But believe it or not, I've been thinking about doing exactly that—checking out the Great Land."

"Brr. Makes me cold to even think about it. Hey, you want me to swing by and pick you up tonight?"

"Nope. I have some errands. I'll catch a ride with Agnes and Marty."

"You call if you change your mind. See you at dinner."

"Yeah." She reaches in the car and grabs her lunch sack. "Ness?"

"Oh, we're finally done with Precious? Well, thank God for small favors."

"Say hi to David Snow for me. Tell him I hope he'll come to dinner one day soon. I'd really like to meet him."

She shuts the door and strides off, the redheaded bird savior who appears to know more of my secrets than I ever will of hers. Did I tell anybody I was going to see David today? Maybe Verde. Then again, maybe I talk in my sleep.

I drive down the Valley road and inland. The traffic's light for this time of day. David doesn't know it yet, but one of these days he's going to be kidnapped and taken to Sadie's farm, and fed an organic vegetarian meal that will knock his socks off. It might even be today.

DAVID STANDS IN THE DOORWAY, a cup of coffee in his hand. He has that look on his face like he's thinking of all the friends he's lost—to this disease, to the prejudice that accompanies it, maybe even just for regular reasons. He's got a cold and a bad mood came along with it. When he offered to come with me to the service for Jake, I took him up on it. The Patrinis were there, and several of the trainers Jake was drinking buddies with. Surprisingly, I was the only woman in the group. David shook hands and listened to stories of a man who surely would have swung a punch at him just as soon as give him the time of day. I thought I knew about prejudice until I met David Snow.

He agrees to let me do the laundry, but only until he's feeling better. I fold his clothes into the dresser, and change the sheets on his bed. His room's decorated entirely in Roy Rogers memorabilia, down to the chenille bedspread and the rearing Trigger lamp on the wagon-wheel dresser. "Feels like I'm in the Roy museum," I say out loud. "Keep expecting Dale any second now."

David comes into the room and sits in his desk chair. "I appreciate your helping me until I feel stronger. I can pack some things away if it bothers you."

"Don't you dare," I say. "Your room is the real thing."

"The real what?"

"I think this is how every man would do his room if he got his way. Cowboys or army men."

"Really?" David says.

"Yes, really. I don't care who you love, you all never grow up."

He laughs.

"You look tired," I say. "Slide under the covers and take a nap. Nothing feels as good as fresh sheets."

"I'd rather look out the window and feast my eyes on those horses."

"Of course you would." I pull the curtains open and there they are, dappled with sunlight, nosing around the corral and spooking at birds—his horses. "They'll be here when you wake up. Take a rest now. You don't want to tire yourself out. That just invites opportunistic infections."

"Yes, ma'am," David promises. He rests his head on the bank of pillows and looks so lonely lying there alone it breaks my heart.

When I move to get up, he stops me with a hand. "Stay until I fall asleep?"

"I was planning on it."

I put my arm around his shoulders, bony from his various battles. Going to have to fatten this one up with biscuits, I think, and thick vegetable stews. I'm remembering Granny Shirley's recipe for peanut butter pie, and how it smells when it comes out of the oven all bubbling hot. David clasps my hand. I raise his to my face and press it to my cheek. He smells soapy and salty, with a hint of horses to his skin.

I slide down next to him in the bed. I press his face to my breasts and hold him there against me until I feel his body relax. We don't say anything, but we're both holding on tight. In any other situation, this kind of woman holding a man would lead to a burst of passion, an exchange of body fluids, and some kind of relationship that would weather its share of storms. But this closeness is softer, meant to be kind. It's two people who each have jagged histories, but choose to embrace anyway. This is what it really means to be somebody's lover, I think, holding on in the face of the big good-bye you both know is coming. We lie there for long, quiet minutes. David's hold on me loosens. I listen to his breathing, and feel my heart slow its beat to move in time with his own. So long as they continue to do that, we're fine, I tell myself, as fine as we can be. Outside, the horses stretch their long necks through the fence rails until they reach the new grasses.

IN THE KITCHEN, I fix a sandwich of broiled peppers and feta cheese, and cut up fruit for a salad. I sit down to eat. There's a stack of paper on the table. I take a bite of my sandwich and turn pages. David's written a script for a television movie. The main character's a gay man who has given up on his life and is considering killing himself—that is, until he meets a cranky black woman who shows up one day to shoe his horses. Thankfully, David is the kind of guy who keeps a box of tissues in every room of the house.

"Hey, Alice," I say to Phoebe's physical therapist as I throw my purse on the table and kick off my boots. "Isn't it kind of late for you to be here? Everything okay?"

She smiles. "Phoebe's fine. We got to talking and I stayed awhile longer than usual. How are you doing?"

"Can't complain. You want to stay for supper? I don't know who's cooking, but we always have extra."

"Love to, but I have to get home to my husband. Take care, Preciousness."

"Oh, that's very funny, Alice." I march down the hall to Phoebe's room. She's sitting on her bed in her black sweats. Duchess is on the bed with her. "Did you take out an ad in the *Herald* about my name?"

"No, but that's a great idea and I bet James can get me a deal. What are you going to do with your thousand dollars?"

"Give a hundred to the church, and throw the rest in the bank. Why?"

"Just curious. You should take a trip. You look a little stressed. How about that spa idea we had a while back?"

"Not now. David needs me. And Leroy and Florencio and you and the flowers and Granny and the worm farm, they need me, too."

She clicks her tongue. "That's a wicked long list, Ness. What about what you need?"

I spread my arms and gesture around me. "Nothing more than this, Phoebe. Believe me, nothing at all."

She smirks. "A year ago, I'd've believed that."

"Pheebs, are you going to marry Juan and move out? Is that why you're selling the property to James?"

She looks at me like I'm suggesting the worst kind of mutiny. "No way. Juan and I are taking things slowly. *If* we ever get married, he'll move in here. I love this house. I'm not going anywhere. But James might build a place. He wants to be closer to the farm. Actually, he says if we put our heads and his money together he thinks we can triple our income with the same amount of effort. Sounds all right to me, but I want to see his five-year plan, and run it past you guys, of course."

"I hate change," I tell her. "I fight it with every fiber of my being."

"Horse poop," she tells me. "You're the most resilient of us and you know it." She takes hold of a crutch and stands up, and begins to walk toward the living room. Duchess leaps off the bed to follow her. I still can't get over the sight of Phoebe upright. I'm always worried it will end in another hospitalization.

"Phoebe? Why won't you walk in front of Juan?"

She stops, her back to me. "I'll do it when I'm ready."

In the kitchen she takes down a package of pasta from the cupboard, and from the fridge, tomatoes and fresh basil we grew in the greenhouse. She pulls up a stool and begins chopping, putting together sauce for spaghetti, a meal we always agree on, and one that keeps us talking long after the last slice of garlic bread is gone. I sit at the table and read the newspaper, skipping over the bad news and taking my time on the good stories. When I have those memorized, I feed the ads to Verde and get ready to solve the *Herald* crossword puzzle. One across is too perfect. I have to ask Phoebe just to drive the arrow in a little deeper. "Pheebs?"

"Yes, Precious?"

"Tell me, what's a five-letter word for faith beginning with T?"

"Trust," she tells me.

"That's right," I say.

The smell of chopped garlic fills the air.

I SPOON VANILLA ICE CREAM into glasses and Beryl pours in the root beer. "Mmm, Ambrosia," she says.

"Incipient carbohydrate overload," Nance admonishes from the sink where she is putting away clean glasses still warm from the dishwasher.

"Shut up," I say. "Don't spoil our fun with that stupid protein talk or I will sit on you and force-feed you Green Magma."

"Lava?" Nance says.

"No, it's this wonderful supplement made from wheat grass."

"Oh, Sweet Jesus, now I've heard everything."

"It gives you tremendous energy," Phoebe says. "You should try it."

"Why? Do I have a bus to catch?" Nance fires back.

"Would that be the *love* bus, by any chance?" Beryl adds.

"Featuring UPS at the wheel," I have to say.

In a heartbeat, Nance and Beryl are on their feet, singing "Love Train." They execute a few dance steps, looking like the worst kind of karaoke duet ever assembled. I cringe at what I've started, but I can't stop laughing.

Phoebe sits at the table peeling an apple. Duchess peeks up over the edge of the table; the dog is mental for apples. She gives the half apple to Duchess, grips her crutches, and stands up. "Anyone ever tell you it's not nice to hassle the handicapped?" She raises one crutch like she's going to whack me and Duchess starts barking.

"You're scaring our dog," I say.

"Ladies," Beryl says. "Let's take it easy, shall we?"

"Oh, my God, is that what we are?" I ask. "Ladies?"

Everyone stops talking for a moment and looks at me. Look at us. With our odd lovers, our difficult mothers, and the endless crops of flowers that keep us here together in this wonderful house. We're the fiercest kind of women, the best, at least Beryl is, but it never occurred to me that we were ladies. We lift our glasses and toast with root beer floats, even Nance, though she takes a pretend sip, because with those sneaky old carbohydrates, you just can't be too careful.

# Spring

Hard is the heart that loveth naught
in May.

—CHAUCER
*The Romaunt of the Rose* c. 1440–50

# 17

## *New Plumage*

THE PHONE CALL COMES just as Marty and I are getting ready to release the bats. Agnes holds the receiver out and yells, "Hey Beryl, it's your breather!"

Marty's fingers hesitate on the latch. This is a now-or-never moment for him. If I take the call, his resolve will crumble like the Big Sur highway sometimes does in rainy season.

"Tell him I'll call him back."

Agnes cackles like a Bingo winner, delivers my message, and replaces the receiver. She goes back to wrapping the wing of a goose that tried to break up a dogfight. The stubborn bird still believes he needs to prove his point, but Agnes clearly has the upper hand, which is wrapped firmly around his beak. "What do you know, Beryl? He hung up."

"Good riddance," Marty says. "Lunatic calling here pestering the daylights out of us. What's the world coming to?"

It's spring. The world is coming to exactly what it does every year—single entities searching for mates. "Let's get a move on, Marty. You want your babies settled in before nightfall, don't you?"

He kisses Agnes good-bye and before we drive

off in his Honda hatchback, he tapes up one of BBR's CAUTION: RESCUED BIRDS ON BOARD signs in the window. The sign's an excuse for Marty to drive ten miles under the speed limit until we are deep in the Valley, miles past the farm, where there're any number of good places for bats. We turn onto a gravel road and drive for two miles until we arrive at the Creekside Nature Center where Ranger Derek Twombly is waiting. Bats roost in the eaves of his office. Someone's here twelve hours out of each day, giving tours, writing reports, and generally enjoying the perks of an under-paid job. The bats will be watched, coddled, fed if necessary. If they have to leave Marty, this is pretty much bat heaven.

The ranger greets us in his army-green clothes, his Dudley Do-Right hat set square on his head. I wish everyone wore hats. I like how Ness's granny always wears one. They're so self-defining, with their various plumes and well-worn creases. If Earl wore a hat, I think it would be one of those woolen Russian deals with the ear flaps and brim so he could walk twenty miles in a snowstorm. Me? I'm a water-proof Tilley hat with a lifetime guarantee, something that if it lands in the water, floats straight toward the falls, tumbles right over and surfaces downstream. Ranger Derek opens the front of what looks like a bird-house tacked midway up the wall. It has a skinny, slotlike opening. Marty removes the lid of the box the bats are in. Little mouse faces protest with open mouths. For the millionth time, I marvel how you can see their bones through the thin wing skin. We slide them gently inside the wooden box. Later, when they're comfortable with the idea, they'll roost up high with the others, but for now this is a bat halfway house. "I'll check them daily and call you if there's any problems," Derek promises.

Marty takes one long last look before the ranger closes the bat house. "You got yourself a nice location here," he says to Derek, pointing down a path where the rushes grow tall enough for shy animals to hide and still drink. "The creek's down that way?"

"Yes, sir," Derek answers. "Bad Girl. Running pretty high with all the rain we've had lately."

Marty kicks the dirt. "Bet that sure brings the animals up."

Derek nods. "Oh yeah. Saw a couple of real nice foxes yesterday."

"Well, I'll be. You get any mountain lion?"

"One, last month. Don't see too many of them anymore."

"You sure don't."

"I'd like to see the creek," I say. "Mind if I take a walk and check it out, Marty?"

His mouth trembles. "You go on, Beryl."

Oh, Marty. Not one single good-bye in this world is said easily. I leave the men to talk critters the way some men would talk stereos, and hike the trail to the water and stand at the muddy edge. Ripples quilt the surface of the water. Mossy brown rocks glisten beneath the silvery flow in a pattern like that stone, tiger's eye. By summer, the current will reduce to a lazy trickle shallow enough for Leroy to drink from. If I walk hard for a couple miles, I'd end up at the farm by dinnertime. If I kept on going, eventually I'd arrive at Crossroads by the River Grill, where a larger creek empties into the ocean. I guess if not above ground, then somewhere near the water table, all these streams and creeks connect. It strikes me as strange that I live so near the ocean and rarely take the time to visit. So many excuses— it's hard to find parking, who wants to brave the tourists, and of course, farm chores take precedence. My life's going great, but when it comes to leisure I feel hopelessly retarded. If I don't have a book in my hands, I have to be repotting something. Nance, who is addicted to vacuuming, says I'm "avoiding dealing with core issues." Ha. Who at the farm isn't? I pick up a stone and toss it, listening to the froglike plunk it makes as it settles on the creek bed. Ness slept on these banks last summer, before she met Phoebe. Imagine hearing water lull you to sleep—even better than rain, I bet. I think about my freebie plane ticket and wonder if and when I should use it. Maybe before I'm too old I can find the time to roll out a sleeping bag near a river.

When I get back to the ranger station, Marty's done yakking with Derek. "Guess we should get going," he says.

I nod yes, and we get in the car.

He turns on the radio and a burst of classical music fills the car. Then, just as quickly, he snaps it off. "Those damn bats got under my skin, Beryl. I'm going to miss them like crazy."

"That's the great thing about working at BBR, Marty, new guests arrive daily."

"I know. But nobody can take their place."

"At least not for awhile." I pat his arm and he slows when we near the turnoff for the farm.

"Want me to drop you home?"

"Actually, could you take me back to town?" I say. "I have some business in Sierra Grove."

"Sierra Grove? Sure thing."

We drive back past the bird center, funded by the wealthy denizens of Bayborough-by-the-Sea. The first day I came to work, the sight of their homes overwhelmed me. Dollhouses with curving slate roofs complete with a blush of decorative moss on the north side. Lush landscapes trained to complement the dollhouses. Nice cars in the driveway, the kind that age well, that you give a nickname like Big Blue, take care of, and pass down to your kids. I felt like an illegal crossing the border. I never imagined that by answering an ad in the paper and taking a left turn into the Valley I'd be living in my own sprawling dollhouse. And yet lately, what with Phoebe coming so close to checking out, I feel itchy inside. Spring fever. Restlessness. It's hard to explain. While she was in the worst of times, I spent a part of every day sitting at her bedside. I held her hand. I sang songs I'd never have the courage to hum in regular life. *Won't you come home, Bill Bailey?* When Phoebe was in the coma was the closest I felt to anyone since my real mother killed herself. And now that Phoebe's up and walking, the farm's doing so well, that same closeness—well, how can I say this so it makes sense—that I feel her good fortune is pushing me to take some kind of walk of my own.

Marty drops me on the boundary of Bayborough and Sierra Grove. I travel the few blocks it takes to get to downtown, past the antique stores and the Victorian homes turned bed-and-breakfasts and the realtor with the color pictures taped to the window. FIXER-UPPER: $390,000. Somewhere, I smell pizza cooking and think I should make that when it's my turn to cook next. Sausage up one side, mushrooms down the other, olives across the board, everyone's happy. The wind's picking up now. Fog swirls overhead and gets ready to settle in for the night. The salt in the air frizzes my hair even worse than usual. Long ago I learned that with hair like mine, there are good days and bad, and that how I move my comb has very little to do with either. Nance pays seventy-five dollars for a haircut and I do mine with nail scissors. We both look presentable. You prioritize according to what you can afford. Outside a drugstore, I find a phone booth that works—no small miracle in a resort town—and drop in a quarter and dial Earl's on Ocean.

"Bookstore," his tired voice answers.

I hesitate, long enough to let him say "Hello?

Is anybody there?" and see how that feels. Then, because my heart understands the toll courage takes, I give in. "Sorry I couldn't talk before," I say. "I was getting the bats ready for their big day. I'm done now. It went real well, I think. They'll be happy at Creekside; what bat in his right mind wouldn't? But that doesn't mean Marty won't miss them. Poor guy, he really got attached this time."

Earl doesn't respond. I imagine him sitting there utterly dumbfounded—he's been found out but isn't getting yelled at. Men are not comfortable with this kind of consequence.

"If I played guitar," I say, "I'd know what to do next. But I'm afraid the most I can offer you musically is my whistle." Which I then demonstrate with "Michael, Row the Boat Ashore." I don't know why that song; it just came to me. I listen as Earl laughs quietly, like I imagined he would. "So," I say. "I'm coming over. Just thought I'd warn you in case you decide to flee, because even though I owe you for the raven book you slipped into my bag, I have a feeling this isn't about books anymore."

Silence, then he says, "Okay, Beryl."

"Okay. Bye, Earl."

I walk seven more blocks, stopping once at Java the Hut for a mondo decaf latte with extra foam and a shot of almond and the fortitude only a hot drink delivers. I pick up a plastic knife and study its serrated edge, and think how when you need it to, the most ordinary item becomes a defense weapon. Much as my lawyer tried to get me released without jail time, I probably deserved that sentence. From chopping onions to stabbing my husband—it all happened so fast that I couldn't really explain to the police why it should be called an accident. But when a man gives you his last name, that doesn't mean a world of grief should come along with it. J.W. called me every name in the book—probably why Verde's worst doesn't faze me—but what he said that night—that was what made the knife leap up.

"Do you *realize* how big a favor you'd be doing the world if you saved me the trouble and took your own sorry self out, Beryl Anne? You can borrow my daddy's shotgun or I can get you the pills. Come on, if your own mother could do it, you ought to be able to—"

And hearing him use her like that, just take her name and run his drunken tongue all over her struggle, well, it was as if somebody else's hand was on the hilt. The knife went in, just the tiniest bit; then J.W. slipped in the beer, hit his head, and suddenly there was blood soaking his shirt and his life was over in less time than it had taken him to tell me to end my own.

"Want a bagel to go with this? They're half price this time of day," the counter guy asks me, so politely that tears come to my eyes. "I can warm it up, throw some cream cheese on it."

"No, but thanks for the offer."

*Beryl, you are alive and free. You have a*

*thousand dollars,* I remind myself, and order a coffee to go for Earl.

Through the windows of his store, I see Hester Prynne sitting on the counter cleaning her paws. She's a skinny tabby with bedroom eyes. All cats sport that look—incipient Audrey Hepburn. A long time ago, Earl told me how he found Hester on the street, all barrel-stave ribs and big meow. Earl's helping an old man at the first shelf with Steinbeck hardcovers that sell to tourists for ten times what they're worth. I open the door and set the coffee on the counter. Hester bumps me with her head and I pet her while I wait for Earl to be finished. I like cats all right, but they're not parrots. Horses, well, someday I'll sit Ness down and tell her that whole long wild chapter in my life, but not just yet. We need to save some secrets for other nights if we're going to be friends for the rest of our lives. Pretty soon the cash register clanks shut and the store is empty except for us.

Earl and I look at each other. Neither of us is sure where to begin. I feel shy, which is ridiculous behavior for a woman forty-five years old with prison under her belt. I squint my eyes. "Earl, how old are you? Fifty?"

"Fifty-two."

"Have you ever been married?"

He grimaces. "Once. Didn't go too well."

I take the lid off my coffee and run my finger through the foam caught on the side of the cup. Licking it off, I say, "I hear you. But I think it's important to remember that one failed marriage doesn't necessarily indicate crash-and-burn the second time around."

He sips his coffee. "Assuming there is a second time."

"Yes, that is a big assumption."

"Gargantuan, if you ask me."

"Oh, I don't know. Many things are possible."

He shrugs.

"Earl? Are you so afraid you can't call me up on the phone and talk? Does it have to be guitar music? You know, there's some serious speculation at my house that you're secretly this Buckethead fellow, and if that turns out to be the case, the least we expect is free tickets to your next gig, now that I've listened to you practice. Are you Buckethead?"

He blushes. Watching a fifty-two-year-old, gray-haired cat owner blush gives me hope for the world. I try to think of clever stuff to say to make him do it again, but I'm tired and it's been a long day. "Talk to me, Earl. Tell me what four months of phone calls saying nothing is all about."

He sighs, opens the register, and throws the money from the till into a zippered bag without counting it. He turns the OPEN sign to CLOSED and pours Hester a bowl full of kibble. He spends a long while petting her while she eats. "Guess it's the time of night when people eat, too. Sometimes I forget, and then I look up and it's midnight. Beryl, you want to have dinner with me?"

"How do I know you won't strangle me and leave me in an alley somewhere?"

He smiles. "For God's sake, if I'm too shy to talk to you, how am I going to get up the nerve to kill you?"

"I'm pretty hungry," I tell him. "I might want a big dinner."

"Then I'll watch you eat, and when you're full, we'll talk."

"Deal."

He switches out all the lights except for the one that illuminates a high-backed, upholstered reading chair near the window. Hester, familiar with the routine, races to the back of the store. She sleeps in Historical Fiction, on a pad set high on the top shelf. We turn and walk toward the front door. Earl reaches above me to get the latch and uh oh, there it is, tucked in that inch or two between us, the exact thing I've been trying my best to avoid. To some people that kind of movement communicates a dent in your personal space—take two steps back and phew—you're comfortable again. But to Earl and me, it's the kind of heat that lets us know that someday, no telling when, we are going to touch each other and it will be the start of something to remember. He smiles like it's about time I figured this out. I force myself not to move away, to stay there even though the soles of my feet are humming *run, run now, while you still can.*

The thing is, I don't want to make a mistake like I did with J.W. Up until right this moment, I've been doing pretty well without a man. No reason I can't continue that way, is there? Sure, there are occasional nights when I feel an ache below decks, and if I think too hard about Phoebe and Juan in the other room, I have to get up and walk through the fields until the cold air knocks some sense into me. But Earl and me that way? Success instead of a jail sentence? I might as well ask for a complete pardon.

"For dinner," Earl says. "We have any number of options. A fancy, sit-down place? Take-out food and a walk at Point Anne? There're always ethnic restaurants. The contest of who will be brave enough to try the weirdest dish."

"How about burgers?" I say. "In a sit-down place, but nothing fancy, and maybe a root beer float?"

He nods and we walk down the hill toward the center of town.

I reach over and tuck my hand into the space between his upper arm and his jacket. He gives me a squeeze to let me know he likes that. Earl and me—we're just two people now, moving through a foggy Sierra Grove night, free to while away the hours how ever we decide.

I SWITCH ON THE LIGHTS and fill my Alaska mug with tea and add honey. It's early, and nobody else has clocked in yet. The birds are starting to raise a ruckus; they know our schedule. Dr. Llewellyn will be by today, making her rounds and picking up a peregrine falcon that, I'm sorry to report, appears to be blind in one eye. What havoc a kid with a BB gun can wreak. The falcon will end up living a pampered life in a bird sanctuary, but that's a far cry from picking your dinner out of the chaparral. I sip my tea, blackberry flavored; I think the new girl brought in the box, so I use my stolen moments to ruminate on various thoughts.

In the bird world, song is the best means of identification, especially with birds that like to keep their distance. It takes considerable patience, and one has to listen with a careful ear before naming names. Birds are wary. The slightest movement can startle them away. They have idiosyncrasies when it comes to nests, mate-taking, and choice of food. The sooty shearwater, the American wigeon, and the red-shouldered hawk, even the common snipe—everyone receives the same treatment at BBR. Sometimes the orioles are hooded. Sometimes they lift their heads and turn out not to be orioles at all, but the western tanager, his distinctive strawberry top feathers ducked into a bush foraging for insects. Oh, give me the good old house sparrow, the wings of the linnet, the surprising size and color of the Arctic loon—when I close my eyes, beneath my fingers their feathers blend to a universal color, one common skin, the type I dedicate my life to saving.

Last night, with half-eaten burgers on the plate between us, Earl said, "Beryl Anne, you have the most infectious laugh. I could listen to it for thirty years and not get tired."

Earl's some kind of hamburger purist, pronouncing onions essential to the experience, along with a beer on *tap,* no foreign bottled nonsense for the Earl of Books. He insisted on buying me a sundae for dessert, and then he ate half—but he saved me the cherry. He held it in his fingers until I took it in my mouth. He grasped my hand across the table and talked about first edition J. D. Salingers, and how amazing it feels to open any book to the title page and see the author's signature there. How it gives him a little thrill each and every time that happens no matter if the writer's famous or not. How even though it meant losing a five-hundred-dollar sale, he refused to sell an illustrated Longfellow to some advertising agency that wanted to make a sign out of it. He mentioned that his guitars are his most prized possessions, and worth more than his car, which got me to wondering what he drove, and not really caring but hoping it wasn't going to be a rusted-out Subaru filled with fast-food wrappers. Turned out to be a turquoise vintage Ford pickup that Florencio would lose his mind over, and it looked pretty darn valuable to me, but what do I know of trucks? At the farmhouse porch, he held my hand, and said, "I sure would like to kiss you" and I said, "Then why don't you?" and by God he did, my first kiss in seven years. I am happy to report it did not disappoint.

I sip my tea, remembering.

I can't get over the fact that I have money and that plane ticket. And as if to remind me, today's

*Herald* has an advertisement for cheap fares to Anchorage. Nance threw it on the breakfast table and said, "That's a sign. The Holy Spirit is at work, Beryl. You can't get much clearer direction without a neon arrow."

I know the advertisement is a pre-tourist-season come-on, and there's bound to still be snow in the shadier places, but would that be so bad? It's March now. My birthday's coming up. I'd like to turn forty-six in Alaska. If I don't go now, I have a feeling I'll never do it. I think about asking Earl along. He looks like he'd travel well. For people our age, taking a trip is a terrific way to get to know each other. I'm pretty sure I could talk him into it since I know it's him who sent me the ticket. *Earl, imagine two thousand eagles in one place, fishing in cold, clear water born from snowmelt. All around you, there are mountains in every direction. Glaciers between them like tongues of blue ice. Three kinds of bears waking up from hibernation. You and me, feasting on locally gathered chanterelles at the Marx Brothers' café. Kayaking in Prince William Sound, where otters and porpoises swim alongside you, asking What's up, Doc? Walking down Fourth Avenue past the tourist shops and not buying anything because your heart is already full up and brimming over with souvenirs you can't pay money for. Yes, I know it's too late for the Iditarod, but it's a big state, and chances are there's probably somebody out there still mushing. Rubbing my nose against Earl's, that old cliché of how it is Eskimos kiss.*

*Come with me, Earl.*

But in my heart, I think I need to do this alone. If I'm ever going to understand all its chambers, this is one adventure I probably have to make by myself. I think of Steinbeck's words, before he took off with Charley in the camper of his truck, how he knew that a change of venue wasn't just a good idea, but utterly necessary for his writing. For some people, only the earth can provide that kind of healing.

I pick up the phone and make the call. In ten minutes I've booked a window seat on the right side of the plane on the way up, the left on the way back, to maximize my views. All I have to do is go to any travel agency and exchange my ticket for the booked flight. That's easy enough, as is breaking the news to the girls. The hard part? Going.

The bell chimes and in walks a woman with a cardboard box. Her face is tight, concerned, a look I've seen so many times I can't begin to count. I set down my tea and walk over to help her. "I didn't know what else to do," she says. "The vet I telephoned gave me your address. Please say you can help them."

In this business, there are no promises. I peer inside the cardboard box and two nestlings look up at me, barely feathered, mouths gaping, faces so ugly only a mother could love. There's always the one moment I want to kill whomever started the rumor that fallen babies can't be put back into the nest.

"Mockingbirds," I tell her. "They're fairly hardy."

She stays awhile, chatting about how much she loves birds, how she hopes they can be released, and to say what a good thing it is we do here, how grateful she is, and can she leave a check.

Cat owner, I think, and know without asking what happened to Mama Mockingbird. I tuck her money into the donation box and give her a couple brochures and a sticker for her car window. When she leaves, I fill syringes with formula, and welcome the first spring arrivals to Bayborough Bird Rehabilitation, where saving avians is our business, our only business, unless there are bats. In the back of my mind, I'm imagining how it will feel to step off that plane and find my way to wilderness.

The phone rings, and when I answer, there's guitar music.

"Good morning, Earl," I say. "Did you sleep well?"

"Not really."

"Oh? Is insomnia a chronic problem? Maybe you should cut out coffee."

"I already have. But I can't cut out redheads, and that's what kept me up all night. Thinking."

I smile. "That *is* a problem."

"Look, Beryl. Can I see you again? Like maybe for lunch?"

"I'm all alone here. And you have the bookstore to run."

"That's true. What about dinner? Or breakfast? Do you take a nutrition break?"

I tuck the phone into the crook of my neck so I can keep feeding the babies. The mockingbird babies trill beneath my hands. "Earl, you're funny when you talk. I like that."

"Well, I'm glad you're amused. I'm scared to death is what I am. Say no and I'll probably quit talking to everybody, even Hester."

"Yes, you can have dinner with me. And sometime soon, breakfast. Nutrition break, well, I don't know. That's getting awfully intimate."

"Which is the general idea, Beryl."

Male birds in springtime, I think. They'll dance for you every which way. "What was Plan B last night? Ethnic take-out? Point Anne?"

"I believe I mentioned both. Do you like Chinese food?"

"Definitely. Egg rolls especially."

"Me, too. I'll pick you up at five."

"I thought the bookstore stayed open until seven."

"It used to, but not anymore. Jeez, I have to go. Believe it or not, I actually have a line at the register."

"That's great. See you later. Bye, Earl."

When Agnes and Marty come in, they're arguing about the fox sparrow versus the golden-crowned sparrow, the merits of each, and which is superior. "The golden-crowned sparrow," Marty insists. "For Pete's sake, Agnes, the bird's not only gorgeous, but he can sing 'Three Blind Mice.' Can your boring old fox sparrow do that?"

"The golden-crowned is practically domesticated," she argues. "Hangs around the feeder all the time, changes color in the spring, big deal. The fox may be plainer, but he's superior in a dozen ways."

"Name one."

She turns to me. "Beryl, can you explain to my friend here how entirely wrong he is?"

In my book, it's the fox sparrow hands down. Also known as *Passerella iliaca*, it's the tiniest bird, but chunky in the stippled breast. Similar to a towhee, it makes a kissing noise in winter, but in summer, oh, my gosh; he sings a song to his mate that will bring tears to your eyes. Once you've heard it, you never forget. "Sorry, Marty," I say.

He calls me a traitor, Agnes laughs her Bingo winner's laugh, and we get back to work.

When Dr. Llewellyn comes in, I mention in passing that I have some questions when she has a moment. She works for two hours, and then stops at my station.

"If a person were to take a parrot out of state, would a health certificate suffice? Can birds fly cargo on planes, or what? I mean, commercially, they have to get places some way, but what about in the case of domesticated birds?"

She gives me a look. "What are you planning on, Beryl? Kidnapping the falcon?"

"Nothing like that," I assure her. "I was thinking of taking my parrot to Alaska."

She laughs and laughs. "Now I've heard everything. Why don't you leave him here and let us babysit? Less trauma for the bird, easier for you in case you can't find parrot-friendly digs."

"I don't know. I hate to leave Verde out of anything."

"I trust you'll make the right decision," she says, moving on to her other charges.

I'M PORING OVER A MAP, running my finger across the strangest names: Yakutat, Seldovia, and Matanuska, when Nance drops a glass fishing float on my bed. "Here," she says. Verde hops down off my shoulder and begins giving it the business. I look up at her face, perfectly made up, but that doesn't hide the sorrow.

"What's that?"

"My past. I'd like you to throw it in the Bering Sea for me, Beryl. Either some kid will find it and call it a treasure or it will make its way down here via the currents. Who knows? One day it might even end up in Bad Girl Creek."

I smile. "Yeah, I guess if whales can migrate, how hard can it be for a glass bubble?"

She sits down on my bed. "You know, I read someplace that the otters that came this way from Alaska stopped when they got to our peninsula. Scientists can't say why that is, exactly, but my feeling is they didn't see any reason to go any farther when they were already in paradise."

"It's only a vacation, Nance. I'm coming back home."

"Right. You're going to take one look at those bald eagles and forget Bayborough ever existed.

No doubt they have a bird rehab up there that will welcome you in with open arms and never let you go."

"Maybe, but they won't have you guys."

"Still, it's the wilderness up there. You could be sorely tempted."

I roll the float across my quilt. Verde crow-hops after it, enjoying the new game. "I guess I won't know until I see the place."

"I'll be holding your parrot hostage," she says pointing her finger. "You remember that if you get any ideas about relocating."

At dinner, I serve up the salad onto the good china. We use it willy-nilly, not just for holidays. Ness grates hers with Parmesan cheese and sits picking up strands with her fingers. "So, caribou head," she says. "What's your first stop? Mount McKinley?"

"The natives call it Denali," I say.

"Uh oh," Phoebe says. "She's already practicing the language. You know what that means, she's going to try to pass for one of them."

"What's wrong with being one of us?" Nance says. "Jeez Louise, Beryl, were you ever skimpy on the olives on this pizza. I'm going to add a few more."

"Me, too," Ness says. "And maybe a jalapeño or two."

"For what it's worth, I like this pizza just fine," Phoebe says. "Overloading it with condiments is like plastering on too much eye makeup, painful to look at and just plain tarty."

Nance and Ness look at each other and then at Phoebe. "Oh, really?" they say, and we are off to one of our crazy nights of teasing and friendly jealousy and much raucous laughter. Verde throws in a few experimental curses, and Duchess seizes the opportunity to swipe a crust.

A thousand dollars—how far can it take me? Motels, camping, the courtesies of strangers notwithstanding, I am going to spend a lot of money on postcards and presents.

I stand back and watch them doctor my pizza. They're like three bossy kindergartners fighting over finger paints. Once upon a time, teaching school was my biggest ambition. That business with J.W. and the knife got in the way and I went about my life like a beaten-down failure. Since coming to Sadie's farm, I've had to take a long, hard look at what I thought I wanted and make new goals. Okay, so maybe I still don't know what it is I need, but one thing's for certain, I know what I can't live without.

"Like a moose just took a dump," Phoebe says. "That's what putting fifty olives on one slice of pizza looks like. I can't believe you're going to eat that."

Nance throws an olive at her. "How's forty-nine look?"

Alaska is our forty-ninth state.

Phoebe fires back a jalapeño. "I challenge your olives with this pepper of fire."

Ness shakes her head, picks up an olive, and

the fight begins. And me? I get out the paper towels to clean it all up.


*Nance*

# 18

## *Atomic Structure for Dummies*

"BERYL, I THINK YOU SHOULD take a cell phone. Let me show you how mine works. That way, if a bear threatens you, you can—"

"She can what, Nancy Jane?" Ness says. "Dial nine-one-one? Stop talking like an insane person. Let the girl go on her trip with a light heart. Honestly, all she needs is clean underwear. But don't take your good undies, Beryl, take your ratty ones and throw them out as you go instead of washing them. Then every day your pack's a little lighter, see?"

"And in the airport gift shop you can fill your pack back up with mementos for the present slut who doesn't want you to take a six-ounce cell phone," I say.

Phoebe laughs.

Ness scowls. "Ha ha, Phoebe. Ha ha, Nance. I didn't mean it that way and you both know it."

"Yes, you did," I say. "Beryl, you have to

promise to call every day so we know how you're doing. Plus Verde needs to hear his mother's voice."

"Last time I checked Beryl was a grown-up," Phoebe says from where she sits on the bed helping to fold Beryl's clothes. "She only needs to call if she feels like it. However, postcards are mandatory."

"What's a postcard besides a slow phone call?" I say. "Look, I have fifty free roaming minutes a month that I never use."

"Take your own trip," Ness says.

"And don't you think I won't, one of these days."

"Ooh," she answers, "I'm holding my breath."

"Ladies," Beryl says, finally responding to our protective melee. "I'll call. Postcards will be dispatched. Knickknacks will be purchased and brought home. Can we not spend the few minutes I have left here arguing over stupid stuff?"

"Take the cell phone, Beryl," I beg. "Even if you never use it, I'll sleep better knowing you have it."

"Nance, it probably won't work in half the places I'm going."

"Take it anyway. And you'll need the adapter for recharging." As I begin to amass the necessary equipment, including the instruction manual I've never mastered, I realize the folly of my ways. "Lord forgive me, I'm a worse nudge than I thought. You don't have to take my phone."

Ness puts her arm around my shoulders. "We're all going to miss her, Nance."

Phoebe rolls a pair of blue jeans into a tight column she secures with rubber bands. She sighs, and this makes me shut up and poke Ness to stop her chatter, too. "Pheebs? You feeling okay?"

She lies back against the pillows. "I was just thinking how all this reminds me of when Sadie used to get packed for Europe. I'd sit on her bed trying not to show how jealous I was of all those foreign countries. Inside, I wanted to bomb Paris, I mean, blow it clean off the globe. Imagine a teenage girl whose biggest enemy is adventure. That was me, entirely selfish. She always sent postcards and brought me great presents, but my whole world felt out of whack until she came home, to the farm, I mean. Sadie lived other places, but this was the only place of hers I ever knew her in. Beryl Anne, I hope you know this is your home."

"I know it, Phoebe."

Beryl shoves the rolled-tight jeans and shirts into the bottom of her pack. When the pack is full, she buckles it shut. Into the outside pockets she tucks breakfast bars, a photo of us, one of Verde's feathers, and a rock from the creek bed. Talismans, I think. I have a few of my own. She'll be back. Then I notice the glass ball sitting on her dresser. "Um, you forgot the fishing float," I say.

"I didn't forget, Nance. I didn't want to take a chance on the airlines smashing it when I can

452

keep it in my purse. Now, can I talk somebody into a ride to the airport?"

I look at my watch. It's a Swiss Army brand; a present from James, who somehow figured out it was my birthday when Phoebe was in the hospital and surprised me. I don't dare dwell on how much he spent because then I might have to stop loving it. "Why, when your plane doesn't leave for hours yet?"

She hoists the pack to her shoulders, looking like she's setting out for nothing more strenuous than a week in the Sierras. "Nance, I know what time my plane leaves. I've woken up every night for the past three weeks afraid I'd miss it. I want to get there early because I need some time to sit by myself, to decompress between this world and wherever it is I'm going. And I don't care much for long, weepy good-byes and airport scenes. That kind of drama will make me stay home."

"Oh, you're just saying that," Ness says.

"No, Ness. I'm not."

"But we have to stay there until the plane takes off."

"Why?"

"For one thing, to make sure the landing gear gets tucked up properly."

Now it's me putting my arm around Ness. "That's right, Beryl. You can't get rid of us. You're going to look out your window seat and see our faces plastered up against the terminal window."

"That's what I'm afraid of," she says.

"Look," Phoebe says. "If Beryl wants it

that way, we have to respect her wishes, even if it ruins our fun and we have a terrible evening."

"Beryl?" I say. "You want us to clear out so you can say good-bye to Verde alone?"

Finally something we say hits home. She blinks hard, and nods, and we leave the room, all three of us walking to the kitchen trying not to cry.

"I'll drive her to the airport," I tell Ness. "Unless you have your heart set on it."

"No, you take her," she says. "I'll lunge Leroy and let Phoebe ride him."

"Really?" Phoebe says. "Do I have a choice in this?"

"No way," Ness answers. "You need to ride my horse and that, my dear, is that."

Phoebe shrugs. "So this is what it's like having three mothers."

The phone rings and I rush to get it. "Hello?" I say, and then I hear a familiar voice on the other end.

"Hey there, Mattox. Got an assignment on my desk I'm betting you can't say no to."

"Just a second, okay?" I put my hand over the receiver. "Work. I might have to go out of town for a day or two."

"Well, leave us a note if we're not here when you go," Ness says, holding the door for Phoebe.

When it shuts, I put the receiver up to my ear. "Hello?" I say, wondering if it's somebody playing a joke, or if after all this time, it really is Rick Heinrich on the other end.

"Hey, babe," he says. "Sorry I missed your birthday. But I'm about to make up for it in a way you'll never forget."

I HANG UP THE PHONE after saying maybe I'll be there, maybe I won't. The minute I set the receiver down, it rings again. I figure it's Rick using redial, but it's James.

"Just the person I wanted to talk to. You feel like dinner out, maybe going dancing? I want to see you," he says, his voice thick with desire.

"I have to go out of town on a last-minute assignment," I say.

"You can't get out of it?"

I hesitate; want to say yes, and then leap directly off the cliff and say, "No, I really can't."

"Call me the second you get back," he says. "Drive safe, sweetie. I'll be waiting when you get back."

It feels like I've swallowed one of the huge rocks on the beach in Oregon, like I've stepped over a line from good taste into my mother's territory, like my brain fizzed right out of my head. I walk back to Beryl's room expecting Verde to call me a slut, but he's preoccupied, trying to get enough affection out of Beryl to tide him over until she returns.

She turns to me. "I'm ready to go. Are you?"

God, what a question.

THE PENINSULA AIRPORT IS TINY and services mainly those commuter planes with turboprop engines. Bayborough's elite flies them to San Francisco or Los Angeles, where international flights leave at all hours. But occasionally a 737 lands, its engines booming, and a few Peninsula souls climb aboard. Beryl's taking the turboprop. I try not to think of plane crash statistics. In San Francisco she'll catch a direct flight that goes to Anchorage without even stopping in Seattle. She says that's good because it means she can't change her mind halfway there. We ride along in silence as the sun begins its descent, and the sky goes the color of an agate marble.

"Should anything happen to me—"

I refuse to let her finish. "Nothing is going to happen except you're going to have a good time, without us, I might add."

"But if anything did—"

"I would swear on my life to take excellent care of your parrot and I know you'd do the same for me, with Duchess."

"Jeez, Nance. All I wanted to say was thanks. These last six months have been the happiest times of my life."

I shush her, but I feel the same way, too. Beryl doesn't know this, and neither does Ness or Phoebe, but I'm catching the plane that leaves right after hers, to Portland.

At the airport, I park and walk in with her. "You don't have to stay."

"I just want to see you to the gate, okay? Deep down, I'm Southern, remember?"

"Right, afflicted with manners."

She shows her ticket to the woman at the window, who glances at her ID and rattles off all the mandatory bomb-in-your-luggage questions. Beryl listens closely and answers no to all of them. "Nance? I have a confession to make."

For a second I'm startled, then catch myself—it's my guilty conscience, not hers. "Well, I already know about your husband. How bad can it be?"

We walk on, then Beryl stops by the bank of newspaper dispensers to adjust her pack, and that same old heart-stopping ache hits me— Rick, editor-in-chief of *After-Hours Magazine*, the past it seems I can't swallow or spit out. In just a few hours, I'm going to see him. My heart is beating crazier than Phoebe's did when she was on the monitor.

"The reason I wanted the time alone at the airport is so I can be with Earl. We're having dinner. He asked to come over and sit with me until my plane leaves, and I told him that was okay."

For a nanosecond, I'm taken aback. Then it occurs to me that over the past few months each of us has shifted in exactly this way, making room in our all-girl world to include men. Phoebe with Juan, of course, but also Ness spends a lot of time at David Snow's. Up until today I would have said then there's James and me—this budding, promising, healthy relationship. But If I catch this plane like I told Rick I would, I'm guilty of the worst kind of duplicity—not just lying to James, but lying to my girlfriends. Beryl deserves a boyfriend. We all do. Am I such a round heels that the minute Rick called me and said come up here I said yes, without even considering how my roommates might feel? "It's perfectly fine with me," I say to Beryl. "Somehow I take it you don't want the others in on this."

"Not just yet, if that makes any kind of sense."

Beryl Anne Reilly, terminally afflicted with shyness—without fail, she makes me grin six or seven times a day. "Well, honey, I'm honored you shared it with me, but you'd better warn Earl if he isn't treating you like royalty, there will be hell to pay threefold."

She looks up. "He's good to me, Nance."

"I believe you."

As we reach the gate I see this tall, silver-haired man standing there, his face breaking into a smile when he sees Beryl walk in. In his hands he holds a picnic basket, and I have a feeling everything will be okay. I hug my friend and kiss her on both cheeks. "You go get your fill of that wilderness," I urge her. "Take in as much as your heart can hold, then you get your butt back here. We have flowers to plant, sales to plan, animals to love, and each other to keep relatively sane, if such a thing is possible."

"I will. Anything special you want me to bring you?"

I hold her hands and look into her eyes, worried she can see my deceit. "Yes, I want a dopey refrigerator magnet with a moose head on it."

"Done."

Beryl passes through the metal detector without setting it off. The irony of this might have escaped her, but it doesn't escape me. This free woman heads straight for Earl, who hugs her, then opens the picnic basket. They bend their heads together talking. I could disappear in a puff of smoke and Beryl wouldn't notice. It's every woman's wish to find a man like that. But there's a bittersweet taste to it from her girlfriend's point of view. For a moment, I have to stay and watch, even though it's the worst kind of eavesdropping. I guess if Beryl Anne can trust a man after what she's been through, that means at some point, I can, too. But Rick? Does he deserve another chance? Maybe in the last six months he went to therapy and learned how to be tactful, although that is not a quality common to newspapermen. Maybe he set the refrigerator-recliner on fire. For the next two weeks I'll be praying on auto pilot, because that's how long Beryl will be gone from us, and if anything happens to her, God had better have a crackerjack team of attorneys, that's all I can say.

Then, as easily as if I'm turning to a life of crime, I blithely walk to the next gate to purchase my ticket to Portland.

"Flight's full," the counter clerk tells me. "All we have left are first-class seats."

I slap down my Visa, thinking, Lord God; I just paid this thing off. "Could I have the window seat?" I add, and sign the receipt without looking at the cost.

THE FLIGHT ATTENDANT BRINGS ME a complimentary glass of wine before takeoff. I try to make it last as I look out the window across the terminal tarmac. "Of course I've missed you," Rick said, and the sound of his voice pierced me deep in the heart, like the organ was made of shale. Six months of silence and in five words he erases my resolve. I remind myself he also said there was a photography assignment involved, but we both know that's not why I'm going.

All the way there I try to read the in-flight magazine, but the words blend together. All I can do is replay the good moments we had together. Skiing all day, stopping at the end of one particularly good run, face to face, his skis spread apart so I can ski into that space. Watching him eat an apple until it's reduced to the core, at which time he throws it into the woods for some lucky deer that will leave not even a single seed behind. The story he wrote a week later, with bits of what he saw on our ski trip sprinkled into the prose. It's like I've suddenly been demoted to about an age-sixteen maturity level. Why does he do this to me? Is it love or is it some deep-seated, self-destructive core in me, thanks to my mother's DNA?

Rick's there when I walk down the jet way into the terminal. He leans against the ticket-taker's counter, dressed in black Levi's and the Polar Fleece pullover I bought him two years ago for his birthday. It's black, too, and he's one of those men who look incredible in that color—his dark, lightly dusted with silver hair set off by it, his clear, pale skin craggy and masculine. The smile on his face makes me feel light-headed, and I clutch my camera case to feel something real. I walk directly into his embrace and stand there trying to read in his arms what this reunion means to him. No kiss, but he never was demonstrative in public. No words of what he wants to do to me later whispered into my ear, but I notice he doesn't let go until I do.

He drives us away from town, onto the 5, and we're in Washington State before I've had time to tell him everything about the farm and Phoebe and all the photo shoots I've done since I moved. He says he thinks it all sounds like a good feature story for the Sunday section of the paper—Phoebe inheriting that farm, all of us working so hard to bring it back to life. Mostly I listen to his tales of the latest rock stars he's met, and how he's come to the conclusion that current blues musicians are a bunch of phonies, all the good ones died along with Robert Johnson and Mance Lipscomb. I love the blues, but I don't say anything lest I interrupt the conversation, which is one of the longest ones we've ever had without arguing. I figure out that we're headed for St. Helens, the mountain that blew its top in 1980, taking whole forests and a few human lives as well. Finally, like a tape wearing down, I have to ask. "Rick, is there really a photo assignment, or are you taking me across state lines for illicit purposes?"

He leans over and kisses my cheek. "Like your new haircut," he says. "But I liked your hair the other way, too."

"So I take it you're not going to tell me where we're going."

He smiles. "Babe, we're almost there. Be patient."

I was patient for three years and look where it got me. I can't stop thinking that I've made the biggest mistake of my life saying yes to this man while James is back in Bayborough thinking, How practical that Nancy is, she chose an out-of-town assignment over a night with me, look how committed that girl is to her work. Rick sings along with some special tape of songs he's made, nobody I ever heard of. His voice, when he relaxes, sounds like John Lennon's. I close my eyes and listen. I wonder why it is men like music so much that they practically choreograph their lives to it. If you listen to the lyrics, it's as if they're all either madly in love or brokenhearted idiots. Talk to them and it's an entirely different story. It's dark when we reach the town of Castle Rock, population 2,100. He pulls into the parking area for a small inn, leaves the motor running, and hops out of the car long enough to pull an envelope with his name on it off the office door. "We're staying here?" I ask.

He smiles. "Looks that way."

"I hope you reserved a room with two beds," I say.

"Absolutely."

He parks in front of a small cabin farthest from the office. Just down the road is the Cinedome Theater, with its thrice-daily shows on the volcano and its devastation. This area is a complete tourist trap, but it's too early in the season for tourists; the roads haven't been open long enough for motor homes to clog them yet. We have it all to ourselves.

"Rick," I say. "We can't just go back to where we left off—"

"How about we let bygones be bygones?" he says, and kisses me.

"I guess I could try."

He hauls his backpack out of the backseat and travels up the steps to our cabin. I follow along, dragging my camera case, into which I've stuffed a nightie and a clean pair of plain old cotton panties, not the silky thongs I usually wear. When he opens the door, I take note that this place is equipped with only one bed.

"Must have been a mix-up," he says.

"Oh, give me a fucking break," I say.

He looks at me soberly. "Nancy, it's one night. All we have to do is sleep here."

"That's all we're going to do," I say. "I mean it, Rick. If you think I flew up here to fall into bed with you, you have another thing coming. There had better be a real photo

463

assignment, too, or I am going to find a ride back to the airport."

He cocks his head and grins. "How are you planning to do that?"

"If I have to, I'll walk."

He laughs. "Okay, tough girl. Here's your assignment. Tomorrow morning, right here, I'm interviewing James Taylor," he tells me. "After which, you get to take his picture. He *never* gives interviews. This is the coup of a lifetime," he hoots, and falls back onto the bed, one arm out, his hand patting the mattress like he's calling Duchess to join him.

I stand there amazed at my own idiocy. A thousand questions come to mind. What's James Taylor doing in Castle Rock, Washington? If indeed he is here at all. Why did you not call me for six months and then reserve a room with one bed? Just who do you think you are, Rick Heinrich, and better still, who do you think I am to come along with you after five minutes on the telephone?

Verde has a one-word answer for that.

"I'm going to take a shower," I say, and duck into the bathroom and lock the door behind me.

I stand under the water and soap up, but an oily slick coats my skin even after I rinse. Using all the bath towels, I dry off and slip my nightie over my head. It's what I always sleep in this time of year, a red DKNY T-shirt that ends just above my knees, hardly sexy, but tonight it looks racy. I stand there awhile wishing I'd brought a robe, then sigh, open the door, and slide into bed. Rick stands by the window, looking out. "Wish this place had a TV," he says, coming closer.

"You sleep on your side of the bed," I tell him.

"Why?"

"Because I said so."

He smirks, and begins undressing. Off comes the pullover, to reveal a black T-shirt. He unbuckles the horsehair belt I bought him, and pulls the T-shirt away. When he pushes his thumbs into the waistband of his jeans, I grab my pillow and put it over my head. When I feel him get into bed, I take the pillow off. He's reading a book he's brought along, some history-of-rock tome. I curl around my pillow and try not to move. Eventually, he puts the book down, shuts off the light and lies on his back. I can feel him right there next to me, the man I lived with, the man I could turn to whenever I felt like making love and know that he'd generally accommodate me, take me to the place I wanted to go. Worse yet, I feel my own body aching to touch his. It's as if every nerve ending I own has burst into flame. The desire to run down the path I know is almost overpowering. I can just see the glint of the watch James gave me as it sits on the bedside table. I wish I could hear it ticking. "You are one beautiful pain in the ass," Rick says. When I hear his breathing become slow and regular, and I'm sure he's sleeping, I am shocked. For the life of me, I do not understand how men can fall asleep like that.

I lie there in a cold sweat, terrified. More than anything, I'd like to wake Rick up and beg him to hold me, but if he touches me, I know we will make love, and if we do that, there will be no going back to the Nance I was this morning, the one who felt like she owned her perfectly reasonable life. Rick sleeps naked, always has, wakes up every morning, shall we say, ready for action. Some of our most memorable sessions occurred just before daybreak, which certainly made for a nicer wake-up call than the alarm clock. I miss my dog, my double bed in Sadie's house, the way I know its rooms so well I can find my way to the kitchen and get the coffee maker going before I've fully awakened. And I miss James's politeness and the sight of his profile, and the way he puts his hand on the small of my back, intimate but not intrusive.

The hair on the back of my neck stands up because I think of Bunny, and how this is just like something she would do—walk out on a perfectly decent man in order to scratch an itch. Right there on the spot I pray hard that no matter what, if I make it through this night, I won't lose everything I've worked so hard for. I don't want one man to drive us roommates apart, and Rick could. I am still in love with him and always will be. I am in no way ready to live without my roommates. I love those women; I want to grow old with them. I want to wallow in those golden years when we give up on our thighs and eat pie à la mode with every meal, and wear sweats all the time because they're comfortable and who gives a rat's ass about having a pot belly when you've earned it. I also want the impossible— Rick.

Rick sleeps; I say Hail Mary's until it begins to grow light outside. I slide out of bed and pull my jeans on, pull off my nightgown, and put back on the shirt I was wearing. I pick up my shoes, intending to sneak out the door and slip them on in the parking lot, but Rick catches me just as I'm about to make a clean getaway.

"Where are you going?"

I turn back to see his face lit by the light of a new day. He's so handsome. For the rest of my life when I see a man with the set of his jaw, I will feel a sharp pain and wonder if I made a mistake. It's cold, the air coming in the cabin makes my teeth want to chatter. "To the office," I lie. "I started my period and I don't have any, you know, tampons."

"I should have known," he says.

"Known what?"

"You're always weird when you get your period. The crankiness, the mood swings, the bloating and all. For a minute there, I thought it was me." He laughs, and I assume I'm supposed to.

"Good-bye, Rick," I say, and walk out the door.

I'm in tears, almost to the office when Rick catches up to me. "What about James Taylor?" he asks. "Aren't you going to stay and take the picture?"

I turn around and look at this man I spent three years of my life loving. Even with his clothes thrown hastily on, the belt I gave him undone, and a nastier mouth on him than Verde, he can write a story to break your heart. I always dreamed it would be his children I'd bring into the world, sassy, good-looking brats who'd run me ragged and make him smile for real.

"They probably sell those throw-away cameras in the gift shop," I say.

He laughs like I've told the best joke ever. "Nancy, this assignment is once in a lifetime," he says.

I answer him the only way I can. "So was I."

I WALK INTO THE CENTER of this itty-bitty town, surrounded by Doug fir and bait shops. I come to a mom-and-pop grocery where there's a phone booth. Then I remember that Beryl refused the offer of my cell phone, so what the hell am I doing hiking to hell and gone? I sit down on the steps of the market and call James, knowing I'm going to wake him up, knowing that he isn't going to understand why I'm in the middle of nowhere at five in the morning, crying my eyes out, desperate to tell him to meet me at the airport.

When he answers the phone, I say the first thing that comes to my mind. "I love you."

"No kidding?" he says.

Then, while I wait for the taxi, like an idiot,
I tell him the rest of it.

"JESUS CHRIST, NANCE, I don't care that you
didn't have sex with him, the fact that you went
there at all is a betrayal! You knew that, too,
didn't you, or you wouldn't have left without
telling me first. God, Nancy, how could you
do this?"

"Because I had to know. I know that sounds
stupid, but I don't have any other defense,
James. Please try to understand."

He sighs. "I need time to think about this.
Let's hang up now."

"No, please," I bargain. "Just talk to me until
the taxi gets here."

"Look, I have stuff to do today. Real stuff.
I'm meeting with my lawyer to get the papers
filed for the business with Phoebe. I can't
blow that off just to comfort your guilty conscience."

"I know, James, but just say you understand me a little. I'm not asking you to forgive me, believe me, I'm not that selfish, I just
want to know that you comprehend why I
did it."

"I can't say that, Nance. Not at this time.
I really have to go now."

Oh, God, I pray. Here I went and listened
to my conscience and all it got me was bupkus.
Should I have fucked Rick's lights out, at
least gotten laid for all this trouble? I'm bewil-

469

dered, out in the middle of nowhere. James freaking Taylor. Was Rick lying? He never lied to me before. "Okay, James," I say. "You go get ready for your meeting. Sorry I woke you up. Bye."

I click END on my phone and throw it into some bushes. The lights come on inside the grocery and I could go in, get an orange juice or something, but my stomach is so twisted I know it wouldn't stay down. I wait for the taxi, and when it comes, I climb into the backseat and tell the driver to take me to Portland Airport.

"That's a long way, ma'am," he says.

Boy, is it. "I have the money for the fare, sir. But if you don't mind, I really don't want to talk. So I'll just shut my eyes, and you wake me when we get there, please?"

He's a decent guy, doesn't even turn on the radio. He's wearing a wedding ring. Some woman knew a good thing when she saw it and claimed it for her own. Well, good for her. I cry the whole way to the airport, but quietly, I'm good at that. Then I wipe my eyes, head to the United counter and charge up my Visa once more. "Have a pleasant flight," the clerk says sunnily.

Easy for her to say. She's probably married to my cab driver.

Home, I think, looking out the airplane window at the clouds. Shower, then bed. I'll pull the covers over my head, give myself a day to feel sorry for myself, then I'll go beg Florencio to give me some really horrible back-breaking task involving a pickax and rocky earth. Duchess will help me. For my stupid actions I deserve a little time on the chain gang. And then I think about Rick, and I let myself cry.

"LET'S REDECORATE THE SPARE BEDROOM," Phoebe says one morning at breakfast. "It'll pass the time and that way, if we ever want another roommate, it'll be ready."

Ness says, "Can't today. I'm taking David to the movies. But I want a vote in the color. How about egg-yolk yellow? I've always wanted to have a bright yellow room with white furniture and antique quilts."

"It's not your room," I say. "Why not wallpaper? You certainly can't go wrong with pink cabbage roses, and a white wainscoting halfway up the wall."

"Hey," Ness says, her hands on her hips. "Anyone ever tell you this ain't Tara?"

"Fine, paint it yellow. Who the fuck cares?"

"Jeez, Nance, what's got your undies in a knot?"

"Nothing," I say.

"Liar," she says back.

Phoebe holds up her hand. "Enough bickering. Nance, you bring home some wallpaper samples. Ness, you find some paint swatches. We'll look at them at dinner and then we'll vote."

"But how can we vote when Beryl's off chasing caribou?" Ness says.

"Does everything need to be run by her?" Phoebe asks.

"No, but it just seems like—"

"Let's just go ahead and do this," Phoebe says. "I'm bored. All this bed rest's made me crazy. I need a distraction, something for fun. And I have the feeling that we need to get this room ready for some reason. Humor me, won't you?"

A few nights later, it's settled, the room will be painted a *pale* yellow halfway up the walls, then a strip of white molding will define the edge, and the most wonderful wallpaper with pink and yellow roses will reach all the way to the ceiling. It's going to look brilliant, like a room a woman might spend years planning in her mind, but put off making a reality while she raises kids, feeds her husband, works too many hours, for fear she will step inside and never want to come out. I've been home two weeks and still no call from James. I'd like to move into the room myself. Never come out. Instead, I send Rick sunflowers, with a note that says, "I'm sorry."

Juan shows up to make sure we get the molding level, and fool for love that he is, when he's up on the stepladder, he asks about the wallpaper. "That pattern looks complicated. Who'd you hire to hang it?"

"We're going to do it ourselves," Phoebe says cheerfully.

"Phoebe," he says, "no way are you getting yourself all worn out with this mess. You leave that wallpaper to me, you hear?"

So of course Juan ends up hanging it all in one night and it turns out utterly perfect, just like I imagined, a mirror reflection of his love for Phoebe. That is what good people get by behaving in accordance with decent morals.

The next day one of the photographers I work with gets food poisoning, and it's up to me to get the job done, which is taking group portrait pictures for a private school in Bayborough. The classes are small, ten to twelve kids per every one underpaid, enthusiastic teacher. Peter and Celeste, two of the teachers who are friendly and bring me coffee, say this is a great school, with lots of extras, but wouldn't it be great if I could come back and talk about photography? The children are bright and shining in their favorite clothes, open the way only kids who get plenty of attention paid to them can be. They're all over my cameras and asking so many questions I have to promise to come back and see them, to give a talk and maybe even a beginning workshop. It's not for pay, of course, but I'll find a way to do it. It takes me a half hour just to say good-bye to everyone. In the car, the silence overwhelms me. There's nothing like smiling children to push all my buttons, so when I get home, I take down the can of paste wax and polish the wood floors in the guest-room by hand. Then, with Duchess at my side, I stand back to examine my work.

"What do you think, girl?"

She leaps up on the double bed, a bare

mattress sitting in a cherry four-poster bed Phoebe found at a garage sale. Its tall posts could easily support a lace canopy. A canopy bed is my and every other girl's childhood dream idea of the bed she never got. Ness scrounges an antique end table from David Snow, and Granny Shirley contributes yellow throw pillows made from old quilts too tattered for traditional use. Juan brings over a high-backed wingchair upholstered in a faded blue-and-white stripe he says some lady on his route asked if he wanted. I hang an oil painting of horses grazing in a meadow that Rick said—in a voice like John Wayne—always made him want to whistle "Happy Trails."

"Finished," Phoebe says.

Then the beautiful room sits idle. Some nights Phoebe and I end up in there talking, wondering out loud how Beryl is doing up there in the forty-ninth state where eagles fly overhead and salmon struggle upstream in order to further the species. Every day Ness reads the newspaper and checks the temperatures in Alaska. "Forty-two degrees in Anchorage," she says. "That is damn cold, don't you think so, Duchess?"

Duchess barks.

"Not even thirty in Barrow," she comments. "Was Beryl going to Barrow?"

None of us can remember.

The oddest thing is, since Beryl left, Verde hasn't said one single word. At first we tried teasing him. "Hey bird, cat got your tongue? One cuss word will earn you a peanut." But no cursing, no wolf whistles, nothing. Every morning I offer him his dish of seeds and fruit, and he takes it, but he no longer squawks his ebullient thanks. When I ring his parrot bell he cocks his head at me as if to say, "What? That old thing?" I take him out in his parrot harness and walk the fields, telling him the names of all the flowers. Phoebe says if this keeps up, we'd better have the vet take a look at him, just to be on the safe side.

Beryl hasn't called. I think of Earl with her at the airport and wonder if he kidnapped her or something.

"Let her have her adventure," Phoebe says. "She'll probably call from the airport, needing a ride home."

"Yeah," Ness says. "Maybe she's climbing a mountain."

Maybe it's just my bleak outlook, but I wonder if she'll come back at all, if my grim prophecy about bird rehabs up there will indeed seduce our Beryl. Maybe I'll call Earl tomorrow, after the mail gets here.

Phoebe, Ness, and I pass the one postcard we've gotten back and forth like the Old Maid playing card. It's the ubiquitous joke postcard of the state bird depicted as a bloodthirsty mosquito. Would that it were the Anchorage skyline, or bear cubs the color of honey. When I'm not working, I scout the Sierra Grove antique stores and decorate the spare room with a vengeance. On top of the dresser goes a lacy dresser scarf, an antique ceramic ring box in the shape of a horseshoe with only a little of the gilt decoration missing. I frame three antique Valentines and hang them next to the mirror. Finally, I splurge and buy a hooked rug with a moose embroidered in the center and set it on the floor near the bed. I sit down and put one foot on it, and come to the realization that dissecting the days down to hours and minutes and air miles until Beryl comes home is what this room frenzy is all about. Not Rick. I almost believe it.

When I look up, Ness is standing there looking at me. "We're all three trying to create a space so perfect Beryl will take one look and never want to leave," she says. "Think this is good enough?"

"I don't know."

ONE NIGHT JAMES COMES OVER and he and Phoebe sit in the great room passing legal papers back and forth, talking money details and investments. I do what I always do when James shows up—I grab Duchess's leash and take her outside. Tonight I walk all over the empty property where James is planning to build his house. Maybe when it's summertime, I'll look for a place a little north of here. Not Primrose Cottage, but a place small enough for one bad girl and one good dog. I'm standing there in the moonlight when James shows up.

"Hi," he says.

"Hello," I say back.

"How have you been?"

"Fine. You?"

He smiles. "Pretty good. Had a cold for a while, but it's gone."

"That's good."

"Yeah." He picks up a stick and drags it through the dirt, showing me the outline of the floor plan, and where each room will go. "I want the downstairs to look like a cabin," he says. "Rustic, lots of wood, one of those big stoves designed to look old and European. A bathroom with a tub big enough for two people, and dual shower heads with steam." He looks up at the stars. "Upstairs, a loft. You know, lots of wide-open spaces, and the mother of all fireplaces, some kind of native stone, with two openings, one down below and one in front of my bed."

"Sounds romantic as all get out," I say. I can't help it, I'm bitter and miserable and sometimes the worst of it just leaks out.

"Nancy," he says, and shakes his head.

"Look," I say, "I'm not flirting."

"I didn't mean to imply that I thought you were."

"I know that."

But I'm lying. James, I want to say, I want you to take me right here in the dirt. I want your hands in my hair and your leg thrown over mine, claiming possession for all time. I know I have no right to ask, and I won't, but dammit all, that's what I want in my stupid heart of hearts. Can't you make me forget Rick?

James just stands there twirling the stick in his hands, saying nothing.

"Have you seen the owl babies?" I ask him when the silence starts making me nervous.

"In the barn? No. You have time to show me?"

"Sure." I have all the time in the world. Mostly I used it to stand around feeling like the dumbest woman in the universe, but I can squeeze in some owls.

Leroy neighs. We climb up the sacks of feed as quietly as we can, peeking into the nest, where the babies are nestled together like twin ugly ducklings. "Mama must be out getting them some food," I say.

"Yeah," James says. He's close enough I can smell his breath, cinnamon, those mints he keeps in his car. I wonder if he popped one in his mouth for any particular reason and I turn to ask just as he turns to me and we bump noses.

"Ow," he says. "That was awkward."

"James, I—"

"Nancy."

I look into his eyes and mine start to overflow. "You say what you were going to."

"No, you first."

"I miss you," I say.

He smiles. "That's funny, that is exactly what I was going to say. Don't you think it's time we did something about it?"

"Like what?" I ask. "Go into counseling?"

He laughs. "Your smart mouth is one of the things I've missed most. I never knew a girl who could match me quip for quip, besides Phoebe, I mean."

All it takes is a little encouragement and I tip right over. I'm more like my mother than I care to admit. "What else have you missed, James?"

He places one hand in the small of my back and pulls me close, right there on top of the feed sacks. "This," he says, and kisses me.

So that is how we end up in the barn, lying down on a broken bale of hay, breathlessly kissing like teenagers, driven to mutual lust by witnessing the miracle of baby owls. Leroy hangs his head over the railing and watches us fixedly. Probably the only thing going through his brain is the idea that the presence of humans generally results in carrots, but I wonder what he makes of our silliness as he stands there staring. Up above in the rafters, one of the barn owls swoops in, bringing dinner for the babies, I imagine. I mean to point this out to James, but instead I take his hand and close it over my breast.

He groans and pulls it away.

"What in the Sam Hill's the matter now?" I ask, picking straw from his recently cut hair that smells of shampoo and shaving cream. "Don't you want to touch me there?"

"More than just about anything on earth I want to touch you there."

"So?"

He takes hold of my hands and strokes them like they're covered with down. "Are you familiar with the color ultramarine, Nancy Jane?" he whispers into my hair.

"The one that's just this side of violet?"

"Ah, the very same. That, my dear, is the exact shade of my testicles, I'll have you know. Nevertheless, the way I see things, sex is too important a step to take until you're one hundred percent with me."

"But James, I am—"

"Shh. You aren't over that stupid journalist and you know it. God knows I'd like to take him out and pound him flat as the cage liner he writes for. But until you can look me straight in the eye and say you are finished with him, I'm not, I repeat, I am not taking you to bed."

Fury boils up in me and over. "Oh, and you think only men get blue balls? Let me tell you something, Mr. DeThomas, women ache, too. Particularly women who—"

But I stop there, because not only is he laughing at me, we both know he's right. And sex, while it would go a long way toward helping me sleep at night, isn't the cure-all I want it to be. "Jeez," I say. "Can we at least still kiss?"

He sighs. "Sure, Nance. Why not? I've always wanted to see what they'd look like purple. Let's kiss all night and find out when the sun comes up."

But that night we don't kiss anymore. We lie in the straw and ask Leroy whom he'll vote for in the upcoming primaries, and make up crazy answers.

James says, "That's a no-brainer. The horse will likely go Republican."

"Not so," I say. "Given all he's been through,

I think we have a Democratic gelding on our hands."

"Well, Nance, whoever he'd vote for, I'm sure it would be a candidate with a tendency to buck the system."

"Oh, that's awful," I say, and search for tickle spots on his body.

"Stop it," he begs. "Every time you touch me, I get excited all over again."

"And this is a problem?"

Our discussion ends when Ness comes out to the barn to put Leroy's blanket on. Duchess barks like a maniac. Ness stands there looking at us covered in straw and says, "It's about damn time."

We endure the lecture that follows about seizing the day and giggle and pet Duchess because we're both embarrassed. Desire and respect as bedfellows—imagine—throw in a dollop of "I don't want to get hurt" and you have James and me, snug as two bugs in our moral dilemma. Damn Rick Heinrich anyway.

"Big meeting tomorrow, Nance. I have to go home and sleep," James says, as he walks me to the door of my room and looks in at the bed just once. Longing, sorrow, and patience fill his blue eyes. Then he turns away, and in a few minutes I hear him drive down the gravel road. I'm alone in my sheets with my dog and instead of the emptiest feeling in the world inside me, I feel full.

RICK HEINRICH RETURNS TO ME at the strangest times. I can be driving down Highway One with the radio on Monterey Jack's all-jazz drive-time hour and one minor note hits my heart the wrong way and I'm so done in I shouldn't be driving. Or standing in the shower in the morning, I nick my ankle shaving and picture the scar on Rick's right forearm from when he worked in a factory when he was a teenager. Seven inches long, stippled with stitch marks, he really should have had plastic surgery. Men enjoy parading their scars so what's it matter except that I remember it, or more accurately, can't forget it?

James. James matters.

When I check the farm's Internet orders, just the sight of stacked up e-mail reminds me how Rick, when he was feeling uncertain, would send me his rough drafts, ask for my opinion, and actually listen to my ideas like they mattered. When he was in the mood to make me soar—not often, but often enough to keep me hooked—he wrote me one-line messages like "Babe, you rock my world," and no matter what I was doing after I read that I had the best kind of day.

It's all such a freaking cliché, falling in love so hard with the wrong man, the one brimming with potential yet overburdened with his painful past. You lie in his arms looking up at his tight-lipped face, and you're sure if he'd quit bringing up women who hurt

him and how disappointing his life turned
out, and just *let you love him,* you could coax
him out of all that shadowy pain, and encourage
him to shine in his own perfect light. What did
I see in Rick Heinrich? Here is my list:

- A man who could lie on the couch
  with you and read books while a
  fire roared in the fireplace. Discuss
  them afterwards!
- A man far too attached to the drug
  called television.
- A well-meaning fellow with a big
  heart, too quick sometimes to be
  generous, yes, but the kind of man
  who'd stop his car to help a stranger
  dig out of the snow.
- A man reeking with that primal
  masculinity women crave—the way
  it's kind of breathtaking when a
  man can entertain himself with
  secondhand skis or a one-speed
  bike ride or hike into the mountains without nine million pieces
  of equipment with Nike labels plastered all over them.
- How gentle he was with children
  and respectful, always giving them
  his complete attention, and easy
  smiles that I remember thinking,
  Lord, if I could make him smile
  like that four or five times in my life
  I'd die happy.

So, fine, I tell myself. All that's in the past. Tied up neat with a freaking ribbon on it made into a four-loop bow. That's your doing, Nance. So why do I dream about him three times a week? Why, in the dreamscape, are we always torqued up to a fever, just about to make love when something interrupts us—a hurricane, an earthquake, or nuclear war?

ON SUNDAY, I GO TO CHURCH at the Bayborough mission. The sermon's about trust and blind mysteries, Catholic specialties. The priest's Irish, and no matter what anyone says, they make the best orators, and so I really listen. He spreads his arms wide when he blesses us, embracing the congregation like he means it. I don't go up for communion because I haven't for so long I'm sure I qualify as the blindest mystery of all. After mass ends, he walks out into the courtyard and shakes hands. Like I have every right to do so, I walk up to him and ask him does he have ten minutes to talk?

We sit on the bench just outside and watch birds bathe in the fountain and tourists rushing around taking photographs of all the cacti just starting to bloom.

"What's troubling you, child?" he asks, and no doubt the moment I start talking he wishes he hadn't asked.

"Well, you see, Father, I loved this man," I explain, "even though I don't think he ever really truly loved me back. I don't know, maybe I was a diversion, or maybe what really happened is I reminded him of the ambitions he tried to bury, so he was bound to end up hurting me, you know? And there's this perfectly decent other man, you see, and he loves me for real, and I kind of love him too, but I have to admit, not with the passion and fire of the one who doesn't love me. It's kind of a dilemma."

The priest frowns. "Perhaps you'd be better off discussing these matters with a psychologist, definitely a woman..."

"No, Father," I say. "This is coming out all wrong. It's not like that, not a sexual thing, though there is that element, but really, I think it's something else entirely. I mean there are days I have to tell you I wonder if I have a brain anomaly. My mind is going Rick Rick Rick for hours on end, and I mess up two rolls of film I'm trying to develop and endanger my job, and I need that job; it's not like I'm rich even if I do live in this county. It's like being infected with malaria, only there isn't any specific quinine available to fix it."

Looking bewildered, he touches my hand. "Dear, sometimes life is very confusing. All you can do is pray—"

"But, Father, that's just it! I pray so doggone much it scares me. Sometimes I get the idea that when God hears me cry for understanding He just sends me more confusion to toughen me up. Things have gotten so I'm afraid to ask Him for guidance. So I make a fool out of myself with complete strangers. Does that make sense to you? Please tell me you get what I'm saying a little. I just want somebody to say they understand."

He looks at me uncertainly. Then he stands, his beautifully embroidered robe shining in the sun. "I have some wee babies to baptize. Why don't you come watch? Perhaps it'll take your mind off things."

Yes, babies. That's a *great* idea.

I stand in the back of the church and watch as the newborns are named and their foreheads painted with holy water. Some of the mothers are still puffy from pregnancy, and I want to know how that feels so deeply that it makes my flat belly ache. At the very least, a baby gives you perspective; and the worst thing is, watching them and knowing not one of them is mine gives me even more perspective.

On my way out, I stop in an alcove and light candles for my father—whoever he may be—and for Phoebe's continued good health, Ness's immune system to stay strong, and for Beryl's trip to be satisfying and over soon; get her safely home, dammit all. Lastly, I think of Rick and wonder if it's wrong to pray that someday I can be delivered of him for good, so I don't pray for that. All around me are new parents taking pictures of their babies, people who came here to give their tiny ones that much more good fortune. The Irish priest intones the names of the newly passed away and announces the marriage banns; he probably will mention me in his prayers tonight—Lord, straighten out that confused blond woman in the courtyard—send her to a psychiatrist because the man problem sounded far beyond my ken.

I kneel on the bench and look at the flames. Rick Heinrich was an altar boy.

If I had my cell phone instead of those bushes in Castle Rock, Washington, I'd call him up right now and say this: *Rick, I've attempted to hate you, but that accomplished nothing. Physically, I left, but you're still hanging around. Every so often I commit the childish sin of calling your work after hours and listening to your recorded voice tell me your one believable excuse:* I'm not in right now... *Were you ever in, Rick, for me, anyway? James is waiting patiently for me to take his hand and I know what he wants to give me besides his body includes the white picket fence I've dreamed of, as many babies as my body can handle, and all his love. Only one thing stands in the way—your ghost. Rick Heinrich, I'd like to bless you and let you go.*

This should be as easy as blowing out the candles on a birthday cake.

But when you love someone, maybe they become part of your atomic structure. I have come to believe that love gets deposited deep into every cell of the body, the same way that grief settles in, and no matter how much wine you drink you can't chase it away. That's got to be the answer, even though my mother never learned this. There is simply no other sane explanation left. I used to think that these feelings wouldn't let up, this always thinking of him, they were signs from God that I should pack up Rhoda, uproot Duchess once again, drive all night, and just fling myself at him repeatedly until he gave in and started loving me the right way because that was the way it was meant to be. Then I met Beryl, and I heard about what she put up with when she was married to J.W. So abuse wears different cloaks, I discover, in the end it's still a gut-punch. Rick, a part of my heart will always love you.

So I do what I can, I keep on saying good-bye out of my mouth, waiting for my heart to catch up.

# Once Again, Almost Summer

*E. B. White on hot weather:*
The first day of spring was once the time for taking the young virgins into the fields, there in dalliance to set an example in fertility for Nature to follow. Now we just set the clock an hour ahead and change the oil in the crankcase.

*Sadie DeThomas on hot weather:*
Take off your shirt. Drive the tractor. Afterward, lie down in Bad Girl Creek, and play tag with Florencio's daughter.

# 19

## *A Brief History of Tulips*

"PHOEBE?" JUAN ASKS IN THE DEAD OF NIGHT, when we're lying spent from making love, our limbs entwined, the sheets twisted around us. "You sleeping?"

I'm dazed out of my skull, so satiated I'm beyond dreaming. His touch on my hand barely registers. I smile and squeeze his fingers. In response, he slides a ring onto one of mine. Whoa. That cool metal circle wakes me right up. I touch it with my right hand, feel the stone, and recognize without benefit of light he's just given me an engagement ring. It's like the most wonderful dream, and I guess he meant it to feel that way. All I know is I'm shaky, scared to death, and don't know what to say.

"Um, Juan?"

"Yeah, baby?"

"Aren't you're supposed to get down on your knees? Not to mention give me roses?"

He makes a sound in his throat like I have to be kidding. "What do you need with roses? You got an entire flower farm."

"Well, that's true. It's just that I think roses are a woman's constitutional right."

He laughs, kisses my cheek, and I can feel his guy parts stirring against my thigh, once again coming to life. My UPS deliveryman is seemingly inexhaustible. "Fine, you want roses? I'll carry you outside naked and throw you in the garden."

He starts to slide his hands under me.

"Don't. I'm all snuggly and the last thing I want is to move. But I'm curious. How come you waited until I was almost asleep to do this?"

"Shoot, Phoebe. I've been carrying this thing around for months. It's burning a hole in my pocket. You're not gonna give it back, are you?"

"Good lord, no. Why on earth would you ever think that?"

He raises up on his elbow. Every place we were touching before is now chilled by the night air. I pull the covers up and turn toward his body. Then in a rush, all his worries come out. "Because I'm not the perfect catch. I'm short, I come from Salinas, I'm Mexico Mexican, and I sure don't have a Bayborough pedigree."

He takes a breath, and I study his profile, the sharpness of his brow, his strong chin, and all the places I love to touch. Salinas? John Steinbeck lived there. Me? I come from Shriners' Hospital, where the only common ground is limbs that don't work.

"All I ever want to do is work for UPS and love you. I don't feature going to college and getting my MBA, or becoming some Internet millionaire. Shoot, I can't even type. And I don't know nothing about art, but

491

I do know that your naked lady mobiles tickle me to death even if they will shock my mother into making the sign of the cross."

I muss his dark hair and kiss him all over. "You'll pry this ring from my cold dead body," I say. "And I haven't even seen it in daylight yet."

"It's not that big a rock," he warns. "The setting's new, though. The diamond came from my *abuela's* wedding ring. She left it to me when she passed away. Her and my grandfather were married fifty-one years. Sometimes they fought like wildcats, but they took good care of each other and they had my dad and his brothers, who turned out to be good people, with the exception of *Tio* Elisen, who went to jail a couple times."

"I'll marry you, Juan," I say. "If we can live here, and I can keep on with the farm. Would that bother you, moving into my place instead of me into yours?"

He laughs. "Phoebe, if you saw my place, you wouldn't be asking that question. I'm easygoing; I can live anywhere. Here would be great. But let's get married right away," he says. "Let's not wait. How about next month, when the roses bloom, so you can have your constitutional bouquet?"

"In the garden?"

I can feel him nod. "Where else? Soon as Beryl comes home."

"I miss her."

"Me, too. Beryl and me, we cut through the BS. If she don't have Mexican blood in her, then she's honorary *hermana,* you know what I mean?"

"Yes. Okay, the minute the roses bloom."

"But my mother's going to want a priest. That okay with you?"

"Sure, Juan. I'll say a prayer to the Virgin, but I don't think I can do it kneeling."

"I got that covered. Picture this, baby. We lace ribbons and flowers through your wheelchair. Whatever colors you like. What do you think?"

I ponder that idea from all directions. Yes, it would look pretty, kind of like streamers on a kid's bike. I bite the bullet and ask him, "Juan? What if I walk down the path to meet you instead?"

As soon as the words leave my mouth, I think, Oh God, huge error. One look at my funky gait and he'll run for the hills. But he kisses me long and deep, and strokes my breasts until the nipples rise up and I shiver and forget what I was saying. "Phoebe DeThomas, I will take you any way I can get you."

I sit up, naked, my thighs sticky from our loving. I ease my legs over the edge of the mattress until my toes touch the carpet. Then I brace myself against the nightstand and stand up, push my chair away, and walk across the bedroom and stand in front of the window. It's light enough I can catch a glimpse of my diamond sparkling in the moonlight, my own personal star planted there on my finger, handed down from Juan's grandmother. My eyes brim with tears. With my hand, I push the curtain aside and by moonlight, I let Juan take a good, long drink of me upright. Then I walk toward the bed, for the first time in my life unembarrassed at my progress.

*PHOEBE? ARE YOU LISTENING? There's something I forgot to tell you while you were in the hospital. Listen to me, because this is important, and tomorrow Howard and I are off on a trip to Switzerland, so I won't be around for some time.*

I turn in the sheets. A second later, Juan turns with me. Already our movements are synchronized, like swimmers. It makes perfect sense to our resting selves, which married each other a long time ago. I have no way of knowing what he's dreaming, but I feel him there with me all the same.

I'm listening, Sadie. Tell me what it is you need to. Then have a wonderful trip, and don't forget to send postcards.

*Okay. This is it. My wedding gift, if you will. A recipe for a good marriage from the perspective of an ageless old broad that is still several ranks below angel. Number one: Make love every chance you get, especially in adventurous places, because those are the times you'll remember best. Like say, Scotland, in the ruins of a castle. Your bodies are the perfect reminders of your partnership, sweetie. And sex is the glue that will hold you together.*

Gotcha.

*Number two: Welcome children as the phe-*

494

*nomenal complication every life requires to become truly rich. Even if they aren't your own off-spring, they're still treasures. Take them traveling. Serve them lemon cake for breakfast. Always tell them the truth, even if it makes them temporarily sad. Read to them every chance you get, and allow Juan's mother to fill them with Mexican legends and* pan dulce *and cocoa. My single regret of my life is not having babies. But I did have you.*

Yes, you did. More important, I had you.

*Yes, we were lucky that way. Three: Invest your money in several pots. Sock away a certain amount for the future, certainly, but take chances, too. You can never go wrong with buying art. While it appreciates slowly, it brings you enough day-to-day pleasure that in the end you won't give two poops about equity. And when you have a surplus of cash, send some to outrageous causes like I did. Why, just the other day Joe Redington and I were talking, and he informed me that Susan Butcher has retired from the Iditarod—a pity in my estimation, but Joe says any number of Alaskan women could use a hand-out where her dog team's concerned. Besides that, and we both agree here—Doug Swingley's a Montanan, dammit all, and three years in a row is plenty enough wins for someone who lives out of state. Of course, I accept (reluctantly) that dogsled racing may not be everyone's cup of tea. So what I'm proposing is that you decide whatever crazy thing is your passion, and experience the singular joy of telling someone who also loves that same wild passion, here, have a check, and no, you don't have to pay it back. Just aim for the finish line without so much worry.*

*Four: Never forget to plant a row of sunflowers for the crows. I believe Beryl Anne will back me up on this.*

*Five: Remember the tulips.*

ON THE DAY that the reporter is coming to interview me about my art, I wake up and find Nance next to me in bed. Duchess is lying along the foot of the bed, too, and there're signs—throw pillows and a blanket on the floor—that Ness slept here, too. Gee, and to think I started out the night with my boyfriend. I get up quietly and go into the bathroom to run a bath. This whole interview deal is the work of Mr. Toad, who insists it will help me sell more sculptures, and though I'm not real keen on letting a stranger into the house, he insists it won't kill me to expose my art to a wider audience. All day I plan to move slowly, take a long nap, eat only my favorite foods, do nothing more strenuous than behave like a queen. I'm in the tub, soaking when Nance comes in the bathroom and sits on the bathmat. "What's up with my bed partners?" I ask.

"I got lonely."

"Why don't you go sleep with my brother? He obviously wants you to."

She sighs. "It's complicated, Pheebs. I have a feeling James might even make me wait until we get married."

I whistle. Who would have thought James,

once he found a girl this gorgeous would suddenly turn traditional? "So, does that mean you're engaged, like me?" I smile and flutter my fingers at her.

"Enough about your ring already. We've heard nothing for days now except for how it's the perfect ring and how romantically Don Juan presented it to you. Ever think maybe a few of us are just a little sick of romances where everything proceeds smoothly?"

I squeeze out the washcloth and lay it over my face. "Fine," I say through the steamy terrycloth. "Not one word more. What else do you want to talk about?"

"Beryl. I'm worried, Pheebs. It's been a month. No card, no phone calls, nothing. I'm afraid something happened to her."

"I think she's probably having a good time, that's what happened."

"But maybe she fell into a glacier while she was hiking. She could perish there and not be found for centuries, like that television special on the woolly mammoth."

"Nance, Beryl didn't fall into a glacier."

"What if some crazy old Alaskan fart kidnapped her and is making her his love slave in a cabin with no heat in the middle of nowhere?"

I laugh so hard I suck the washcloth into my mouth. "Nance, have you ever thought of writing a book? The places your imagination runs readers would definitely enjoy visiting."

"Phoebe, I can't help it. I just want to know if she's coming back."

I peel the washcloth off and abandon my fantasy of starting my day with a long, dreamy soak where I picture my wedding day, plan the music, and decorate each tier of the cake with crystallized violets—I'm back to loving purple again. "Fine, throw me a towel. We can start by calling over to BBR, and then go see Earl at the bookstore."

"Um," Nance says, "I'd like to go in person."

"Okay, fine, we'll drive over."

"Bless you, Phoebe."

Now I feel like a total selfish brat because I see she's worried sick.

Ness makes us each breakfast to go: almond butter on multigrain bread, and a quartered and peeled orange. "I'll stay here by the phone," she says.

Nance drives us to Bayborough Bird Rehab and introduces herself. The old man, Marty, shows us his postcard from Beryl—a fierce-looking eagle, wings outspread—and I check out the postmark, maybe a week after ours. "I seem to remember the new girl took a call a week or so back," he says. "Something about Beryl changing her ticket and staying a while longer?" He squinches up his face in a grin. "Expect she met a mountain man?"

"I seriously doubt that," Nance says. "She was just starting a thing with Earl."

"First I ever heard of any Earl," Marty says.

"He runs the used bookstore," I put in. "Down on Ocean Avenue?"

"Sorry, it doesn't ring a bell."

498

After BBR is a washout, we drive to Earl's bookstore, but are met with a CLOSED sign and no number to call. Nance peers in the windows as if she'll find him there hiding. "I can't see anything but books," she tells me. "There might be a kitty litter box way in the back, but no sign of a cat. I can't really make it out well enough to tell."

"There's a coffee place up the street, Nance. Let's go ask if they know him, or who the landlord is for the building. Although I gotta tell you, I still feel like we're overstepping our boundaries here. So Beryl wanted to stay longer. Big deal."

She looks at me with blinking eyes. "She would have called, Phoebe. She promised she'd call, didn't she? I knew I should have made her take my cell phone."

"She would have forgotten how to use it. I know I would've. Why on earth you need a cell phone is beyond me."

The coffee place is very little help, just a pair of teenage boys behind the counter who jitter their way through eight-second espresso shots and say "huh?" every time Nance puts a question to them. I peek at my watch. My interview is in less than two hours. I haven't fixed my hair, I still need to iron my shirt, and I had in mind that I'd dust off the cabbage-head ladies, and make certain everything was displayed the way I wanted. *Adios* to that plan.

"Hi," Nance says. "Do you know who the landlord is for the bookstore?"

"The used bookstore?"

She sighs. "Yes. Earl's on Ocean. The one you can see if you step outside and look to your left. The one you'll walk smack into if you take a few steps in that direction."

They look at each other and laugh. "Oh, the *book*store. I think Earl owns it."

Hence the sign! I watch Nance barely contain her impatience.

"Yeah, Earl," the other boy continues. "He owns most of this block. Earl's our landlord, isn't he Billy?"

"You mean the pony-tailed old gomer we give the rent check to?"

"Right! The same dude."

"Yeah, his name's Earl. I'm pretty sure it's Earl. Or maybe it's Ed."

"Thank you," I say. "You guys were a tremendous help."

"They were not," Nance hisses hotly as we return to the car.

"Sure they were. We learned that the guy who's got the hots for Beryl is a rich man. Do you have any idea what real estate goes for in this neck of the woods?"

"Rich, schmich. He could still be a murderer."

"Write a book, Nance. I'm telling you, it'd sell for sure. Can we go home now? I have that little interview, remember?"

Nance taps the steering wheel nervously. On the radio, Monterey Jack is cueing up *The World Saxophone Quartet,* reading from the liner notes about who's playing what and where the song was recorded. I can tell the Nancy Drew in Nance is extremely unhappy not to tie up this whodunit in fifty pages. I reach over and pat her hand. "It'll be okay."

"How do you know?"

"I just have a feeling. Lately, I'm an optimist."

"These Sierra Grove lights take for-freaking-ever," she mutters, and we head back to the farm.

MR. TOAD IS STANDING THERE by the kitchen table when I arrive. "Where have you been?"

"Relax, I'm here now," I say, ducking into my bedroom and hurrying to change clothes. I've decided to wear jeans and a long-sleeved T-shirt; forget ironing a blouse and dressing up for a reporter. I'm also using my wheelchair, for a couple of reasons. One, I know I'm going to get tired. Two, savvy cripple that I am, I know there's an advantage to surrounding myself in metal. The journalist is less likely to slay me outright if I've got wheels. *Slut!* I can hear Verde thinking, even though he's still not talking. I bring him along for color, and when I wheel out into the great room, the screen door is just swinging open and in walks this good-looking reporter with his notebook and pen. Duchess likes him, but dogs are easy. And I notice his presence doesn't do much to perk up Verde.

"Hello," I say, and shake his hand. He's short, like Juan, but longhaired, with little John

Lennon glasses, and a flirty smile I don't trust for one minute. Only Ness is here with me, but Nance, parking the car, will be back any minute, and thank God for that.

Wine is passed around, but minding Lester, I say no to it, and Ness brings me a glass of iced tea.

"Mind if I look around first, ask questions later?" he asks, already doing so.

"Be my guest," I tell him.

Mr. Toad smiles. It's something, watching the reporter examine my work. The cabbage ladies have been brought in from the garden, and scrubbed clean of their mossy covers. They sit on the table like newly plucked vegetables, stark-white, blinded clay women, and that's what the reporter seems to spend most time with. He blithely skips over the mobiles Little People passed on—my nightmare horses—imagine carousel horses in rebellion, and my mermaids because bare breasts offend certain members of the buying public unless they can look at them in private. Then he makes furious notes in his book, keeping the cover turned so I can't see what he's writing.

"Why clay?" he asks, when he's finished.

"Why not clay?" I demur, but then I feel Nance arrive at my side, giving my arm a little pinch. I think about how hard she worked on the ad for the *Herald* when we were taking a gamble on all those poinsettias. Thumbing through her thesaurus, she pounced on various words, compared and contrasted, and chose the best. Me, I have only the words in my heart. Will that be enough?

"Well, it's simple to work with. Working with clay's sensual; I get in there with my hands like a kindergartner and play. Most of the time it's therapeutic to pound out air bubbles, or painstakingly create a face using a few tools."

"That's all fine and well, but I'd like to know where your inspiration for the legless women came from."

I study the take-no-prisoners face of this pushy young man and wonder how Nance must feel, face to face with the enemy.

"I spent a great deal of time in Shriners' Hospital when I was a child."

"And?" He sighs, as if instead of revealing my heart I've told him a great big phony-baloney, feel-sorry-for-me lie. Jeez Louise!

"In case you haven't noticed, I can't walk very well."

"What does walking have to do with the flowers?" he argues.

"It's kind of a subtle metaphor," I say. "Remaining planted."

Maybe this goes right over his head; maybe he's been trained to ask the maximum amount of questions in the minimum amount of time, because he immediately fires from the hip, changing subjects.

"What about the cabbage women?"

"What about them?"

"It's not just the clay that's different, but the expressions of the faces inside. They look so emotional, almost looks as if they're strug-

503

gling. What is that? Some kind of feminist statement?"

Why, that cocky little able-bodied booger. I'd like to stick his pen where the sun doesn't shine. Nance smiles and nods *Go ahead, Pheebs, clean this guy's clock.* Mr. Toad, however, is tapping his foot. He wants me to say the right thing, come up with the most amazing, articulate, engaging explanation of why it is I folded petals of clay around porcelain faces that indeed, look as if they are women not terribly eager to be born.

"What if that's just the way they came out?"

"Too easy," the journalist replies. "Why women's faces? Why are their eyes closed?"

"Listen," I say. "You know how you close your eyes when you're the most scared?"

"I suppose some people do that," he concedes.

"These women are in transition. I see them each as having just come through a really difficult period, but surviving. The next step is being born, and from what I've heard, that's not the most pleasant experience." I think of my own birth, my spine getting twisted, and decide, no way am I telling this so-called journalist one more tidbit. He can just make up the rest of his story; he will anyway. "Just out of curiosity, do you close your eyes when you're frightened?"

"I THINK THAT WENT WELL," Mr. Toad says when the reporter's driven away in his politically correct Saturn hatchback.

504

Ness gives him a look that could freeze-dry his heart. "Saul, let's you and me take a walk outside and see what flowers are blooming. You look like you need some air, and I know I sure do."

She hustles him outdoors and Nance and I sit at the table exhausted. "Are they all that bad?" I ask her.

"Who? Reporters?"

"No, reptiles."

She laughs. "Some of them are, yes. It's the job, mostly. That and the fact that deep inside they believe they're all repressed Steinbecks, and they're pissed off they lack the courage to write their precious novels."

She looks world-weary, but somehow never more beautiful than at this moment, with one well-manicured hand resting on the cheek of one of my cabbage ladies. "Nance? Do you love my brother or not?"

She looks up at me, startled. "Yes, Phoebe. I believe I do. But there's a part of my heart that will always belong to Rotten Rick." She shrugs. "That's just how it is, I didn't plan it. I don't know whether James can live with that. I know I sure find it hard to do."

Verde makes a noise like a creaking door.

"This has gone on long enough," I say. "Tomorrow I'm taking him to the vet."

"Amen," Nance adds.

Then the back door opens again, and Ness flies in, with Beryl in tow.

Nance jumps to her feet. "Now how did you do that?" she squeals. "Get rid of ugly Mr. Toad and bring us back something so wonderful?" She rushes to Beryl and folds her in a tight hug. "You're home, oh God, I missed you!"

"Don't get too excited," Ness says, and I can see in her face that we only have Beryl back long enough to get her suitcases packed for real.

But the real reunion is just beginning. Verde hops down from the arm of my chair to the table, and drops the car keys he thought were such a prize. He looks up at Beryl like she's the door out of prison, not quite sure if he should believe it. She raises her arms the way he raises his wing stubs in greeting, and she says hello the same way he does. He cocks his head, rolls to his side, and sprays her with every curse word in the English language. By the time he gets to the Spanish one we're all crying, and he's climbed into her arms, rubbing his beak against her face, Madonna and parrot, reunited. If I were a painter, this is the portrait that would be my masterpiece.

"Are you really moving to Alaska?" I say after things have settled down.

"Yep. Me and Earl."

"Are you getting married?" I ask.

"Oh, don't answer her," Ness says. "She has marriage on the brain."

"It's okay," Beryl says, grinning. "Maybe someday, Pheebs. But for the time being, we'll live in glorious sin."

Nance stands up. "I can't listen to this one more second. This single girl is going to the market to buy herself a T-bone steak."

"ALASKA," NESS LAMENTS when I tell her all we have to do is run the ad again and Beryl's room will be occupied before she knows it. "It won't be the same."

She's sitting at the table and I'm mixing up ingredients for a broccoli and tempeh casserole that is so out of this world even Nance likes it. "Of course it won't. Nobody can replace her."

"But it's more than that," Ness says. "We were the originals. And when this whole thing started, men weren't a part of it. I can't tell you how I loved that; it brought me such peace. It was like being ten years old again, and going swimming without a top and not giving a hoot who saw. Now, well, it's like everyone's fallen victim to men again. You and Juan, that's forgivable. Nance and James, well, they're going to do the shall-we-marry dance for a year or more."

"You and David Snow," I gently point out.

"Loving a gay man, that's a whole other animal, Pheebs," she tells me as she absently clutches the cross she's lately begun wearing.

"Be that as it may, Preciousness, it had to happen sometime. And look at Beryl—she's deliriously happy. You yourself said she more than deserved this chance. Be glad for her. Figure it was meant to be and something good will replace it." I dip my finger into the bowl of cheese sauce, breadcrumbs, and slivered almonds. "Mmm. This recipe of Sadie's is so good I could eat it raw. We'll work on the ad tonight, after Nance gets home."

Ness doesn't look too sure.

But I know better. A day will come in the not too distant future when we've outlived our men, or maybe given them the gate, who knows? This farm will be here, and our rooms will be waiting. If you ask me, I think we are well on our way to becoming terrific old ladies.

"ALL I'M SAYING is the age parameters seem a tad narrow," Nance points out. "If you lower it to twenty-nine on one end and fifty-two on the other, we offer a wider range of women opportunity."

"Twenty-nine-year-olds?" Ness shrieks. "Why not ask to be afflicted with migraines?"

"How do you figure?" I ask.

"Loud music, men coming and going, makeup on the bathroom counter…"

"Well, well, well," Nance says. "Who would have thought Precious Butler would turn out to be such an ageist?"

"I'm not ageist, I just remember what I was like at twenty-nine."

"I like the idea of somebody young," I say. "But even better, I'd welcome somebody older."

"Enough carping," Nance says. "We're going to miss the deadline if we don't write the ad."

*Attention: Have you been the victim of denied housing because of your pet? Seeking women ages 29–52 to participate in a study. If you qualify, you will receive compensation for your time while simultaneously contributing to the great body of women's studies. Write in care of* The Blue Jay, *Box 192488, Bayborough Valley, 93955, for questionnaire. You will be notified by return mail if your responses admit you to the study.*

"There," Nance says as she e-mails the ad to the weekly where Ness and I first ran the ad. "Now all that's left is to wait."

BERYL'S LEAVING IS A GRADUAL THING. She spends a couple of nights a week at Earl's, then she's back with us, working in the garden. When it's her turn to cook, she fixes the best dinners, stuffed potatoes and thick stews, always with some kind of homemade bread that's risen overnight in the fridge. We sit at the table long after the food's gone and laugh over stupid things.

"Anchorage is just like San Jose," she says. "Traffic, crazy drivers, box stores, fast food. But you get twenty miles outside the city and things are really beautiful and wild. I saw moose running alongside the highway. Earl must have shot a hundred rolls of film."

"When did you know you loved him?" I

ask. "Was it before you left? Was that why you asked him to come with you?"

She smiles. "No, it was definitely after we got there. We were standing at this scenic rest stop along the Cook Inlet, looking out at the water and he had just lifted his binoculars up to look through them. I watched his face, saw how he smiled at what he was seeing, and carefully adjusted the focus. I thought, yep, this is a man I want to be with. He's quiet and strange and kind and he makes me laugh." She rearranges her silverware. "I know that's not as romantic as getting a ring slid on your finger in the dark, but you take what you can get."

Nance sighs.

"Will you guys visit?"

"Just try and stop us," Ness says.

WHEN BERYL SPENDS TIME at Earl's, it feels like something huge is missing from the house. Nance lives on chocolate, she and Ness argue, and I use my chair more than I need to. I can't imagine how we will ever find the right person to fill her space when she moves for good.

The responses to the ad trickle in, but none of them grab us—they're full of pushy comments—*What's in this for me? I don't see why people have such an attitude when it comes to pit bulls. Do you pay for the completed questionnaire?* These are not the kind of answers we want, that tell us here is a woman to be reckoned with, one who will challenge us as much as we will her.

"Be patient," I tell Ness and Nancy. "The right one will come along. I know she will."

James's house is framed, the wooden skeleton of his future. I love to sit on the porch and smell the newly cut lumber. I get postcards from Mother. She thinks she might visit, but not until after her latest cruise—the Caribbean this time. I hope she has a king-size blast and falls in love with some lonely geezer who's just aching to have his sock drawer color-coordinated.

THE DAY BERYL LEAVES to drive up the Alcan Highway with Earl and Verde is wetter than El Niño, and we end up spending the morning staking plants. We try to be brave, but we all cry, Beryl, the hardest of any of us. "We can stay," Earl says, not understanding what it is Beryl is mourning, or even why it's so important that she go. Maybe no man can truly grasp that kind of woman-friend loss, but it's awfully nice to see him trying.

"I promise this time there will be postcards, phone calls, and lots of visits," she says as we embrace each other for the last time.

"Be happy," I say. "No one deserves it more than you."

She looks so young sitting in the shotgun seat of Earl's truck. Verde's in his harness on her shoulder, and he lets out with the Spanish curse before she rolls the window up. Earl turns on the ignition, puts the truck into gear, and it rolls slowly down the gravel driveway and soon is out of sight.

"Chocolate," Nance says.

"Kleenex," Ness sobs.

Luckily we not only have both to console us, but also the fields of flowers. Stake us up, they cry. Give us mulch. As soon as we get the least bit selfish, the farm reminds us it needs us more.

"POSTCARD FROM BERYL," Ness says, dropping the mail into my lap. "I gotta go shoe those draft horses again. Then I'm having dinner with David. See you tomorrow, Pheebs."

I finger the card without looking at it. "Tomorrow? Since when does dinner with David last all night?"

She smiles. "Since it does. Gotta run, don't want to be late."

I shake my head and look at the card. It features a dogsled team in the snow, even though it's nearly summer. I think of Sadie's passion for the Iditarod, and how she used to have those parties. Maybe Juan and I will go visit Beryl one of these days. I suppose they'll let girls with wheelchairs on airplanes. There's no way I could manage my crutches in the narrow center aisle, but I could check them as baggage.

Dearest Phoebe, Ness, and Nance,

Driving the Alcan Highway with a parrot is not for the faint of heart. The scenery along the way was incredible, but it's good to have finally landed. We rented a house—a cabin, really. It's classic log design, but bigger, and the kitchen reminds me of Sadie's. It has this great old Aga stove with three ovens. Earl says he'll buy me whatever I need for the kitchen, so I asked for a set of Ginsu knives, ha ha. Anyway, this is my, or rather, our address. We have two spare bedrooms, so you had all better make your reservations soon. Summer is going to be here before you know it. If you can't make it for summer, then come for fall. Earl says the fall here is brief but exquisite. I'm looking forward to all of it, even the snow. He promised if I don't like the cold, we can go to his place in New Mexico, or come back to Sierra Grove, but nothing on earth is going to make him miss fishing season. Give my love to Duchess and Leroy, and to each of you. I miss you and the garden—our growing season is about six weeks!—but I am so dog-goned happy I can't stop smiling.

And remember, Phoebe, we have your wedding to plan!

Love,
Beryl Anne

I read it again, then sit staring out at the fields.

There are tulips in multicolored bloom across the fields as far as my eye can see—such abundance it almost hurts to look. Every so often, I can smell the first hyacinth blooms. Late spring is such an unpredictable season—there can be whole days of solid sunshine, or it can rain like crazy, and sudden romance may bloom as thickly as flowers you forgot you planted. Years ago, while Sadie and I sat on the porch drinking Long Island Iced Tea, a beverage that struck me silent but loosened her tongue in the most wonderful way, she told me the history of tulips.

"Observe, Phoebe," she said, raising her glass to the panorama of colors—red, white, yellow, orange, pink, bicolor and that magnificent royal purple that verges on black. "I'll bet you didn't know that tulips got their name from the Turkish word for turban; that's right. *Tillibend.* All because some genius of nomenclature observed the shape of the flower and was struck by the resemblance."

No, I hadn't known that, or a multitude of other truths Sadie taught me. I had, however, by that time in my life, begun the passage through my various stages of tulip affinity. For example, the puppy love I felt for the scarlet variety had recently departed, replaced by a passionate infatuation with the purple, which impressed me as both exotic and deeply romantic. Oh, hell, I was sixteen years old and I thought the more unusual things were the sexier. "What's your favorite color tulip, Sadie? Confess."

I was so sure she'd say purple, too. We agreed on just about everything else—black-and-white movies being superior to color; that Chinese food always made a good meal, even for breakfast; that American mysteries beat British because since Agatha Christie stopped writing, things were altogether too finicky and uppercrust for both our palates.

My aunt regarded her flowers through sleepy eyes. I had no way of knowing, but already the cancer was beginning to form in her cells. "Yellow, I suppose, with that deep dark center."

"Really? Yellow?"

She nodded. "To my way of thinking, tulips should be yellow, roses ought to be white, and wildflowers can be whatever the hell shade they feel like because they work so hard to be born."

"I used to favor the red ones," I said, the words coming from my mouth with some difficulty due to the amount of liquor I'd ingested.

"Oh, yes, the red ones," she echoed, and kicked off her shoes, one, two, landing there on the porch with a clunk. She wiggled her toes in the spring air. "Persian folklore has something to say about red tulips, you know."

"Tell me."

"Once a young man discovered the girl he loved had died. How doesn't matter, but it was probably due to an avoidable tragedy—snakebite, poison, an untimely demise at the hands of someone who didn't realize the treasure in every human life. So overcome by grief our poor lad was, he stole his father's best stallion from the stable and ran the poor beast toward the steepest cliff. At the last moment, he had a change of heart and spared the horse. He dismounted and stood a moment, then flung himself onto the craggy rocks below. The horse, knowing full well in which barn his oats were mixed, found his way back to the stable, his reins leaving a trail behind him in the sand. Two tracks, one for the girl, one for the boy, because no matter how brief, every love leaves its mark. The horse was as loyal as he was handsome. He led the father directly to the unfortunate cliff. Oh, that poor man! Imagine his heart as he scanned the rocks, his eyes lighting on his son's battered body, knowing the pain suffered along the path the youth tumbled down, all because he couldn't believe he'd survive the loss of his first love. The father had lived a long time, long enough to realize that life has its ups and downs, and that there are lessons to be learned from both. At that moment, through his tears, he noticed something else there among the rocks, right at that moment as the father was steeped in his mourning. Like magic, it seemed that everywhere the young man's blood had dripped, a scarlet tulip had bloomed."

I remember how she lit a cigarette and blew smoke into the spring air, like she was exhaling her own personal cloud of defiance. Against what, I wondered? The sentimentality of folktales? Howard's death? Maybe it was her heart expelling the last flinty shard of bitterness she felt for Kenny, the playboy husband who beat her. Sadie knew the power of dramatic pauses, and she would never tell me things when it was more valuable for me to figure them out on my own, but she did say this. "That's the way it is with symbols, Phoebe. Valentines or tulips, they're all made of the same red blood of the lover's heart. Although I must admit, my favorite part of that story is the young man's thoughtfulness in not sacrificing such a wonderful horse."

Then she laughed, from deep in her belly, the sound arcing like a gilded frame around the story. I remember agreeing about the horse, even though at that time I only loved horses from a distance, as symbols, ironically. And how my aunt swirled the ice in her glass, and the brown eddy of liquor that frothed and rocked and beckoned to be drunk. Buzzed from alcohol I was still five years away from being allowed by law to drink, I poured mine out. No wonder my poor mother had such reservations about Sadie.

My aunt would fight her illness for nearly a decade, but I didn't know anything yet about that kind of ordeal. I'd lost my father in such a tidy way—one day his heart simply stopped. He died at the hospital when I was living at Shriners'. When I saw him in his casket, he was wearing his good gray suit and his hair was combed to the left, same as always, and my mother came quietly undone. Howard, the love of Sadie's life, had been dead several years by this time. Sadie'd moved to

Europe, spent time in Mexico, and finally come home to the Valley for a long enough stretch that I could visit. But her spirit was with Howard, and although I distracted her, I believe it was growing flowers that gave her the deepest solace.

Now those same flowers, or at least their descendents, are mine. I'm sipping the mint iced tea Nance makes since Lester has put the kibosh on alcohol, saying that I can drink it for special occasions, like tragedies and weddings, but in-between time I had better think twice before I put my body through the strain. Sadie's legends remain with me, but I've collected a few more facts about *Tulipa liliaceae* I find pertinent.

Tulips prefer cold-winter climates, but with effort, do pretty darn well here in the Valley. They come in bizarre varieties, like the wildly ruffled red-and-blue parrot species, and my old love, the purple, but as nifty as those tulips may look, they don't sell as well as the old standards. After you cut a tulip, it continues to "grow," up to two full inches—kind of like me since I decided to get up out of my wheelchair. Of course, four feet, six inches may not seem like much to some people, but to me it beats four-four all to hell and then some. After I got out of the hospital, Alice talked me into going to a Rolfer—Grant—this wiry ex-wrestler who hums along with classical music during our sessions. He tells me stories about what it was like to grow up in cold, remote Canada as he stretches my muscles from their long-sleeping beds, kind of like some master gardener himself, I tell him. Sometimes I talk, too. I tell him that tulips were once considered a manifestation of great wealth and power, at least when the Ottoman Empire was in full swing, but nowadays a person can buy a potted one for about eight bucks retail in any supermarket. Of course, ours are a few dollars cheaper, if you skip the middleman and come directly to the farm. Also, ours are hardier, stronger, more brightly pigmented. I think that's because Florencio sings to them.

It's a year now since Sadie died and left me this place. Ness, Beryl, Nance, and me, we've turned it around. With James's help I think it will end up being something to hand down to our children, when we have them, and I know for sure he will. My poor brother reminds me of a long-dormant volcano, getting ready to rumble. When he and Nance are together they exude this ancient fertility that announces one good DNA has met its perfect match, so what in criminy here is the holdup? They move so slowly toward commitment they make me laugh. The tulips on the other hand bloom like it's the easiest thing in the world, which makes me wistful for good times gone by and hyperaware how truly fleeting the present is.

Of course, weather's always a factor for the small-scale farmer, and in tough times, it's a given that people don't buy as many flowers, but just look around—this county's so full to the gills with old money I can't imagine we'll go out of business any time soon. So next season I guess we'll plant more bulbs, and Nance will enter our sales into the computer and print out spreadsheets that show what sold best and what to plant for the coming season. Then she and Ness will argue about something and I'll step in like a peacemaker, and all will be great until the next squabble.

Another tip I try to pass along to our customers: If your cut tulips begin to droop, try dropping a penny in the water. Then, stand back. Watch as they perk right up. Is it the metal? Are tulips impressed by money? Who cares, so long as it works?

When I finally get back to the mail, I see an envelope with no return address, but it's postmarked Anchorage. Maybe Beryl forgot to write her address on it, I think as I slip my thumb under the flap. Inside are four tickets to a café in Palmer, Alaska, called Vagabond Blues. On the enclosed map I see it's about forty-five miles from Anchorage. The attraction? *Buckethead.*

I laugh so hard Duchess comes out to make certain I'm okay.

A while later, James drives up and pulls to a stop in front of the porch. He gets out of the yellow Mercedes and stands there looking pissed off until I ask him what's the matter.

"Nance here?" he asks.

"Haven't seen her."

He sighs disgustedly. "Well, that figures."

I set the mail down. "Now what's happened?"

He pinches the bridge of his nose. "I don't know, Phoebe. One minute she's all lovey-dovey and everything is going fine, then the next we're fighting about something really stupid like what kind of tile she wants in the downstairs bathroom. I mean, I'd like her touch in the house, too, you know? I want her to help me choose everything. All I did was mention how instead of a couch we could always get two matching recliner chairs to put in front of the television and boom, just like that, she got so mad that she up and left me at the tile shop. Just left me there with my hands full of samples and the salesman staring. I had to take a cab to my house. Cost me twelve bucks."

"Ooh, that must have broken the bank."

"It's not funny. I swear, when she acts like this, I don't know if we have a future."

"Shut up about the future, James. It generally takes care of itself. Why don't you sleep with her? I have a feeling if you did that, all these absurd squabbles would disappear."

He kicks the gravel. "I do not want the ghost of that stinking reporter in our bed," he says. "I believe I made myself clear on that particular score. If Nancy can't come to me having made a clean break, then maybe she shouldn't come to me at all."

I fold my arms across my chest and shake my head back at my big, stupid, overly proud idiot of a handsome brother. "You bozo," I tell him. "Hasn't forty years on earth taught you anything about women? She'll never be over him, not until you give her something else to fill up her heart. Stop talking like a nine-teenth-century duke and go pick her some flowers, feed her a steak, and take her to bed. I don't want to hear any more about this until you do."

"But it's not fair, Phoebe."

"What isn't?"

"Her still having feelings for him. After how badly he hurt her..."

I let James rant on for a while. Pretty soon, after he's run out of gas and started repeating himself, I'll say something. But until then, why bother? I mean, really. If you think about all that's unfair in the world you can drive yourself loony in no time. You want unfair? Tulips bloom only once a year. People you love die too early. That's not just unfair, it's a damn crime.

"You're right, James," I say. "So much unfairness it calls for a dirge. Now where did I put my violin? Good thing neither of us wastes one second of our precious time on earth, isn't it?"

James sighs. Then he smirks. He bends down and kisses my cheek, and heads off to the barn where we keep the buckets for the cut flowers.

"Hey," I warn him. "The roses are just starting to bud out. You stay out of them, you hear? They're for my wedding," for which Beryl promises she'll fly down, as soon as I fly up there for hers.

"Not fair," he says.

And I think, Oh, Stinky, you big in-love lug.

What ever was fair? What ever is? You put one foot in front of the other and you walk through all of it. And if you're lucky, like I am, on either side, you plant flowers.

# *Acknowledgments*

WRITING A BOOK is a strange process, with alternating periods of solitude and frenzied collaboration. Each time I finish a book, I am struck with the feeling that the title page should reflect many more names than my own, because the details that make my stories breathe generally come to me when others generously share with me their lives and struggles. The acknowledgment page becomes the only repository for such a list, so if it goes on like a bloated Academy Awards speech, forgive me.

Firstly and always, to Deborah Schneider, my long-time agent and forever friend. Bless you for your faith, your caring ways, your fierce support, and your vision. Somehow you always manage to guide me through the difficult times back to the sunniest days. Also, you are responsible for the best line in this book, but even better, you believe it and incorporate it into your daily life. When we get old, I hope we can live on a farm just like Sadie's.

To my editor Marysue Rucci and to David Rosenthal for the warm enthusiasm for this project, and to everyone at Simon & Schuster for their welcome, kindness, and efforts. To

Marysue, thank you for believing in me, for your careful editing and your unwavering support. I look forward to a long relationship and many books together. To Margaret Wolf and Nancy Inglis, for great copyediting.

To my medical doctors: Daisy Tint, who always takes the time to answer my questions, no matter how odd. To Robert Linden for his gentle guidance and support. To Lois Kennedy and Jamie White—how you both toiled to patch up two incredibly stubborn people—your gold stars are already in place in the heavenly firmament.

To my writerfriends (there is no division) Earlene Fowler, Judi Hendricks, Jennifer Olds, Rachel Resnick, Alexis Taylor, and Joyce Weatherford. Bless you for your encouragement, for listening to my plot concerns, reading my manuscripts in record time, and especially for lunches at Chester's, where the food was always great and the conversation even better. A special and separate thanks goes to Jodi Picoult for taking my hand when I was afraid to begin this journey. You yanked me into Bayborough kicking and screaming, we reached the coastline together, and you still haven't let go. To Wilton Barnhardt for e-mail correspondence and for urging me to go back to Alaska—were you ever right, buddy!

To my Alaska friends who kindly took me in, fed me, walked me through the wilderness at a difficult time in my life, and continued to say come back so convincingly that I did—on a permanent basis. Walter Bennett, Susie

Blandin, and their dog, Harmony, have created the perfect writer's retreat in Palmer. Some of my best ideas took form while sitting at Susie's kitchen table, enjoying delicious vegetarian meals, strong cups of tea, and sharing laughter. Harmony, my buddy, is a wonderful guide to the woods. To Debi Cole and her dog, Destination Unlimited, for opening their warm and comfortable home in Anchorage to me whenever I needed shelter from the storms and great conversation. To Mark Dudick, for reasons he alone understands.

To Alaska, for remaining wild.

To my sisters, Lee, C.J., and Ruth, for being there, and allowing me to steal from their lives and still loving me in spite of it. Lee, for sisterly wisdom and encouragement; C.J., for true stories that rival fiction; Ruth, for having a heart so large and wise that the birds of America are lucky, indeed.

To my brothers, Jim and John, you're both insane, it runs in the family, but I love you anyway.

To my mother, Mary, strong of heart, salty of tongue, and increasingly hard to beat at Scrabble. You make the best potato salad in the universe. I apologize for being such a difficult child and hope at least being a productive daughter makes up for some of it. You are a wonderful and wise woman and I love you. Please come visit me in the Great Land. In summer the golf courses are open until midnight.

To my son, Jack, for being willing to relive

three scary cardiac experiences to assist his mother once more in the name of story. I feel blessed to have you back in my life. Please stick around and take your medicine. To his intended, Olivia Barrick, for loving my boy, and in addition, maintaining ocelot status of the very first order.

Lastly thanks to the dog man, who has an old soul that is best friends with mine.

# About the Author

JO-ANN MAPSON is the author of five previous novels, including *The Wilder Sisters* and *Blue Rodeo*, which was made into a CBS TV movie starring Kris Kristofferson and Ann-Margret. She lives in south-central Alaska.

'He's trying to kill me,' she whispered. Tears rolled thinly down her pale cheeks.

'Sorry?' Cassie put her head closer to Naomi's.

'I know he is . . .'

He? Cassie looked round the ward. Nobody in it looked homicidal. Nor were the beds occupied by anyone male. The only man in sight was a good-looking young doctor standing by the door exchanging clipboarded information with the ward sister. 'Who is?' she said.

'John. He's . . .' Propped against pillows, her thin face drained of colour, Naomi seemed not to have the strength to finish the sentence.

'Your husband?'

Naomi nodded.

'And you think he's trying to kill you?'

'Not think . . . know.'

'Why on earth would he want to do that?' Cassie felt uneasy. It was not simply the hospital atmosphere, with its intimations of mortality, its brisk smells overlying an uglier odour of apprehension and the anticipation of pain. There was also the fact that Naomi appeared to believe what she was saying.

'. . . wants a younger . . . someone to give him children . . .' Naomi managed. Still recovering from the effects of sedation, she licked her dry lips with a white-furred tongue.

'Don't say such things,' Cassie said. 'Don't even think them. John loves you. He only wants the best for you. We all do. When I spoke to him about coming to see you here, he kept saying how much he'd missed you and that he couldn't wait for you to get back home.' She figured the lie had therapeutic value and was therefore worth telling. In actual fact, the conversation she had held with Harris prior to making this visit had contained neither of these sentiments. She had no idea what he really felt about his wife. With some couples, it was easy to determine either passion or dislike; with the Harrises, the only thing she could have reliably said about their relationship to each other was that they were married.

Disbelief spread slowly across Naomi's face as though it was being painted on with a brush. She frowned. Wetting her lips again, she struggled to speak, though at first the effort appeared to be too much for her. Finally, she said: 'Of course he did.'

Cassie took Naomi's narrow hand in hers. Dark spots showed on the sallow skin, not freckles but the beginning of age. 'Why didn't you tell us you were going in for a hysterectomy? You should have said something. I didn't even know you were in hospital until I telephoned about setting up a game of bridge and your husband told me.'

The tears trickled again. 'I suppose this is better, in a way,' Naomi murmured. 'At least now there's no hope left . . .'

'Naomi—'

'You've no idea what it's been like. So awful. What we've put up with . . .' The sentence floated away, adrift on a tide of awkward suggestion: rectal thermometers, sperm counts, ovulation charts.

'There are worse things than not having children,' Cassie said gently.

'Not if that's what you want.' The effort of talking was obviously exhausting the other woman. 'If it's *all* you want.'

'There are other things to strive for.'

'No!' Naomi struggled against the covering sheet. 'No! I wanted a child. I want . . .' She turned her head restlessly on the pillows.

'But you and John have so much going for you.' Another lie. Cassie had no idea whether they did or not. They certainly seemed to, but other people's relationships were always inexplicable to outsiders and the public face of any marriage did not necessarily mirror the private one. Although she had nothing against him, John Harris had never struck her as a particularly nice man. Maybe Naomi felt the same way. Maybe she wanted children because she needed something to love. Or to be loved by.

'Had.'

'What?'

'We *had*,' Naomi said, her tongue too big for her mouth. 'We used to have things going for us.'

'I'm sorry.' Cassie wished she had been more aware of the marital problems, the baby problems. She and Naomi had played bridge together for two or three years on a more or less regular basis, and not until very recently had it occurred to her that there might be a reason why Naomi wore that perpetual frown of worry between her brows, why she seemed so discontented.

'If you could look into the future . . .' Naomi muttered.

'How do you mean?'

3

'When you're young . . .'

'Yes?'

'. . . wouldn't do things, would you?'

'It's probably best in the long run that we can't,' Cassie said. 'See what's going to happen to us, I mean.'

Naomi's fingers scrabbled, dry as scarabs, across Cassie's hand. 'I wish that . . .'

'What?'

'. . . I was more like you.'

'Sometimes *I* wish I was more like me.'

'Strong. Fearless. I'm always . . . afraid.'

'Oh, Naomi.' Cassie felt like crying. 'Most of us are afraid most of the time. Including me. It's how you deal with it that counts.'

'Mmm.' Naomi suddenly fell asleep. Her mouth dropped open a little. Cassie waited a long while then tiptoed away.

She walked along the hospital corridor to the nursing station. Wards fanned to the right and left; a group of smaller rooms lay on either side of the passage, their large windows Venetian-blinded to the gaze of the world bustling by. The white-coated doctor was still holding his clipboard as she approached. A badge on his lapel announced his name. On impulse, Cassie stopped beside him.

'I'm a friend of Mrs Naomi Harris,' she said.

'Yes?' A bleeper protruded from the breast pocket of his coat. Pushing it further inside, he waited politely, head on one side.

'I just wondered how she was.'

'Absolutely fine. No reason why she shouldn't be,' the doctor said heartily. He took Cassie's elbow and steered her towards the reception area. 'Perfectly fine, or will be, once she's recovered her full strength. A certain amount of emotional resistance to overcome, perhaps.'

'Understandably.'

'Of course,' he said, male, not understanding in the least. 'If you want to be of any help to her, the best thing you can do is persuade her that she made the right decision to have the operation.' He moved into jocular mode. 'After all, what use is the baby-carriage when there are no babies to fill it?'

Cassie pulled her arm away from his fingers. 'Nobody asks sterile men to have their dicks off, do they?'

He raised his eyebrows, smiling, unaware of her anger, thinking she was joking. 'Perhaps not an entirely apt analogy.'

'Good enough, though. After all, what use is a baby-making *machine* when it's not producing the goods?'

He laughed, showed strong white teeth. His handsome face creased with tolerant amusement. 'It's a subject we could debate much further. For one thing, it has not yet been established that prior to the gynaecological problems, the husband was at fault.'

'Was the wife?'

'That seemed fairly clear, though I will admit that the root cause hasn't been determined to our complete satisfaction, either.'

'I see.' Cassie wanted to take issue with his uncaring tone about a distressed patient, his damnably patronising attitude, but his skin was clearly centimetres thick. Seething, she left, reminding herself as she did so that, as a taxpayer, she paid this man's salary and so was technically his employer.

★　★　★

5

The man was out there again, waiting for her. She stopped. Behind her, the automatic doors swished back and forth, open and shut, their mechanism activated by her presence. He was leaning against the side of his car, nonchalant, dark glasses hiding the direction of his gaze. But she knew he was looking at her. That he had followed her here.

She walked to her car and got in, locking the door, pushing down the knob with unnecessary force. Was she being paranoid? She wasn't rich or famous enough to have attracted her own personal fan. She hadn't had the kind of public exposure which would catch someone's eye, or have dragged her into anyone's private fantasies. Starting the engine, she debated whether it was the article which had appeared in the local paper a few weeks earlier that had brought her into this man's cognisance. There had been a photograph of her, unflattering, taken from the wrong angle, emphasising her chin. Hardly the stuff of dreams. But fixations were not based on any acceptable rationality.

If, indeed, fixation was what lay behind these more than accidental encounters. It couldn't be merely a coincidence that he was here today. He had obviously been waiting for her to come out. She fumbled in her bag for her sunglasses and put them on, stared into the rearview mirror. Sweat gathered in the hollow above her buttocks. To know she was here, he must have followed her.

Stalked her.

*Stalk* . . . Images tumbled in her brain. Stags, noble against the sky. Indian trackers. Men with slogan-painted headbands crawling through tropical undergrowth. Hard breaths and pounding hearts.

But this kind of stalker was different. This kind went after human quarry. High-profile people had them: they went with the territory, they were almost part of the contract. Film stars. Tennis players. Pop idols. Not ordinary citizens. Not women like herself, with jobs to do, places to go, ten pounds of unsightly fat to lose. Backing out of her parking place, she knew she was deceiving herself if she really believed that only high exposure attracted the attentions of the lunatics. There had been cases in the papers, women who had inadvertently imprinted themselves in the crazy fabrications of a weirdo or men pursued by deranged women. Phone calls, hundreds of them, night and day. Letters, rambling, making impossible claims and written in elaborate curling hands with gold ink or green. She'd read about it in a magazine. They even had a name for it: erotomania.

The man made no attempt to get into his own car and follow her. She had to pass him to get to the exit from the parking lot but he did not even turn his head as she went by. When she glanced in the rearview mirror, he was still there, arms folded across his chest.

Her hands were limp on the steering wheel. She forced herself to concentrate on the road but instead she found herself thinking about him. Her own personal erotomaniac. If that was what he was. It was about a month ago that she had noticed him for the first time, standing outside the public library in Bellington. She had barely registered the person sitting on the wall beneath the cast-iron lantern in front of the building until he got up and followed her down the street into the supermarket. He had collected a cart and pushed it behind her, not taking items from the

7

shelves, simply stopping when she stopped, waiting, following again. At the frozen food cabinets, he had grinned at her as though they were joined in some doubtful complicity. It was only then that she really took him in. Since then, she had seen him several times. On each occasion, he had made it clear—or so it seemed to her— that he was there because she was.

Stamping on the brakes as a football from some street game rolled into the road from between two parked cars, she tried to laugh at herself. Ha ha. *Très* droll. They must be putting something in the water. First Naomi accuses her husband of wanting her dead. Then Cassie Swann convinces herself that she is being hassled by a nutcase. If she had believed in a Divine Presence, she would have pointed out to It that she already had one psychopath in her life, thanks; she didn't need another. Though to be fair, Steve, the first one, the ex-prisoner who had been in her bridge class at HMP Bellington, and who had taken a fancy to her, had been lying dormant recently. It was some weeks since he last rang her up in the middle of the night, waking her from sleep in order that she might endure his obscenely violent whispers. Perhaps he had found some other unfortunate woman to torment. Better still, perhaps he was back inside somewhere, doing some more bird.

'*He's trying to kill me . . .*' Why would Naomi say such a thing about her husband? Was she suffering from some drug-induced hallucination? Turning left at the traffic lights, Cassie considered the Harrises. Their defining characteristic was that they were rich. Only the seriously well-off could have afforded to buy Bridge End, their perfect little manor house with its beautiful